KINCHEN

*To Claudia
Hope you enjoy a journey into my family's past!
John F. Burgwyn*

BY JOHN FANNING BURGWYN

Copyright 2003 John Fanning Burgwyn
First Edition

COVER PHOTO: Kinchen and Hawkeye, circa 1863. Photograph taken by John F. Engle of Oxford, N.C.

Designed by Tammy Deane and Marshall McClure

McBride Creative, Inc.
P.O. Box 1071
Virginia Beach, VA 23451

www.johnburgwyn.com

ISBN 0-9743926-0-X

Printed in the United States of America

TABLE OF CONTENTS

Foreword • 4

Family Tree and Glossary • 5

A Fine Summer Day to Remember • 8

The Descent • 37

The Cottage on the Neuse • 46

The Legacy • 64

Hillside: Comings and Goings • 76

On Southern Manners • 95

The Hills and the Soul • 107

The Experiment • 115

Thornbury • 128

Letters Home • 143

White Sulphur Springs • 153

A Fool's Dream • 170

A Peculiar Situation • 177

The Boy Colonel • 186

A False Christening • 195

Riches Among the Dead • 214

A.L.D. • 243

This Valley Leads to Freedom • 250

Walking Blind • 268

Where Is My Sword? • 277

Always Faithful • 290

The Gift's Burden • 302

At Paradise's Gate • 323

Afterword • 337

Acknowledgments • 352

FOREWORD

THIS IS AN OLD STORY, a family story, told with the benefit of scores of letters and nearly a dozen journals that have been preserved for over one hundred and fifty years. Many eyewitness accounts also add their support. Because of the unusual number of primary sources that form its bed, the main current of this story should be considered true. However, since there were many gaps in my sources that I filled in with my imagination, and since the main sources were subject to my interpretation, the tale also should be considered fiction.

To aid its plausibility and effect, the story is not told with a modern voice. For that reason, I found it necessary to use words, slang, and phrases that some people will not find particularly endearing. This was done without malice toward anyone or any group, and I beg for indulgence.

This chronicle of the Burgwyns and of a slave named Kinchen is set in the mid-nineteenth century and mostly in America's Southland. It does not pretend to sum up life in that time and region, but deals with just a small part of the confusing whole. The story deals with, among other things, the sensitive subject of slavery. An ancient institution, human bondage was unjust and cruel, yet it is an important part of our past and current culture. Its influence can not be denied and should not be disregarded. Furthermore, slavery shouldn't be cleaned up, smoothed over, or hidden. Nor, should its darker aspects be overemphasized. Instead, slavery should be studied, understood, and the truth, as best as we can disclose, should be available.

Again, the story of Kinchen does not, by any means, tell the entire story of slavery in America. But it does run contrary to many people's perceptions. My purpose in this is not to challenge concepts, but to widen them.

THE BURGWYNS

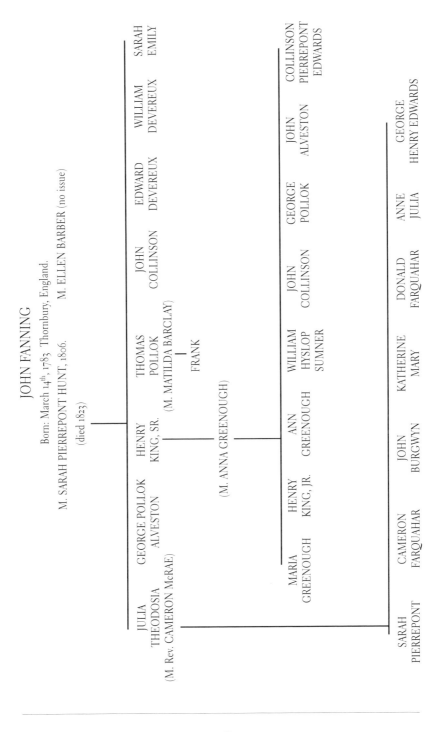

GLOSSARY OF CHARACTERS

JOHN FANNING BURGWYN

Born March 14, 1783 at Thornbury, Gloucestershire, England, he was the son of John and Eliza Bush Burgwin. Reared and educated in England, he inherited his father's shipping business in Wilmington, North Carolina in 1801. Also through his father, who was the progenitor of the Burgwins in America, John Fanning inherited two plantations near Wilmington (Castle Haynes and The Hermitage), which he later traded for other plantations near New Bern, North Carolina. John Fanning became very wealthy, owned many ships, and traveled extensively. He resided in New York City, Boston, Philadelphia, Wilmington, and New Bern, and also at times in England, and Florence, Italy. The father of eight, three of whom died in infancy, at the time of this story he was a remarried widower, but estranged from his second wife who was English and had been a childhood sweetheart. During his senior years he resided almost exclusively near his offspring in North Carolina. Legend has it that he changed the spelling of his surname from Burgwin to Burgwyn before his first marriage when he learned drafts were being forged on his bank accounts in Europe.

HENRY KING BURGWYN, SR.

Born in New York City in 1811, Henry was John Fanning's oldest son to reach maturity. He was raised in the South, but was largely educated in the North.

ANNA GREENOUGH BURGWYN

Henry's wife and a New Englander from a prominent family in Boston.

HENRY KING BURGWYN, JR. (Harry or Hal)

The second child and oldest son of Henry and Anna. Born in Jamaica Plains, Massachusetts in 1841.

KINCHEN

A slave of African decent who was owned by Henry Burgwyn. A stable-boy and jockey, later he would serve as the body servant of Harry Burgwyn during the Civil War.

To Nat, Margot and Ellen

"Self trust is the essence of heroism."
—*Ralph Waldo Emerson*

❊ 1 ❊

A Fine Summer Day to Remember

WITH HIS MIND'S EYE ONLY, he saw a figure on a distant ridge, a horseman, still and solemn, in the shade of a sprawling maple. The haunting image annoyed him, made him anxious. It had appeared to him in one form or another nearly every day since the regiment had left Fredericksburg, and that night it wouldn't leave him. Had swelled up clear and firm, and had so engrossed him that he would not satisfy himself with sleep until its message was found. The sum of his efforts came to one conclusion: a great battle was imminent. Just the day before, a sighting of the enemy had convinced him an encounter was very near, and only then had the figment become ominously vivid.

    The Colonel sat alone on the edge of a dark grove, his back against a great white oak, his head resting on its trunk. The dawn revealed a pensive expression, the dim light flattering to the boy's handsome, troubled face. His blue eyes were bright and alert, not a line of obvious wisdom around them, the mouth drawn tight under a neat, well-trimmed mustache. Overhead, a little finch commenced its steady chirp; wings fluttered, rustled the leaves. Another finch lit on the eaves of a nearby barn and answered. Harry heard the merry exchange, its melody breaking his muse, and the foreboding image made a hasty escape.

    He watched the dawn, ribbons of mist, the muted colors. There was a familiar scent in the air, the smell of wet earth. It reminded him pleasantly of the gray mornings at Thornbury, and the dew falling over Occoneechee Neck. He followed the passive light as shafts touched a roll of pasture, and then splashed eight hundred men slumbering in a tangled mass within the clover. The Colonel, still shrouded in the darkness of the oak, gazed at the outlines of his soldiers, the clumped folds and lumps that resembled deep furrows in a freshly plowed field. He thought of the hundreds of dreams flowing through their heads at that instant. What could they be? Images of home, of lovers and wives, of children, of terrible battles? They wouldn't remember the visions when they woke, he judged. They were much too exhausted for that.

Harry brought the heels of his palms to his burning eyes and rubbed them. He drew in a deep breath, rose stiffly from the oak, arched his back, then brushed the loose dirt from his uniform. After raking his fingers through wavy, auburn hair, he reached down, grabbed his hat and tucked it tightly on his head. Noting the strengthening light again, he pulled a gold watch that dangled from a silk chord around his neck and checked the time, then reflected on the date. The first of July, exactly a year since the charge up Malvern Hill. It seemed so long ago now. The four seasons more like years. And even though the war had lost its shine, he was satisfied that his regiment was no longer a rabble of green country boys. Bearded, patched and lean, it was the largest in the army, and in his mind, the most disciplined, the best, and the climax of his own tireless efforts.

Yesterday, his regiment had been tramping east along the pike from Chambersburg and Cashtown, and when they rounded a ridge with a stately Seminary nestled near the top, a town rolled into view, a place called Gettysburg. Dusting a brown road to the south and cantering over a ridge just beyond the town had come a body of blue riders. Not an unexpected sight, if they had been militia, but Harry's looking glass had revealed cavalrymen of the Army of the Potomac. An alarming discovery given that all reports placed the entire Union army in Virginia.

Oddly, the Yankee horsemen maneuvering on the hills had been similar to the rider of his own disturbing image, yet his vision contained a solitary rider on the crest of a hill. His phantom would appear outlined by stark gray clouds, wearing dark clothing, not necessarily blue. Still, the similarities between the image and the Yankee cavalry were marked, enough to make him ponder.

Harry tugged at his coat front then turned and slipped into the grove's shadows. He searched for his body servant, Kinchen, and found him curled up under a woolen blanket, within the massive roots of another glorious oak. He decided not to wake him yet. No need; he wasn't hungry, hadn't had an appetite for some time. Instead, he peered deeper into the grove and spied Hawkeye and Cora staked out by mossy rocks. Kinchen had sheltered the horses in the trees for the night, away from the clover. Their diets had been poor of late, and the slave had felt too much rich Pennsylvania grass would be bad for them, knot them up. Kinchen knew his horses. He called them his "baby lambs."

The horses stood silent, asleep, but woke when Harry approached. Ears twitched, hooves stamped, and their eyes flared at the closing shadow. Finally, they recognized their master, and they shook their heads and burbled. Harry touched Hawkeye's velvet nose, drew his hand down the length of the chestnut's massive back, then gave his flank a solid slap. He was a tall, muscular brute with a small head, big ears and a mule-like snout, not a tint of blue blood in his veins, but a horse well suited for army work.

The Colonel kicked around in the dark for the gelding's riggings. Wanting to escape his haunting image, he saddled Hawkeye, then guided him slowly through the grove and into a decaying orchard, aglow with the orange hint of sunrise. His urge for distraction did not last. Harry mounted and rode for his pickets.

A Corporal stood and listened by a twisted fruit tree. His brother, a Private, lay prostrate nearby, his head resting on a knotty log. The muffled pounding of hooves on the orchard cart-path echoed through the fog.

"Who's that?" asked the Corporal.

The Private didn't answer.

"Who is that, Josh?"

"An officer," the Private finally mumbled.

"Yeah, yeah, an officer, but which one? Better get up, he's comin' fast."

"Does it matter? Calm down there, Jason. You sure've been on the jump since we seen them Yank cavalry," the Private poked. He got up, brushed away the dust, wandered sleepily toward his comrade.

Harry rode up quickly and brought Hawkeye to an abrupt halt. The Corporal saluted. "Mornin' Colonel."

Harry dismounted, returned the salute, and handed the Corporal Hawkeye's reins. "Good morning, Corporal. Jason isn't it?

"Yeah sir, Corporal Jason Carr, sir."

"Any sign of that enemy cavalry?"

"No sir, nothin' stirrin', but they's out there, sure 'nough."

The Corporal pointed a filthy finger to the east. "Think they's clingin' to them hills yonder."

The Private stepped forward, came to attention, saluted. "Mornin' Colonel."

"Ah, well, they've got you twins out together this morning, huh?"

"Yeah, sir, Colonel."

Harry thought of his own twin brothers. Only one, Sumner, was still alive. He was in service back around Richmond, a captain in Ransom's Brigade. The other twin had died as an infant, when Harry was just five. That summer, up in Boston, the whole family had been sick, terribly sick. He barely remembered the little boy now buried in northern soil.

He didn't mention his brothers to his pickets, but fumbled in his coat pocket for a looking glass, then climbed a slight rise. From there, he looked off to the east, toward Gettysburg.

He had come to look for the image.

"Careful, sir, sharpshooters." the Corporal cautioned.

Harry ignored the warning, squatted aside a rotting apple tree and engaged the glass.

"Ahh," he blustered. "Can't see a thing with this," and he shoved the glass shut, put it into his coat pocket. He then pulled out a pair of delicate little opera glasses and scanned the reddening horizon.

They had actually seen several regiments of cavalry the day before, but there had been strict orders from General Lee not to spar with the enemy, so

Pettigrew's brigade had reluctantly returned to Cashtown. However, Harry's regiment, the Twenty-sixth North Carolina, had been ordered to picket Marsh Creek, a few miles west of Gettysburg. Yankee vedettes had followed Harry's Carolinians, were now keeping an eye on the menacing gray infantry.

The little opera glasses scanned out into the dawn and captured the creek flowing lazily to the south. On the other side were open fields of hay and wheat, and about half a mile further was a mature grove of hardwoods blocking Harry's view of the ridges beyond.

A solitary rain drop pelted his hat. He lowered the glasses, and glanced up into the still sunless sky. Dark clouds were moving in from the southwest. He shook his head, recalling yesterday's mountain showers that had kept him and his men damp and uncomfortable all day. It appeared this day would be a repeat performance.

It was really too dark to see much, but Harry was sure none of the enemy was close to the stream. He lowered the glasses and turned to his pickets, reached for Hawkeye's reins.

"Want to water my horse, Corporal."

"You sure 'bout that, Colonel?" warned the Corporal as he led Hawkeye up the rise and handed the reins to his commander. Harry handed him the opera glasses.

"Keep a look out."

The Corporal's forehead folded into soft wrinkles as he studied the strange ornament. He mumbled something, cocked his head.

Harry walked Hawkeye over sodden ground, while the drizzle gained momentum. A steady breeze swept in from behind him, and he felt the cool sprinkles on the back of his neck. The creek was flat and deep, unlike the many rocky streams he had come across of late, and the big gelding waded in and began to suck up the inky water. With measured eyes, Harry peered across the hay and wheat and strained for shadows in the great grove. Seeing nothing of consequence, he turned and followed the creek south until it disappeared into a tangled rabble of willows. Harry pivoted, and barely made out the dark silhouette of a stone bridge that housed the Cashtown Road to the north. His eyes then followed the road east, until they focused on a shack along the pike, perhaps an old smith's shop. He thought he saw a wisp of smoke curling and a glimpse of movement. His eyes blinked wider, straining through the mist. Hawkeye raised his ears, sensing his master's alarm.

Harry wished he had the opera glasses, but yanked out his looking glass, focused on the shack, and saw the wisp of smoke again. He thought he saw a rider and several men on foot, but a heavier shower suddenly passed through and wiped the images away. He waited for a long, tight moment, then aimed the glass again, but saw nothing.

"C'mon, c'mon!"

Harry jerked on the chestnut's reins, pulling him out of the creek. He quickly mounted and galloped toward his pickets. The Corporal saw him charging, called out.

"See sump'n, Colonel, see sump'n?"

Harry brought Hawkeye to a lurching halt at the Corporal's side, then lunged with his right arm.

"The glasses, Corporal, the glasses!"

"Yes sir, yeeah sir!"

Harry snatched them from the Corporal's hand and quickly focused on the bridge, then swept them up the road to the shack. The Private rushed up.

"What yuh see, Colonel?"

But the mist had set again, and he could see no smoke, no movement, and no image.

"Have you seen any enemy vedettes around that shack?"

"No sir," the Corporal fumbled. "Only Yankees we've seen were four horsemen late in the evenin' yesterday, 'bout dark. They rode up to that bridge, and we were 'bout to take a shot at 'em when they turned round and rode off into them woods yonder."

"You sure? Haven't seen anything about that shack, no fires, no smoke?"

The Corporal shook his head. Harry leaned back in his saddle, pocketed the glasses, then looked down at his soldiers.

"Probably nothing, but I thought I saw something. Hard to tell in this drizzle."

He took a deep breath, rubbed a sore eye, looked down at his pickets again.

"Keep a sharp watch, and if you see any enemy cavalry, fire an alarm."

"Yeah sir."

"Our division will be marching into that town we came near yesterday. They'll be coming down the road from Cashtown here shortly, and when they reach the bridge, pack up and come back to the regiment."

"Yes sir," the twins said in tandem.

"Keep a sharp look out in the mean time."

Harry wheeled Hawkeye toward the dying orchard as he returned a salute from his two pickets.

"Colonel, sir? Sir, you reck'n you could get someone to bring us some breakfast?" piped up the Private.

"I'll send someone presently," Harry assured, and he cantered down the orchard path, vanishing into the mist.

"That boy is all intens- intens...."

"Intensity."

"Yeah, that boy is all intensity," exclaimed the Corporal referring to his colonel.

"Yep," agreed the Private.

"Was a time I'd just as well shoot that son-of-a-bitch as look at him."

"Yep, but you wouldn't do it now, would yuh?"

"Nope, couldn't pay me. That boy knows how to run and fight a regiment. You hear what he done yesterday?"

"Nope."

"Well, those Fontaine brothers from Company C went off—you know 'em?" Josh shook his head.

"Well, they went off and pilfered a farmer's beehive."

"That right?"

"Yep, and it weren't long 'fore that damned Yankee farmer came to camp complaining to Colonel Lane, and the Colonel asked the farmer who done it, but he hadn't seen the culprits. Well, pretty soon Colonel Burgwyn got wind of it, and he commenced to askin' round, but all he could find out was that a couple boys from Company C had done the deed. So the Colonel had them fall in, the whole company, and he asked them who done it point blank in front of that farmer."

"Um hm."

"Wouldn't yuh know, no one 'fessed up, so Colonel Burgwyn asked the farmer what was the worth of the honey taken, and that Yank said twenty dollars."

"Whoa!"

"Yeah, twenty dollars, so the Colonel paid him on the spot, and that damned farmer had the gall to take it, but I reck'n nobody's gonna be stealin' anything anymore if it means comin' out of the Colonel's purse."

"Don't know. The Colonel comes from stately stock," exclaimed Josh with a scornful tone in his voice.

"Yeah, that's what they say, but he's on a Colonel's pay now, and nobody wants any harm to come to him, finan'- finan'..."

"Financial."

"Yeah, financial or otherwise. You know they say he learned soldiering under the great Stonewall up at the Virginia Military School."

Josh nodded, the Colonel's association with Stonewall had been common knowledge since the camp of instruction.

"Yep, Colonel Burgwyn knows how to run a regiment," the Corporal said one more time as he jammed a ball down the barrel of his Enfield rifle.

"Sure does," said Josh. "But right now all I hopes is for 'im to 'member to order up someone to bring me some food. My gurglin's gonna bring on the whole Yank army."

Harry rode out of the hazy orchard and into the clover field, began to wake some of his men. He glided among their tired, grimy faces, and dispersed their dreams. Near the oak grove where he had slept, Kinchen was starting a fire for breakfast, but Harry still was not hungry.

At sunrise, the Colonel called a meeting of his company officers. Throughout the gathering, he kept a restless eye on the Cashtown Road. Eventually, Harry's brigadier, General Pettigrew, appeared out of the drizzle. He was a dark, handsome man, had a formal, studious look about him. The General was usually quite composed, but this morning, Pettigrew was as jumpy as his spirited gray gelding. Like Harry, his commander had taken yesterday's sighting of enemy cavalry as an ill omen. They had no cavalry of their own, not a single mounted company to check what might be hiding beyond the distant, wall-like ridges, and their blindness had given all the brigade's officers fits of uneasiness.

Pettigrew had reported the enemy's sighting to his division commander, Henry Heth, but his warnings had been taken as the ramblings of a nervous, inexperienced brigadier, and thus ignored. In some respects Pettigrew was considered brilliant, but he did not belong to the West Point elite, so rarely received his due respect. After the long tramp from Virginia, the Third Corps desperately needed shoes. Now, General A. P. Hill was ordering Heth's Division to blindly sally forth into Gettysburg to find a stockpile rumored there.

Pettigrew's field officers, whose eyes had not failed them when they spied the Union cavalry the day before, believed General Hill could be marching them haphazardly into battle.

BROWN HANDS POURED THE LIQUID eggs into a skillet, and Kinchen listened to them sizzle in the hot grease. Knowing his master's fondness for eggs, he had gained permission to go into a Pennsylvania village to purchase some a few days back. Harry had also provided his servant with enough money to buy some sugar, and Kinchen had just sprinkled a liberal pinch of the white gold over some freshly fried apples. Camp fare had improved a great deal since their arrival in Yankeedom.

He'd been holding off on cooking, but shortly after the eastern sun rose, the gray host came twisting into the light on the Cashtown Road. Kinchen figured it was time to cook; the regiment might march off before Colonel Harry could eat. He stirred the eggs until they became fluffy and golden. Every few seconds he glanced up at the huge mass of marching white men. Being from lowland plantation country, he'd never seen so many white folks all at once, and wasn't quite used to the sight. He'd been with his master throughout most of two years of war, but Harry's brigade had not been with General Lee's army long. Just two months before, the brigade had been posted to the defenses of eastern Carolina, and it wasn't until late May that it was attached to Lee. Kinchen was used to being among two or three thousand of them, but there were over eight thousand soldiers on that road, and behind them another two divisions. Somewhere out there, back at Chambersburg, and further north somewhere, were two more Corps. Then there was the cavalry, spread out every which way. The Colonel had said there were close to eighty thousand boys. Astounding. Who had tallied them? Must have been like counting stars.

Kinchen lifted the skillet off the hot fire, and the eggs tumbled on to a tin plate, smothering the freshly fried bacon and apples. Kinchen stood and looked for his master. Harry and the General had been watching the column, and the Colonel had just ordered the regimental band to strike up a tune, "The Campbells are Coming." All of Harry's soldiers had eaten breakfast, and were lounging about in the clover field, watching the procession. Kinchen spied the Colonel easily. Six feet tall and sitting erect on the massive gelding, he stuck out of the clump of mounted officers like a pine among hollies. The slave proudly marched toward Harry, with the delicious, hot meal in hand.

The early morning drizzle drifted away, leaving damp, heavy air in its wake. The sun streamed through the hazy clouds, threatening a dreadfully hot, sticky summer day. Yesterday, Pettigrew's Brigade had been at the head of the division as it marched for Gettysburg, but today, as was the custom, the brigade of North Carolinians would rotate to the column's rear. They would have to watch the entire division march past before taking their new position at the end of the line.

Harry sat regally on Hawkeye, all his attention focused on his brigadier. Pettigrew, just twenty yards away atop his dapple gray, was speaking to General Archer, whose brigade now led the column. Harry strained to listen, couldn't make out much, but knew Pettigrew was describing what they had seen yesterday near Gettysburg. He was warning Archer there was more than just militia out ahead. The General's right arm repeatedly jabbed to the east, emphatic gestures. Archer gave the appearance of polite interest, but wasn't asking questions. The tall and slender Pettigrew removed his hat, waved it through the humid air, and with a long graceful sweep, directed it toward the distant ridges. Archer's following glance was apathetic.

Harry's eyes were riveted to Pettigrew's hatless head, his black hair, his olive skin. His name and his dark complexion had convinced some folks into thinking the General's roots were French Huguenot, but Harry knew his people were mostly Irish. Some of the brigade's officers were beginning to draw comparisons between Harry and Pettigrew. Both were aristocrats, and both had finished at the top of their classes at the University of North Carolina. They were aloof, handsome, and highly intelligent. But the General was fourteen years Harry's senior, and had acquired a brilliant reputation that the younger man had yet to achieve. At just thirty-five years of age, he'd already become a successful lawyer, state representative, writer and diplomat, and had traveled and studied abroad extensively. A talented linguist, he could converse fluently in more than four languages, and could also read several Arabic dialects. He had yet to prove his mettle as a soldier and commander, had no formal military education, and very little pre-war experience. Nonetheless, his bravery had never been questioned. Just the year before, at Seven Pines, Pettigrew had experienced a near brush with death. He'd been bayoneted, left for dead, and captured, but survived to be exchanged. The

General was a southern gentleman, and considered a genius by some who thought him capable of replacing the great Lee himself.

The Colonel observed his brigadier critically. He didn't share such a high opinion of his commander, was aware of his shortcomings, and resented the fact that he rarely considered Harry's suggestions and advice. In truth, he thought Pettigrew overrated and unqualified for his position, particularly in tactics. The young Colonel had the audacity of youth, the confidence and ambition to think himself better suited to command the brigade.

The meeting broke up; Archer and Pettigrew shook hands before turning their mounts in opposite directions. Pettigrew was looking down, tacit, contemplating. When he looked up, Harry could see the disgust and the anguish in his black eyes. The General drew near; Harry spoke first.

"Gather you were describing the ground ahead to General Archer?"

Pettigrew nodded, then spoke earnestly. "Told him there was Union cavalry in that town, no doubt about it, and that infantry could be close."

"Did you tell him of that road coming up from the south, on the right, the one they'd likely be on?" Harry asked.

Pettigrew nodded again quickly. "I told him to go in cautious, with skirmishers thick, and to keep a sharp eye on his right."

"Did he listen?"

"He listened—'fraid he didn't believe."

Both officers felt a powerless, crawly feeling about their necks and shoulders. Harry looked at the long, gray column marching deliberately toward the sun. He knew what the absence of cavalry meant. Infantry were as shortsighted as bookkeepers. Moving unescorted in enemy country was flirting with disaster.

Rumors had been milling around the last couple of days: Jeb Stuart was killed, his brigades destroyed or captured. Harry gave the rumblings little credit. The cavalry was off on a useless raid again, that was his mind. They were the most inefficient and undisciplined arm of the service and didn't deserve the laurels that had been heaped on them. Without a sorry word from them, Stuart and the cavalry had left the Rebel infantry groping in the dark.

A single, sharp shot cracked from the direction of the stone bridge over Marsh Creek, followed closely by two more shots from beyond the old orchard, where Harry had visited his pickets earlier. All the mounted officers quickly turned their heads, as a low moan rose up from the marching column and swept to its rear. The officers stood high in their stirrups, tried to peer over all the shouldered rifles, finally realizing the shots had been an exchange of fire between pickets. Harry sat back in his saddle, then immediately directed a question to his second in command, Lieutenant Colonel Lane, who was mounted beside General Pettigrew.

"Do you know what that sound was?"

What a silly question, Lane thought. Of course he knew what it was, picket fire. But Lane knew better than to answer too quickly. Harry often taught lessons in the field, and typically started the lessons with strange, tangled questions. John Lane was nearly illiterate, but nonetheless very intelligent. He had enlisted in the Twenty-sixth as a private, but had moved up quickly. Harry had detected his talent as a drill sergeant, had sponsored and pushed him, and now Lane had become a worthy officer. The two weren't friends though. Their backgrounds were too diverse for that, but there was mutual respect, and on Lane's part, admiration. He had never met one so mature and bright at Harry's age. After the war, he would describe his colonel as "sharp as a tack, and steady as nail." He would also admit that he had feared Harry at first, but eventually had come to trust the stern boy, as nobody before or since.

Harry continued the lesson, which was meant for Pettigrew as much as Lane.

"That first shot was a carbine, the carbine of a Unionist cavalryman. Did you notice the difference between it and the reports of our pickets' Enfield rifles?"

"No, no sir, can't say that I did," admitted Lane.

"Do you know why the carbines are significant?"

Lane deliberated a moment, then admitted he didn't know.

"Well, if the enemy's infantry had come up yesterday afternoon or evening and relieved their cavalry occupying those distant ridges, the first shot you heard would've likely come from a rifle, not a carbine. The enemy cavalry would have pulled off to the flanks, and would be probing our own flanks. Infantry pickets would have replaced the cavalry vedettes. The fact that the first shot was a carbine probably indicates their infantry is not yet up."

Lane nodded in comprehension. Pettigrew was impressed, and realized the lesson had been meant for himself as well as Lane. He knew of Harry's resentment toward him, but decided to let the boy have his triumph.

"Very good, Colonel," Pettigrew commended. "I wasn't aware the carbine had any consequence."

Harry blinked, embarrassed by the compliment. He dropped the lesson, turned and looked to the west. He spied a second gray brigade coming up in the column.

"Is that not General Davis's Brigade?"

Pettigrew squinted into the glare of many shining rifles.

"So it is," and the General begged pardon before guiding his gray into the swirling dust.

Kinchen witnessed the conversation from twenty paces away while fighting his own fierce engagement against marauding flies determined to have Harry's hot breakfast. The slave was not supposed to be at the regiment's forward bivouac, but with the brigade's supply wagons back in Cashtown. The slave was holding back; he didn't wish to embarrass his master by serving him his breakfast in front of so many ranking officers.

He had come up the previous evening with several wagons, and had helped deliver rations to the regiment. Of course, he'd noticed all the excitement about, as the men had chattered of the enemy sighting all evening. He'd been around long enough to know when there might be action, knew that words spoken in the army's rear bore little truth, and preferred to see developments with his own eyes. A slight cut on one of Hawkeye's hind legs needed doctoring, and that had been his excuse to stay the night.

Kinchen waited patiently; he hoped one of Harry's officers would notice and relieve him of the Colonel's food. He was still waving away the flies when more shots rang out, nearly causing him to drop his morning's work. As if invisible, he stood but twenty feet away, silent, watching. He looked at Harry closely, felt a flash of pride. Just the prettiest soldier he'd ever seen, he thought. Colonel Harry sitting so proper up there on that big Hawkeye.

Chaplain Wells slid into view, a gaunt man with dark sagging bags under his eyes. Kinchen recalled his last sermon, the whole regiment attending divine service up on that rocky hill outside Chambersburg. The Chaplain's words had moved Harry. Kinchen remembered the look on his master's face, resigned, peaceful. Then he'd heard whispers. A soldier was talking to another, and Kinchen had caught the words "...afraid we're gonna lose the Colonel on this trip."

The thought of it had spooked him. He'd never seriously considered losing Harry, but ever since that sermon, he'd been infected by a sense of impending tragedy.

Suddenly, down the great column, a Mississippi Sergeant trumpeted an order to unfurl his regiment's colors. The voice jarred the thoughts from Kinchen's head. He watched as a brand new flag was unsheathed and carried to its regiment's front. It was the Stars and Bars, recently adopted by the Confederacy as its new battle flag. Kinchen thought the crimson beautiful, waving in the sunshine, and he watched the flapping banner intently, until it fell limp in the thick morning air.

Kinchen returned his gaze to Harry who still looked magnificent on the gelding. The servant's black face beamed again, but then, very suddenly, his cheeks went smooth. The horrible thought sparked in his mind again, that unexplainable premonition. He shuddered, and the words flashed in his head, "Massa Harry gonna die ta'day."

His knees went weak, his hands cool and clammy. The feelings were involuntary and they stuck with him like a growing sickness.

Davis's Brigade tramped by. Brockenbrough's small brigade of Virginians followed, and behind them, the balance of Pettigrew's Brigade made their approach. Harry motioned to his adjutant.

"Prepare the regiment to fall in, Lieutenant."

As the adjutant peeled away, Harry noticed Kinchen standing alone with a plate of food. It dawned on him that he had not eaten, that the morning's activities and excitement had caused him to ignore his stomach's pleas. He turned Hawkeye, excused himself from the covey of officers that surrounded him, and walked the great gelding toward his servant.

"You've been very kind this morning, Kinchen. I've failed to ask you to make my breakfast, but I see you made it anyway."

Kinchen's mind was still preoccupied by the premonition, but he managed to stammer a reply. "Oh, yeah suh, Colonel Harry suh, I - I fixed yo' breakfast, but I's 'fraid it's got a bit cool."

Harry reached down and gently took the tin plate from his servant's hands.

"Eggs! They look delicious Kinchen, thank you!"

Kinchen didn't respond, and Harry noticed he wasn't smiling. There was a strange softness in the black eyes, and he seemed troubled.

"You feeling all right this morning?" the Colonel asked.

Kinchen jerked, quickly looked up at Harry, and beamed his signature smile.

"Oooh yeah suh, I fine. Just a lookin' at all dem soldy'as, suh. Just can't get over all dem soldy'as."

Harry glanced at the dusty column while preparing to put a spoonful of yellow eggs in his mouth.

"Magnificent, aren't they? But there are many more than what you see there."

"Oh yeah suh, dare's a great multitude mo' just a marchin' from dose hills yonder," Kinchen said as he pointed to the blue mountains.

Harry nodded as he chewed on a mouthful of eggs. Kinchen fell silent, and his smile disappeared.

A sputtering of shots rang out again, and instinctively the two looked off in their direction. But the firing didn't elicit further response; Harry continued his breakfast, while Kinchen stood in silent vigilance.

Finally, Harry put the last delicious bite into his mouth, then handed the plate back to his servant.

"Kinchen, I believe that was the best breakfast I've had since the war. Aunt Ruthy has done just a marvelous job in teaching you the art."

Kinchen smiled.

"Oh, dank yuh Colonel Harry, suh, twurnt not'n, suh. Did yuh taste da suga' on da apples, suh?"

"The apples were delightful."

The servant beamed, but a troubled expression returned. Harry noticed.

"Something on your mind, Kinchen?"

The slave jerked.

"No, suh," he said as he scratched his cropped hair with a nervous finger.

Again there was a pause. Kinchen scrunched his nose, thinking.

"Colonel Harry suh, I's fixin' to go on back ta da wagon camp wid Cora."

"Yes, you do that," said Harry. "The wagons will be following shortly, and they'll need you there. Do your best to help them."

Shyly, Kinchen gave his master some advice. "Well, Colonel suh, seein' dat dare might be some trouble ta'day, thought I'd take Hawkeye wid me."

Harry sat up in the saddle, looked off towards Gettysburg. The image of the lone, dark horseman on a distant hill returned. Trouble, will there be trouble today? The sun shone bright in his eyes, perspiration stinging them, and he rubbed them, then he looked down at his servant.

"No, won't be necessary. There's just enemy cavalry ahead, and the Twenty-sixth will be at the end of the column. No fighting today. Hawkeye will stay here with me. Thank you for tending his cut, and for my breakfast. Now go on back with Cora."

"Yuh sure, suh? Y'are a mighty invitin' target on dat big Hawkeye, suh! Yuh sure I might not better take him wid me?"

Harry's face showed pleasant appreciation for Kinchen's concern, but he answered immediately.

"No, won't be necessary. You go on back with Cora. I'll see you this evening."

Kinchen hesitated, gave another nervous look at the marching gray column.

"Don't worry, go on back now," said Harry again.

"Yeah, suh," the slave said resignedly. Kinchen made his way back toward the grove, but glanced one more time over his shoulder at Harry, who was making his way toward the column, the image of the dark horseman still firm in his mind.

General Archer's Brigade veered off the Cashtown Pike and deployed on its south side near the orchard, while General Davis' Brigade formed on the north side. With a thick screen of skirmishers out in front, both brigades advanced beyond Marsh Creek. A battalion of artillery trailed along the pike behind them. The occasional pop from a carbine indicated the Confederates would meet resistance.

The sun had cleared away the mist and had long dried the morning showers. The Rebels were engulfed in dust; sweat and humid air caused a brown cloud to stick to the soldiers' uniforms and faces. It gave the entire division a butternut hue.

Harry observed the Eleventh North Carolina marching past. It was a well-drilled unit that competed with Harry's for the best in Pettigrew's Brigade. It brought up the rear of the column. Harry gave a nod to its commander, Colonel Leventhorpe, then pivoted in his saddle and watched the Twenty-sixth step forward in perfect unison. Colonel Lane was mounted near him, and Harry made an address.

"We've worked hard, Colonel. We've the finest regiment in the army. I am proud of it, and I am proud of you. The Twenty-sixth is large and strong and disciplined, and they'll obey us, and follow us wherever we go. Today, we'll enjoy the fruits of our labor. We'll lead them into battle, we'll fight, and we'll prevail."

Harry had not believed his own soothing words to Kinchen. There would be a fight today, he was sure. He removed his hat, applied a handkerchief to his brow, and looked reproachfully to the heavens and said, "And a hot day it will be, Colonel Lane."

Lane also looked up, shaded his eyes from the glare, and smiled sentimentally.

"Yes, sir, Colonel Burgwyn, a fine summer day to remember."

Beyond the troops, and about fifty yards off, Harry caught a glimpse of a black mare pawing at the earth. It was Cora with Kinchen perched atop her, standing at the fringe of the grove. The slave was staring at him; he had not yet left to join the wagons. Harry detected an anxious mood about him, tried to catch the black eyes, and stole a small wave. Kinchen stood motionless and unresponsive, yet it was obvious the servant was looking directly at him. Queer, he thought, Kinchen's apparent remoteness. The Colonel raised his arm, held it upright, and showed the palm of his stained white riding glove to Kinchen. The slave remained perfectly still, but finally removed his fuzzy, black derby and held it shoulder high. A slight grin came to Harry's face, a small moment of affection, then a throbbing bolt, as Kinchen swept the faded hat over his head with a flourish and reapplied it to his head. He wasn't smiling though. Normally he'd be smiling, and Harry crooked his head. For a few silent seconds their eyes met. An officer called out, distracting the Colonel. He turned aside for a moment, then looked back anxiously, in time to see Kinchen wheel the mare and canter away. Harry watched him through a thin veil of dust, and was suddenly beset by a vision of home, of past days at Hillside and Thornbury Plantations. As a boy, he had fancied himself king of his domain, Kinchen his prince, lording over thousands of acres of cotton, corn, and wheat. They had fished and skipped rocks together in the great Roanoke River, had hunted ducks in the swamps and squirrels in the forest. Kinchen, a little older, had taught him how to whistle. A rare friendship despite a gulf of differences had grown even tighter through the war.

Harry watched until the dust settled, absorbed, and finally suppressed his nostalgia. The Colonel tugged Hawkeye's reins, turning toward the regiment, then puckered his lips and gave a low whistle.

From the east came another sputtering of shots. Archer's skirmishers were pushing the Yankees out of the distant hardwood grove. The terrible Battle of Gettysburg had commenced.

A REBEL BATTERY FIRED ITS VENOM from atop Herr Ridge, trading blows with Union horse-artillery on the next ridge over. The enemy skirmishers had given Archer and Davis little trouble at first; their small coveys had been pushed back rather easily. A much stronger line of dismounted cavalry had been encountered along McPherson's Ridge however, and they were holding it with uncharacteristic stubbornness. Strange—one battery, and one thousand horsemen dueling with heavy columns of infantry. Perhaps they did not know that more than half the Rebel army was bearing down on them, stacked up and choking the Cashtown Pike all the way back to Chambersburg. Making a nice show on their home ground, most of the Rebels thought. They'd give way soon enough.

Below, mounted in the shade of a tall poplar on the south side of the pike, John Lane observed the guns firing, recoiling, and discharging their milky smoke. He watched at length as the gunners handsomely operated their cannon, while Yankee shells tore up the hill around them. Such discipline, such superb execution while under fire. Lane studied them intently, admiring their rhythm and nerve, hoping the Lord would spare them a direct hit.

Beside Lane was a sunlit hayfield ripening in the July heat. It contained a quarter-mile-long line of men, Pettigrew's Brigade, close to three thousand Rebels. The Twenty-sixth was situated on the far left of the brigade, followed by the three other regiments of Carolinians. The troops were standing at ease, a casual look about their line, yet most of the boys were peering skyward over the hazy ridge to the east, carefully measuring the progress of each enemy round. Most of the sizzling balls were landing near the Rebel guns, but some were crashing into a thin grove at the base of Herr Ridge, which was about one hundred yards to the brigade's front. Other missiles were sailing long, a threat to more Confederates moving up on the Cashtown Pike. These new arrivals were the first elements of Dorsey Pender's Division, the second of three in A. P. Hill's new Third Corps. Filling the road behind Pender were the rest of Hill's Corps and most of Longstreet's, more than enough men to deal with a handful of spirited, yet foolish blue cavalrymen.

Lane's attention shifted away from the lurching guns, turned to Harry pacing his big gelding up and down the line, a sign of his growing impatience. Lane decided he'd join his Colonel, try to calm him.

Harry had his gold watch in hand, a gift from his father the Christmas of '55. As Lane drew near, Harry flipped the watch open, and looked at its ornate face. It was 10:25 AM.

"How long ago, Colonel Lane, did Archer go over the ridge?"

"Oh, 'bout half hour, I'd say."

"Really, I thought longer."

"Could be, Colonel, not much longer though."

No sooner were the words out of Lane's mouth than a long, loud rattle of musketry ripped through the air from the opposite side of Herr Ridge. It was off to the right, to the south. The two Colonels listened as the firing escalated. Lane was the first to comment.

"Sounds like they've run into more than just cavalry."

Harry nodded. "That's Union infantry volleys, and they sound like they're on Archer's right."

The firing began to sweep up, and heavy fighting could be heard directly across the ridge, not a half-mile away.

"General Pettigrew said they would be on the right, didn't he?" Lane asked.

"Pettigrew told Archer just what I told him. They'd be coming up that road from the south."

The Confederate battery began to fire in earnest. Now, more musketry could be heard on the left.

"Sounds like Davis is engaged too."

Harry tried to gauge the progress of the battle from sound alone. He wanted to ride to the ridge top and look down on the fighting beyond, but instead motioned to his adjutant and dismounted. The Lieutenant rode up, saluted, and waited for Harry's order.

"Gather up all the officers' horses and assign some men to take them back to Cashtown. Send Michie's band members."

Harry handed Hawkeye's reins to the adjutant, then turned to Lane.

"Dismount, Colonel Lane, and give the Lieutenant your mount. I want none of my officers on horseback today."

A SLIGHT BREEZE CAST THE HIGH HAY ABOUT like soft waves in an ocean, a small relief from air growing thick with damp heat. The sounds of battle had drawn closer, but were not as intense. Archer's Brigade was falling back on Herr Ridge.

Harry continued his restless pacing in front of the Twenty-sixth, jerking, stopping, listening, then off for short rambles. He checked his watch again. At last glance it was just after eleven o'clock. Lane was still standing near.

"Why are we waiting? We should be going to Archer's support! We need to expel the enemy from that far ridge before they're reinforced!"

Lane nodded, agreed.

A rider on a big chestnut was approaching the line at a leisurely pace. Harry recognized Captain McCreery from the brigade's staff.

"General Pettigrew's compliments, sir."

"Thank you, Captain."

"Colonel, the General has ordered the brigade forward, and we are to occupy that grove there at the base of the ridge. We are to wait there in support of General Archer. I am to direct you to deploy your skirmishers on the ridge top."

"Very good, Captain. Anything else?" Harry replied.

"No, sir."

The displeasure in Harry's voice was obvious as he aired his own opinion.

"Captain McCreery, please advise General Pettigrew that I believe we should press the enemy and take that far ridge before they can reinforce the position. Remind him we have General Pender's entire division here in our rear as support. Tell him we should attack this instant!"

The Rebel battery on Herr Ridge fired a salvo as McCreery replied.

"I will respectfully pass your message, sir, but Colonel, I should advise you that General Pettigrew has orders from General Heth not to attack, and he has instructions from Headquarters. It seems General Lee doesn't want a battle today, as our entire army is not yet present and the strength of the enemy beyond the ridges is not known."

Harry absorbed the information, realized that perhaps he was being a bit impetuous.

"Captain, disregard my message to General Pettigrew," he said reluctantly.

"Yes, sir, Colonel... Colonel, will you advance your regiment into the grove?"

"Yes, Captain, immediately, thank you."

The two exchanged salutes, and McCreery rode back down the line. Harry watched the battery on the ridge for a moment. Their pace had slackened and there was no response from the Yankee battery. The battle, at least temporarily, was dying away.

"Colonel Lane, take charge of the right, and advance the regiment to the grove upon my signal."

"Yes, sir."

"Lieutenant!" Harry motioned to his adjutant. "Advise Major Jones that he has command of the left, and to advance the regiment to the grove upon my signal. Tell him to keep the companies in line of battle, and to advance his skirmishers to the ridge top."

"Yes, sir, Colonel."

Harry looked back at his watch: 11:17.

A SUBLIME VIEW, THE ROLLING LANDSCAPE, the tidy little town nestled among the green folds. It was all in plain sight from Herr Ridge. Harry stood among his skirmishers, looking over the enemy position on McPherson's Ridge with his opera glasses. Earlier he had sent Lieutenant George Willcox from Company H to observe the battle, and now the young officer was at Harry's side making his report.

"General Archer was advancing over that creek when they attacked. See that creek there, Colonel? It's hid 'tween those thickets and willows."

"I see it, Lieutenant."

"Well sir," Willcox scratched his chin. "'Bout half the brigade was in the thickets and creek when the Federals attacked, most unlucky, sir. The Yanks swung around out of those woods there and hit Archer on his right. Those 'Bama boys, they were in a bad way. Then the Yanks attacked Archer's front directly through those woods. That's where the General was captured sir, and near half a regiment."

Served him right was Harry's silent conclusion. Pettigrew had told Archer to go in cautiously and look out for his right. His carelessness had made him a prisoner, the first Brigadier General from the Army of Northern Virginia ever to fall into enemy hands.

Willcox continued.

"Well, the brigade was in a bad way. They were stuck in that creek, and the Yanks, they were just picking away at 'em, but Colonel Fry took charge, and I believe he did just a fine job. Got the brigade out of that creek and retreated here to the ridge, fighting all the way. Killed one of their big Corps Generals they say."

Harry lowered his glasses, and looked at the young officer.

"A Major General, is that confirmed?"

"Well, no sir, not confirmed. Just a rumor, I suppose. But I was talking to some Tennessee boys earlier, and they say some of their sharpshooters picked him off his horse earlier this mornin'."

"Do you know the General's name?" Harry asked.

"No sir, they didn't say his name."

"Do you know what enemy Corps that is on the ridge there?"

"No, sir, don't rightly know... But those Tennessee boys said some were wearing them black hats."

Harry thought, "black hats." He knew of only one Union brigade that wore black hats. They were in General Reynolds' Corps. It must have been John Reynolds they had killed; that is, if it wasn't a rumor. Reynolds! According to the Yankee papers, he was one of their best!

"What happened over on the left, Lieutenant? What happened to Davis?"

"Well, General Davis advanced right smartly, sir. One of his regiments struck off to the left, and flanked the enemy while they were on that bare stretch of the ridge. See it there? Well, those Yanks skedaddled sir, and the Mississippi boys pushed on 'em. But they needed support, Colonel, they had no support. See that red clay there in the distance, sir? See it there, that red clay?"

"Yes, Lieutenant, that's a cut for a railroad."

"Yeah sir, well, that's where the Mississippi boys held up, in that ravine. And a pile of Yankees, better than three regiments, I'd say, came from behind those woods there and trapped them. Better than a regiment gave up, sir. Disgraceful! Matter of fact, not much of Davis' Brigade came back at all. What's left of them are hunkered down the line, sir, to the left, opposite that farm there. 'Fraid the Yankees have had the day, sir."

The day wasn't over, was Harry's first thought, but he didn't say it. Willcox seemed to read his mind though, and supported his claim. "That's a mighty strong position they hold there."

"Yes, but not impregnable," said Harry, a little irritated. "Very commendable report, Lieutenant. Thank you, you're dismissed. Please return to your company."

"Yes, sir, thank you, Colonel."

Willcox saluted, turned quickly, and scrambled down the western side of the ridge.

The summit of Herr Ridge was a bald, old pasture with ancient rocks randomly jutting out of the thinning soil. Harry squatted on one of the gray sleepers as he trained his glasses on the enemy position and the valley between. He studied the contours carefully.

Down the eastern slope of Herr Ridge was another grove that rambled about fifty yards, until the ground leveled off into a golden wheat field. Harry looked through the ripening tassels, through the debris of the previous engagement, and then slowly brought the glasses upon heavy brambles that shrouded a shallow ravine housing Willoughby Run. On the other side of the creek was yet another grove that stretched up to the top of the opposite ridge and beyond. Harry guessed the wood lot was four hundred yards wide, and at least a third of a mile long. Within the woods he could see movement and the occasional flash of sunlight off bayonets and gun barrels. The reflections gave evidence that this was where the Federals were massed.

Slowly sweeping his glasses to the right, Harry's eyes locked on a blue battle line extending out of the grove to the bare ridge top beyond. An enemy battery was posted there, and was now lazily trading blows with a Rebel battery on the opposite ridge. Beyond the battery, several companies of horse soldiers guarded the enemy's far flank.

The crack of random picket fire to the north caught Harry's attention. He lowered the glasses, then refocused them to his left. Here he caught sight of the Edward McPherson Farm. Yet another blue battle line extended from the northern edge of the grove all the way to the Cashtown Pike. Behind the farm was another enemy battery.

Looking beyond the pike, Harry could see the northern extension of McPherson's Ridge, which was open, yet void of Yankee soldiers. The ridge continued to meander in a northerly direction, until it rose up to a high hill timbered by towering hardwoods: Oak Hill.

A formidable position, Harry thought, but the Yankees had left their right unguarded. It was dangling there at that farm. Even if General Lee wanted no battle that day, General Hill should come up and make plans to envelop their right. Certainly the army would be united by the morning, and should attack that flank at first light.

Harry peered over at McPherson's Grove. As General Archer had just proved, an attack through that valley would be costly indeed. However, if they could line the top of Herr Ridge with batteries, they could blast that grove to bits. Heavy artillery barrages and a flank attack would help a frontal assault immeasurably.

Harry knew that his regiment, along with the rest of Pettigrew's Brigade, were now in the best position to spearhead any assault against McPherson's Grove.

At that instant, J. B. Jordan, the regiment's adjutant, came puffing up the ridge. Jordan had been Harry's adjutant from the start, and was six years older than his commander, but the age difference had never affected their relationship. Harry always carried an air of authority, even in the presence of men three times his age.

Jordan picked the seeds and briars off his uniform, cleared his throat. "Pardon me, Colonel."

Harry lowered his glasses, but didn't turn, recognizing his adjutant's voice. "Yes, J. B."

"Orders from General Pettigrew, sir. Captain McCreery informs me that General Pettigrew would like you to advance the Twenty-sixth to the top of this ridge, sir."

"Now?"

"Yes, sir, immediately."

Perhaps there would be more fighting after all.

"Are we to take a defensive posture, or are we to prepare an attack, Lieutenant?" Harry asked.

"Ah, Captain didn't say, sir. Said just to advance the regiment to the ridge top."

Harry finally turned and looked at Jordan.

"Very well, inform Colonel Lane and Major Jones. Tell them to advance at their discretion, and to post their skirmishers in the grove at the bottom of the hill near the edge of that wheat field, see it there?"

Jordan peered down the ridge, nodded.

"Tell them to stay alert, and to keep the regiment in line of battle. I'll be down presently."

"Yes, sir," Jordan saluted, hurried off.

Harry turned and looked again at McPherson's Grove. It bristled with men in blue who wore the black hats of the famous "Iron Brigade." The Colonel hoped there would be no naked assaults against them.

His eyes squinted at the heavens. The sun was high and hot. It was mid-day.

THE CLICK OF BREAKING BRANCHES, THE SHUFFLE of feet, and the occasional clang of a canteen were the only sounds, as eight hundred North Carolinians emerged from the shaded grove. Bathed in sunlight, the long line advanced slowly up Herr Ridge. Harry's regiment kept to the far left of Pettigrew's Brigade, which now held center stage. Archer's Brigade, under Colonel Fry, had surrendered their post and had moved to the right.

Brockenbrough's Virginians were moving up from Harry's left, and what was left of Davis' Brigade was supporting them. Henry Heth's entire division, with Pender's in reserve, was aligned against the Union First Corps on McPherson's Ridge. The Rebels were still under the restraints of General Lee, who had not yet arrived on the field.

A little more than a mile to the east, at Gettysburg, ten thousand more Federal troops were arriving. In fact, well over one hundred and fifty thousand gray and blue clad soldiers were converging on the village. A battle had started that morning, quite by accident. Now the fighting had lulled, and Lee had regained control, but it would quickly slip away from him. The brawl would open fresh.

The sun's momentum had just turned, early afternoon. The shallow valley between Herr and McPherson's Ridges was still and hot, and Harry had assumed it would remain that way for the rest of the day. Tomorrow would be when the real fighting started. The Twenty-sixth was at its post on Herr Ridge, the Carolinians lounging in the sparse shade. Harry was still vigilant though, and it was he who glimpsed the first puff of smoke on Oak Hill. Surprised, he shaded his eyes and stared at the distant hill. Powder flashes and more puffs of smoke burst from the trees. Then came the explosions, as rounds screamed and landed behind the McPherson Farm. Harry knew of no Third Corps batteries that far north! Who had fired those shots? He scurried to a higher rock, and on tipped toes, searched the rolling fields to the right of the wooded hill. He saw them! Long gray lines twitching in the sun. He aimed his glasses at them, grinned. There were thousands of troops, and dozens of red battle flags. It was the van of Ewell's Second Corps arriving from the north.

Suddenly, everything had changed. The Colonel's excitement bubbled over. Ewell had arrived at the most opportune place, the rear and flank of the Yankees on and behind McPherson's Ridge. Oh, how the enemy would suffer if Ewell, Heth, and Pender attacked at once.

It was a time for speed, a situation that demanded quick decisions, yet no orders came. Lee was still not present, and knew nothing of Ewell's arrival. General Heth was, on the road searching for him as the time wasted away. The Yankees realized their peril, reinforced and altered their lines, and when Ewell finally attacked, he used just five brigades. It was a bloody repulse, for the Rebel division gained no support from Heth or Pender, and the attacks were uncoordinated and piece-meal.

The Carolinians watched the fight from their ridge-top perch. The anger and frustration sparked hot in Harry as he observed the slaughter, and the missed opportunity. When his adjutant, Lieutenant Jordan, finally came panting up the ridge with new orders from General Pettigrew, they merely instructed Harry to move his regiment into the shade of the trees at the eastern base of Herr Ridge, nothing more.

THE SHADE OF THE GROVE OFFERED LITTLE comfort to the Carolina boys. There was no wind, and a fresh hatch of biting black flies was feasting on the sweaty men in gray. Occasional shells whistled overhead, and stray sniper rounds cracked into nearby trees. Tension filled the air.

Harry stepped to the eastern edge of the grove for a clear view of the north. There had been quite a bit of racket up that way, while the regiment moved down off the ridge, but the firing had died down. The last of Ewell's five brigades had been repulsed. The Colonel looked back across the valley to McPherson's Grove. He had been studying the enemy position since before noon, but he had yet to find an obvious weak point to exploit. No doubt the Federals had brought up reinforcements, and it was evident that General Heth would try their front again. Harry was certain that Pettigrew's Brigade would spearhead the assault. A bloody mess it would be, he thought, a bloody mess.

Balls began to whistle and whine overhead. The shots were coming from an old barn on the western side of the run. Yankee skirmishers had ventured over the stream, and had been making a nuisance of themselves ever since the regiment had occupied the grove. There'll be no more of that, Harry determined. He jaunted back to his regiment, yelling for his adjutant.

"Lieutenant Jordan! Jordan!"

"Right here, Colonel. Yes, sir."

"There's a barn over there, Lieutenant, full of enemy skirmishers," Harry barked. "Kindly gather a detachment and remove them. Assign Lieutenant Ashe from Company G."

"Yes, sir, Colonel," the Lieutenant saluted and hurried off.

"And Lieutenant!"

Jordan stopped in his tracks.

"Have them burn the barn." There was a distinct seriousness to the Colonel's voice.

"Right."

Harry turned back toward the edge of the grove, but was immediately hailed by Colonel Lane, who was approaching with Pettigrew's adjutant, Captain McCreery.

"Captain's here, Colonel, with new orders."

"General Pettigrew's compliments, sir."

"Thank you, Captain."

"Colonel, our brigade has been ordered to attack with Colonel Brockenbrough and Colonel Fry in support."

It was about time, Harry thought, and perhaps not too late.

"Our brigade is to lead, and the Twenty-sixth is to commence the assault. We will attack in echelon; your regiment is to step off first, and the rest will follow."

Harry nervously cleared his throat, pleased and excited with the honor.

"You are to advance directly across the valley, and drive the enemy from the woods."

Harry nodded.

"You will inform the General when your regiment is ready."

"I have just now sent a detachment to remove some enemy skirmishers from a barn on our flank. When they return, we'll be ready."

"Very good Colonel, send your adjutant to me. General Pettigrew wants this attack to be coordinated, and he will not give you permission to advance until he's heard from all the regiments. I will come back personally with the order to advance."

"Understood... Captain, we will have artillery support, I assume."

McCreery hesitated, "Yes, Colonel, I believe so."

"I don't see them deployed on the ridge!"

"They are on the way, I believe," said McCreery with a tone of doubt.

Harry shared his apprehension, but made no sign of it. He looked at his watch instead, then back at McCreery.

"Expect to hear from my adjutant in a quarter hour."

"Very well, sir." The two saluted, and the Captain quickly cut back through the shade of the grove.

Harry turned to Lane, gestured for him to follow, and set off at a fast gait for the edge of the grove. He stopped at the fringe where there was a field of the glowing wheat, took a deep breath, then addressed Lane with eyes focused on McPherson's Grove.

"I've been observing the enemy position all day."

"Yes, sir," Lane replied.

"It is strong. I see no weak points. No weak points except possibly one."

Lane stepped up to show that he was listening, while rifle fire cracked from the right. Boys from Company G were clearing the Yankees from the old barn. Harry raised his voice over the clatter, and pointed to the right.

"See that enemy battle line extending out from the far end of the grove?"

Lane squinted, then nodded.

"See how it falls diagonally from the woods and down to the stream?"

"I see it."

"Well," Harry used his hands now to aid his point. "I believe that flank is exposed, and I believe our far right will come against it. If we can turn and collapse that flank, then our assault will drive them out of that woods."

Lane nodded in approval.

"Colonel Lane, I will be at the center of our line. You will be in command of the right. I will rely on you to turn that flank."

Lane felt the pressure, a stinging stab in his shoulders, but masked his anxiety well.

"Yes, sir, Colonel Burgwyn, I'll do my best."

"I have no doubts that you'll succeed if the opportunity is there," Harry replied. He gave Lane a confident smile, then quickly returned to the business at hand.

"We have one more advantage, Colonel. The enemy batteries are to the right and left. None are on our front. I trust Colonel Brockenbrough's and Colonel Fry's brigades will absorb most of their fire. That means our fight will be one of rifles. After our artillery barrage—if there is an artillery barrage—I will advance the regiment. We will then deliver concentrated and coordinated volleys as we go. I will rely on our superior firepower to break the enemy, and only after they have broken, will I give the order for independent fire. Understood?"

Lane nodded, "Yes, Colonel, very good."

"It'll be a desperate assault. But we will prevail," Harry concluded gravely.

Smoke suddenly began to bellow out of the old barn on the right. Harry spied it, and cut Lane off before he could respond.

"Ah, I see Ashe's detachment has removed that little nuisance. I'll be sending Jordan to see General Pettigrew presently. Any questions, Colonel? Are we ready?"

Lane gave a nervous nod, but could find no words. Harry moved back into the dark of trees and left Lane staring into what had once been a peaceful glen.

THE CANNON FIRE ROARED AND ITS RUMBLINGS reverberated through the little valley. Shells cracked in the grove. Branches and leaves spiraled down on the Twenty-sixth North Carolina.

Ewell was advancing again, and fighting had started anew on the left. The regiment had been in silent anticipation for hours, and they could take no more. They were ready to spring. Harry had sent his adjutant to Pettigrew, and he was expecting the arrival of Captain McCreery at any time.

The Colonel stood silently erect at the regiment's front. His mind racing, grasping for last minute details. Had he forgotten anything? He looked across the wheat, across the thickets and the creek, stared at the menacing dark grove and the enemy within. They were just shadows, and Harry took pleasure in the realization that they didn't yet know of the fury that would soon be unleashed upon them. He had complete confidence in his men, in his officers. They would obey him. As long as he was resolved to go on, they would follow. If the grove could be taken, they would take it.

Everything was ready. He had forgotten nothing. He began to relax, but the image was back. It crept along the edge of his consciousness like a shadowy apparition, then flooded his mind. The lone horseman again. Harry shook his head. There was no horseman, no cavalry. There was no bare hill to his front, just a wooded ridge. The image meant nothing, nothing at all.

Someone was vomiting close by. The loud retching startled him, but he tried to ignore it, and reached for kinder thoughts. They beamed into his mind like golden rays through stormy clouds. His mother's face. His father's elusive smile. A giggle from Annie Devereux. Bonfires on a cool October night. Negroes dancing by the light. Kinchen... Kinchen. He was back at Cashtown worried sick. He saw an image of him on black Cora. The flourish of his derby. He was on a hill, a distant hill, a sprawling maple shading him. Harry's eyelids began to flutter, his mouth opened ever so slightly. The realization snapped in his mind. The dark horseman in the image. It was Kin—

"Colonel Burgwyn."

Lane had interrupted his thoughts. Harry turned to him and tried to focus on his face. His milky skin came into view. He was wiping his mouth, and was standing there with hat in hand, visibly shaken.

"Colonel, I feel just horrible, sir, just horrible. I'm afraid I cannot do my duty, sir. I must ask for permission to go to the rear."

It was Lane who'd been vomiting, and for the first time, Harry showed his youth to his second in command.

"But you must, Colonel Lane—you see, I can't—I can't—I can't think of going into this battle without you!"

Lane was taken aback. Harry's reaction had been that of a pleading little boy. Now, they stood before each other in knotty silence. Then Harry quickly reached into his coat and pulled out a flask, unscrewed the top and brought the silver close to his lips.

"Here, Colonel, here is a little of the best French brandy, which my dear mother gave me for just this very purpose. I haven't had a drop since the war, but it may do us both some good."

Harry took some of the sweet liquor into his mouth, and swished it about, then handed the flask to Lane, who immediately did the same. The color came instantly back to Lane's face.

"Here, stand here with me, Colonel, and we'll toast our dear mothers while we wait for Captain McCreery."

Lane was already feeling better, and he poured more of the warm liquid down his dry throat. He handed the flask back to Harry.

"Colonel Burgwyn, what's your mother's name?"

A pleasant little smile shone on Harry's face.

"Anna, Anna Greenough Burgwyn. And your mother's?"

"Elizabeth Lane. Papa calls her Liza."

"Lovely," Harry responded.

"Colonel Burgwyn... I can go in with you."

"Thank you, Colonel," Harry replied. He took another sip of brandy, and gave the flask back to Lane.

"Here, Colonel, you keep this. If you feel that twinge again, just help yourself."

"Thank you, sir."

The roar of artillery bellowed out again, this time to the left and to the right. There were no Rebel batteries on Herr Ridge to the rear of the Twenty-sixth. McPherson's Grove was hardly being scratched. Harry knew it would make their work that much more grim. He sighed.

"Oh, what a splendid place for artillery, Colonel Lane. Why don't they fire on them?"

THE DAY HAD DRAGGED INTO MID-AFTERNOON. Long hours of tension and frustration had passed. The moment had finally arrived. Pettigrew's Brigade was in line of battle in the grove at the base of Herr Ridge. Eight hundred men of the Twenty-sixth North Carolina stood at attention. The battle for McPherson's Grove would start on Harry's word.

"Post your colors, Sergeant Mansfield."

The Sergeant saluted and unfurled the regiment's brand new silk battle flag spun by Harry's older sister Maria and her school friends. The soldiers in line nearby proudly observed as Mansfield raised the colors, then pointed them eastward. Eight color guards followed Mansfield to the edge of the grove, where they halted. Harry adjusted his coat, removed his hat, and strutted forward. He walked beyond the color guard and into the sun-drenched wheat, then stopped and unsheathed his sword. Holding the silver saber high, with his head still bare, he turned and addressed his regiment.

"Soldiers of the Twenty-sixth... We have pulled the enemy from our homeland. We will fight them now on their own soil. If we defeat them, they will never despoil our homes again... The Old North State calls on you... Carolinians forward!"

He turned and stabbed his sword toward McPherson's Grove as a great chorus reverberated from the line. Harry could almost feel the sound waves pass his ears. His jaw tightened.

At attention, as if on parade, the regiment surged forward. They hustled out of the cover of the grove. The broiling western sun splashed on their necks, but their long-billed hats still shaded their faces. The golden wheat engulfed the gray host, as Sergeant Mansfield waved the Stars and Bars.

Soldiers from the Twenty-fourth Michigan, mostly mill workers from Detroit, but now members of the Iron Brigade, watched the Confederates come forward. They would bear the brunt of the North Carolinians' attack. But since Harry's regiment was so large, the Michiganders would need help from the farm boys on their left, the Nineteenth Indiana, and from the Second and Seventh Wisconsin on their right. Harry's regiment would be taking on almost the entire Union brigade.

Their grip on their rifles tightened, as the northerners prepared for combat. Since the Rebel attack was in echelon, four gray lines instead of one seemed to be advancing against them, giving the impression of a much larger force. The troops in blue held all the advantages however. They occupied a defensive line, and they were nearly hidden in the cover of the grove. They could see their enemy, while the Carolinians could only guess where the Yankees crouched.

Harry's smart line was not fifty yards into the wheat when the Union batteries opened on them. He had assumed wrongly that the enemy artillery would take on the Rebels at their fronts. Instead, they had turned their guns in, choosing to enfilade Pettigrew's advance. Exploding shells churned up the wheat field before them. But the regiment did not flinch, moving right into the storm. Then came the hot, black balls of solid shot bounding through the field, threatening to toss the men around like sticks. The cannonade was utterly unnerving, but Harry and his troops moved forward.

A tremendous crack now came out of the grove, then a sheet of smoke, and minie balls, whistling. Most flew overhead, too high. With precision and discipline, Harry brought the Twenty-sixth to a halt and barked out his orders for volley fire.

"Fire low, men, fire low, just over the wheat! Ready—aim—fire!"

Flames flashed from the guns, then blinding smoke. The Rebel balls skipped over the yellow tassels. They broke through the thicket, but were thinned by the many trees in the grove, some landing with thuds into the Yankees.

"Reload, reload, quickly, quickly!"

Another crack came from the grove. The balls whistled by. Too high again, but Color Sergeant Mansfield was down, a bullet through his left eye.

"Steady, steady. Ready—aim—fire!"

Again the Twenty-sixth sent in a heavy volley, but exploding shells began to find their mark, and crashed into the gray line, sending torn limbs and screams through the heavy air. A shell exploded directly overhead, raining shrapnel, its roar deafening. Harry instinctively bent over, put his hand to his right ear, tried to shake out the ringing. Keep moving, he thought, got to keep moving. They have the range.

"Reload, Reload!"

"Shoulder arms! Forward... march!"

Shaken, but with perfect discipline, the Carolinians lurched forward. They went twenty yards, then another volley came from the grove. The balls whined and whistled, and collided against the regiment with the gruesome sound of iron on flesh. A second color bearer went down. The regiment did not break stride. Another fifty yards, and Harry answered the Iron Brigade with two more volleys. He looked left and right, down the line. It was straight, steady, and resolute. Lane was to the right, Major Jones to the left. Harry moved them forward again. Two more color bearers had fallen.

With shaking, perspiring hands, and a tight grip on hot barrels, the Michiganders were ramming another charge home. The Rebel volley fire had been amazingly accurate. Their rounds had pierced the grove, and almost all the Yankee casualties had suffered abdomen wounds. The Iron Brigade had been matching the Rebels volley for volley, but the Twenty-sixth moved on, seemingly unaffected by the waves of shot and shell.

The Federals pulled out their ramrods and aimed their weapons. The inside of each gun barrel was grooved, and when the spark ignited the powder and ejected the ball, the grooves caused it to spin in a tight line. The balls spun out of the muzzles with tremendous velocity, and the rotation caused them to whistle, hum, and whine. The Rebels first heard the rattling explosion of burning powder, then the horrible whistle. They heard the balls coming, but did not try to avoid them. Discipline was the key in this warfare. It was what Harry had worked so hard to instill. Their concentrated and coordinated volleys were having a telling effect on the Iron Brigade. The Twenty-sixth was closing in on Willoughby Run.

At close range now. The Carolinians delivered another demoralizing volley.

"Dress that line! Dress that line! Reload... shoulder arms... forward through the creek!"

Harry and his officers now had the difficult task of keeping his regiment organized as they negotiated the thick maze of briars and willows along the run, always under decimating artillery fire from their flanks, and volley fire from their front. Once across, the Yankee cannon no longer had the angle on them, but they'd taken a toll; the regiment's ranks had thinned terribly. They had bunched to the center at the creek, and Harry was trying desperately to get his companies realigned. The Iron Brigade took advantage of the pause, and poured sheets of lead into them. The eighth color bearer went down.

The sweating Rebels seemed stunned, but they still responded to their officers. Harry raised his sword high.

"Carolinians... forward!"

They advanced into the grove, soon to halt again. The enemy line was barely visible through the smoke, and the Twenty-sixth sent another devastating volley. For the first time, the Yankees did not respond with their own fusillade. There was a trickle of independent fire. Harry felt a lightness in his chest, a twinge of joy.

"We have them! Reload! Quickly! Quickly!"

The men's sweaty hands slipped on their ramrods. They were having trouble jamming the charges home. Many turned their guns upside down and desperately slammed the rods on rocks.

"Ready—aim—fire!"

Blinding smoke filled the woods, and Harry could not see the destruction. No return fire came. Had the Iron Brigade broken?

Colonel Lane came bounding out of the smoke. "All in line on the right, Colonel!"

"All in line on the center and left," came Harry's reply. "We've broken their first line."

"We came across their exposed flank, Colonel! Just as you said! Just as you said! They fell back, sir, and the last volley sent them runnin'," Lane hollered exultingly.

"We must stay on them," Harry yelled. "They'll reform. We mustn't let them. We'll have to break their second line—prepare to advance."

Lane saluted and scampered off back to the right.

About fifty yards below the wooded crest of McPherson's Ridge was another dry creek bed. It ran approximately north to south, a natural trench. Here, the remnants of the Iron Brigade were rallying.

Drifting smoke filled the grove, causing eyes to burn and tear, but the Twenty-sixth advanced up the wooded slope, and made their way blindly through the swirling haze. The soldiers choked, their faces caked, nostrils black with powder, mouths burning, and throats parched. A clump of Wolverines, Hoosiers, and Badgers waited for them, tamping their charges. A line of fire lashed out. A ball shrilled by Harry's head, and one found yet another color bearer, the last of the guard. Harry was close. He snatched up the flag, and turned to look for another bearer. Just then Captain McCreery from Pettigrew's staff came rushing up, out of breath. Harry barely recognized the Captain covered in grime. McCreery yelled over the den, had a message from Pettigrew. Harry cocked his head, could not hear, and signaled with his hands for the Captain to repeat the order. But the adjutant was infected with zeal. He grabbed the colors from Harry's hands, stepped forward, waved the flag frantically. Another volley of balls hummed, one ball cutting through the Captain's chest. He sprawled backward, fell on the colors, and stained the banner with his blood.

Lieutenant Willcox jumped forward, the same boy who had described Archer's and Davis's battle so vividly to Harry. He pulled the flag from near McCreery's body, and advanced it three steps. The balls whistled in again. Two grazed Willcox's head, and he went down. For the first time, the Carolinians wavered, wilting under the fire—Harry grabbed the colors.

"Rally to the colors! Dress to the colors!"

A Private from Company F bounded forward. "You ain't gonna carry them colors, Colonel."

But the Private quickly perished, the twelfth bearer to fall, and Harry caught the staff before it hit the ground. His mind was clear, uncluttered of images. No thoughts of home or family. The instincts clicked in his mind; they had to rush the enemy. He held the colors aloft, waved the flag high.

"Charge! Charge! Charge!"

The Carolinians hollered like demons, and charged with bayonets. The Yankees rose from the creek bed. Powder exploded. The whistling balls came twisting through the smoke. That horrible, murderous whistle.

⁂ 2 ⁂

THE DESCENT

A SHRILL WHISTLE PIERCED THE MORNING AIR. The sound startled her, bore into her; gloved hands flew to sensitive ears, and she looked at Henry and laughed, said she wished she'd worn the fur earmuffs packed away in her trunk. The steamer began to pull away slowly from the crowded dock and, braced against its deck railing, Anna looked down at the teeming throng. The sights, smells and sounds of the waterfront absorbed her, like a Fourth of July parade, except that the balmy summer had long been blown away by December's crystalline snap.

She and her new husband were off on their first voyage, and it seemed all of Boston had gathered to see them depart. People were dressed in all their traveling finery, the ladies maneuvering their fashionable skirts through the mob, and gentlemen thrashing their walking sticks with occasional pokes toward idle, mischievous boys. There were polished porters, their black hats and calm composure slipping in their struggles with stacks of trunks. Muscle-bound sailors labored, their tired eyes framed by radiating lines as they handled thick ropes with the ease of girls handling hair ribbons. Fishermen competed in voice and price, their buckets laden with their day's catch. Cooks gathered up black, glistening mussels, and gray clams, then sniffed and prodded row upon row of silver-green cod before wrapping them in last week's headlines.

The well-wishers on the dock began to resemble colorful bits of parade confetti, until the colors blurred and ran together. A tear welled up in Anna's eye. She tried to focus on her mother, stepfather, sister, and brothers, their excited faces growing dull and smeared. She bent at the waist, her arm reaching out over the water as she vigorously waved a handkerchief. Henry saw her emotion, gently put an arm around her small waist. She looked up at him with a crooked, watery smile. He lifted her chin and kissed the end of her nose. She looked at the man she had married just three days before, and a tender expression came to her face.

He was tall and attractive, with thick wavy brown hair, a long face, and bright, blue eyes. She listened to his soothing voice. It had a tint of southern culture: warm, smooth, and gentle. His voice and graceful manners had first caught her attention, and his singular and devoted affection toward her had brought on a wedding just six months after they had met.

Anna looked away from the kind face, shifted her gaze back to the Boston skyline, and watched her lifelong home fade away. She felt empty already. Part of her was being left behind and would not be recovered, perhaps not even after she returned. This moodiness had come over her the day before, and not just because her home held all that was familiar. Her destination, the South, was a mystery, a maze of cloudy visions, most of them unflattering. It was part of her country, yet remote, and lacking a grasp of the place, she feared it.

Her mother had had doubts about the marriage. She had never uttered a word against it, but Anna had seen it in her eyes and in the curve of her lips. It wasn't Henry. No, she was very fond of him, admired him. Mrs. Sumner had terrible prejudices against the South though; she feared its influence, and was anxious it would steal her daughter away. For the moment, it had. Anna was leaving her family's reputation and wealth behind. All that was familiar would take their leave. Gone, also, would be Boston, its culture and vitality. In its place would be a land of strangers, one that she had often disdained. Her own social circles had spoken about it with trepidation. Hot and humid. Filthy and wild. A world of ignorant people with alien religions and lazy habits. A section of the country that was stuck in the past, regressing perhaps. It was also a paradoxical kingdom, possessing a clan of wealthy, cultured, and highly educated princes: the landed aristocracy, the South's saving grace, and also its greedy benefactors. A class of people who embraced America's sense of fair play and freedom, but at the same time, set itself high over other peoples, and treated them like dirt. The proprietors of black slaves, of beings who were not considered human at all. Mistreated, ill-fed, whipped and murdered. Their women, objects of lascivious and immoral acts. Chattel they were. Thought to be no better than a horse, a cow, a pig. In Anna's mind, this was the South, her husband's home.

She watched the Massachusetts coast disappear, and hoped the time spent away would be brief. After all, she consoled herself, she was just going to meet and winter with Henry's family.

Anna knew she had just married into the South's dubious aristocracy, but in Henry Burgwyn, she was certain she had an exception. He possessed their gentlemanly charm, but lacked their mean spirit. Henry's father was a planter, but had shown less interest in that aspect of his estate than in others; he had not played an active role in the management of his plantations. Mr. Burgwyn was also a merchant, who owned a fleet of ships in Wilmington, North Carolina, and had traded and traveled around the world. Henry had described his father as eternally restless, a man with short roots, as much an Englishman as an American. Anna's new father-in-law had been born in Britain and educated there, and had lived there on several occasions. His second wife, now estranged, had been from Bath. Anna was sure his son fell within a similar category, for he seemed as much a northerner as from the South.

Henry had been born in New York City and only a small portion of his youth had been spent in the warmer climates. True to custom, he'd been tutored on his father's plantations near Wilmington and New Berne, then, during his adolescence, his education had shifted to the North, with only occasional forays back to the plantations. At seventeen, he had received an appointment to the military academy at West Point, New York, and had spent three years there. He had grown restless however, and left before graduating. But he had remained in the North, and for the next seven years worked as an engineer in the construction of the Boston and Providence Railroad. He'd been so employed when Anna had first met him at the Astoria in New York, while both were visiting relatives and friends. So, clearly, her new husband was not a real southerner. He couldn't be anything like the devils of her indoctrination.

Henry took Anna's arm and led her out of the blustering sea winds. It would be a long journey, and he wanted no sick wife on his hands while in North Carolina. He was excited with the prospect of going to his father's home in New Berne and introducing Anna to his family, more excited than he cared to admit. But a blot tainted the happy homecoming he envisioned. Although he was certain all the Burgwyns would love Anna, and that she would love them, he wasn't so sure she would admire his homeland, for Anna did not know that he and all the Burgwyns considered themselves, in heritage and attitude, true southerners.

THE NEWLYWEDS MADE THEIR WAY DOWN the coast, with a quick stop in New York to board a ferry for the Jersey shore, where they stayed the night. Early the next morning, they arrived at the station just in time to catch their train for Philadelphia. Thus began Anna's southern descent, her first move into unfamiliar territory. Both anxious and happy, she fancied herself an adventurer, but the pace of change overwhelmed her senses. She had never felt so alive. A married woman now, she was being introduced to all the new intimacies.

She held out her newly ringed hand to Henry, and looked up at him, reaching out for her from the iron passageway, at the top of the car's steps. Her burgundy sleeve, a lace cuff at her wrist, and delicate hand with long, tapering fingers stretched out for his grasp. The gap between their hands closed, as if in slow motion, just before he captured her and pulled her up. The moment seared into her memory, an inconsequential instance at the time, it seemed, but it marked the moment when a fork in her road was reached. And whether hesitantly or boldly, a path is chosen that forever changes the rest of her journey. The moment passed, and Anna boarded the car.

They walked down the busy aisle, bumping into settled passengers and against the fruit and cake sellers hustling their way through the cars. The couple found an empty seat toward the front, which, although made for two, turned out to be a tight fit. Anna looked about with quick, jerking motions. The windows on either side of the car, along its entire length, were constantly being opened and shut as passengers said their goodbyes. The frosty air sent chills up her spine, so she leaned closer to the front of the car, to capture the warmth generated by a sheet iron stove filled with glowing anthracite coal. Then, with all the windows up, the train began to vibrate, the engine softly huffing and puffing, like a racehorse gathering strength for a run down the track. The coal's heat and foul smell grew intense. Anna put a handkerchief to her face, and watched a woman across the aisle stuffing her uncomfortably hot child with heavy pound cakes to keep her quiet. The tactic worked, until the cakes were gone. Then came the grating wails; the mother jumped up, and tried to open a window to release some of the stifling air, but bitter blasts and indignant protests rose from other passengers. Anna was glad her kerchief covered her amused grin at the woman's tart response.

"Death of cold or death of heat, makes no never mind to me."

After a trip that seemed much longer than its five hours, the couple gratefully clambered off the train only to board a steamer resting in the Delaware River bound for Wilmington. Once there, they again caught a train, destined for Baltimore, then yet another steamer, the *Albemarle*, for an overnight trip down the Chesapeake Bay to Portsmouth, Virginia. Anna felt like a ravaged potted plant, set out to drink from a gentle shower, but left forgotten when the shower turned to a squall.

She was exhausted, but the numerous new and strange places kept her from closing her eyes. The vast Chesapeake, its waters and shore swirling with life, was as busy as a bee hive on a warm spring day. Water weaved through the yellow marsh grass that framed the Bay. The Laughing Gulls, their summer black hoods now resembling moth-eaten winter caps, ha-ha-haaahed in delight, as they swooped near the steamer's bow. Pelicans flew by in a V-formation, looking awkwardly majestic with white heads up and ungainly beaks pointing the way. Their round bellies skimmed the Bay's undulating surface, the leader's fringed brown wings flapping, and signaling them all to flap. Then they held their wings still, soaring in unison. Anna watched an osprey hover high over the water, its bent wings fluttering, its tail fanned out. It plunged feet first, then came up with its slippery prey agleam, a golden treasure in the light of the magnificent sunset. These were the scenes of her first southern evening.

"It's so beautiful, Henry."

"Yes, isn't it?"

"And peaceful."

"Um hmmm," Henry agreed, as he leaned languidly on the rail and puffed on his pipe.

They looked out across the water, watching the day slowly come to an end. Anna let the sights and smells enrich her senses. A warm glow filled her eyes, and she caught the spicy scent of sea water. Comforting, almost familiar.

"It's not at all what I expected," she said moments later.

Henry looked at his beautiful wife, the smooth skin of her youthful face reflecting the setting sun.

"What did you expect?" he asked.

Anna didn't answer. An embarrassed smile told the tale. She had spoken too fast. She had never disclosed her anxieties about the South to Henry, unwilling to offend, wishing to hold judgment until she saw first hand. She would stay to her vow, smiling, saying nothing, yawning exhaustedly. Henry saw right through her reluctance, and picked up yet another clue to the discomfort he'd been sensing.

Henry returned the pipe to his lips, and together, he and Anna gazed across the Bay. They watched the earth roll on its belly, a molten sun dipping into a radiant horizon.

Alone in her small cabin since Henry was in a separate sleeping berth, Anna was getting ready for dinner. She had had her bath, making due with the basin, ewer, soap and small towel in her compartment. She had tried in vain to get more towels from the Negro stewardess, but after being rudely informed that one towel was more than enough, she had been soundly ignored. Anna had never received such treatment from a servant, and she was more than a little exasperated. She pondered whether she should have listened to her mother and brought her Irish maid, Madie, along with her.

Later, over dinner, Henry introduced her to a Mr. Collins, also a Carolinian. They talked about her first impressions of the South, and Anna, still offended, told the two men of the stubborn stewardess who had refused to give her an extra towel. Upon leaving the dining room, Mr. Collins made a special effort to track down and admonish the stewardess, telling her to take care of Mrs. Burgwyn.

"Burgwyn? Dat's Miz Burgwyn?" the old Negress asked, as Collins pointed to Anna still sitting at the dinner table.

That night, Anna was valiantly fighting back sleep, still trying to read, but the words kept blurring and fading to black as she fought her weary eyelids. Then came a startling knock at the narrow cabin door. Her eyes widened.

"Yes?" she called.

The door opened, and the Negro stewardess' round, black face peered around the edge.

"Miz Burgwyn, does you needs any'ding 'fore you retires?" she asked sweetly, her brilliant white teeth bursting from her wide smile.

Surprised, Anna just sat in the chair, staring at the now good-humored Negress.

The woman laughed at Anna's reaction, her musical peals and hoots sailing down the passageway, across the deck, and out to the Bay, warming the chilly air before dissipating in the salty night mist.

Anna recovered her composure, stammered, "Excuse me?"

"I says, does the Missas needs any'ding? I knows how you ladies like to use up my wash towels, and lawdy I tries to understands why a clean white woman needs so many a' dem towels, but I figger yuh needs some extra, and Cook tells me you didn't eat much a' yo' beefsteak so I come ta see if'n you needs any'-ding like biscuits or towels 'fore you retires."

Anna was fascinated. The black woman, so sullen and closed before, appeared as accommodating as a king's footman. Anna marveled at the animation in her open face and musical voice, her high cheeks, wide nose and thick lips, the rich ebony skin that wasn't really black at all, the pink palms and dirty fingernails, the long eyelashes and soft, fuzzy curls that escaped from under a faded red kerchief.

"Thank you, but I'm quite comfortable."

"Lawdy chile, yuh look like yuh gonna fall right over. Git on in dat bed and let ol' Grace tuck yuh in," the Negress said, as she walked into the cabin, laid a second towel on the tiny dresser and pulled the bed covers down, her movements unhurried, but deliberate.

Anna stood up, the book nearly falling from her lap. "You don't have to do that. Thank you, I can take care of myself."

The black woman stopped and looked at Anna with a knowing smile.
"Well, you just calls ol' Grace if'n you needs her," and she almost bowed, while slowly backing out of the cabin.

Anna's surprise at the change in the stewardess lingered, and she put the book aside, taking up pen and paper to write to her mother.

"This is the first time I've felt away from home. But here everything is southern. Not a white person of the serving description to be seen, & the ladies with their blackies & southern accents & manners, to say nothing of crying children, not at all interesting. However, Henry introduced to me a Mr. Collins of N.C., the first gentleman other than Henry from that state I have ever known I believe, whom I found to be extremely conversable, intelligent & agreeable. He told the old stewardess of the steamer who I was, and I can assure you, Dear Mother, I never knew the force of that expression 'what's in a name' before. The old blacky treated me like a child."

They arrived in Portsmouth the next morning. As they steamed into the working harbor, Anna walked out on the deck, refreshing herself after a much-needed sleep and eagerly eyeing the new surroundings. She sauntered around the deck a few times, trying to make the most of the weak December sunshine, before she stopped and watched the shipping activity in the busy dry dock and Navy yard. It looked functional to her, and even with the rosy hue of the sunrise, the scene was quite unpicturesque. She was watching sailors scrub, paint, and repair scratched and barnacled hulls when she noticed dark, shrinking shadows against the climbing sun.

She gasped. They had to be slaves, she thought, dirty, black slaves who had melted into the shadows like puddles of grease and tar. These were the creatures she had imagined she'd see. They were poorly clothed, some with tattered rags hanging off bare chests, and they crawled off barrels and out of corners with a slow nonchalance that telegraphed, only too well, their reluctance to start the day. She was both horrified and fascinated. Her expressions of mingled repulsion and curiosity went unseen by Henry, who had moved up behind her. But he knew what she was looking at.

"Slaves," he said, in a guarded tone.

She quickly averted her eyes from their nakedness and looked at her husband. A chilly wind kicked up, and Henry seized the opportunity.

"Let's go inside," he said, and pulled her gently into the passageway. An uncomfortable silence overtook the couple as they made their way to shelter and warmth. Anna had fully expected to see slaves while in the South, and thought she would be prepared for the sight. But this was different.

Wrong, she thought, a crime, keeping people in such a state. How do they justify it? How do they sleep at night? But she kept her tongue. She huddled against Henry on a bench, his arm around her, a hand stroking her arm. They sat, waited, and did not speak.

The couple disembarked the *Albemarle*, and took the cars for a short journey to the Blackwater River, passing through the Great Dismal Swamp on the way. Forlorn, dark, sorrowful, Anna thought, as she peered from the car's window. Black pools of stagnant water, gnarled cypress roots like arthritic knuckles of witches, the fetid stench of rotting things: A place where nightmares were born. Spanish Moss drooped and clung to the matted branches overhead, like moldy cobwebs, making the snake-infested, dreary swamp forest even more horrifying than she ever imagined the southern landscape could be. Built nearly in the swamp, were several dilapidated Negro huts squatting around a rough framed building with brick chimneys on the outside. A house, she guessed, where squalid white people dwelled. Anna's visions of a filthy, miserable land of heathens had, in one morning, come rushing back.

Later that day, they disembarked the train, only to board the little steamer *Fox*. It would carry Anna and Henry down the Blackwater River into North Carolina, then down the Chowan River, across the western end of the Albemarle Sound and into Plymouth. Anna figured she had been on one ferry, three trains, and three steamers in three days. She was tired of traveling, and disheartened by some of the things she had seen. Yet, there was the thrill of others. It was a great adventure, and she was reluctant to miss any of it by sleeping.

They steamed along at ten miles an hour down a river, which seemed much too narrow and shallow for the steamer. Anna could reach out and touch the overhanging tree limbs from both sides, and the surroundings were as thick a jungle she imagined could only be found in darkest Africa. She took in every bit of it, marveled at a curious kingfisher with its ruffled crest, long, sharp bill, and white collar. Its loud chatter amused her as it darted about and perched on dying cypresses at every bend in the river, as if showing the boat the way. She breathed in the fresh scent of southern pine, filling her lungs, and held a handkerchief to her nose when the winter breeze brought in a smell of rotten eggs, the natural scent of the marsh. She saw wild myrtle and holly bushes, their green leaves polished to a high sheen and dotted with brilliant red berries. She leaned over the steamer's rail and watched a Great Blue Heron, its soft gray plumage cascading down its curved neck like the pen strokes of a capital "S." It cocked its long beak, ready to snatch a plump frog. When they reached the Sound, she saw great rafts of waterfowl, and overhead the startling beauty of thousands of white swans flying in splendid, purposeful formations. She listened to their mournful calls, spellbound, until the flock finally faded away in distant clouds. And as Anna watched the southern landscape flow by, Henry eyed Anna. He wondered if she saw the beauty as well as the wildness, the repulsion as well as the intoxication that was the South's charm.

THE COUPLE DESCENDED A WOODEN PLANK, to set their feet on Carolina soil, and Henry danced a little jig, making a fuss about finally being on home ground. Anna couldn't resist a giggle, amazed at seeing her husband, usually so controlled, kick up his heels. She wished she could feel as lighthearted.

Trunks were loaded onto a stage and the weary travelers climbed into the four-horse coach that would take them on the final leg of their trip. Four other adult passengers and a child also boarded, ensuring tight quarters and no privacy.

The day had opened cloudy, dreary, and all of it would pass before they reached their destination. Anna, tendrils of hair escaping their pins as her hat bumped against the back wall of the coach, wondered how she could stand a full day of jostling over pitted paths. She managed a loose smile at the little boy sitting opposite her, as he was pummeled between his heavy-set, full-bearded father and his delicate, but plump mother. Gradually, she turned her attention outside and saw more swamps, drippy trees melting into swirling, inky water that reflected the muddy sky. The opposite window offered the same drab view. Recent heavy rains had raised the water levels; the swamps overflowed, covering the road in places, and turned it into a muddy quagmire.

The coach began to bump violently, a loud rattle from vibrating wheels. Anna found the sound unnerving. Had the wheels fallen off?

Henry explained. Numerous logs that resembling corduroy wales had been laid across the road to help keep the stage from getting stuck in the deep mud. Unfortunately, the touch was nowhere near as soft as fabric, and Anna felt every bump down to the marrow of her bones. No such roads were needed in New England's rocky soil, and she wondered for the hundredth time how she would survive the trip.

The clouds swelled like thirsty sponges, grew darker, and unleashed a cold drizzle. Anna thought it strange. At home, in Boston, the tiny drops would surely be fat white flurries in this season. Was there no snow in the South? Henry laughed.

"Of course we have snow, but hardly ever before January," he exclaimed with a definite tone of relief in his voice.

"Why, no snow at Christmas?" Anna asked.

"Rarely," he replied.

"My first Christmas without snow," she lamented.

The stage plodded along, making slow progress despite infrequent stops. When they did pause, it was usually to board precarious looking ferries that offered the only passage over brown, swollen streams. Occasionally, they took respite at hamlets: dingy, mud-soaked little back-washes of dilapidated hovels. More evidence of the uncivilized and wild country she had anticipated.
The countryside was no better. The same monotonous scenes of fields infested with broom sage, abandoned farms, and shaggy pine forests, set against a gray, soggy day. It was a vision of tedium and depression, and Anna's heart sagged.

The light grew dim. The short December day was drawing to a close. During the last hour, Anna had been staring out the window for what seemed an eternity. Time had simply stopped. She had gotten used to the pain in her rump and lower back, but a powerful urge for sleep filled her.

Finally, she heard Henry's voice coming from far away and realized she had actually drifted off. From exhaustion, or simply to keep her eyes in her jostled head, Anna's eyelids had quietly closed, and her face had nestled into the soft wool of Henry's shoulder. The carriage continued to stumble on, and Anna lifted her head.

"Pardon?" she looked up at Henry and asked sleepily.

He smiled and caressed a fallen curl back into place, as the carriage finally slowed to a stop.

"New Berne," he whispered. "We're home."

❧ 3 ❧

THE COTTAGE ON THE NEUSE

New Berne, N.C.
December 8th, 1838

My Dear Mother,

 You never need have any doubt, dear Mother, that I should forget my home, & ever for a moment cease to wish to return to it again. I would relinquish everything earthly except my husband's love, it appears to me, for the sake of being settled once more amongst you all.
 Henry & I arrived here yesterday evening terribly fatigued from our long journey. Despite the most uncomfortable carriage ride of my entire life I should think, somehow I fell asleep, and was awakened by my dear husband just as we entered the gates. It was very dark, & when we drove to the door the house looked like an illumination. There were lights in almost all the windows, & Mr. Burgwyn & Thomas ran down to meet us & caught me in their arms most affectionately. Oh Mother, I am delighted with southern manners thus far.
 After many gentle hugs and tender kisses we were ushered into the parlor, which is, I assure you an exceedingly cheerful one. It has three large windows opening on to a piazza fronting the Neuse. It is carpeted with a delicate blue & white carpet, & on one side of a large hospitable wood fireplace lies a handsome sofa; on the other a handsome reclining chair. Then there is a central table with pretty books, a side table ditto, & the piano which Henry sent from New York. The ensemble is externally very handsome & the house internally perfectly charming. But, dear Mother, this is nothing compared to my apartments when I was shown them. They are fitted altogether by Henry's taste, & he has not omitted the slightest article which could conduce to my pleasure or comfort. I have a dressing room very prettily completed, in which stands, to begin with, a spacious mahogany wardrobe reaching to the ceiling (which, by the way, is not very high, as the house is a cottage). Then a charming easy chair, then a very beautiful rosewood work table, French, & the prettiest thing I ever saw of the kind, & on the mantel piece are two dear little night lamps. There is a spacious closet

I take great delight in. Then comes my sleeping room which is carpeted like the other and contains a French head stand with a canopy of scarlet & white, confined in a circular form over the bed & hanging most gracefully around it. The pillows are ruffled & like the covering, white as snow- then I have a mahogany end table & a bureau with a marble slab & a mirror on top. There is another cozy fireplace & on the mantel are my candle sticks & flower vases. Next is another closet with shelves for my books & a mahogany wash stand also with a marble slab at the top. Then I have a rocking chair & a small rosewood bureau with French perfumery. Henry has forgotten nothing I could desire, and this morning I have been fully occupied with arranging my little domicile. My chamber has an easterly front, towards the river, which offers bright sunshine and cheerful prospects. The whole house is very cheerful in fact, nothing magnificent or costly, but very comfortable.

As for the family, about whom you must feel the greatest curiosity. I can say nothing, except that I expect that every day will make me more & more fond of Julia. She has a sweet voice & face & must have been very beautiful, before she had so much sickness. She reminds me continually of Mrs. Chas. Inches, whom I think she very much resembles, except with Julia you have all the Lamb without fear of the Lion. She is a treasure & already I think of her as a sister. I very much like Thomas Burgwyn. He is one of the handsomest young men I ever saw in my life & is a very fond admirer of Byron. Collinson, the youngest of the boys, has been confined to the house, his room, & is by no means well yet. He refuses my company when in such a state. As you know, Sarah Emily is off on the wings of the winds, as is a common occurrence with her, & I shall not meet her here. As for Mr. Burgwyn, well, he is one of the kindest-hearted men who ever lived.

I know you will think this strange at this season of the year, but the weather is enough to enliven anyone. The windows and doors are flung open with pleasure and, in looking out, I notice the Ladies walk about with shawls only. I am having my flowers attended to with all expedition, for I intend to have a fine display in the spring. Henry is exceedingly interested in the matter & plans to construct a miniature green house for some fine japonica & geraniums. I have six bulbs in my room which are growing beautifully.

Soon I will be devoting myself to visitors, and this evening I had a very pretty serenade, which I think quite famous for New Berne. We are to go to Ravenswood Plantation next week for one night to visit, & I am very much looking forward to the pleasure. Thomas & Mr. Burgwyn propose going there tomorrow to announce our intentions.

I am not in the least bit homesick or unhappy & am surrounded by the most considerate family. New Berne, if it were peopled with New Englanders, would make one of the most beautiful towns in the world. The streets are exceedingly pretty, being lined with trees & open to one side, & the other to the river. There are very pretty homes in the town which would make a fine appearance if they were nearer each other and weren't so few- three or four ugly buildings for each pretty one, and most surrounded by Negroes. There is not a hill to be seen, nor rock or stone. I have seen beautiful specimens of cotton and have procured seeds of jasmine for you. Oh, and this morning I ate a delicious fruit I had never before heard of called a Persimmon. It must be eaten when perfectly ripe or it is as disagreeable as you please. It is sweet as a preserve & has a stone very much like a tamarind.

You must write often and keep me up on all at home. How is the General? Give him my love. Will Janey come visit? You must tell John to come to New Berne while on his tour of the South, & tell David I plan to compose all my letters to him in Latin since he shows little interest in those I write in English. I shall keep my promise and keep you informed of all our little frolics here in the South. I shall write as often as possible, with all my love, your most affectionate daughter, Anna.

THEY STROLLED IN COOL, MORNING sunshine, arm in arm. Anna was delighted with the weather; she was quite comfortable in her shawl. Henry waved at a finely dressed old gentleman sitting on a nearby portico.

"Judge Cash," he whispered. Anna smiled and bowed her head gracefully.

The streets were almost clear, with very little carriage traffic, and they had nearly all of it to themselves. Her eyes scanned the town, taking in every little detail, anything that was inconsistent with New England. There was a cow ahead, eating some old grass by a fence post, its hind end protruding into the dirt lane, its waving tail posing an obstacle. She pulled at Henry's arm, indicating a desire to give the animal a wide berth.

"Won't find any cows in Boston's streets," she declared with a slight hint of indignation.

"Um hmm," was Henry's nonchalant reply.

Anna focused on a large, fine-looking house diagonally across the street. It resembled a castle.

"And what strong prince dwells within that abode?" she asked.

Henry grinned.

"The proud resident of that estate is not currently present in New Berne, and I would hardly call him a strong prince. Weak king perhaps, but not a strong prince. The castle, my dear, is owned by my half-uncle, Mr. George Pollok."

"Ahhh, I see."

Henry had told her all about George Pollok, before they were even married. The richest man in Carolina, he owned forty thousand acres and a thousand slaves. He was considered a highly cultured, well traveled, elderly gentleman, and a mysterious bachelor.

"I've been contemplating writing Uncle. He has an extraordinary library that I'm sure he'll allow you to visit, in exchange for putting it in order. It has been rather neglected of late, if I recall."

Anna beamed; she coveted books.

"Oh please do, Henry, write him. I adore dusty libraries."

Henry smiled down on her, patted her hand. "I will, this evening."

There was one unexpected inconsistency in the town that Anna couldn't help but note, and which made her quite uncomfortable. The streets and houses were full of loitering Negroes. She had expected the slaves to be on the plantations, with just the occasional house servant roaming around the town. The blacks she saw seemed to be quite tribal: a clump here, mumbling, a cluster over there, laughing. They appeared to have nothing in the world to do, yet they looked strangely content. Anna asked about them.

"Free Negroes," Henry said. "Because of the season, the plantations aren't hiring, so they're in town looking for work, some of them. You won't see as many come plowing time though, and—"

"What is that?" Anna interrupted. She had stopped abruptly and was pointing at a shack. Henry looked over, toward a huge sow sleeping underneath the structure, a sow that was rather famous in New Berne.

"That's Dr. Avery's brood pig."

"He's gigantic!" she exclaimed.

"She," Henry corrected. "Would you like to see her? She's quite impressive."

Anna scrunched her nose, "Will she bite?"

"Not likely; she's in a pen, see?"

Henry led her over. The shack was of a considerable size and the sow was hanging out from underneath on all sides. Her giant snout snorted, as if she had a cold, and the fine dust in the bottom of her pin scattered.

"My, is she sick?"

"No, no, she's just so big her breathing is difficult, so she takes a deep breath now and then. Let's see if we can get her up."

Henry saw some filthy sweet potatoes at the edge of the sow's pen, reached over, and flipped one toward her. It rested near her snout. She didn't move. He picked up another, tossed it, and the potato hit her on the head and rolled away. The sow wiggled, opened her eyes, looked at her distracters, but still made no effort to get up. Henry reached for a long handled rake leaning against a post, and poked at the sow's flabby back. With snorts of protest, she kicked her legs.

"No, no, Henry, she doesn't want to get up; let's leave her alone."

"She'll get up," Henry poked her several times, then spied some dried apples on the other side of the pen. He used the rake to push some against her snout. She ate one, while staying prostrate, so Henry moved some more just out of her reach.

"Suppa', pig-pig, suppa'," Henry chattered.

Anna giggled, as the sow began to squirm out from under the shed, kicking, and snorting, and causing the little structure to shake. The sow got on her front legs, pulled, and with great difficulty managed to get her hind legs out and up. She wobbled, hardly able to stand. Henry kept tapping her with the rake handle.

"Pig-pig, Pig-pig."

There she was in all her glory, a speckled sow.

"She must be three hundred pounds," Henry speculated.

Anna stepped back, and covered her gaping mouth with a hand, her eyes wide as she watched the mammoth attempt to walk.

Suddenly, there was terrible growling; a big scraggly dog had come from Dr. Avery's back yard.

"Henry!" Anna screeched. She grabbed his arm. The dog's hair bristled, his growls turning vicious, as he threatened to attack. Caught off guard, Henry stepped back, and Anna panicked. Releasing her husband's arm, she started to run. The dog saw her fear, and leaped after her. Henry swung around with the rake handle, smacked the dog on the shoulder, and the cur careened into the dust, where it got up and stood its ground. Henry jabbed it in its chest repeatedly, sending the dog reeling backwards, still barking, and snarling. Anna stopped about twenty yards away, now recovered from her fright, and heard a crowd of Negroes laughing at the ruckus. Henry worked his way between the dog and Anna, then raised the rake high over his head, as if he would smash it down on the dog's head. It cowered, growled one last time, then scurried away. Henry walked calmly over to the pen and placed the rake exactly where he had found it, then he turned and glared at the still laughing Negroes. They ceased their chortle at once and went back into their protective huddle.

Anna tried to suppress a laugh, covering her mouth as Henry came toward her.

"Never, never run from a dog," he said very seriously. "It will sense your fright, and its instincts are to chase, attack."

Anna still managed to cover the grin, but her amusement showed in her eyes.

"It's not at all humorous. That dog could have hurt you. Always stand up to dogs, retreat slowly."

She could hold them no longer, the giggles rolled out. Henry tried to act annoyed, but a smile escaped him. Anna hugged him, apologized through her snickers, and promised never again.

They strolled down to the river, and since the tide was out, walked in the packed, moist sand along its bank. Again, Anna noted differences.

There were no rocks and little vegetation, just mussel shells, mud, and sand. Occasionally there was a clan of cypress knees, and around the tide line, countless cypress draped with mournful Spanish Moss. The river had a distinct brackish smell. The only sounds were of its weak waves swashing at the shore. The river was very peaceful, a little sensual.

The cypress gave way to some young pines, and beyond them were fields of harvested corn, the stalks cut, but the stubble still in neat, long rows. The couple strolled into the field, hand in hand, each following an indented path. They came across an old two-wheeled cart used to haul shucks, and

Anna jumped in, begging Henry to push her.

"My feet are sore. I've got corns," she laughed.

Henry gave in, grabbed the handles, and pushed slowly.

"Faster, faster," she urged.

Henry jogged.

"Faster!"

He began to run and Anna squealed. Suddenly, he purposely turned against the grain, pushed the cart quickly over the rows, and Anna bumped violently, giggling while she jostled. Suddenly, Henry stumbled, the cart turned sideways, and Anna went tumbling into the dirt.

Henry got up chuckling, but Anna was laughing so uncontrollably, that she rolled in the stubble, holding her sides, unable to rise. Henry dove in and began tickling her. Her tears streamed, and out of breath, she begged for mercy.

"No quarter! No quarter!" he yelled, and she began to scream hysterically. Finally, Henry relented. They embraced, kissed.

A rust-colored sporting dog came bounding up. They heard him panting as he approached, and he tried to lick their faces. Anna wasn't scared, she could tell he was friendly, with his flashing tongue, waggling tail, and panting smile. Henry got to his feet, threw a corn stalk, then helped Anna up, as the rusty dog jumped after it. He came running back, wild-eyed and smiling, ready for more. The dog made numerous retrieves, and Anna admired his determination and beauty.

They turned back towards town and encouraged the dog to follow. He pranced ahead, his nose skimming over the ground. When they neared the river, he shot into a briar patch and a hare flashed out into the stubble. Anna watched the cotton tail bouncing over the rows, the yelping dog fast behind it. She clasped her hand to her chest, and hoped the dog wouldn't catch it. Henry teased her.

"Watch," he said. "The dog has no chance."

Sure enough, the darting hare circled back around and jumped back into the very thickets from which it came. The rusty dog pounced in, whining, barking. He rooted around, his busy nose puffing. He dug, jammed his muzzle into the dirt, snorted, but the hare was safe in its hole. Henry and Anna chuckled at the flying dirt, then left the dog behind.

They turned down New Berne's main street and headed for the church. Henry wanted to take her up the steeple, and show her the view. A young Negro with closely cropped hair and a pointed head, made his way toward them. He was carrying something behind his back, and when he drew near, he stopped, bowed politely, then displayed his wares. It was a rough cage made of sticks with a handsome red bird perched inside. Anna thought the bird marvelous, but she didn't want it. She whispered in Henry's ear.

"Very sad, such beauty in a cage, let's free it."

Henry paid the boy twenty-five cents and instructed him to deliver the bird to the cottage. The couple then continued on to the church, climbed the steeple, and sighed at the vista until they grew hungry.

Back at the cottage, Anna found the bird on the portico and immediately snatched up the cage; she stole for the backyard while Henry asked Bella the cook to prepare some tea. Anna placed the cage in the middle of the lawn. She opened the make-shift door tied with string, then slowly stepped back. Freedom was just a hop away, but the bird made no effort to escape. Instead, it sat quietly on its perch, its tufted head twitching from side to side. Anna watched for a while, then lost her patience. Perhaps it was afraid of the ground. She gently lifted the cage and placed it within the "V" of a young elm. The result was the same. Henry came up behind her.

"It's been a captive too long," she said.

"Perhaps, but probably it's forgotten how to fly. The boy must have trapped it when it was just learning. Without its mother and confined as it has been, the talent never developed."

"Should we break the cage around it and force it to relearn?"

"No, it's too vulnerable to predators; it wouldn't live."

Anna thought about the dilemma.

"Would you make it a larger cage, a wire cage? It could strengthen its wings. Then we could free it."

Henry's eyes squinted, he raised his head, poked out his chin. "Of course, good idea. It might just work. I'll construct it at the same time as the green house."

She looked at the glowing red bird with orange beak. We'll soon have you flying with your friends, she thought. Anna retied the cage's door just as Bella announced tea.

SHE WAS IN THAT WONDERFUL STATE of half-sleep, her head snuggled into the soft, downy pillow. She thought she heard her mother's voice down the hall, listened to the sound of her own gentle breathing, and relished the comfort of home. She drifted off, then heard the creak of the door and the padding of soft footsteps across her bedroom floor. She opened her eyes a crack, noticed the light and the smell were strange. She wasn't home at all. The chamber maid had come to light her morning fire.

Henry had told her never to show signs that she was awake when Tamer made her morning rounds. It would hurt her feelings immeasurably. She had dutifully obeyed for the last week, but this morning Anna was determined to thank her. She rolled over, sat up, stretched, watched the servant crouched at the hearth, and heard the match strike.

Tamer stood up, but kept a slight crouch to her back and shoulders as she turned to leave.

"Good morning, Tamer!"

The servant jumped, squeaked, then turned and saw the mistress.

"Pardon, pardon me, I didn't mean to startle you." Anna blinked, looking at the wide yellow eyes and coppery face.

"I's sorry, Missas."

"I was already awake; I just wanted to thank you for your comfortable morning fires."

Tamer smiled shyly, and lowered her head. She was a handsome girl, Anna observed. But Tamer's smile quickly turned to a frown followed by a frantic dash for the door.

"Sorry, Missas," and she was gone before Anna could reply. Anna hoped she hadn't hurt her feelings; she stretched again, then noticed there was bright sunshine behind the curtains. She threw off the covers, jumped for the window and pulled away the drapes. Her eyes squinted against the brightness. She admired the shining river, the horizon beyond, rows of cypress, live oak, and cedar. A glorious day, but Henry was off on a hunting excursion at the plantation, and it was bound to be a lonely one. She thought of the day's coming activities, the social calls, and the prospect deadened the beauty of the view. She looked back at the bed, but duty beckoned.

Her northern impatience was showing. She paced around the parlor, waiting for Julia. Sweet, gentle Julia, she thought. How does she do it? She'd been making social calls in this dirt-road town for years. A few nice houses, a few nice parties, but really, nothing at all to keep one stimulated.

She heard the delicate footsteps coming down the hall, then saw her at the parlor's entrance: the once beautiful face now pock-marked, the warm, gentle smile. Julia seemed tired, listless, but she insisted on the calls. Anna helped her with her shawl, and the two women stepped out into the chilly air.

The town was perfectly silent, without a hint of urgency, cemetery-like. Anna tip-toed around some bovine droppings, fresh, steaming. Then she saw the horned fiend moving slowly toward her. For three straight days this quadruped had been particularly attracted to her person. It seemed not at all docile in its character, and Anna had been cautiously diffident. Escape wouldn't be difficult, since she was rather fleet of foot, but Julia was accompanying her, so she would have to be brave. She attempted to ignore it, hoping it would lose interest, and hung close to Julia, thinking strength in numbers might prevail. But what if it assailed? She saw its approach from the corner of her eye, and her feet took charge; without further thought, she took to her heels. Once she had successfully evaded its path, she stopped and frantically motioned for Julia to run. The cow had halted lazily between them, chewing, slowly cutting its head back and forth.

"You know a cow won't attack," called Julia. "She is paying you a compliment, just being friendly."

"I am not overly fond of her perfume," Anna retorted. "And not at all courageous enough to make her acquaintance. Make haste, Julia! Please run!"

Julia cut a glance at the cow, smiled coyly, then sprinted for her sister-in-law. Anna caught her, and they both ran on and giggled. They stopped, and looked back at their slow-footed assailant, who hadn't budged.

"I don't think she has malicious intentions," Julia suggested.

"But still, a cow is a cow, and to me, terrific," said Anna.

"You have no cows in Boston?"

"Not the four-footed kind," Anna shot back teasingly. Julia gasped and looked at Anna in mock horror, put her hand to her mouth in gleeful shock, and wondered how a proper woman could utter such an indiscretion.

"Oh, you're mad!"

Anna grinned.

In the Watson home's drawing room, Anna watched her frosty breath. Why did southerners wait until they had callers at the door before they had their darkies light a fire, she wondered? She leaned towards the smoking logs, wishing, wishing for the chill to let go. She rearranged her skirts for the third time, took another sip of the steaming tea, and looked at Julia over the rim of the cup. That smile, that interested expression as she listened to the Watson sisters tell the story of Joshua Rudd taking a carriage ride with Lucy Coefield for the third time this week. Surely they wouldn't talk about that again. What else could be said? How could Julia be so politely interested? Didn't they have something, anything, else to discourse? Was this the most important event in New Berne or anywhere else?

"... about your thoughts, Anna?"

"Pardon me?" she blinked and turned to face Frances Watson with her own polite smile.

"I was asking Julia how she would have responded to Mr. Rudd's invitation. Would you have answered?"

"Well, first I would have informed him I was a married woman."

The sisters tittered. It was the right thing to say. Just enough indignation. Trying to decipher the magnolia delicacies of southern manners, the proper balance, was difficult indeed. Yet she admired the rhythm and grace, was determined to support the character of a lady whether she was in the Great Dismal Swamp or the polished circles of home.

But this was extremely tiresome, horribly irksome. They were total strangers and she cared not a straw for them. She was a northerner, and they were obviously disposed to think somewhat unfavorably of anyone from that clime. In fact, every female New Bernite often gave the appearance to think she would bark and bite. On the other hand, at times, it seemed they were beginning to like her. After all, she had married a southerner. She might have been too stiff and invincible at first. Now, she was endeavoring to be diplomatic. In her heart, however, Anna rejoiced that she was a Yankee, she was more proud of it every day.

"...ruined her dress, I'm sure."

Anna listened to the feathery talk; she looked at Frances Watson as she would a common fruit, with total ambivalence. Incredibly bored, she looked as empty and flat as the Queen of Spades, not that anyone here would know what that royal woman looked like, she thought. It was practically a sin to have such amusements, and the fact that she could play cards, dominoes, chess, checkers, dance and laugh like a living mortal put Anna past redemption. Why, a game of cat and rat would simply give them a fit of the horrors.

"...reading parties!"

Anna's thoughts returned to the parlor.

"I propose the reading parties that existed one or two winters previous should be revived," Frances was saying.

"Yes, that's a marvelous idea!" agreed her sister Meredith, nodding rapidly.

"We could meet every Thursday evening at a different home, read a chapter or two and discuss it."

"That sounds fine," said Julia putting down her teacup. "And every lady would have a turn at making the next selection."

"You mean every lady and gentleman," Anna interrupted. They looked at her. She steadied her cup and cleared her throat. She was about to give her opinion, as forthright as she had been her whole life. After all, with both ladies and gentlemen present, there would probably be very little reading, and the party would be all the more enjoyable.

She swallowed hard. "I'm sorry."

Julia's eyes widened in sympathy, her little smile blossomed.

"Please, Anna, don't be nervous. You'll fit right in."

HENRY WAS HOME FROM THE HUNT with the spoils of the chase. There would be a joyous reunion, then a bridal party at the Thornton's, and the next day, Christmas, a dinner party. On New Year's Eve, the Burgwyns were to dine at Judge Clarke's, and on the eighth of January, there would be a ball to celebrate the anniversary of Andrew Jackson's victory at New Orleans, to be held in the hall over Mr. B's Counting Room. Finally, there was Henry's upcoming birthday party to prepare. Anna couldn't have been happier with the prospects of so many frolics, and her guest lists were nothing short of extraordinary. All of Henry's family would attend, including Mr. B's brother George, fresh from his plantations near Wilmington, and their Devereux cousins who were staying at Mr. Pollok's castle. All the prominent persons of the town would be there of course, including all the talented young girls. Most importantly, Anna would welcome her brother John, who had just arrived from Boston, in the opening stages of a tour of the South.

The Thorntons' Christmas table was delectable. First came pickled oysters and a round of toasts to the new bride and husband, then came oyster soup and beef soup followed by roasted turkey, boiled fowl and ham, and beef with accompanying vegetables. For dessert, lemon, apple, and mince pies; custard, jellies, and syllabub; preserved apples, peaches, and limes; then lastly, delicious coffee.

Anna was quick to note that the young reverend Mr. McRae was in attendance, which made for a sad occasion. Just the previous Sunday, he had executed a long dissertation on the sin of dancing, so his presence would deprive them of any such joy. It was just as well, she sighed, for the cause of dancing in New Berne was a constant subject for discussion and not worth the trouble. The young ladies just wouldn't partake, and the gentlemen would get very angry. To hear the fuss, one would think that if any mortal would so much as hop a jig he would be subject to eternal damnation. She thought of home and was thankful that there were some parts of this world that tolerated such escapes.

Just as she feared, after dinner the sexes split. The ladies formed a circle and discussed the coming fair to benefit a parsonage for the Presbyterian minister; the gentlemen retired with their tobacco to the drawing room where Henry showed his Grecian design for the new Roman Catholic Church, at the request of Judge Clarke. Anna looked at all the solemn faces. There they were, dressed in their finest, at a party—yet all were deathly quiet.

Sweet Julia was the savior. As if by cue, and when the clock struck ten o'clock, she feigned illness and asked the Reverend to escort her home. No sooner were they out of the fine double doors, than one of the Thornton's servants came in with a heavy bowl, and another brought a tray of sparkling glasses. The men looked over; skirts began to rustle. The whiskey punch was served and the sinning began.

Tongues loosened quickly to verses and puns. The first singing was a rendition of the Huntman's Chorus by some visiting German friends. Anna was glad when it was over and didn't care to hear it again, German being such an unmusical language in her opinion. The young men of New Berne stepped up to the piano, including Henry's brothers, and from somewhere there even appeared a flute and a fiddle. Lively dancing soon commenced: waltzes, cotillions, and the Virginia Reel. Even Mrs. Samuels, looking like the devil himself, short, fat, and hideously ugly, danced with her elongated husband.

Anna danced with Henry's Uncle George who was tall, stout, amiable, and to her eye, more handsome than his older brother, Mr. B. He asked her opinion on the subject of dancing, and she candidly told him she was a Unitarian, and consequently that she thought it conducive to her health and happiness. Therefore, she highly approved. He, by no means, objected, as was evidenced by his talented feet.

She spied her brother John conversing with the beautiful Todd girl. Nearby was Melanie Thornton, another Carolina beauty. Both were intelligent and delightful in spirit, and she worried that John might lose his heart to them. However, she knew they were proud and scornful, and not easily flirted with; they expected much more attention from their gentlemen than northern ladies did, and at the same time, were more reserved. So far, John had had no success in persuading a Carolina girl to dance.

As the night waned, the guests turned to games: dominoes, backgammon and chess. Then came the sentimental songs, *Auld Lang Syne* and *Home Sweet Home*, and after dancing into the morning, the honored couple finally departed at two AM.

The dark was still and silent, the sky like velvet, and the moon nearly full. It was but a short walk to the cottage, and Henry carried Anna's scarlet cape and lace scarf, for the December air was summer like.

"It's too beautiful not to extend our walk, not to make it last," Henry said as he looked at the glowing moon. "Let's stroll down by the river."

Anna breathed in the night air, and nodded her approval. They made their way to the Neuse, a wide silver ribbon, and walked along its bare banks. A cool breeze kicked off the water, and Henry wrapped Anna in her cloak. They ambled along in comfortable silence, slowly growing moody, a little melancholy. Anna paused, and gazed at the black satin water, the ripples, the cool shimmering light.

"Sometimes I feel I'm in a different world," she said quietly. Henry glanced over the water.

"I can look up at the moon and see the same gentle face I used to see at home, but everything beneath is different."

Henry nodded; he could feel the burden of an unwanted conversation.

"This is such a..." She searched for the word. "... a confusing place. Not to be disrespectful, but I feel a chilled aloofness, and at the same time, a warm welcome. It's both dirty, and yet pretty. The people are generous, yet they hold others in bondage... How can that be?" She looked at her husband in earnest.

Henry shuffled his feet in the sand. It was best, he thought, it was best for them to live in Boston, but the possibility made him shudder. He saw himself as a small man there, a feeble man, not in control. There would never be a fortune, and he would never be able to guide his life in a desired direction.

"Life is different here," he responded. "It has to be."

"Why?" She asked in a frustrated tone. "We live under the same rules. We all worship the same God. Can't you see that slavery is a terrible wrong?"

Henry grimaced, looked up into the dark. "It's not a question of right or wrong. It just is." He paused, knowing she wouldn't be satisfied with that, and expanded.

"It's a question of geography, climate, and... and tradition."

Anna cocked her head.

"Can't you see?" He swept his hand out across the river. "Haven't you noticed the differences? This is a land of wide rivers, fertile plains, and long growing seasons. It's best suited for planting, and so the society has to be different."

"Of course," she said. "But we have farmers, and we have no slaves."

Henry shot back. "You did fifty years ago."

Anna bristled. "That was then, and we learned to do without them as you must here."

"You just don't see." Henry shook his head. "This is a hot country, scalding. You've never experienced it. Whites are unsuited for the kind of labor this land demands, and the blacks, they're from a hot country, they thrive here. This land, this climate, it requires a special labor force and the Negroes provide it; it also requires special management, intelligent caretakers, and the whites provide that. We take care of the land, and we take care of the blacks, and the system works here, and without it, the South would have never developed into the country it is today."

"Of course, I understand that perfectly," she said with confidence. "But why not pay them wages, why not let them have their own homes with the freedom to move to different jobs?"

"And give them the vote too, I suppose."

"Of course."

Henry turned away, paced. She was so naive. She hadn't been around them long enough, hadn't seen they were different. In his mind, they were unmotivated idlers, most of them. The free ones proved that.

He didn't want to go into it, didn't want this conversation in the first place. He spun around, impatient.

"Listen, I don't wish to defend slavery. I'm just trying to make you understand why it's here. I appreciate what you say, but the Negroes have been here two hundred years, eight generations. Freeing them is not at all as simple as you imply, trust me."

Anna felt victory, but she graciously agreed to let the topic pass.

"I own no slaves, and suppose I never will," Henry added. "My father owns many, but he will pass them to my brothers, I believe. They are suited for that lifestyle, they want to be planters. I, I am good with figures and numbers. I think of myself as a builder, not a planter. It's a foreign occupation."

Anna felt relief. She had never been sure of Henry's motives, and he had never been so open.

"We'll go to Boston in the spring. While there I'll think on it. I make no commitment mind you, but I promise to consider staying."

She felt a shot of joy. She knew she could never ask him to stay in the North, and must not pressure him. But his considering it was all that she could have hoped for at the moment. She hugged him, thanked him, felt a huge weight lifted, while Henry, Henry felt it all the more.

The day after Christmas they took a buggy ride to Glen Burney Plantation, passed the race course surrounded by haunting, vacant buildings, then bounced through the piney woods, where holly, mistletoe, and evergreens grew in abundance. In the afternoon, they shot arrows in the garden with Collinson,

Thomas, and John, while the red bird chirped in its new cage, and flew up and down from its perch to feed on the seeds that Anna had so thoughtfully flung there.

Their peace was spoiled by a fire in the town. A worker had accidentally caused a spark to fly into a barrel of spirits and the turpentine distillery went up. All in town assisted in extinguishing the blaze, but there was no saving the building. The boys retired back to the cottage, sweating, and coughing, but they soon recovered and bathed. After dinner, Anna taught Bella how to make Pumpkin Pie, which was declared delicious, and would thenceforth be called Yankee Pie in her honor. Henry unloaded some crates sent from New York and found his watercolors of Italian and Venetian scenes. He hung them in Anna's chamber as she supervised. Late that evening, Henry brushed Anna's hair, as Collinson read a play out loud, *The Lady from Lyons*. All the household, servants and all, gathered 'round and enjoyed until Collinson's eyes grew blurry. They all scattered to retire, and the cottage grew dark.

On the morning after New Year's Day, Henry woke his wife early, brought in some oversized boots stuffed with puffs of cotton and insisted that she wear them.

"I will nurse your corns until your feet are better, but you must wear the boots."

It was a ridiculous sight, and since they walked about the town at least once a day, Anna's footwear soon became the talk of New Berne.

On that particular morning, Henry had another surprise for her. He loaded her up with brooms, dust pails, and dusters and they made straight for Mr. Pollok's castle. They passed Judge Cash again on his portico, and he couldn't resist making a comment on the boots. He praised the particular way Anna navigated. At the castle, they met Mr. Pollok's servants, Billy, Tassy, and Spence, who escorted them to the grand library. Anna gasped at the sight of what she was told was the finest collection of rare foreign books in the country. She licked her lips and went right to work, first attacking the dreaded cobwebs, then sweeping away the dead moths. Armed with a rag and duster, she removed each volume and rubbed the leather until it shone. The servants assisted, while Henry, with arms folded and at a safe distance from the flying debris, chuckled with satisfaction. At final inspection, Anna noticed that quite a number of books had been returned to the shelves upside down or out of order. She pointed this out to Tassy before realizing the errors came not from laziness. Not a one of the servants knew their letters.

Upon her return to the cottage, she was astounded to see ol' Tom Sandy, the gardener, planting peas. Tom was a feisty old soul, and when she questioned his endeavor at so early in the season, he was offended.

"Massa reads da almanac, says gonna be a mild win'na, so I's a sowin'," he grumbled.

She looked at the puffy cheeks under his wrinkled eyes and was glad he never smiled. He possessed the worse teeth she had ever seen.

"Did you feed the bird today?" Anna asked.

Tom Sandy shook his head, murmured something inaudible, and waved at her, as if to suggest not to bother him with such trifles. She looked at the bird, its lovely red feathers fluffed up against the chill. There was plenty of food in the cage, but that day, the bird had not eaten, sung, or flown.

THE GRAY RAINS AND BLEAK WINDS of January and February came and passed, and during that time she practically lived in Mr. Pollok's library. She read the classics, all the books in Latin she could get her hands on, then went home and practiced the piano. Henry was working in his father's Counting Room during the days, and the rest of the family was in and out, never around for more than several days at a time. Julia had taken a long sabbatical to see her Devereux kin in Raleigh, so Anna took on the responsibility of mistress in her absence. She had been apprehensive about housekeeping, knowing her inexperience in such matters, but with firm determination she managed. Actually, she was a natural, and the bywords for the servants became: "Missas Anna, yuh don't loves to see no dust no place does yuh?" She arranged and rearranged twenty times a day.

There were still little parties, visitors, and afternoon teas. Henry took her on carriage rides on the few pleasant days, but her life was becoming intolerably monotonous. To overcome her growing homesickness, she wrote home often.

Reverend McRae was a frequent guest, but always failed to cover his disappointment in Julia's absence. He was determined to make Anna a good Episcopalian though. Anna admired the prayer book, and thought the service much better than the Unitarian, but in all other concerns, Reverend McRae did not succeed with the conversion. At nights, Henry read poetry to her by the fire, or her brother John's letters from the deep South. They always declared wherever he was "uninteresting."

In the latter part of March, Henry brought home some Negro children from the plantation to liven up the cottage—two of Tom Sandy's grandchildren. Anna was instantly infatuated with the three-year-old girl, little Polly. She thought her a perfectly beautiful, funny little thing, and loved to hear her talk and giggle. She went on frequent shopping expeditions, buying Polly shoes and frilly dresses. John Fanning couldn't help but notice the attraction, and proposed Anna take Polly to Boston that summer. She grudgingly refused; she couldn't think of separating the little jewel from her family, even for a month.

Eventually, she came to notice that the black children avoided Tom Sandy, their grandfather, so she questioned the older boy.

"Da meanest ol 'man dare is, scares me, beats us all da time."

A ritual developed during the first afternoons of spring. Just after Henry's return from work, he and Anna immediately set off for the garden "a la Carolina," with a troop of Negroes fast behind, large and small. They carried hoes, rakes, and shovels, and the rite took on an almost regal character. The townsfolk took notice, gathered and watched, and even clapped when the garden was transformed into a gorgeous bed of tulips hyacinths, and other colorful flowers.

One fine morning in early April, Anna went out into the gentle breeze to harvest peas. She filled a basket, got up to take it in to Bella, and felt light-headed. She looked down at her belly, and rubbed the little growing bulge. Tom Sandy was sitting on a bench by the fence. He had just finished eating, and was picking at his teeth. Anna waved. He scowled at her, got up, and slowly shuffled off.

Everyone seems to have the blues, she thought, everyone but me. The household was in a funk, yet it was spring time. All the family, white or black, seemed to lack energy and spirit. In a sudden burst of defiance, she thought: I will always keep my New England habits, and on no account lose my Yankee traits of character. I shall never become a Southerner, or ever like living among them.

Anna looked at the birdcage, the green sprouts of grass, and saw a red feather trapped in the tangled blades, waving in the breeze. She stared at the empty perch, and sighed.

April 6th, 1839
New Berne, N.C.
Cottage on the Neuse

My Dear Mother,

I confess that I am wicked enough to wish time away. I long to see you all so much & I believe were I to live here a thousand years I should always feel like a stranger & a sojourner in the land; but such, Dear Mother, is not my intention. My thoughts are bent upon spending my days in the land of my birth & among those I love, & if I do not carry my point it will be the first time I ever failed. Would you like to know one of the air castles I build when alone? It is to be at housekeeping in a neat little house in Boston, & to have you & the General with the rest of the family come to see me as often as you would. When you go to the theater to come & pass the night with me, when you come in town to drive right to my house & stay there with me, & to make all your appointments there. To have Janey come & stay whenever you could spare her, & have my brothers consider themselves at home there. I would study order & good management to please you, cooking for the General & whatever would be most agreeable to the others, & I would always have an open heart & ready welcome for ole

Henry's friends. And last, though not least, it seems to me that I would strive a thousand times more than I do now to make Henry happy. I know he hates the idea of living in Boston & from my soul do I regret it, for he is so kind & affectionate to me here, that I cannot ask it of him. I know he would have to work much harder than he does now, but my sacrifices would become as light as air to me. Now living in Boston does not seem unreasonable in my opinion. However, I know that whatever is, is right & cannot therefore complain or feel unhappy.

I must say, I am growing more and more impatient with my Negro servants. Tamer, my chamber maid, is not quite equal to welding a ruffle iron, and when I showed her how to iron cuffs I burned myself starching & all the sympathy I received was a roll of the eyes & an amused grin. I am opposed to Slavery more each day & think I would rather be reduced to poverty than to have anything to do with it. If I were not in Carolina I think I would be an open abolitionist, for I would rather have one white servant than sixteen blacks. But the trouble is to be relieved of such a curse. I believe every slaveholder in the Union would be glad to abolish them if he could, and I have yet to meet one lady of the land who condones the institution. I have seen nothing of the cruelty that had been described to me as a youth. On the contrary, I see much spoiling and coddling, which, as you know, ruins all those thus treated. But Henry assures me abuse does exist, only not with the occurrence we northerners tend to believe. I have little fancy for southern institutions & none at all for slavery. If asked to describe it in a word I would call it "bear-trap," for as much as they defend it as beneficial to all, I tend to believe it quite the opposite. It will be the ruin of both races.

The wondrous animal, Mr. Pollok, arrived at his castle this week & created quite a sensation. Fortunately for some poor mortals he was too fatigued to dine with us that evening as we expected, for I think the knowledge of his arrival & his actual presence would be too much for one day. Well, when I finally met this august personage I soon recovered my wandering senses. Mr. Pollok is very tall & thin, almost emaciated, but he has the manners of a courtier. His hair is thin and perfectly gray & he has a fine Roman countenance & I think a sweet expression about his mouth. He rose and shook hands with me when I entered & he told me that the Carolina air had not been injurious to me, he should suppose. He spoke of travel, climate & provisions and I found him not the least frightening. He is precise and reserved and very handsome for his age & when he talks with Julia, whom he has known from childhood, he speaks the same as with a stranger, such is his formality.

When Julia excused herself, our conversation turned to religion. He said that in Boston he believed the talent, generally speaking, was confined to the Unitarian Church, & that the reason the people here were not Unitarian was because they had not sufficient understanding to be so. On climate, he acknowledged that here was not more healthy than at the North, that he had never passed but two summers here & then he nearly died. We agreed admirably on all points & when

I left I was more pleased with him than I had ever hoped. I had misgivings of him before because I feared he would prejudice Henry against Boston, but I must say I do like him now, & all I hope is that he never will leave Henry a cent of property in plantations or Negro flesh.

Soon after breakfast this morning Mr. Pollok came by to say good-bye, for his visit here was to be brief. He is going to the Roanoke to inspect his plantations there. He has been quite ill of late and Mr. B. tried to persuade him to let him accompany, but Mr. Pollok said he was much better & I believe he is. Still, he is a frail man. We talked very pleasantly, but he seemed sad when he went away. He told me he hoped I should leave Carolina without any reason to speak ill of it, and I expressed a desire to see him during the season in Boston. He said yes, towards the autumn. But I should not be surprised if he never returned to New Berne again, or if he lived ten years longer.

I have been thinking about coming home for so long I have the hysterics— I laugh, I cry. Yet, this is such a pleasant season in New Berne. We have delicious green peas and strawberries & a variety of flowers & the wonderfully fragrant magnolias. The weather is warm and the surroundings couldn't be any more pleasing, but I wish with all my heart to leave it. Just imagine, in a month I shall be sitting in the parlor, beside you, or playing the piano, or singing with all my family, & all my favorite people will be near. Henry is as eager to go as I, and he says we must leave by the middle of May at the latest to save my health. I will never set foot in this town again. Give my love to all, and tell them I will be among them soon. Your most affectionate daughter, Anna.

P.S. I send you this confectionery to convince you the people here are not so bad as I have portrayed or as you imagine. I enclose below a recipe for Syllabub which southerners use in place of ice cream & I find quite delicious.

"Season milk with sugar and white wine, but not enough to curdle it; fill the glasses nearly full and crown them with whipped cream seasoned with the same."

TWO DAYS AFTER ANNA COMPOSED THIS letter, Henry's Uncle George Pollok died after a fall from his horse, while riding on his plantations near the Roanoke River. He had no will and no direct heirs.

In May, after an easterly storm delayed their departure, Anna and Henry left New Berne for Boston. On September 21st, while at the Greenough family home in Jamaica Plains, she gave birth to her first child, a girl, Maria.

⁂ 4 ⁂

THE LEGACY

THE FABLE BEGAN MANY YEARS AGO, more years than can be counted. No one will ever know exactly how or when it came about.

They came from the grassy savanna, near the middle of the earth, on the dark continent, where men first walked on two feet. The game was abundant on the plains, and even before the taming of fire, they thrived. They spread in all directions, and to the north and east they came in contact with people of sharper features and lighter skin. The Greeks and Romans would later call them Berbers and Libyans, and they dwelled near the sea. Those with dark skin came among them, and lived and mixed with them for centuries, until the dry winds swept over the savanna and turned the grass to sand. The Great Sahara emerged. Those with dark skin retreated south, and those with lighter skin clung to the sea. They were separated once again.

On the savanna they grazed their flocks, grew millet, and traded with the caravans that traversed the sands. But there were some among them who took the fire and the metals, and went west to dwell in the rain forest. They settled along the wild rivers and by the ocean. They fished and hunted in the dense jungles. Many villages sprang up, many tribes, and they worshiped many gods, and spoke a thousand tongues.

Like all men everywhere, and in one form or another, they consumed themselves. There came an era of kings. Great cities rose near the edge of the forest, so magnificent they rivaled those of the better known civilizations far to the east. They traded gold and silver, ivory and spices. They built great armies, conquered new lands, spread their ways and language, and adopted those of whom they overcame. Then the great cities vanished, soon to be forgotten.

Isolated by the sands, the thick forest, the treacherous coast, and the unnavigable rivers, the petty kings and princes held sway. Their words were law, and under them they nurtured a hierarchy. The noble, the priest, the warrior, the hunter, the fisherman, and the serf; only there, on the dark continent, in the forest and along the deep rivers, they were not called serfs. They were slaves.

Far to the north there came the great awakening, nurtured with the belief that there was but one God and his son. With this belief came the ideal that their God was for all men, everywhere. Of course, with this notion came, too, the desire to spread the word and to civilize. Great wooden ships with puffy white sails took to the seas, and armed with their new instruments that read the stars, the people of the North came upon the dark continent. There they found a race of men that, to their tastes, would make good servants. Soon, people of dark flesh appeared in every noble court within the white world.

Long after finding a new western land of vast riches, but not long after the aborigines had died off from disease, attrition, and war, the great crusaders gazed back at the dark continent with hopes it would save them from their sweat and toil. Among the peoples with the dark flesh, were lords all too willing to help and comply, for the feudal domains of the black princes were not rich. Their soil was not suitable for crops. The fetid swamps and black forests could not be tamed. There was gold and ivory, yes, but the land's greatest resource was its people.

With dreams of wealth and power, the new merchant princelings swallowed their neighbors. They took to their canoes and ravaged the villages that thrived along the river banks. Great wars flared. Tiny empires grew, only to be devoured by others. Anarchy spread, and all for the cause of gathering labor for the great white fleet.

There was a great exodus: Eboes, Coromantees, Mandingoes, Foulahs, Whydahs, Pawpaws, Nagoes, and Gaboons. They were herded to the shores of the wide ocean and a stretch of land that would become known as the Slave Coast. Jammed into great fortresses, stockades, caves, and pits, they would suffer until the wooden ships came. Only the strongest survived.

When the white captains came and moved among the captives, they would pick only those they felt could endure the long voyage. Those too old or too weak were made slaves of their captors, or rotted in the pits, until a ship came that found them acceptable. The strong were crowded into the dark holes below the decks to live among their filth, to die of disease, to starve, or expire from thirst, as the ship rolled over the stormy sea. Only the strongest survived.

They were spread over thousands of miles: from the great cape to the South, through the Indies, to the deep snows of the North. The ships sailed in great numbers, and the supply of their cargo seemed endless. Two hundred years the fleets sailed. Ten million came to the new land. So many were their numbers, so little was the regard for their lives, that they worked until they dropped. Seven years is all that most suffered. Only the strongest survived.

Finally, the great white queens came to believe that the trading of human flesh was a mortal sin and offensive to their one God. The ships found new cargoes that carried greater profits. Passage of the ones of dark skin slowed to a trickle. Suddenly, those who had lasted under the lash had great value. They were husbanded. The strongest were bred for their stout offspring. Laws were made to protect them, only to make sure their chains remained in place. A new society evolved that bore a strange resemblance to all that had come before, and all that would come after. It consisted of those with wealth, those without, and those who were consumed.

In the year of our Lord, 1839, there came the cry of a new life. The wail swelled up from a cold, dirt floor, and sprung out of the only passage in a dark, wooden shack. It spread both joy and sorrow to those who heard it within neighboring shelters. So loud was the cry that it traveled over the furrowed fields, where the dry stalks of harvested corn stood barren and bleak. Through the veins of this new life flowed the blood of the strong. Within his genes were a mix of the millions who had survived the pits, the voyage, and the lash. They called the new life Kinchen, only Kinchen, for those with the dark flesh had but one name.

Other than his blood, the little boy had no connection to his native land, for the old ways had long been forgotten. Even his name had its roots in the Island Kingdom, whose natives had once dwelled in foggy glens, and who had once worshiped rocks, trees, and air, before turning their grace to the pure one who died on a cross for mankind's shortcomings and weaknesses. Someday, Kinchen would also worship the crossed planks of the tormented, and receive great comfort from it.

Despite the tested blood of his sires, this boy was not destined to grow physically large or strong. As for intelligence, he had more than most, and less than many. But there was something special about Kinchen. He had a gift. A gift from birth perhaps, from God maybe. More than likely it was a gift unto himself.

The gift is elusive. Most who seek it never find it. Many grasp it, only to lose it. There are untold numbers of impostors. Recognizing and attempting to learn from those with the gift is difficult, for they are not the usual pillars of society. They are often meek, and do not possess a stature that one is prone to emulate. Furthermore, the one who possesses it may be unaware. He may take it for granted, or not think it special. For that matter, perhaps many more have it, and are heedless of it, until the reward is fulfilled.

So what is the fate of one who has the gift? What becomes of a boy with the strong blood of ancestral slaves, a boy with a tortured heritage, a good heart, and an unassuming nature? What is his reward?

THEY MARCHED UP THE MAIN STREET OF JACKSON Indian file, looked like a little brown army. There was one large wagon hauled by five horses carrying their clothes and implements. One small covered cart conveyed their food. There were seventy of them, and they were quiet and in good order.

The company filed out into the lot below the window of her hotel, a sprawling frame building in the heart of the little town, clean and white, the whole structure a pattern of neatness. Anna looked down on them, tried to count them. Where would they sleep?

The Burgwyn brothers were transferring the contingent from Ravenswood, to augment the troops already on their new lands along the Roanoke. The

Court had handed down its decision on Mr. Pollok's estate, and it had favored Henry's family. The conclave at last was dissolved, and its members were fast scattering to the four winds of heaven. The great business of division was concluded, and each began to look after himself. The Burgwyn brothers decided to pitch together, form their own little society along the river. Henry got Bull Hill, over 4,000 acres of prime land, and 108 Negroes. Thomas took Occoneechee Wigwam, and Collinson, The Levels and The Lake Plantation. Sarah Emily received Green Hill, which John Fanning would manage for her. Julia would have the castle in New Berne, and the Burgwyns all the furniture. Their Devereux kin got the remainder of the estate, more sizable tracts.

The late winter skies turned dull and dark early, the air cold and breezy. The troop went about kindling large fires in the lot and began to cook their provisions. Anna watched them intently, curiously, until squeaks from her little one distracted her. Maria was waking from a nap, rocking in the arms of Madie, Anna's Irish servant brought down from Boston. The baby babbled, ready for nourishment. She was fat as a porpoise, had a full head of curly red hair and a pug nose. Madie was devoted to her, and Anna enjoyed her dotage.

The mother was preparing to nurse when there came a rap at the chamber door, and pink-cheeked Collinson, with his own curly locks, walked in. His appearance was very different from that of his older brothers who were tall, dark, and fine-featured. Collinson was blond, and stocky; much more manly, but not nearly as handsome. He wore a constant smirk, and he was so grinning when he entered.

"Pardon me, ladies." He had no idea Anna was about to nurse. "A Negress has an infant with a bad cold. I wonder if you object to her bringing the child in for the night?"

"Bring a sick child in here with little Minnie, certainly not," Madie responded indignantly.

"Don't forget, we have the drawing room," said Anna calmly. "Yes, of course, bring her and the child in. Madie will build up the fire, will you not?"

Madie glared a cross frown, then nodded.

Satisfied, Collinson's strolled over to the window, and looked down at the slaves.

"A fine looking group, wouldn't you say?"

Anna tried to settle Maria who had started to fuss from the sound of Collinson's strange voice and the delay of her meal.

"I suppose."

Collinson sensed her aloofness. "You may have to get used to this sight," he snickered. "What with Henry and his ways. In six months he might be going over to the plantation to persuade every one of them to say they wish to live with him. He takes as much care of them as if they were his own children."

Anna smiled politely, still struggling with Maria.

"Will you please go get the woman and her child," Madie interjected.

"We must feed the baby now."

Collinson bowed, made his apologies, and thanked the ladies for their graciousness.

The glow of the huge fires lit up the darkness outside the window. Anna was continuously drawn to it, constantly looking down at her new possessions and listening to their soft murmurs. They were quite well behaved, she thought.

She had heard Collinson bring the Negress into the adjoining parlor, and waited a few minutes for her to get settled. Then she decided to offer her some hot tea.

The Negress was sitting on the sofa and as close to the fire as she could get. She rocked the baby gently, humming. When Anna tapped on the door, and entered, she jumped to her feet, and looked away shyly.

"Good evening," said Anna pleasantly.

The Negress gave a short, jerky nod, "Evenin' Missas."

"I'm Anna, please sit down."

The woman kept her eyes toward the floor as she sat, then held the baby loosely on her lap.

"And your name?" Anna asked.

"Nancy," was her quiet response. "But dey calls me Nan."

"Very pretty." Anna looked at the baby boy asleep in a soiled green blanket. "Your baby appears to be resting well. Is he very sick?"

Nan looked at the fire, "Not bad... It was Massa Henry, he say I should bring 'im in."

"That's fine," Anna assured. "Glad to have you. What's his name?"

"Kinchen."

"Kitchen?"

"No ma'am, Kinchen."

"Ahhh, that's a different name. How did he come by that?"

Nan looked up at the ceiling, tapped one leg nervously. "My man calls him dat."

"Your husband?"

"Yes-sum, my man."

"Is his name Kinchen?"

"No ma'am, York."

"I'm very curious, how did the baby come by that name?"

Nan looked about the room, and took a long breath. "It was my man's papa's name."

The baby sneezed a tiny "chew." Anna stepped back.

"Oh, he does have a cold, doesn't he?"

Nan pulled him tight. "Not bad."

Madie came in with a pot of tea, poured some in a cup, and offered it to Nan. She just looked at it.

"Wouldn't you like some tea?" asked Anna. Nan shook her head.

"Please do, it'll warm you up." Nan took the cup and Anna watched her put her thick lips gingerly to the delicate rim and take a sip.

"Dank you, Missas."

"We'll let you rest now. There's a blanket there and a pillow, and if you need anything just tap lightly on the door. We have a baby too."

"Yes-sum."

"Well, good night."

"Night, Missas."

The next morning Anna rose before the sun. She cleaned up and dressed, then quickly went to check on Nan and her baby. They were gone. The parlor was in complete order, the blanket nicely folded and in its proper place. After breakfast, she promptly joined Madie in her room and fed the baby, but not long after, she was unexpectedly called outside. The fires had all been extinguished; the wagon and cart were packed, and the yard neatly put back in order.

Anna stepped out on the porch in her shawl and was surprised to see the entire black contingent in one long line, all smiling up at her. One by one, each slave came up to her, shook her hand, and gave his or her name. She was quite taken back. Not having gloves on, she felt their rough, unkept hands. After the Negroes had filed past, they gathered round, smiled at her timidly, bowed, then bade her good-bye in grand style. Anna felt so strange being at the center of their attention, like a queen, or some holy saint. Was this a ritual that had to be done? They all backed away from her, bowing, averting their eyes, then reformed their line in the road. Henry waved at her from a buggy at the column's head, while Thomas and Collinson were mounted as outriders, one in the rear, one out in front. Anna watched them march off. The little brown army had walked all the way from New Berne; now they had only five miles to go to their new homes.

Anna gazed at her husband, the builder who had once thought planting foreign. But he was so excited. She had never seen him so full of life. "Now I can make my fortune," Henry had told her. Yet, as far as Anna could tell, he already had one.

He had also told her of his plan for manumitting their slaves, but had not gone into specifics on just how that would be done. She did not think he really knew.

Anna watched the procession draw off, until they were well out of sight, then rushed upstairs and scrubbed her hands thoroughly.

THEY WOULD STAY IN WHITE'S HOTEL in Jackson until a suitable dwelling could be found. The hotel was comfortable, and Anna was perfectly satisfied, though not with the country hours. Breakfast was at 6:30, dinner at 12:30, and late tea at 6:30 PM.

None of the plantations on the Roanoke had an acceptable house, except for Thomas's Occoneechee. He was no better off for it though, since he lived with no one but his servants. His solitude had been the price of a New Year's Eve impulse. On that eve, he had been in New York, and, according to some, had attended the first-ever masquerade ball in that city at the Brevoort Mansion on the corner of 5th Avenue and 9th Street. He was attired as Feramoz and, while there, met a beautiful girl dressed as Lalla Rookh. She was actually the charming, young daughter of the British Consul in New York, and her name was Matilda Barclay. The two fell instantly in love, and at four o'clock the next morning, left the ball and were married by break of day. The affair was the talk of the city.

All was fine, until Matilda's father returned from recruiting activities back in England. He had the union immediately annulled, and Thomas returned to Carolina broken-hearted and disgraced. Since then, he had repeatedly sought an interview with Mr. Barclay, but had been consistently denied. He had even returned to New York for the same purpose, and had been turned away at the door. Now, he would pace around the old house, lovesick, writing Matilda sixteen times a week. He claimed she was answering; still, his cause seemed hopeless.

The marriage bug seemed contagious, for as Thomas paced the pine floors at Occoneechee, John Fanning received a sorrowful letter informing him that Julia had married the Reverend Mr. McRae in Raleigh. She had not acquainted the family with her decision, and the only relatives who attended the ceremony were her Devereux cousins. None was more upset than Anna, for she thought the Reverend unworthy of both Julia and the Burgwyn family. John Fanning remained calm, returned to New Berne and treated Julia tenderly when she arrived. She seemed very happy, and her father gave her the cottage as a wedding gift.

ANNA LOVED MUSIC, BUT THERE WAS NOT a musical instrument in the newly rented house. It was a rambling, airy old place, but in a town as sparse as Jackson, they had but few options. The dwelling had been Dr. Cross's house before he had married, and was the most suitable in a town that existed only because it had been designated the county seat. There wasn't even an Episcopal Church.

Henry brought three old women, field hands, from the plantation to help put the house in order. If they displayed aptitude, he would retain them to be trained as house servants. Laner, Old Sally, and Penny were so alike they could have been sisters. They were tall, long-armed, with big hands and feet. Their shining faces were dark as coal, and their broad bottoms made navigating in the small kitchen and narrow doorways sometimes bruising.

There was also a boy, a stable hand and general errand boy. He was fifteen, very small for his age, and had an infirmity about his eyes that rendered him perfectly blind after dark. Anna supposed he had never been inside anything but a Negro cabin, for he had the utmost curiosity for the house and all its contents. He was also delighted with his new town clothes. Madie had made him a shirt, and Henry had another one made by a tailor, with a checked vest and yellow jacket. With new, clean handkerchiefs, he looked quite reclaimed. Jimmy was his name, and he carried a perpetual smile along with a disposition that was quick to amuse.

Since Dr. Cross had been a bachelor, the house, of course, was a calamity. Anna's first item of business was the elimination of spiders for, of all of God's creatures, there was not one she despised and feared more than the hideous little carnivores. Every nook and cranny was checked for webs, egg sacks, carrion, and the nasty, spindly monsters themselves. Even the pots and pans were thoroughly perused.

After a week-long campaign, the house began to take shape. Henry, who had been staying some nights on the plantation with his overseer, and others at Occoneechee with Thomas, was very pleased on his return. He also brought the unexpected tidings that Mr. Barclay had agreed to an interview, and that Thomas would soon be bound for New York. His numerous letters, and pressure from Matilda's mother had at least given him a second chance.

Eventually, a routine began to take shape. Each morning Henry would be up before the sun and off to his plantation, not returning until after dark. Anna, with help from Madie, trained the servants, knitted socks, and sewed clothes for the hands. She also waged constant battles with the bugs that infested the furniture.

An intricate system of color coordination was developed for the servants' benefit. Green, blue, and yellow ribbons were tied to their utensils, and towels. Cleanliness was emphasized. Ebony hands were checked and rechecked.

Little Maria, whom everyone called Minnie now, was constantly attended to. She had flaming red hair, a fiery personality to match, and was totally infatuated with her grandfather, who spoiled her unmercifully. John Fanning had become a frequent visitor, and he and Anna took many walks together, since other than reading, there were almost no other sources of recreation. The two grew terribly fond of each other.

Anna desperately sought company and fun, but there were very few parties in the town, and very little socializing. The one church held services only on certain Sundays, and she had found them so drab and alien that it took all her motivation just to attend. She begged Henry to take her to the plantation, but he had categorically refused, sighting that it was not ready for her eyes. For now, she would remain its mistress from afar.

Finally there was some excitement early that spring; Thomas Pollock and his new bride arrived in Jackson. The family met at White's Hotel and dined there. The couple could not have appeared more content. Matilda looked lovely and was lively to the extreme. Anna thought she had the wildest spirit of anyone she had ever met. She also wondered how Matilda would adjust to the monotony that would soon engulf her. Thomas announced that they would live at Occoneechee, and that they had vowed never to be apart again.

The initial reports of Matilda's adjustment to her new domestic discomforts were good. She seemed perfectly happy, and was striving to remain good-tempered. The hands at Occoneechee were delighted to have a mistress among them, and there was constant debate between them and Henry's hands on who had the prettiest mistress. Eventually, word spread that Matilda was thought to be fairest. This really didn't affect Anna, who had abandoned fashion and vanity of late, but Henry, in contrast, was quite miffed, especially since many of the hands had never laid eyes on his wife. The next day, he had Jimmy arrange the buggy so he could take Anna among them.

It was almost a full year after Mr. Pollok's untimely death, the event that had dictated that the South would be forever Anna's primary home. The ride to the plantation was enlivening, full of the scent of the pine and hardwoods, the dogwoods and redbuds just starting to bloom. Along the way, there were deep, lazy creeks and rickety bridges, wide swamps, and an old millpond that served as a perfect rendezvous for ducks and Canada geese in the fall. Near the gate, a gang of wild turkeys crossed the soft road just ahead of the buggy, their flight so quick Anna had never dreamed that creatures could literally vanish. The buggy rolled through the dilapidated gates and down a sandy lane; it passed a fallowed field, then climbed a wooded rise. Anna saw a country house, the overseer's dwelling, and gazed at the thick, twisting forest that protected it from all manner of wind, cold, and heat. She had thought John Fanning's Ravenswood stunning, but this, with its wild beauty, far surpassed it.

They bounced down a narrow, wooded road lined with colorful wild flowers and running cedar and, at the bottom of the gentle hill, jumped into the sun, on to flat bottom-land that seemed to stretch for miles. The field was in perfect order and uniformity: deep furrows of black, rich dirt, and not a stump or stubble to overturn the buggy or break the constant view of the little black waves in the earth. They rolled over the furrows then turned down a road that rose like a dike and cut right through the sea of terra firma. The lane led to the river and, as it came into view, Henry and Anna paused on a low bluff to watch its greenish brown water swirl within its unyielding current. The smells were indescribable. Henry did not say a word of embellishment; he did not need to. Anna admired the scene in silence.

He led the team down the furrows closest to the river, turned and skirted a shallow pond. Then they headed for the village. Every Sunday was a holiday on the plantation, and nearly all of Henry's one hundred and fifty slaves could be found among the rows of little frame houses. The slave dwellings had been the first project for Henry when he had arrived on Bull Hill back in October. The previous huts had been deplorable and, in Henry's eyes, totally unacceptable, so the time between last year's harvest and this year's plowing was spent in repairing, replacing, and building new shelters. All were sturdy now, some were painted, and some were even raised with wooden floors. Eventually, Henry planned to build all of them in this manner.

The arrival of the Mistress was a huge, greatly anticipated event. Henry's hands had been fussing at him to bring her for months. Some had even accused him of not really having a wife, suggesting that she was a mythical apparition of his imagination. These were not their words, of course, but this was how Henry had described their taunts to Anna. As the buggy wheeled through the village and halted in its center, the slaves scurried out of their homes and little vegetable gardens and quickly gathered around. Henry stood in the buggy and addressed them, while they listened attentively and respectfully. Most of them stared at Anna. Henry introduced her and asked her to stand. Many of the slaves pushed forward to shake her hand, or to get a closer look. She said a few, nervous words, then handed out some presents she had made, some socks, scarves, and several vests. A precious few gifts, she thought, thoroughly embarrassed at how quickly they disappeared. She promised to have more very soon, then smiled very gently and tried to look as many in the eye as she could. She recognized some of them from New Berne and Jackson, but she had never seen most of them and was amazed at the great variety of colors, sizes, and features. They all seemed in good health and spirits and not the least bit downtrodden and she suddenly felt a great responsibility for them, a great desire and need to see them all as happy as they could be. Henry stood and bade farewell and promised to be among them on the morrow, which seemed to delight them. When they pulled away, Anna waved and sighed both in release and in satisfaction. Henry had acquired the habit of calling them his "people," or his "black family," and Anna determined, at that very moment, to do the same.

They rambled up the hill to the overseer's cottage where Henry stopped and took Anna for a walk. There, on the hilltop was where he planned to build their home and the construction, he promised, was to commence very soon. He said he would clear away the brush, plant a pretty lawn and garden, burn the cottage or convert it to stables, and build the overseer a new one. He planned to remove all the trees facing the river and bottoms, so they would have a fine view, and the house, he said, would be made of brick, spacious and elegant. Anna thought the place uniquely beautiful and with the hand of art it would become a show place. She was about to tell him this, when he turned to her abruptly— somewhat like a nervous suitor, once more—

"Would you like to live here?" he asked. "Do you think it tolerable?"

She looked over the great expanse that was nearly void of anything manmade. She said, "We'll be merry as crickets. And the crickets, with their wild cousins, I suppose, will be our only neighbors."

THERE WAS TO BE ONE MORE WEDDING that spring, and Henry announced its coming several weeks after Anna's first trip to the plantation. One of Henry's hands had asked permission to wed, which was granted, and the slave had also requested that the ceremony be from the holy book, which was likewise granted. Anna grew very exited about the prospect and was determined to aid the frolic. She had placed sewing for "her people" among her priorities, and now she went about earnestly making the bride's attire, a dress of purple and red calico with a yellow belt, a white cape and a scarlet neck ribbon. Henry provided the groom a light pair of linen pants, a buttoned white shirt, and high stockings.

They set out in a large open carriage borrowed from Dr. Cross, with both Madie and Minnie within. It was the first Sunday in May, the weather fine, and when they reached the home site at the plantation, Anna saw the new frames of her future home laid out on the ground; they were serving as seats for the gathering throng. The hilltop was a perfect location. A fresh breeze blew, and the high trees shaded it delightfully. All the people had been ordered to the site, and the men, women and children were dressed in their tattered, Sunday best as they waited with anxious anticipation. Anna thought the sight of the cheerful hands gratifying, as she watched Henry climb some newly constructed scaffolding that was much too high for his audience.

Just before Henry's first matrimonial service, Laner showed up, having arrived after a five-mile walk from Jackson. She was sort of the elder stateswoman of the group and she begged Henry for the floor. He nodded his approval, and she climbed a pile of planks, cleared her throat and started her address.

"We have a good Massa, a good Missas." A general humming of agreement came from the gathering.

"It be our duty to works good for 'em, try ta do good in all dings. Don't be quarrelin', don't do no fault-findin'. If'n we live good n' right, we'll die good and satisfied." There was a nodding of heads. Laner looked at Anna sitting in the carriage.

"We gots a good Missas. I don't say it cause she's here, fo' I've lived wid her dese months back and she a good woman and I knows da good ol' creature ta acts from principle and mo' pure dan most white folks would do in her position."

There was reverent silence. Laner looked about, had suddenly lost her train of thought.

"So do good, no runnin' away cause dese are righteous folks and will do good by us."

Laner was quiet a moment, as if she might have forgotten something.

"I's through."

Everyone clapped as she stepped down, and then all eyes were on Henry in his black suit and on the wedding party in their colorful attire below him. The bride and groom looked up, stretching their necks, squinting into the sun, and looking as if they did not dare breathe. He read from the book, asked them to repeat the vows, and to say I do, finally announcing they were man and wife. The groom raced through the company shaking hands, smiling, and everyone laughed, and began to dance. Some biscuits were distributed, and even a small amount of spirits. Anna handed out gifts, mostly children's clothes she and Madie had made themselves.

Henry boarded the carriage. Madie and Minnie had stayed within it throughout the ceremony, and just as Anna climbed to her seat, a young hand approached her with a basket containing some red calico. He spoke in a low voice.

"Missas, I's York... Dis gown here, it's my woman's."

"You're Nan's husband?"

"Yeah, ma'am." There was awkward silence for a moment.

"Well," he spoke again. "Dis gown here, it's been outgrowed by my woman since da baby, and I's, I's axin' if'n you'll make it bigg'a since she don't knows how herself."

"Why certainly," Anna said. "I'll do it myself," and York smiled the most grateful smile she had ever seen.

On the ride back to Jackson, Anna praised Henry on his debut, but Madie iced their jovial spirits with the announcement that Minnie had a runny nose and she thought a fever.

"You must leave for the North right away," Henry declared. "It's quickly approaching, the season, and if the bilious attacks you once, you are done for."

"Won't you be coming?" Anna asked. She looked at the back of Henry's head while he drove, and saw it shake.

"Too much work here; I can't leave until the harvest is well under way."

Disappointment flooded over her. She had hoped to stay in Carolina until after the first of June, and realized Henry had to remain until then because his presence affected a great deal. Unlike most planters, he worked with his hands as well as his head, and he was gaining a reputation for being truly a driven man in this part of the country. A reputation Anna thought he very much deserved. But now that little Minnie had a fever, he would insist they leave, and as was their arrangement, she must obey. While they were in the South, Henry was master; in the North, she was mistress. Henry went North in the summer to please her, and she wintered in the South to please him. They had agreed on it; that's how it would always be.

5

HILLSIDE: COMINGS AND GOINGS

THERE WERE EIGHTEEN PLOWS RUNNING in the Snowden Low Grounds, pulled by ten oxen and thirty-one mules and horses; the hands were using the new plows and the new leather collars instead of the old shuck. The weeds were head-high, but the teams were working fine; the plows were turning them over and covering them up. Rawls, the overseer, was laying off the rows. More hands were planting Collins Corn over in the Gee Low Grounds and in the Uplands. The young women were setting winter squash with the corn, and more were sowing sugar beets and carrots in the Orchard Field. The older men were among the peas over in the Cherry Field, gathering ten bushels of red and three of black-eyed, while others hauled manure to the fields to be harrowed before the plows. Older women were planting sweet potato slips near the house site, where ol' Tom Sandy was superintending the children clearing brush. Britton, the brick mason and twelve of his hired men were laying the foundation for the new house or making more bricks down at the kiln. Carpenters were framing Mr. Rawls' new house, but he'd never live there; Henry had already decided his overseer wouldn't suit him another year. Hired carpenters, free Negroes, were down working on the new gin house, and Ricks, the painter, was eyeing the new stables. There were five foals running in the paddock, and fifty-seven sheep grazed nearby with eleven lambs. Boars, sows, pigs and piglets were down in the shelters, and beef cattle were over in the clover fields. The Flodden Field barn was finished except for shingles, and Turner was underpinning the Snowden Field barn and attaching a small porch. Williamson, the surveyor, was walking off the Spring Lot and evaluating the shallow lake where Henry had plans for experimenting with rice. The master himself was near the river in a sprawling grove with eight hands, cutting a new road to Occoneechee. Brother Thomas had sent over four of his own hands to help. Two of them were cripples though, and Henry had them busy burning stumps. Most of Thomas's labor was building a dam for his new mill, and the others were doing the same things Henry's were. It was planting time at Occoneechee Wigwam and Hillside Plantations.

He heard the whistle blow shortly before noon, peered down the river and saw the steamer *Poplar Point* round the bend with a load of lumber, shingles, shoes, and fresh herring from New Berne. Henry broke up the road work, rushed his hands for wagons and carts and used some of his blooded stock to haul them. He'd planned on giving the hands a holiday in the afternoon, but the steamer's unexpected arrival canceled that. Besides, the weather was good for plowing and planting, and they had the momentum.

Driver Jim supervised the unloading of the steamer, while Henry rode over to check on Rawls and the plowers. He was fairly pleased, saw some maverick weeds that needed covering and ordered Rawls to plow a half-inch deeper. He then rode over to the Galled Field where chintz bugs were in the Dutch oats in myriads; once again the oat harvest would be a disappointment. The nearby tomatoes hadn't come along enough to be affected by the bugs though, and Henry crossed his fingers.

A rider came down the hill from the house site and across the bottom land. Henry watched him coming, made him out, was half expecting him. It was Sheriff Peasley.

"I got your boy, Henry! Got 'im in jail," Peasley hollered as he approached. One of Henry's hands had run off the day before yesterday, a good hand, Oliver.

"Any complaints?"

"None yet," said Peasley. "I think he stayed out of trouble. He was awful hungry."

"What'd he say?"

"Won't say a word, but wants to talk to you."

"I'll talk to him tomorrow morning, first thing. Let him spend the night, think on it," said Henry.

"That's fine, got room for 'im." Peasley said as he took off his hat and wiped his brow with a round, bare arm. He was a stocky fellow in his mid-forties, with a fat face, shiny red. His eyes were always bothering him, and he bit at his lips frequently.

"Where'd you find him?" Henry asked.

"Didn't. Arthur Fox found him in his barn last night. You know where Fox's is?"

"Up towards Garysburg, isn't it?"

"Yep, he was heading noth for Virginia."

"Odd," said Henry. "His wife's here. Tamer."

"Um hm." Peasley squinted into the sun, eyed Henry's plows running, then replaced his hat and put a hand to his forehead.

"Place looks good," murmured the Sheriff. Henry looked at his plows, nodded.

"Think you're plowing too deep though."

Henry grinned. Everyone in this part of the world plowed too shallow, he thought. He'll learn.

"Passed your cotton land on the way in. Looks like mine, cracked and parched up."

"No rain since the eighth," Henry replied.

"I'm gonna have to replant. You too, eh?" asked the Sheriff.

Henry nodded again.

They rode over Henry's bottom land until it grew dark and the plows quit. Peasley invited him over to his neighboring farm to dine and spend the night. It was taxing— cutting and hauling logs for the road all morning, riding around the plantation through the afternoon, and then going home to a house full of women and a screaming child. Henry accepted the invitation and sent a boy back to Jackson to tell Anna he wouldn't be home.

They had a fine meal, nothing extraordinary, but filling, then had their whiskey and played backgammon at five dollars a game, until it was time for sleep. Peasley won thirty bucks.

They rode into Jackson in the morning, straight for the jail. Peasley opened the chamber, and let Oliver out. He was a big man, very dark, with large black eyes and wide lips. He was a good plower; he didn't overwork the oxen or mules, and was one of Henry's best cotton and corn pickers. He never said much, never complained; Oliver was the last hand Henry thought would run off.

"The sheriff said you wanted to talk to me," Henry said as the two stood in a narrow hallway between the chamber and Peasley's office. Oliver just rubbed his nose and looked at the floor.

"Why'd you run away?"

Oliver just shrugged.

"I haven't treated you badly, have I?"

"No, suh."

"Where were you going?"

Oliver shrugged again.

"Has Mr. Rawls done anything?"

The slave hesitated a moment, finally shook his head. "No, suh."

Henry put his hands on his hips, looked exasperated. "Mr. Peasley here says you wanted to talk to me— what about?"

Oliver leaned against the wall, refused to look at Henry, kept his eyes to the floor.

"I wants yuh ta sell me."

"Sell! Why? You're not happy?"

Oliver rubbed his nose again, thought for a moment.

'Yeah, suh, I's not happy.'

"Why? You said I haven't treated you badly."

Oliver wouldn't answer, and Henry couldn't get it out of him. The slave's face showed nothing; it was impossible to tell what he was thinking.

"I'd rather not sell you, Oliver. You're a good hand. And Tamer, well, Rawls is very happy with her, she's a good maid and cook. You both have been with the family all your lives."

"Wants yuh ta sell me, Massa," Oliver repeated.

"You and Tamer both?"

"Yeah, suh."

Henry was angry, couldn't understand it; he had to get to the bottom of it. "You stay in here one more night, Oliver, think on this. I'll come back tomorrow, and if you still want me to sell you and Tamer, I will, but you have to tell me why."

Oliver slid back into the chamber, never looked at Henry, and didn't say another word. Peasley locked him in.

"Ever heard of such a thing?" Henry asked Peasley. The sheriff shook his head.

Henry rode home for a mid-day meal, and came upon little Minnie in the front yard riding Blind Jimmy like a horse. The boy was pretending to stalk the fowl, chickens and ducks, and Minnie was quacking and waving a stick. Henry couldn't resist a chuckle.

Her eyes turned big as saucers when she saw her daddy ride up. She rolled off Jimmy, fell down, teetered up, wobbled. Henry dismounted, scooped her up and kissed her, and as he made for the door, he called on Jimmy to feed and water the horse.

Henry ate his meal with his babbling daughter on his lap, and managed to tell Anna about Oliver. She was shocked, sympathetic, for she knew Henry had known Oliver since the slave had been a boy. On the way out Henry asked Laner and Ruthy if they knew anything about it. Laner cut her eyes.

"No suh, not a ting," Laner said.

Henry looked at Ruthy; she gave him a silent shrug.

He trotted back to Hillside and supervised the last of the plowing that day. A little shower had rolled through earlier, but had done little more than settle the dust. The plows were doing fine in the bottom land, though still not running deep enough to suit the master. Before returning home, Henry rode up to Rawls' cottage to speak to Tamer. She knew, of course, that her husband had run off and had been caught. Henry told her what Oliver had requested. She answered him straight off.

"No Massa, don't wanna go."

"Do you know why he wants me to sell the two of you?"

Tamer shook her head, but unlike Oliver, looked Henry straight in the eye.

"You don't know?"

"No, suh."

"Don't know why he ran?"
"No, suh."
"Will he change his mind?"
"Don't know."
"Will he tell me why?"
"Don't know."

He was getting nothing out of her, but he sensed there was something very wrong. "I told him I would sell him and you together."

"No, Massa, I don't wanna go."

"You don't want to go even if I sell him?"

"Yeah, suh."

"You're not happy with him?"

Tamer wouldn't answer, but Henry knew that had to be it.

That evening he went to the jail and talked with Oliver again. He hadn't changed his mind; he still wanted Henry to sell him and Tamer both. Henry told him Tamer didn't want to go, and the slave's eyes dropped, but even through his tears, he insisted he wanted to be sold. A week later nothing had changed, so Henry charged Rawls to take Oliver to Halifax where he was sold for six hundred dollars.

IT HAD ALWAYS BEEN A CAUSE FOR CELEBRATION for those who dwelled along the Roanoke: the coming of the rockfish. Each spring they swam up from the Atlantic's depths and rushed into the sounds, and against the river's current, for the sole purpose of spawning. They were a good eating fish, and had nourished many a red, white and black man.

That spring, about three weeks after Henry sold Oliver, Anna, Madie, and little Minnie would enjoy their first romp along the Roanoke with a "muddle party." Henry loaded them up in Dr. Cross's open carriage, since his own buggy couldn't hold them all, and pointed his team of bays toward Captain Flower's Plantation, down river from Hillside and just this side of the ferry to Halifax.

They passed through their own plantation on the way, stopping in to check the house's progress. Anna cooed at the pretty little purple wildflowers that dotted the lot. The day was perfect, and with breathtaking cloud formations scattered in a brilliant sky. A warm, sweet wind moved through the tops of the trees, carrying clean, diverse scents, mixing them all together, and filling nostrils and lungs.

The house was coming slowly, the brickwork not nearly complete. The kiln had not been able to keep up with the demand, and Britton's layers had been called off on another job. The house would be grand though; they could see it taking form—two stories, several piazzas and an English basement. Anna couldn't wait for its completion, hoped to move in during the coming autumn, after her annual summer retreat to the North.

They doubled back to the main road and made for Captain Flower's. It was an historic road, the very route Cornwallis and his redcoats had used on the way to their fate at Yorktown, Virginia some sixty years before. Not much had changed in that time. Northampton County was still a wild, harsh country, the trees still thick and tall, the forests full of bear, deer, foxes and the like, and swamps too dense to be explored. The human population had experienced little growth to speak of. No railroads cut through Jackson, and the steamers that chugged up the river were a recent occurrence. Since the Roanoke was a narrow river with treacherous currents and shifting bars, it had taken quite a bit of persuasion by Henry and his brothers to get the first ocean-going steamers to come up as far as Hillside and Occoneechee, and much to their benefit, they had succeeded. Now the brothers could sell their crops as far away as New York, and at much better prices.

The gentry had rolled in to Flower's place; carriages lined the grassy flats near the river. Young boys with bamboo poles were already stationed along its banks trying their luck, while their fathers and older brothers were off in canoes and skiffs in search of the running rockfish. A muddle party was peculiar to the Roanoke. It was named for a concoction of fish, ham, red peppers, and spices that were mixed together in a great, black kettle and stirred over an open fire. These gatherings were usually casual affairs, and Captain Flower's was no different. Rough, clothless, boards were placed on saw-horses and strategically arranged under shade trees not far from the river. Plates lay randomly on the planks with a piece of bread on each. The hot kettles rested on the planks, and there were two barbecued pigs and two boiled hams for those who didn't favor the main dish. Sweet potatoes and peas balanced the meal, while figs, grapes, and preserves gave it sweetness. For dessert, there were pies and candies of every description.

Anna had been waiting for this party with great anticipation. Cooped up in the rented house all winter, she had found few opportunities for fun. Minnie, her household duties, and constant sewing for her people consumed nearly all her time. So, with pent-up Yankee energy, Anna dove into the festivities with her nurse and toddler fast at her heels.

There were a few strange faces to explore, for Anna hadn't become familiar with all the gentry who dwelled in the county. The Burgwyns were there in force. John Fanning always loved a party. Julia was there on a visit from New Berne with her reverent husband. The bachelor Collinson, who had recently acquired a taste in fine horses, had come down on a sleek thoroughbred racer, in which he had persuaded Henry to buy a half interest. Finally, lonely Thomas was present, his wife Matilda confined at Occoneechee and expecting a child.

After the filling meal, guitars and fiddles relaxed the guests, then brought them back to life when the players turned to snappier tunes. There was singing, some light dancing. Captain Flowers had a bowling green up near the big house, and wagers were raised on the competition's outcome. The women toured the estate's grounds and gardens, which were not elegant, but pleasing all the same. Coveys of running, screaming children who had lost their patience for good manners, insured the scene would not be too serene. A clan of men and boys took to fishing again, and several of the adolescent girls complained of their exclusion. The afternoon wore on, the activities continued, and Anna had not quite gotten her fill when dark, ominous clouds appeared, and a thunderstorm swept over the river. Streaks of lightning sent them all to shelters, and after nature had concluded its impressive show, the guests started a slow departure. Henry enclosed the carriage, loaded up his little family, and his black coachman, with the euphonious title of During, guided them home to Jackson through steamy, drippy forests.

They arrived at the rented house around dusk. Blind Jimmy was there to greet them with a message from Rawls at the plantation. Tamer had changed her mind; she now wished to be sold with Oliver. Two days later, a Monday, Henry personally escorted Tamer to Halifax and arranged that she be reunited with her husband. Over the next few months he visited the two on several occasions and found them reasonably content.

THE FIRST MALE CHILD OF THE FOURTH generation of Burgwyns in America was born at Occoneechee Wigwam in early June, 1841. Matilda and Thomas were the proud parents, and they named the boy Frank. Unfortunately, he died three days after his appearance. Within a year, Matilda would leave Northampton. Her lively spirit and polished English ways could not take the banal Roanoke. Eventually, she remarried and moved to Charleston, a city that was more in line with her tastes. Broken-hearted, Thomas would regret his impulsive marriage and remain at his lonely plantation. He traveled widely, like his father, but mostly for health reasons. He would never remarry.

HENRY BOUGHT ANNA A GENTLE OLD MULE and began to teach her how to ride. He also bought a fine new carriage, black and shiny. He purchased it in anticipation of taking his family to the annual horse races at Belfield. Collinson had the new thoroughbred, Alveston, ready for the tests, and had personally ridden the horse to the track in advance, to exercise him and familiarize him with the course. Belfield was some twenty miles north of Hillside, in Virginia, and just across the Carolina line.

It was cool for late spring when they set off at six AM. The new carriage was loaded down with trunks, for the races were a five-day festive affair. They stopped at Hillside on the way out to visit some sick, convalescing hands. Henry also picked up his mare Roxanna, a descendent of the great racer Sir Archie. During, the coachman, rode her as an outrider, and was to take her to an estate near the track where she would be put to a blooded stallion.

The party rumbled to the ferry on the Roanoke, passed over to the Halifax side, and made for the estate of Mr. Thomas Devereux, Conicanarra, which, like Hillside, had once belonged to Uncle George Pollok. After morning tea, they set off again with Mr. Devereux and several of his grown children. It was a lovely, cool day, and little Minnie seemed enchanted with the ride; she continually pointed at new sights, called "Mamma, Mamma," and begged to kiss Anna's and Madie's hands and faces. She was becoming quite a little prankster, thought herself immortal, and made daring lunges as if threatening to dive from the carriage. Henry kept up a brisk pace with the two bays. The first heat commenced at one PM, and they arrived at the track just in time to witness the start.

There were five horses running, Alveston among them. The first heat was won by a beautiful black owned by a Mr. Polk from Tennessee, whose brother, Leonidas Polk, had married Thomas Devereux's sister. Alveston was a close second with another horse just beside him, while the remaining two were overmatched and crossed the line far behind.

The sprint was exciting, but Anna was there for the people. She soon struck up an acquaintance with two Misses Hintons, who were quite pretty. They seemed to have come unescorted, but were actually avoiding their father, who was terribly old-fashioned and perpetually embarrassing them with his presence. The girls were quite polished, having been educated at a school in Petersburg, while their father was a farmer in the truest sense of the word. When Anna finally met Mr. Hinton, she could see why the girls were ashamed of him. He was a plain, old gentleman, and wore a drab home-spun coat which indicated his folly for fashion. Anna commented on his girls' impeccable dress and good manners.

"You can depend on it," he said. "They have spent a heap of money for me."

Anna couldn't get over the abundance of pretty girls at the track, and the amusing flirtations performed by the stumbling young gentlemen. Mr. Blount's large family seemed the most attractive. Two of his daughters had just arrived from a visit to Richmond and were definitely the belles of the place. They pressed an invitation to Henry and Anna for a party that night at their home.

Before the second heat of the day, the third place horse dropped out, so only four horses ran. Mr. Polk's black won again, and Alveston came second. In the next two heats, the Burgwyn horse nosed out wins. The fifth and final heat would decide the day's purse, and the Burgwyns were in high hopes, as Alveston seemed to be in better condition. Anna thought Mr. Polk's ebony the handsomest horse she'd ever seen. It resembled the fairy's steed of her childhood fantasies. She secretly pulled for the opponent. At the far turn Alveston had the lead. However, a mistake by Collinson's boy, the jockey, gave a two-length victory to the black. Henry and Collinson were congratulated on their three-year-old's good show, but both grumbled and complained the entire carriage ride to the Blount Plantation.

The doors and windows of the large house were flung open in gracious welcome, and the grounds soon jammed with guests. Minnie was having a delightful time and didn't seem to mind the many strangers in the least. She never cried as she was passed around and admired the long evening through. She went crazy at the sight of so many playful children. Mr. Blount had nine children himself, and the youngest, a boy of two, was a sturdy little fellow who had never worn a stocking or a shoe. He and Minnie became fast friends and quickly wore each other to a frazzle. Fortunately for the Burgwyns, Mr. Blount invited Henry to stay the rest of the week at his home, and the next day their baggage and trunks were transferred from the town's dusty hotel.

Alveston didn't run again that year at Belfield; Collinson decided he was too stiff and sore from his first day's exertions. The Burgwyns remained and enjoyed the competitions to the end though. Mr. Polk's black predictably won all the heats it entered, but the trip wasn't a total loss. Roxanna the mare was served three separate times by a noble stallion, and eventually a healthy little colt would come from the unions.

A ball was the fitting close to the week's gaieties, and it was held at a small hall in the center of town. The turn-out was wonderful, and the hall crowded. Anna danced her southern blues away to the tunes of a single fiddler, the Paganini of the county, who called out the figures and accompanied himself with song. The dancing was such a thrill that supper passed forgotten, and the guests dined on cake and confectionery, their only refreshment. The festivities didn't close until the wee hours of the next morning, at which time Henry and Anna thanked their host, left Blount's, and started the long carriage ride home with benefit of little sleep.

At Jackson, a note from Anna's brother David was waiting for them. Her mother, Mrs. Sumner, was gravely ill. Thus Anna, with Madie and Minnie, would soon leave for Boston as fast as wheels and steam could carry them.

NOT ALL WAS WELL BETWEEN THOMAS DEVEREUX and the Burgwyns. Trouble had been brewing for months and finally boiled over that summer, after Anna had gone north. Thomas Devereux had a closer kinship to Uncle George Pollok than did John Fanning's clan, and he had always resented the court's judgment that had placed them on equal footing as his heirs. Devereux had long complained about the supposed inequitable division of the land and slaves. He held that he'd been slighted. Actually, the Burgwyns had already paid their kinsman sixty thousand dollars to settle the division, which had put all of them, including Henry, in considerable debt. Devereux's continued complaints raised Henry's suspicions as to his motives, and he started his own research. Hired surveyors soon found that Hillside had been considerably overvalued. This rankled Henry to no end, but he decided to let a sleeping dog lie.

That summer, Sheriff Peasley served Henry a writ naming him, his father, Julia, Thomas, Collinson, and Sarah Emily defendants in a suit of equity.

Devereux was demanding an additional fifteen thousand dollars. The Burgwyns gathered their forces, hired a band of lawyers, and countered with their own suit. Their initial defense was successful, but the legal battles would continue for years. Each side would win and lose, and the whole affair would cause everyone a considerable amount of suffering.

Henry managed to join Anna in Boston that summer, but he had to cut the visit short to attend to the pressing legal matters in Carolina. In October, he did receive some good news. A letter from one of Anna's brothers brought tidings of the birth of Henry's first son.

THE ROCKY, WIND-SWEPT COAST WAS NEAR, and the air carried the delightful scent of salt. The autumn colors were at their height. In the Greenough house, which was cheery and full, Anna rested with her newborn son in her arms. Her three brothers were close at hand, and her teen-aged sister was in the next room sitting with their bed-ridden mother. General Sumner, her stepfather, had heard the news and was on his way.

It was a fine old house, in the little village of Jamaica Plains, about five miles over the neck from Boston. Big oaks shaded the lawn with their auburn, freckled leaves. The house had two stories, and was constructed with old masonry, stuccoed and white washed. There were numerous shuttered windows, nine alone on the front, which allowed plenty of light to penetrate the high-ceilinged rooms. The roof was of sturdy slate; two dormer windows jutted out from the attic, while three chimneys loomed overhead. The home lay near the center of liberal thought in America, and the family it sheltered was likewise progressive. Commodore Loring had built the house in 1760, but after the Greenoughs acquired it, three generations of Harvard-educated professionals would live there. Carrying on the family tradition was David Stoddard Greenough III, Anna's oldest brother, an attorney, and a director of the East Boston Company which was developing Noodle's Island.

General William Hyslop Sumner, Anna's stepfather, added to the fair-minded character of the family. He was the son of Increase Sumner, a judge and three-time Governor of Massachusetts. He was also the cousin of Charles Sumner, a future U. S. Senator, and a founder of the Republican party, an abolitionist who would pay for his views with a brutal caning at the hands of South Carolina Congressman Preston Brooks on the Senate floor. The General never ventured into politics, but instead concentrated on building a fortune. He was well on his way to that end, when he married the widow Greenough, Anna's mother Maria, in 1836. The General would become the founder of East Boston.

Anna's new baby boy's name would bear no connection with his distinguished northern kin. Instead, he was named Henry King Burgwyn, Jr., after his planter father, and to keep the two straight, they would always call him Harry.

Later that fall, Henry ventured to Jamaica Plains in order to escort his wife, daughter, and his little namesake back to their plantation home. Just before their departure, however, Anna's mother suddenly took a turn for the worse. This prompted Anna and the children to remain in the north, and Henry returned to Carolina to concentrate on the building of his estate and the never-ending wars with cousin Devereux. Mrs. Sumner's health remained poor, and little Harry spent the entire first year of his life in Massachusetts with Anna, Minnie, his grandmother, the General, and his Yankee aunt and uncles.

ON THE WAY SOUTH, Henry stopped off in Baltimore and bought some spectacles for Laner, his elderly, near-sighted seamstress. When he arrived in Jackson, he asked Laner to pull out a needle and thread, but she couldn't hit the eye in forty tries. Then he gave her the glasses, and showed her how to put them on. She threaded the needle straight off.
"They're a gift from Anna and Mrs. Sumner," said Henry.
Laner was amazed. "You means my Missas an' my ol' Missas, dey 'members dis poor ol' nigga'?"

A few months later, the Burgwyn brothers sold off several families of their blacks to help offset mounting legal costs. Forty-two slaves in all were sent to Alabama, where prices for prime hands were much higher. Laner volunteered to go. Henry made an entry in his farm journal the day they were to set off: "Edwards took out 42 in all—he takes from me Laner, Primus, Serena & boy, Hymen, Anuisiah, Lanny, Dinah, Richmond, and Mary Dido, ten in all. They all left in good spirits."
Scipio, the hog driver, was also on the list to go, but he ran off a few days before with one of Henry's best mules, Blue Tail Fly. He came home several days after the caravan left, when it was safe, saying he didn't want to go South, he wanted to stay at Hillside with Henry. The master couldn't punish him with that excuse, and decided not to sell him.

Henry finally gave up the rented house in Jackson and moved into the manor at Hillside. The new house was far from complete; there were still scores of little things to be done, but it was habitable.
Wagon loads of furnishings were carted in from Jackson, and all the household servants moved in as well. What furniture was still in New Berne, that which had been left behind before the move to the Roanoke, was now coming up the river by steamer. Still, the rooms would be sparse.
A new contingent of field hands were brought up to the house to be trained as house servants and to augment the existing crew. Ruthy, the cook, would stay at her post. During was still the coachman, and his wife, Rachel, was a chambermaid. Joining her were Old Sally, Isabel, Penny, and her little daugh-

ter Polly. Big Milliken was the blacksmith. Blind Jimmy was demoted to errand boy, while the more efficient York was brought up from the fields to tend the expanding stables. His wife Nan came up too; she was to learn how to sew, and would replace the departed Laner as the seamstress. Coming up to the big house on occasion was Nan's little son, Kinchen, who was then two going on three. Mostly, the boy hovered among his mother's skirts while she sewed, but as he grew older, he ventured out to the stables to be with his father. He was a little fellow, and would always remain small for his age. Eventually, he would gain an intense attraction to horses. He took immeasurable pleasure in helping York, and had a particular talent for painting hooves, since he was so low to the ground. All the stock came to trust him. There wasn't a horse or mule that didn't know his tiny, liquid voice and gentle touch, and they seemed to share a unique form of communication. It was soon recognized that this small boy had a special way with horses.

Anna, Madie, and the two children returned to Hillside in the fall of 1842. The mistress was delighted with her new home, and took great joy in the prospect of furnishing and decorating the numerous rooms. She was also awed by the tremendous progress Henry had made with the plantation. Many new fields had been cleared, and all the stumps had been grubbed from the old. The Negro village was looking up, and had improved in both structure and appearance. There were numerous new barns and outbuildings, a mill and dam were being constructed, and the millpond expanded to nearly four hundred acres. There was a small receiving and shipping wharf down by the river, and Henry had his little army busy digging new dikes and ditches.

Cotton and corn were still the main crops, but Henry had added some variety, in hopes of offsetting the year's poor harvest. There had been a fine stand of corn in the bottom lands that spring, the finest yet, but a terrible flood had wiped it out. Henry then expended the labor to replant, and the crop had been grabbing hold, when a second flood also washed it away. Only the upland corn was harvested that year.

The cotton yield also was disappointing because of the wet season. This frequent flooding of the Roanoke was both a blessing and a curse to Henry. The freshets, or freshes as they were called, deposited new rich earth to the bottom land, but if their timing was poor, they also ruined the crops. It was a dilemma that would obsess Henry all his planting days.

COLLINSON BURGWYN'S AFFECTION FOR HORSES turned to those with power and speed. At a fox hunt on All Saints' Day, with the hounds on the run, Collinson's horse missed a jump. Like his benefactor, his Uncle George Pollok, the youngest Burgwyn brother fell and broke his neck. He suffered from the most excruciating pain for nine days. All the Burgwyns gathered to take turns sitting up with Collinson at his plantation, day and night. Even

Sarah Emily, who had recently arrived from one of her many trips to Europe, made an appearance to lend her support.

On November 9th, Henry expressed these sentiments in his diary: "*Poor Coll grew worse rapidly. I went over in the carriage to Occoneechee for sister Julia & returned about 12 o'clock when we found that my beloved Brother was rapidly drawing near the close of his life. We watched around his bedside, where our family all met for the first time in 20 years until about 2:30, when he breathed his last so easily we could scarcely tell when the breath left his body. He has left us to mourn a loss that can never cease to be felt this side of the grave, and at a time we need every friend.*"

Old Sally, one of the house maids at Hillside, took ill about the same time, and died three days later. Henry attended divine service for Collinson, which was administered by Reverend McRae, and then returned home and personally read the rights over Sally, with Anna, the overseer, and all the hands present.

That same November, Devereux won a suit, and Henry had to set his grief aside in order to procure a loan to pay the judgment. Since the legal battles had already drained him considerably, and since his crops had failed so miserably that year, the first two banks denied him. On his third try, at a bank at Tarboro, he was able to acquire a small sum, but it was not nearly enough.

Thomas Burgwyn also went out in search of funds, to Petersburg and Norfolk. He had not yet returned when Sheriff Peasley made an appearance at Hillside and took thirty of Henry's slaves into his possession to be sold at auction. The sale was held the following Monday, on Court Day, and Devereux was there to collect his judgment. Henry asked him to postpone the sale, until Thomas could arrive with the money, but Devereux refused. Henry had a small amount on hand, and a draft on a bank in Boston, which he offered to his cousin. Again, Devereux refused to take it, and the sale commenced.

Henry had heard that there was a league among the local gentry to keep the price for best hands at below three hundred and fifty dollars, but he planted a by-bidder in the crowd to raise the bids higher. A lump swelled in his throat, as he helplessly watched part of his black family being sold on the block. Children of twelve and fourteen were separated from their parents, and Henry regretted he'd ever taken up planting. He prayed to God never to be put in this situation again.

The worst to endure was the begging and pleading of the parents, who looked desperately toward Henry to save their children from the hands of greedy speculators. Henry bought back as many as he could, with the money he had at hand, but he was unable to prevent all the families from being split up. By sundown, ten thousand dollars worth of slaves had been sold. Henry still owed two hundred and thirty five dollars and twenty-three cents on the judgment. Blind Jimmy stepped forward and agreed to be sold, and that final transaction made up the difference.

With the sale of Henry's slaves, bitterness between the Devereux and the Burgwyns rose to a fever pitch.

IT WAS A RATHER GLOOMY THANKSGIVING that year at Hillside, but the Christmas season brought a special treat for Anna: the Sumners came south for a visit. Anna had been begging her mother to come down for almost four years, but Mrs. Sumner had an aversion to the lower states, and her poor health had also prevented travel. Now she was well enough and finally fulfilled her promise.

The Sumners brought many gifts for the Negroes, and one of the first items of business was to pass them out. In the evening, after the Sumners' first day on the plantation, the troops gathered at the big house. The General stood on one of the piazzas, made a formal introduction, and spoke to the group in a tone and language they hardly understood. When the speech was through, the hands lined up and Henry passed out the gifts from the lower steps. They took the offerings in silence, turned and filed away, disappearing into the darkness and began the long walk back to their cabins. They left the visitors with an impression of order and obedience.

On Christmas morning, Henry took the General on a traditional deer hunt. They stationed themselves near a gut in a swampy low ground, while a neighbor's hounds ran the bucks up from a tremendous pine thicket near the river. The hunters returned to the manor around mid-morning, both galled and suffering from easy shots which had missed their mark.

The children had been keeping the women entertained, and they continued their show after the men arrived. Little Harry was walking now, getting into everything, and needing constant observation. He was a beautiful child. With a head full of thick dark locks and with sparkling blue eyes, he could easily have been mistaken for a pretty little girl. Not to be outdone by her attention-grabbing little brother, Minnie was a terror to the household servants, and possessed a whole library of terrible grimaces, which she used to intimidate them. She literally stalked them, then attacked and whipped them. The servants played along good-naturedly, cowered, begged, and pleaded not to be beaten and punished. Minnie showed them little mercy and pestered them throughout their amazing patience. Mrs. Sumner was appalled.

The feast was at Hillside that afternoon. Thomas came over to dine from Occoneechee, and John Fanning from Collinson's plantation, which had been left to him as a life estate. That evening the slaves joined the festivities. Henry had given them a half-day holiday, had ordered a barbecued steer prepared, and had a barrel of beer stationed for them in the yard of the manor house. There was joy in the night. A large bonfire was lit, and the slaves danced, sung, and performed on the piazza, while the whites watched and clapped. The celebration got a little carried away, however, and the crowding on the piazza caused it to collapse from the weight. Fortunately, no one was hurt.

The slaves' holiday continued the next day, but the hands were ordered to remain on the plantation, until Henry and Anna gave out their gifts and the year's rewards. Up before dawn, During prepared the carriage, and outfitted a little barouche for the Sumners. It was a damp, foggy morning, warm for the season. Henry had the back of the carriage filled with life's necessities: woolen blankets, flannel shirts, guernsey jackets, and shoes of every size; Anna's work of the last few months also was loaded up: shawls, socks, and sweaters. The master planned to provide his hands with the substantial, while the mistress had prepared the ornamental.

Henry drove the carriage, led the way, and During, with the Sumners, followed in the barouche. As they closed on the village, they saw that Mr. Sutter, the newest overseer, had the hands out working on their own little plots. The dark figures walked quietly out of the fog, drew near, and gathered around the vehicles. The gifts were quickly handed out, while the prizes were held out until last. Anna had knitted two good shawls as the rewards for the best two women cotton pickers. One was gray, warm, and sensible, while the other was bright, multi-colored and light. The winner had her choice. Big Hoseanna was the year's honored. She picked the gaudy shawl.

Mr. Sutter cantered up on his shaggy gelding. He was a lanky fellow with large feet and hands, had a hawkish face, and spoke with a raspy voice. He wanted a word with the master. Henry interrupted the ceremony, and the two drew away from Anna and the in-laws.

"Saw a glow in the pines beyond the mill house this morning 'fore light, a fire," said Sutter. "It was Scipio. He'd stolen three of your hogs and was butcherin' and cookin' 'em."

Henry's mouth went flat, and he winced. Scipio had been taking quite a few liberties since he had been lenient with him about running off, but this was going too far.

"Where is he?" Henry asked angrily.

"Told 'im to go to his cabin and stay there 'til I talked with you."

"Fine," Henry said, and told Sutter to remain there, until he was finished with the rewards.

Henry gave out the remaining prizes, then sent the hands on their way. Some who had received money or items they could barter set out for town to do some trading. Henry then excused himself from his wife and guests, told them he had a little business to take care of with Mr. Sutter, and promised it wouldn't take long. During took them off in the carriage and, when they were safely out of sight, Henry and his overseer made for Scipio's cabin in the barouche.

On the way to the big house, Anna told her mother and the General how much she enjoyed the handing out of gifts. She thought it the most rewarding activity on the plantation. She and Henry did it once a quarter, but she wished they could manage it monthly.

Sutter brought the thief out from his cabin, and Henry gave him a long lecture on stealing, while he remained sitting in the barouche. Scipio was apologetic, swore he'd never do it again, said hog cutting was coming, and he was starting early. Henry shamed him for lying and ordered Sutter to tie him up. Scipio was put face down in the muddy lane in the center of the village, his hands and feet were bound, then tied together.

"Leave him there, until an hour after sundown," Henry instructed. He slapped the leather traces, and the little barouche jerked for home.

LATE THE FOLLOWING SUMMER, in Jamaica Plains, Anna gave birth to her third child, another girl. The baby was named for her mother, and she was called Annie. She would grow to be a pretty little strawberry blond, a lively child, better mannered than her older sister and brother. She was sweet as could be, a perfect angel.

The Burgwyns returned to Carolina in the fall, and in November, an unexpected visitor arrived at Hillside. It was Anna's younger brother James. Mrs. Sumner was gravely ill again, and he had come to escort Anna back to Boston. Henry was perturbed that James had come unannounced, and was reluctant to let Anna go. He finally relented, but, except for the infant, the children would remain at Hillside.

Mrs. Sumner passed before Anna could reach her.

Janey Greenough had not reached maturity when her mother died, and the General and her brothers decided that it would be best for her to live with her older sister in the South.

A week of good English weather, rain and fog, preceded Anna and Janey's arrival at Jackson, and there was every sign of a tremendous freshet in the Roanoke. The roads to Hillside were mucked up, impassable, so they boarded in White's Hotel, until they could reach the plantation. It was just as well, the Jackson Ball was just around the corner, and Anna wanted to introduce her little sister to all her southern friends.

The flood waters covered Henry's low grounds and had actually reached the hill where the new home rested. The master was surveying the damage. His wharf and mill were gone, the dam washed out. There would be no grain for the hands that winter, but there was plenty of meat on the plantation; they wouldn't starve. Two large barns were also victims of the high water, and the upland barns had become shelters for refugees; every wood rat from miles around had infested them, had broken into all the corn sacks, and were consuming the year's harvest.

The rain had finally slowed to a drizzle. The river would keep rising, and wouldn't begin receding for another couple of days. All the damage was done, whatever was left of value was on high ground. Henry returned home to make notes in his farm journal on the extent of the freshet, then played with his children until it was time to join Anna and Janey in town. The ball to celebrate Andrew Jackson's birthday, the namesake of the town, was that night. He set out alone, leaving Minnie and Harry at Hillside with the servants.

The roads were little rivers with four inches of mud underneath. Creeks and ditches had become major obstacles, but Henry rode Roxanna, the thoroughbred, so he could jump them. The winter day was short, and darkness closed in early and fast. It started to rain again, white sheets, and the rider bowed his head against the black wind. He feared the bridge over Occoneechee Creek would be gone, and he was right; the stream was raging and impassable. He debated turning back, but instead headed upstream through the saturated woods. It was so black he used the sound of the rushing stream to guide him, and rode a half-hour before he found a place to ford. The mare swam across, filling Henry's boots in the process. He backtracked for the road, crossed into a soggy field and over a rise, and spurred the horse. Still, the dark kept them back.

A great flash of lightning hit a nearby tree, followed by a tremendous crack of thunder. High-strung Roxanna bolted, and Henry held on, out of control. They hit the woods again, this time the rider dodging and ducking branches. Roxanna could not be calmed, and finally Henry jumped off to avoid worse injury.

On foot, he tried to track her down, but in the middle of the dark wilderness he soon became lost. He finally found the mare in a thicket of warm pines. Henry took Roxanna's reins and walked her. Disoriented, he guessed the direction of the road, found it an hour later, and walked through slick mud for the remaining three miles to Jackson.

Anna was worried sick, then relieved, and finally amused at her husband's dilapidated condition when he arrived at White's. He was put in front of a roaring fire and given dry clothes.

Despite the weather, Anna and Janey continued to prepare for the ball. Henry told them they needn't bother; they weren't going in a squall. The women stubbornly insisted. An argument followed, and at last Henry became resigned. He arranged a carriage, a footman, and an outrider with Mr. White, then had planks placed in the yard to protect the women from the mud.

He was shocked with their attire. The women were overdressed; their expensive clothing would certainly be ruined. But with their frockies pinned up around their waists over stockings, and with India rubbers on their feet, Anna and Janey descended a flight of stairs and crossed over the planks with Henry in the lead, sounding the mud with his cane. Madie brought up the rear with candlesticks in both hands. Henry jumped in the carriage first, drew in Janey, then got out and lifted his wife. He climbed over them to the driver's seat, and set off just as the footman jumped on the back. The mud in town was up to the horses' knees in places, so they could hardly trot, but they still managed to keep up some kind of a dignified motion. Once they hit a deep hole, which made Janey screech, but that was the worst the short trek offered.

Removing the women from the carriage was equally comical, but they found the ballroom surprisingly full of guests and decorated for the season. It was a long, narrow hall with evergreens fashioned around the walls and many wreaths of running cedar interspersed with holly berries. White paper covered the large arches on both sides of the hall, and there were Christmas trees with flickering candles conveniently placed throughout. A table served as the stage for the musicians: two violins, a flute, and a tambourine. The Burgwyns entered the hall in the middle of a cotillion. There was no master of ceremony or manager, but there wasn't the slightest confusion or the least difficulty in finding persons willing to dance.

Anna still was feeling the loss of her mother, and not overly festive, but she turned her little sister loose, and encouraged her to interact. A particularly lewd-looking Virginian took an immediate interest in her, and seemed very pleased at her pretty white dress with scarlet bows. He told Janey that he knew her brother-in-law, that Henry had once passed a night at his home. After several dances, the Virginian broke away and asked Anna Janey's status. He begged permission to call on her, a request Anna successfully dodged. Henry had never seen the fellow in his life and found out later he was a married man.

The next day opened clear, cold and blustery; even the clouds had a frigid, purple hue. Henry set off early for the plantation; the river was at full flood, and if he was ever to conquer these freshets he would have to see them at their worse. He arrived at Hillside with difficulty, sent During off to fetch his canoe, and ordered Nan to cut some cotton cloth into yard-long strips. Ruthy cooked him breakfast, and he ate with his children, before wrapping himself in the warmest clothes he could find. The canoe was launched just down hill from the house. During went with him, and they paddled upstream against the current, until they reached the far northwest corner of his property. Here Henry started to tie the cloth around the trees at water level. This was the highest he'd ever seen the Roanoke, and he planned to fight it with levies, dikes, and ditches. The markers would show just how much earth he would have to move. They ran out of cloth just before dusk.

A few days later, the roads cleared enough for the women to leave White's and return to the plantation. Janey settled right in, delighted and surprised at the abundance of good-tasting food. After just a week, she declared she was already feeling a little lazy.

Just like Anna before her, Janey soon became infatuated with Penny's little daughter Polly. She had grown to be a beautiful child, exotic, with long fine hair, tan eyes, smooth yellow flesh, and a turned up nose. Janey brushed her hair for hours, played little games, and indulged the child in long conversations. Janey was shocked to learn that Penny was actually Polly's aunt, that her mother, Cloe, who was a field hand, wouldn't have anything to do with Polly, and was hateful toward her. Out of pure kindness, Penny, had adopted her sister's child as her own, and Polly considered her aunt her real mammy.

DAVID GREENOUGH BECAME THE MASTER of the house in Jamaica Plains after his mother's death. He had a wife and children of his own and was now the head of the family. General Sumner remained nearby, continued a close relationship with his stepchildren and grandchildren, and visited Anna in Carolina on several occasions. The Burgwyns still made their pilgrimages to Boston, but they became less frequent and were of shorter duration. The last of Anna's and Henry's children born in the North were twins, two boys. One was named William Hyslop Sumner, after the General, and the other, John Collinson, after Henry's deceased younger brother.

HENRY'S FARM JOURNAL ENTRY OF NOVEMBER 1ST, 1846; reads:
"Returned home today with my family from the North. We have left one little boy behind, John Collinson, buried in the family vault at Jamaica Plains. The rest are all well, thank God!

We bring with us this year no white servants for the first time since my marriage. This summer, however, has been a most unfortunate one for us. Just after I left, we lost Samuel, my beef driver, worth $1,200. Afterwards, I lost Linton and Nervis, two young hands & I have lost 1600 barrels of corn in the low grounds & all my oats. The summer freshets engendered sickness within my people, and they have suffered. My low grounds have been covered again & again by the river, as often as 9 times on the Gee Low Grounds. My wheat crop, however, is a great improvement over that of last year; my limed and clover land has increased at least 3 times in product from the previous product of the same land, making up in some degree for my loss of corn, though this year has not been favorable for wheat. I have had a number of children born within my black family on the plantation this year, as many as 10.

My sister Emily came home from Norfolk with me. At Norfolk I paid Hall bookseller my bill, $13. Walter Taylor my bill, $48, in full. I also bought from Hall a Chickering Piano, $330. I have also bought a new pair of noble carriage horses."

❧ 6 ❧

ON SOUTHERN MANNERS

QUESTIONS FOR MY SON HARRY to put to himself before going to sleep, and which he must some day answer before the judgment seat of Almighty God.

*Did I say my prayers thoughtfully
on rising this morning and have I
been attentive at family prayer?*

Did I remember my prayers at noon day?

*Have I endeavored through the day
to be kind to my sisters and brothers
and to benefit them by my example?*

*Have I been tempted to say that which
was not strictly true?*

Have I been fretful under any disappointment?

*Have I reflected that young as I am my
words and actions may influence others
for eternity?*

*Have I failed in respect or obedience to
any one whom God has set over me?*

*Have I remembered the command to Honor
my Father and Mother?*

*Do I realize that I am not my own, but
am bought with a price and must prepare
myself to inherit my Father's Kingdom?*

Lord be merciful unto me, for I have sinned against thee. Blessed Savior keep me from the snares of this wicked world—Amen.

HE LOVED THE SMELL OF THE STABLES. It was horses and hay, sunshine and sweat; rich, powerful scents all rolled together, making him feel he was breathing in life itself. Of course, with just nine years behind him, it was hard for him to put all these feelings into words.

Kinchen was cleaning out the stall of Occoneechee, the fastest stallion this side of Halifax, and the offspring of Henry's Roxanna. Occoneechee had won the Belfield race, and Kinchen thought him the most beautiful creature he'd ever seen. Early that morning, when During told him to change the hay in the stallion's stall, the boy's ribby chest puffed out, like he'd been asked to put on green racing silks and ride Occoneechee himself. He silently vowed that it would be the cleanest stall ever.

That was where little Harry found him.

"Kinchen...?" asked the curly-haired white boy, unsure that the little haystack in the corner was really a person. Kinchen looked up, strands of hay sticking out every which way from his nappy hair.

"Massa Harry!" he exclaimed. "I's makin' dis stall fittin' for a king!"

Harry giggled.

"Well, with all that hay in your crown, Occo'll chew you!" Harry taunted as he scooped up a handful of hay and added it to Kinchen's collection.

"Who's done got hay in his head?" Kinchen asked, as he tossed some of the yellow straw on Harry. And the hay started to fly.

During strolled into the stables, and through a strong shaft of morning light that poured through the open window above. Pieces of hay were drifting through the beam, as if there were a golden snow shower. He passed by the stalls on either side of him, murmured hello to a bay and stroked the velvet nose of Judy, a chestnut mare. He continued along slowly, toward the rising sounds of giggles, behind the gate of the last stall on the right. It seemed a hay storm was raging.

"Awl right, ya'll come on out a' dare," said During, resignedly.

The laughter stopped, and the hay swirled down quietly. Small footsteps crunched up to the door; two slight heads with corkscrewed hair peered around the edge.

"Well, if'n ya'll don't look a sight," said During, closing his eyes and shaking his head. He looked at them again and his eyes crinkled. The corner of his mouth began to turn, a chuckle escaped his lips, and then a full belly laugh rumbled up at the sight of the two boys covered with hay. The boys' wide, frightened eyes turned to each other, changed to relief, and then amusement, their childlike laughter harmonizing with During's bass.

"Gwon, ya'll get outta' here," he laughed, and shooed them out of the stables.

They sauntered out to the dirt lane that followed the gut to the river and the southeast corner of Hillside. They'd been given more than an ordinary day. It was warm and summer-like, prime for adventure. Puffs of dust rose with every step of their feet, as they meandered down the lane, one set bare, the other in Yankee-made shoes. They threw pebbles, inspected a dead snake half eaten by buzzards, picked up sticks and dueled. Kinchen whistled and Harry blew air, trying hard to make a musical sound.

"Jus' pucker up dem lips," Kinchen explained as he demonstrated. Harry's rosy lips crinkled like a purse.

"Now, jus' sing a song." With that, a beautiful, pure sound emitted from Kinchen's lips.

Harry tried it. He made a sound like wind blowing across a barren desert and stopped, dejected.

"Don't be blowin' so hard, Massa Harry," encouraged the black boy. "Hol' yuh tongue up a lil' and try again'." More wonderful notes poured from Kinchen's pucker.

Harry licked his lips, stuck them out, blew softly. The faintest tune was heard, and Harry's eyes widened in excitement as he strove to blow a little harder, the whistle strengthening before it faded with the last of his breath.

"Did you hear it? I did it! I whistled!" exclaimed Harry breathlessly.

"Yuh sure did. Yuh jus' keep practicin' and yuh'll be singin' like a field lark," said the older, wiser Kinchen.

They reached the shade of the trees that grew along the river. The sand, protected from the beating sun by the lush canopy of leaves, felt cool and soft between Kinchen's toes. He stopped and wiggled them in pure, simple pleasure.

"What are you doing?" asked little Harry.

"I's dippin' my toes in dis cool pool."

"Sand?" protested Harry.

"It's like the horseshoes mus' feel when ol' Milliken is finished poundin' 'em and plunges' 'em in dat cool water," Kinchen said, his eyes closed serenely. "It's like the lil' ice chip in da drinks Miss Madie done gives us when we's parched."

Harry listened, pulled off his shoes and socks, then drove his toes deep into the shady sand. Kinchen smiled, sat down, felt a twinge of satisfaction as he watched his master's son dig and wiggle his toes in delight.

"It does feel good, doesn't it?" Harry grinned, while making a new discovery. He sat down by the slave, and both enjoyed the cool dirt. Kinchen picked up Harry's shoes and they strolled down to the river.

The Roanoke shone green and gold, silent and saintly, its current lazy, almost harmless. It rolled over and around the great hulks of trees it had uprooted during one of its angrier times. Now the dead branches glistened as they dipped into the shallows. An occasional fish jumped and popped. Dragonflies buzzed recklessly near the water's surface. Along the banks were rounded rocks, and underneath were worms, crawfish, and wiggling nymphs of satin-winged flies. The river and its shore were a liquid playground. Kinchen and Harry rushed to the edge, and began filling their pockets with stones, which had to meet their very strict requirements. Then they rolled up their britches and waded in, knee-deep. Kinchen pointed to a fallen tree that led to a bar, and the two struggled upstream. They negotiated the slick, barkless pine with arms fanned out for balance, then hopped on to the slippery flat. Shading their eyes from the river's bright glare, they proclaimed themselves rulers of all they surveyed. Harry threw a rock, counted the skips.

"When I grow up, I'm gonna be able to skip a rock ten times," he said, as he wistfully counted a meager three-skipper.

"Yuh don't have ta be old ta skip rocks. I reckon' most old'a folks done forgot how's ta skip a rock," said Kinchen. "Why, I's reckons boys like us are da best skippers dare is."

With that, he cupped a four-inch round flat stone between his forefinger and thumb and let it fly.

"Wow, eight skips!" shouted Harry. "That almost went clear across to the other side."

Kinchen grinned. He agreed with little Harry on the rock nearly reaching the opposite shore, but the eight skips, he wasn't sure. He wasn't much good at counting.

"C'mon!" yelled Kinchen. "Let's see if'n any fish done washed up."

They scrambled over the flat and the bare, yellow pine, then waded back and roamed along the bank. They saw the nine-foot high water mark on a river oak, revealing just how serious the freshet had been earlier that spring. Harry heard a squirrel chattering in the branches, spotted him, pointed a finger, aimed and fired.

"Got 'im!" shouted Kinchen, but the squirrel safely scampered away.

"In the tail!" exclaimed little Harry.

Empty stomachs drew them toward home. They were almost there, had passed the Cherry Field barn, and were coming up on the chicken pens when Harry stopped and looked at Kinchen with a knowing glint in his eye. The slave caught on immediately; they'd discovered a new game just the other day, and they raced back to the barn, grabbed a burlap bag of chicken feed hanging in the corner, then ran for the chicken pens.

Kinchen climbed in first, then helped the smaller white boy. They buried their hands into the bag, pulled out handfuls of the dried kernels, then positioned themselves in front of the chicken house, facing each other.

Kinchen knew the call.

"Tut, tut...tut, tut."

A hen stuck her head out, and cocked it. The boys let the kernels fall from their hands onto their bare, wiggling toes. Then they looked at each other, steely determination in their eyes, as a few chickens awkwardly ran over.

Harry closed his eyes, clenched his little fists, his arms tight and rigid at his sides. The hens, pecking at his feet, were tickling. But he wasn't going to laugh, wasn't going to even crack a smile. Kinchen was trying just as hard, but the beaks were hard to ignore. His mouth began to curl, a giggle just below the surface. Harry was fighting a losing battle, too, his lips pressed tightly together, his cheeks rising, his eyes now open and twinkling. The loser would be the first to laugh, and Kinchen broke first. A giggle wailed out, and he jumped high, sending squawking birds scattering over the yard. His laughter tumbled out, deep as his nine years could muster, as Harry screamed in victory and relief. They high-stepped in circles, rubbed their toes to stop the tingling nerves, and draped arms around each other, gasping for breath. Harry had won the first competition the other day, and now the second too.

"Ya'll betta' get on ta da house," called Donas from atop a mule. He was a young field hand whose mother was a washer woman. "Dey sent me out lookin' fo' ya'll. Didn't ya'll hear da bell for suppa'?"

The two boys, startled, turned steely quiet.

"Get on out of dat pen now. Get on ta da house." And the friends scrambled over the fence, walked slowly home, worried, could almost feel the sting of the willow switch on their backsides.

SUCCESS CAME SLOWLY FOR HENRY. His engineering skills helped him manage the destructive floods, but he would never control them. The weather blessed him on occasion, and gave him banner years. The Devereux feud had simmered down, and eventually the two families would bury the hatchet. Henry was becoming an innovative and scientific farmer. He used marl and manure to enrich his lands, and visited plantations along the James in Virginia, studying their methods. Deep plowing increased his yields, and he was able to plant more land without increasing his labor force. He also went against common practices; he dropped cotton, and changed his primary crop to wheat. He employed the new mechanical reapers, the first planter south of Virginia to do so. The benefit was immediate. He could cut his wheat when it was ready, quicker, with fewer slaves, and with less waste. Henry and Thomas began to draw attention to themselves. Other planters came and coveted Occoneechee Wigwam and Hillside. Salesmen from all over the country dropped by to pay their respects, and one such visitor called the Burgwyn plantations the best to be found between Canada and Louisiana.

Most puzzling was the management of his black family. According to some, Henry did better than many planters. Samuel Henderson was a salesman for Obed Hussey, an inventor and manufacturer of a wheat reaper. Mr. Henderson was an up-state New Yorker, and not disposed to slavery. After a visit to Hillside, he wrote home:

"He has nearly 2,000 acres cultivated in corn, wheat, clover, and other crops. Last year, at Petersburg, he sold his wheat harvest for over $50,000, and his corn undoubtedly surpassed that. I think his success lays in the fallow lands he keeps for soiling. His stock is well kept, and his Negroes, well, he provides for them very well. His shelters are the best I've seen, and he's built them a chapel and a little hospital. I find myself summoning up my principles often, for you know I don't approve. But I must say, the system works here, and I've never seen slaves so content."

Cyrus McCormick, a Virginian credited with inventing the first reaper, visited Hillside in 1845. He brought with him a fleet of his reapers built on his farm in the Shenandoah Valley, and they harvested all of Thomas's and Henry's wheat within a week. The Burgwyns ordered several of McCormick's reapers soon after. The next year, the reapers broke down shortly after the harvest began, and Henry looked suspiciously at their shipping crates' markings: "For the Southern Market." McCormick had licensed several companies in Ohio to manufacture his reaper, and they were made with inferior parts.

Henry had also bought one of Obed Hussey's reapers; he employed it, and it worked fine. Hussey's machines were built in Baltimore, by southerners.

McCormick sent several of his agents to fix the machines, and eventually he went down himself, but the Yankee-made reapers never worked to Henry's satisfaction. Hussey's southern-built machines continued to perform much better.

PROSPERITY DIDN'T NECESSARILY BRING good health to the Burgwyn family. In the early spring of 1847, Janey, Anna's little sister, died of fever at Hillside. She was just seventeen, and had never become fully acclimated to the South. Her death severed yet one more of Anna's dwindling roots to the North.

A fine coffin was built at Hillside's sawmill, after which Henry and Anna made the long journey to Jamaica Plains to bury the girl in the Greenough family vault.

Not two months after Janey's death came the Burgwyn's sixth child, a boy. He was born at Hillside, and they named him George Pollok in honor of the man who had made Henry a planter. Pollok was rascally, not the brightest of Anna's children, but was free-spirited and adventurous.

"YOU CAN TRAP MORE FLIES WITH HONEY THAN VINEGAR." To whites, they were a sign of culture and good breeding. To the blacks, they were a necessary part of survival, a buffer against threat and intimidation. The will to live is stronger than the need to impress, so no race had better manners in

America than the southern slaves. Due to close association, the South's whites were a distant second.

If a visitor wished to know a native's social standing, all he need do was ask a black man. If lowly white girls were chattering in high company, the best way to clam them up was to throw a parlor maid into the mix. Good manners among southerners were no myth, just a natural by-product of a society based on class and slave labor.

THE SKY WAS HAZY, WHITE HOT, the sun burning the vapors off slowly as it rolled on its westward journey. There was no wind in the wheat, no sign of its cool lappings. Kinchen had just unharnessed a team of lathered horses, had them in the shade of the long leaves of an old peach tree, and was rubbing them with wet rags, a bucket between his feet. He squeezed the water on to their steaming backs; flesh wiggled, but tails hung still, their necks bent and tired.

From the corner of his eye he watched the ugliest white man he'd ever seen. Hadn't seen many, and the Burgwyns were pretty for white folks, but this man was hideous. He was thick, flabby, had no neck, splotchy skin, and a bristling orange beard. He had big wrinkles on his forehead, eyes that were slits, and a humpy nose. He wondered if the man was a Yankee.

Salmus and Horatio were standing near him nodding their heads distrustfully at his garbled words. The ugly man was pointing at Henry on the reaper, while handing out silver pieces, inscrutably bribing the hands to work harder for him than for the competition.

Salmus pointed toward the young black boy in the shade, Kinchen. The ugly man looked over his shoulder, peered at the boy sourly. Kinchen saw the glare, smiled politely, looked away, glanced back shyly, then looked away again. The man started for him, but fortunately, Judge Ashworth had just ridden up. He had come to see the reapers.

The Judge shifted a huge plug of tobacco in his cheeks, spat, called out: "With these new damned machines, what're we gonna do with our Niggas?"

The ugly Yankee laughed. "Send them to Liberia. That's what I'd do." The Yankee moved toward the Judge, held his bridle as he dismounted.

Kinchen felt a sudden spasm of relief and sighed as he dipped a rag into the bucket. He didn't know what Salmus had said to the ugly man, didn't know why he was coming after him, and he was glad the Judge had happened by.

Kinchen turned his attention to Henry sitting on the reaper, his white shirt stained with perspiration under a floppy, wide-brimmed hat. The master was completely absorbed, concentrating. The reaper's steely blades cut a wide swath through the wheat, as Henry guided the sweating team. A dark cloud of Negroes followed behind, raking. Out in front, another troop of blacks were thinning the crop with scythes and keeping eyes peeled for random stumps and ditches that might damage or clog the machine. Fairchild, the newest of the plantation's overseers, was urging them on, yelling out threats.

Another stranger, sunburned, followed along beside the reaper, studying the machine nervously. He was Mr. Pence, one of McCormick's agents, another northerner. Kinchen let his eyes roam over Pence. He was a slightly built man, who continually dabbed at his forehead with a white handkerchief, as he labored through the heat. Nobody seemed to have much respect for him.

McCormick's reaper had broken down again yesterday, but fortunately, Thomas' reaping was nearly complete, so he replaced Henry's damaged cog wheel with one from his own machine. They had already made five turns around the forty-acre Orchard Field, and the heat had already retired a team. The going was slow, the wheat thick, and perhaps not quite ripe. The main wheel and gearing couldn't keep up, had clogged to a halt twice already. Here, on the fifth turn, it happened again. Henry pulled in the team, hopped off, glanced at the tangled rat's nest within the finger guards, then yelled over to the ugly man.

Hussey's representative, whose name was Birch, had his team and reaper standing at the ready. He excused himself from the Judge, gestured for Salmus, Horatio, and their rakers to follow, then drove the mower into the wheat. The yellow heads flew. The rakers scurried behind. The hands with scythes couldn't stay ahead, and Birch had Fairchild wave them off. Henry watched Hussey's machine with satisfaction, while Pence gingerly crawled under his clogged machine to clear it, said he'd have it cutting again in a quarter hour. Henry didn't acknowledge him, didn't turn his head or remove his hands from his hips. He just watched Mr. Birch cut the thick wheat clean and true. Finally, he looked down at Pence.

"I'm ordering your machine out of the field."

At half past three, a heavy thunderstorm blew through, making the wheat too wet for cutting. After the sun showed again, Henry ordered the women into the field to open and air out the shocks of grain. The male hands also picked up rakes and tried to salvage what McCormick's machine had wasted. The teams were sent back to the stables to be groomed and fed, and Kinchen was told to bring Roxanna, the blooded mare, back for Mr. Birch. Henry took him and Judge Ashworth on a tour of Hillside. Mr. Pence wasn't invited.

That evening, Mr. Birch and the Judge were wined and dined, and treated to the best the Burgwyn household could offer. Henry had all the latest newspapers, and gave Hussey's agent the greatest of comforts. To better combat the heat, Henry had a house-boy continually dose the piazzas with water and hung wet towels over the windows to cool off the breeze.

Mr. Pence was told to board with Fairchild, and not once was he invited to the manor house.

The women and men worked until well after sundown. It was then, a small blaze caught up. God knows why she did it. Perhaps she was drying her clothes, or maybe she had caught a chill after the temperature change. Rhoda, one of Henry's female hands, had carelessly lit a fire in the wheat field. Mrs. Fairchild was preparing a meal for her husband and their guest, and it was the couple's son who spotted the flame. The overseer had a fit. He grabbed a bucket of water, stormed into the field, and extinguished the blaze. Then he pulled poor Rhoda out, cursing her all the way. Brister, the women's foreman, also got a taste of Fairchild's foul language, and was threatened with a whipping. As for Rhoda, the overseer decided he had no choice, she had to be punished.

Fairchild sent his boy up to the big house to tell Henry what had just transpired, and to ask what punishment should be metered out. The master ordered fifteen lashes. Oddly, Mr. Birch wished to witness the disciplining, so Henry and the Judge escorted him down to the overseer's cottage.

Mr. Pence wasn't quite sure what to make of all the commotion, as he stood in the shadows of Fairchild's front porch. Rhoda was in the yard, on her knees, naked from the waist up. A good number of the hands had gathered around, and the overseer stood in the middle of it all, bull whip in hand. The scene didn't change until the master and his guests arrived. Henry gave Fairchild a nod. Pence overhead the Judge speaking to Birch.

"He's an old hand at this," said the Judge. "Watch, he won't break the skin."

Fairchild welded the whip expertly, measured his steps. Leather flicked on brown flesh, burned, and stung, but was done in such a way as to not inflict serious damage. With flabby jowls hanging over a hand resting on his chin, Birch observed intently. Pence winced at every snap of the whip.

"No blood," said Henry. Fairchild nodded, continued the punishment. Rhoda whimpered and cried. Pence couldn't watch; he looked at the other hands instead, about fifty of them. They seemed numb with blank expressions on their faces, unmoved. Pence was curiously shocked.

The fifteenth lash cracked, then all was quiet. Rhoda endured the pain silently, tears streaming down rounded cheeks, her eyes wide and frightened. Fairchild gathered in the whip, pointed it at Brister.

"He's responsible, he shouldn't have let her start it."

Henry shook his head. Brister was a good foreman; he took good care of thirty women, couldn't keep two eyes on them every minute.

"No supper tomorrow," the master decided.

Ashworth and Birch moved toward Rhoda slumped in the yard. They stood over her, and the Judge pointed at the welts.

"See, no blood, they'll heal quickly, no chance of septic. She'll be back in the fields tomorrow."

"A valuable lesson," said Birch.

The Judge nodded, "Damn right."

Pence stepped off the porch and into the yard. He was visibly shaken.

Henry watched him, and said nothing. Ashworth caught sight of him. He grinned slightly.

"She'll start no more fires," he said to Pence, then pointed to the other blacks. "And neither will they."

Pence was speechless, indignant. He turned around and slipped back into the cottage. Three women went to Rhoda, and helped her up. The hands headed for their cabins and their evening meals, without a word. Henry, Ashworth, and Birch turned for the big house for drinks and conversation. Little Kinchen watched them draw off. He had witnessed the whipping from the high loft of the nearby stables.

Sunday, a holiday at Hillside, was the last day of the reaper agents' visit. Mr. Pence had brought McCormick's new hay mower to demonstrate to the Burgwyns, but he had little hope of selling one. Thomas and Henry didn't have much use for it; they didn't make hay. Henry turned his stock out in the clover fields during the warmer months, and in the winter fed them grains. His grass lands were usually turned over with the plow to enrich the soil, and the fields were rotated to prevent erosion and exhaustion. Pence dutifully made the demonstration anyway, using the lawn at the main residence while Henry, Thomas, John Fanning and the other guests lounged on the piazza and observed.

The lawn was the retreat for Henry's turkeys, and they flocked up and challenged the intruder. The birds were territorial, aggressive. To prevent an assault on his rear, Pence had to keep an eye on them as he prepared his machine, a comical scene that entertained the spectators. But once the mower started, it cut the grass in impressive fashion, and the birds took an immediate liking to it. They followed closely behind, and feasted on the crickets and grasshoppers the swinging blades uncovered.

The lawn was cut in neat long rows. Pence stood proudly and waited for a response, the turkeys hovering admiringly around him. The southerners relaxed on the piazza and sipped their whiskey, smoking their pipes and cigars. Henry finally looked over the lawn, expressionless. He called up a boy, told him to fetch some rakers to tote the hay over to the paddocks for the mules to pick at. Otherwise, he had nothing to say.

Mr. Pence was invited up to the piazza, the closest he ever came to going into the house. He was offered whiskey and tobacco, but took only water. The conversation centered around horses, and since Pence knew virtually nothing of them, he drew off and observed. The Judge complained of his bowels, and John Fanning likewise grumbled and grieved of the occasional sharp pains. Bad air and hot weather were the agreed cause.

Pence was annoyed. If they took less of their liquor, and gave more attention to honoring their God, they might enjoy better health.

Henry detected the agent's aloofness.

"You will inform Mr. McCormick, I assume, of his machine's miserable performance," he said.

Pence felt cornered. "Eh-um," he cleared his throat. "The machine did quite well under the circumstances."

"And, I might add, so did Mr. Hussey's," said Thomas with a tone of sarcasm in his voice.

"Suppose they don't grow their wheat quite so thick up north," said Judge Ashworth with an equally sarcastic grin.

Everyone chuckled.

"Your opinion, Mr. Birch?" asked John Fanning.

Birch took a sip of his drink, licked his lips, looked at Pence. "I've seen McCormick's machines do better. You got an inferior machine there, Henry."

Henry nodded, agreed, and looked at McCormick's agent. "I should think the machine ought to be replaced."

Pence stood defensively, folded his arms across his chest. "I cannot speak for Mr. McCormick on that account."

"Why?" asked the Judge. "You're his agent, are you not?"

"You've got another machine in your wagon," said Thomas. "You should give it to Henry and take the broken machine back to McCormick."

"It's only right," said Henry. "I can hardly recommend your reaper, if you sell me one that doesn't work."

So prepared they were, thought Pence. Prepared to tell me what was right and wrong, while just last night they had shamelessly whipped a poor Negress. Hypocrites, these southerners. They speak of honor, proud of their honor, but only when it suits their convenience.

"I can recommend Mr. McCormick replace your machine, but I have no authority to do so myself," explained Pence.

The southerners looked at him with disgust. In their minds Pence was spineless, a lackey.

"Now, now," said John Fanning. "The man says he has no authority to give Henry a new machine. We must take him at his word. I'm sure, he recognizes that a wrong has been committed. You will make a favorable recommendation to Mr. McCormick, will you not?"

"Yes sir, I will," said Pence emphatically. "And Mr. McCormick will either repair your machine or replace it. You will be satisfied, Mr. Burgwyn, if McCormick has to come down again himself."

Henry took the offer grudgingly, shook Pence's hand. But he didn't like the man, and made no effort to hide his distaste. He ignored him the rest of the morning, until the Yankee left.

Pence packed up his hay mower while During hooked up his team. Three little black girls entertained them with a dance. Pence threw them some pennies. None of the Burgwyns said their farewells, and the northerner didn't announce his departure. He had just climbed on the wagon when he noticed a scrappy little black boy staring up at him with a curious expression. It was Kinchen.

"What can I do for you, son?" asked Pence.

The boy shyly rubbed a shoulder against his cheek while cutting his big black eyes skyward. Then he pulled a stick cage from behind his back with a Mockingbird within. The boy said nothing; he meant the bird as a gift. Pence leaned over, reached, took the cage, then smiled at the boy. Kinchen showed a pouty expression, which Pence took as a request for compensation. He removed a dollar from his wallet and held it out as an offer. The boy made no move to take the money. Pence shook his hand.

"Come on, take it."

Kinchen hesitated, then grabbed it and ran off without a word.

"Funny creatures," said Pence under his breath.

He kept the bird until he completed his tour of Carolina, then presented it as a gift to Mrs. Cyrus McCormick.

Pence was despondent when he left Hillside; he thought he had lost the southern market to Hussey. He traveled to Halifax that afternoon, then took a train to Raleigh the next day on his way to Yadkin Valley. There, he demonstrated McCormick's reaper and mower to every farmer who would watch. They all seemed pleased with the result, but when it came time to buy, none would pull out their money. Frustrated, Pence wrote his boss.

"As to the fabled southern honor that you have commonly spoken of, I have seen no evidence of it. I would trust the worse Dutchman I've dealt with before these fellows. As long as they have their Negroes and plows, these people will have no need for reapers. We'll sell ten times more in New England, and one hundred times that on the western plains. A stubborn lot down here. Best we leave them alone."

❄ 7 ❄

THE HILLS AND THE SOUL

A COLONY OF ANTS SWARMED OVER A WOUNDED praying mantis. The teeming mass scurried over it, pulling at the trespasser's legs as it helplessly tried to fend them off with powerful, but weakening claws. Curiosity had Kinchen transfixed on the combat. He squatted overhead, and armed with a six-inch-long stalk of straw, poked and prodded the ants whenever they seemed to be getting the upper hand. The mantis was ignorant of its ally, as it frantically jabbed at the menacing attackers. It was a hopeless struggle.

"Wha' yuh doin' dare, boy?"

Big Milliken, his bare chest sweating and glistening in the warm sun of Indian summer, stood at the edge of the shed and watched the nappy-headed, barefoot boy playing in the dust of the barn lot.

"Yuh 'ad better fine ya'self sump'n ta do. Don't want no shif'less nigger boy hangin' 'round heah."

Kinchen gave a final stab with the straw, slowly stood up while still staring at the battle, then glanced at Milliken sheepishly.

"Gwon and get ol' Windsor outta da paddock dare. I shoed 'im yesterday. Wanna check how deys holdin'. Gwon, get 'im."

Kinchen's eyes widened as he skipped over to the shed to grab some rope. Without a word to Milliken, he was gone in a flash to the far paddock.

Windsor was a wide-bodied gelding, a work horse that mostly hauled heavy wagons from the storage barns to the wharf and back. Old, slow, and nearly blind, he ate his weight in three days' time. Kinchen snuck up on his blind side and gave his rump a slap. The gentle old horse responded with a slow look over a massive shoulder and an irritated swish of his tail. The boy looped the rope over his neck, pointed him toward the work shed, then somehow scrambled onto his wide back. Skinny legs and dusty feet poked from the gelding's sides like tiny wings. Soft kicks got old Windsor to a slow walk.

Milliken was replacing a brittle breast strop to a carriage when the boy returned. Kinchen gave a little whistle.

"I see yuh, boy. Now, yuh stay up dare while I checks his shoes."

The big smith strolled up to the gelding, rubbed under Windsor's chin, and made his greeting.

"How yuh be, ol' man? How dem new shoes?"

Milliken quickly reached around and grabbed a massive front leg. He easily lifted the wide hoof from the ground and began to pry at the shoes with a heavy nail. He repeated the process on the other hooves as Kinchen peered down from above.

"Awlright. Just fine," Milliken then gave the boy a stern glare.

"Now, yuh ride 'im down ta da mill and back. Right now, gwon."

Old Windsor sluggishly turned down the farm lane that led to the gristmill.

A warm October sun shone off his brown face and made him feel lazy. He whistled a slow tune as he alternated gentle kicks to Windsor's rounded sides. Not a cloud was in the sky nor a breeze in the air, and the grasshoppers clicked in their harried flight as the gelding clopped slowly along. They passed the mill, and Kinchen let Windsor make a beeline for the mill pond. The boy listened to him slurp, then slid off the horse's back into the pond, the cool water sending a shiver through him as he sank into the muddy bottom to his ankles. He listened to his feet make a sucking noise where the soft mud refused a deeper wade into the pond.

A grove of pin oaks, maples, and black oaks stood alongside the pond's eastern edge. Their autumn colors created a glorious reflection in the still waters. Kinchen felt along the bottom with his toes until they came to a smooth rock. He retrieved it, then threw it into the reflection. He heard the plop and watched the tiny waves roll away. The colors danced and shimmered, and Kinchen laughed in delight. He waded to the bank with difficulty, scooped up a handful of pebbles and flung them. Red, gold, and orange seemed to leap from the pond, the boy's giggles bouncing among them.

Satisfied with his drink, the gelding pulled himself from the shallow mud, and Kinchen grabbed the rope, led him to the mill house, then used a sawhorse to help himself mount. Windsor was hungry for his paddock and needed no prodding. His slow, steady gait made heavy eyes for Kinchen. The old horse knew where to go, needed no guidance, so the boy scooted his fanny back, then draped his arms and legs down Windsor's sides. His face rested in the mane, and he closed his lids to doze.

Kinchen heard the snort of a sow. It woke him and he jerked up to see dozens of hogs in the road. Someone was driving them. It was Scipio. His devilish grin scared the boy.

"Ha, wha' yuh doin' yuh lazy nigga'? Yuh dink dat blind ol' hoase's gonna get yuh home?"

Kinchen's eyes flared at the startling voice. His father had told him to stay away from Scipio, that he was a mean old soul, and dangerous. Scipio had run off about a month back, toward the plantation of Mr. Thomas Wright where his wife was a cotton hand. The slave got ten miles before he was caught, and jailed in Jackson, where Henry had let him sit a while to think. The sheriff had brought him back about four days ago. Henry didn't have him whipped though. He gave him a stern warning instead, then decided to keep a close eye on him. If he didn't do his work, then Henry would sell him to Wright, where he could be with his wife. Scipio was now driving some of Henry's hogs to a freshly picked cornfield to feed.

Kinchen sat motionless and didn't respond to the slave's digging.

"Boy, yuh gonna get'a whippin' if'n Souter catches you ridin' like dat." Souter was one of Henry's overseers, and Scipio had been threatened with his lash more than once. Kinchen still hadn't blinked, and kept his mouth shut.

"Oh, yuh York's boy, ain't yuh. I's see. Yuh dink since yuh York's boy yuh won't get whipped. Well, let me tell yuh. Souter don't care. If'n yuh black and yuh lazy, he'll whip yuh. Yuh dink yuh Papa hadn't been whipped?"

Kinchen kept perfectly still, and remained silent. He wanted to move on, but the hogs were blocking the road. Scipio gave him a long penetrating look.

"Yuh Papa's been whipped, but you ain't, ain't yuh? Naw, you a sweet boy."

An ugly expression came over Scipio's face as he moved menacingly toward the boy. Kinchen smiled at him, trying to deflect the sneer.

"Wha yuh grinnin' at?"

The smile vanished. Kinchen pulled back, thought of escape, but now saw Scipio's hand wrapped tightly against the gelding's rope.

"Ha," Scipio looked him up and down.

"Ha," Kinchen squirmed.

"Shine da Massa's shoes and yuh gets a pat on da head. Do a good job a' cleanin' da sulky and yuh gets a piece of silva'. Leave da hoases too long in da sun wid no water and yuh gets the lash. Gonna happen. Dat's what yuh gonna get if'n yuh a lazy nigga' boy. Don't yuh dink no other way. If'n yuh lives 'round here long 'nough, yuh gonna feel da lash."

Scipio looked away, off into the colored leaves of a line of oaks, and a sudden change came over his expression and tone of voice.

"Dey ain't gonna whip me no mo'. Nope, no mo'."

Scipio's eyes squinted almost shut and he stared blankly, angrily at the gelding's gentle face.

"Dey dink since dey didn't whip me dat I'll be a good nigga' and not run again. Dey wrong, dey wrong. I's a runnin' as soon as I kin. Only not to Massa Wright's. Nope, not ta Wright's. I's a runnin' for da hills."

Scipio turned and stared into Kinchen's frightened eyes.

"To da hills, boy. To da hills. Yuh ain't ever seen da hills have yuh, boy?"

Kinchen shook his head.

Scipio's voice was a hoarse whisper—"Well, dey like a woman's breast, boy, round and full, but green. Full a trees. No sheriff up dare, no jail, no rid'as, no dawgs. Can't find a nigga' up dare. I been dare. Just a wondrous place, da hills. I calls 'em freedom, cause once a nigga' gets dare, he free."

Kinchen sensed a lie. He didn't believe Scipio had ever been out of Northampton. He finally spoke, a tiny voice.

"If yuh been ta da hills, den why yuh here?"

Black eyes turned up at him, black and lost and simmering in yellow puddles streaked with red.

"Dink I's lyin', huh? I been ta da hills, boy. Dey right over dare. Dey whar da sun falls from da sky. Over dare."

Scipio pointed to the west, and Kinchen looked over his shoulder and squinted into the afternoon sun. He didn't see any hills, only flat fields and the same old dull horizon.

"Can't see 'em from here, boy, but dey dare, dey dare. Never should'a come back."

"Why yuh come back?" Kinchen asked.

"Lonesome, boy, lonesome fo' my woman. Yuh wouldn't know not'ing 'bout dat, would yuh?"

Kinchen didn't respond. He didn't even shake his head.

"But I's a runnin' again. Gonna run fo' dose hills, and I ain't comin' back fo' no woman. I'll find a new one up dare, and we'll be free."

Scipio realized he was talking too much, that he shouldn't be telling this boy anything. He suddenly grabbed Kinchen by a skinny leg, wrapped his massive hand around it, squeezed.

"Don't yuh tell nobody what I say. Not a soul, yuh hear? Not a soul dat we even talked. Yuh hear me?"

Kinchen began to cry, not from pain, but from fear. He sobbed for Scipio to let him go, promised he wouldn't tell a soul. Scipio loosened his grip on Kinchen's leg, then dropped the rope and gave Windsor a hard slap. The old gelding jerked and started a steady walk, as the hogs parted before him. Kinchen wiped the tears from his face, then rubbed his leg. Looking over his shoulder, he watched Scipio shake his fist, raving.

"Not a soul, boy! Not a soul! Go kiss yuh Massa and yuh Missas and tell 'em everyt'ings fine! Stay here and rot, cause I's a runnin'! Don't yuh tell a soul, boy. I'll kill yuh! Kill yuh! Swear I will!"

Kinchen's heart thundered in his chest as he tried to hold back the sobs. He frantically kicked at Windsor's sides, but the old horse refused to gallop, so he raised his hands to his ears to block out Scipio's wailing, and the tears rolled down his cheeks.

York led a team of carriage horses into the barn lot, tied them to a post, then looked about for Kinchen. He saw Milliken in the shed.

"Yuh got dat carriage ready?" York asked.

"Finishin' now."

York walked to the shed, removed his hat, and wiped his brow with his shirt sleeve.

"Sho' is hot fo' dis time a' year."

"Dat it is," Milliken replied.

"Yuh seen my boy about? Told 'im ta meet me here."

Milliken realized that Kinchen hadn't been hanging around just being worthless. He'd been waiting for his father.

"Saw 'im hangin' round da lot here, so I sent 'im on Windsor down ta da mill and back. Didn't say he was waitin' on yuh. He'll be back shortly, I'd say."

"Takin' 'im over to Massa Tom's ta pick up his mama and Missas Anna. Dey been nursin' Massa John," said York.

"Heard he'd been sick," Milliken said as he tested the strength of the new breast strop.

"Nan say deathly sick, but he awlright now."

"Dat's good."

"Yuh say Kinchen be 'round shortly?"

"Yep, I put some new shoes on ol' Windsor, and axed 'im ta ride 'im down ta da mill ta see if'n dey hold. Look on down da lane dare. Yuh should see 'em."

York shaded his eyes from the sun and looked down toward the mill, but Kinchen was nowhere in sight.

Milliken put the final touch to the carriage. "Dare, all ready. Hook up yuh team."

York pulled the carriage into the yard and had the two mares hitched and ready in a matter of minutes.

Windsor and Kinchen strolled into the barn lot slowly. Arms folded, York was leaning against a post waiting for them.

"C'mon boy, get a move on."

Kinchen had seen his father from a distance and had purposely made his pace slow to dry his tears. With head down, he pointed the gelding toward the shed.

"Jump off dare, boy," said Milliken. "I'll take 'im ta his paddock."

Kinchen slipped off the horse, as the smith began to check his shoes. The boy stood silent with his head still down. York grabbed his chin.

"Yuh should'a told Milliken yuh were waitin' on me, boy. Yuh gone and made me late. Why yuh movin' so slow?"

Kinchen didn't answer and his father noticed his eyes were swollen.

"Boy, yuh eyes are red. Yuh been cryin'?"

"No, suh."

"Well, it sho' looks like it ta me."

"No, suh. I ain't been cryin'."

"Den jump up in da carriage. We gonna pick up yo' mama and Missas Anna."

The two climbed into the carriage. York grabbed the reins and slapped them against the mares' rumps. The carriage jerked away as York called out to the smith.

"Evenin' Milliken."

"Yep."

The carriage bounced down the lane toward the gristmill. The same road led to John Fanning's Alveston Plantation.

Ahead, standing beside a fence that ran along the gristmill road was Scipio. His hogs were snorting among the golden stalks in an adjacent cornfield. The carriage approached and York tipped his hat in salutation.

Scipio ignored the gesture and gave the boy a testy scowl. Kinchen was afraid to look at him, and turned his head away, but snuck a glance just as the carriage passed. He caught Scipio's frightening glare, but soon lost it in a cloud of dust. A sense of relief passed through him. He didn't want to see that man ever again.

The sight of Scipio along the lane made York suspicious of Kinchen's red eyes.

"Boy, was Scipio dare when yuh rode up from da mill?"

Kinchen felt a shiver crawl up his spine. He hesitated, didn't answer.

"Boy, I axed yuh a question."

Kinchen stuttered a reply, "Ye-ah suh."

"Did he talk ta yuh?"

"Ye-ah suh," he answered after another short hesitation.

"Boy, ain't I told yuh ta stay away from dat boy? Wha' he say?"

Kinchen swallowed, looked at his papa, then fidgeted in the carriage seat.

"Say he won't take no mo' whippins."

"Wha', dat boy hadn't been whipped in a long time... Why he say dat? Wha' else he say?"

York slowed the carriage down so he could hear his son's shy voice.

"Say he gonna run."

"Wha', run again? Fool, fool, he just get caught again. Won't make it half way ta Wright's."

"No papa, he say he ain't gonna run ta Wright's. Say he gonna run ta da hills."

"Da hills? Dat boy neva' make it. Get los', he will."

"No papa, he say he been dare. Say it a wondrous place. He calls 'em freedom. Can a nigga' be free in da hills, papa?"

York stopped the carriage and gave his son a serious look.

"Boy, don't be talkin' 'bout da hills and freedom. Forget yuh ever talked to Scipio. Forget wha' he say, and don't tell a soul wha' he say. Not yo' mama, not nobody. Yuh hear me?"

Kinchen looked up at his papa. York thought it the saddest face he'd ever seen as he watched the tears well up in his boy's eyes. A deep expression of kindness came over York's face, he smiled, then ran his fingers through Kinchen's hair.

"Boy, yuh ain't got near 'nough years behinds yuh for dis, but yuh listen close. Yuh heah? Listen close, and dinks 'bout it."

Kinchen nodded, and he ran a finger under his runny nose.

"Yuh already free, boy. I's free, yo' mama's free, just 'bout everybody's free."

Kinchen listened, bewildered.

"Yuh hear da preacher talk of da soul, boy? Da yuh know wha' da soul is?"

The boy nodded. He thought he knew, but he didn't really.

"It's da Lord, boy. It's da Lord. He's in our souls and He's in us all. The Lord's free, our soul's free, and dat makes us free, dat is if'n we listen ta our soul. Scipio, he don't listen. He listens ta his mind, and dat boy, is whar da debil dwells. Yuh follow, boy?"

Again Kinchen nodded, but his face still showed bewilderment.

"Scipio's mind tells him da hills are freedom, but it's da debil talkin'. Da debil calls 'im ta run. He blocks out da soul wid vanity. Da hills may be freedom, boy, but yuh gotta get dare through da soul cause da debil makes 'em hills a' sand, da desert. When Scipio gets dare, he'll still be a slave, a slave ta da debil."

The boy still didn't quite get it, but he was trying, trying hard.

"Papa, is yuh really free?"

York chuckled.

"Well boy, not all da time. See, da mind, da debil, it a powerful ding. Don't yuh dink otherwise. When I dink sinful thoughts, den da mind is a blockin' out my soul. Makes me sad. Makes me angry. Den I's a slave again. But I always 'members ta listen ta my soul. It makes me free. I gets a warm feelin', a joyous feelin'. It makes me laugh. When I smile, when you smile, dats when we're listenin' ta our souls. It's a struggle, boy. Fo' whites and blacks, it's a struggle. Massa Henry, he got a soul, but he rarely listens. He so busy takin' care a' his chillens and his black family. He so busy goin' afta' da worldly riches, dat he's deaf ta his soul. But da world, da debil, it has a habit a' knockin' a man down, but da Lord will pick yuh up again if'n yuh listen ta yuh soul. I's free, Kinchen. You's free."

The tears had dried from the boy's face, but he was solemn. He had a vague understanding, and the thought that Master Henry was no better than his father in the greater picture took his mind on a tumble.

"Well boy, dinks on dat."

York hugged his son and whispered in his ear.

"Listen ta yuh soul, boy, and da hills a' freedom will always be 'round yuh."

He slapped the reins on the mares' rumps.

"Haa, Lucy! Haa, Bessy!" We better get goin', boy. Yo' mammy, Missas Anna, dey sho' goin' be mad."

Kinchen was quiet during the rest of the ride to Master John's plantation. When they arrived, he went through the motions of kissing and hugging his mother and his mistress. On the ride back to Hillside, his mind was still full of green hills and talking souls. He sat on Nan's lap in the back of the carriage, Anna beside them. Kinchen didn't budge, and didn't make a peep. Anna noticed.

"York, Kinchen's awful quiet. Is he sick?"

"No ma'am, he fine. He just a dinkin'. We had a talk dis af'ernoon. A talk 'bout da soul. He just a dinkin' 'bout his soul."

Brow raised, Anna smiled.

"Such a serious thing for a young boy to be contemplating."

She reached over and lightly rubbed the boy's cheek with the back of her hand. He looked over at her.

"But a good thing to think of, Kinchen. Think of it often, and you'll be a happy boy."

Anna's pretty smile grew brighter. It made Kinchen feel warm, safe, and he couldn't help but return it. Nan began to hum and he leaned back into her arms, watched his mistress smiling at the autumn colors as they passed, and thought, at that very moment, her soul must be just a' shoutin'. ⁊

⁂ 8 ⁂

THE EXPERIMENT

IT WAS THE BUSIEST DAY OF THE YEAR IN JACKSON, "Hiring Day," the first day of January. All the gentry of the county were there to hire out their excess hands for the year. The free blacks were there as well, selling their services to the highest bidder.

Not yet able to build the great dam that could hold back any flood, Henry went to town to buy ditchers and dikers. Last October, another disastrous freshet had killed all his peas and pumpkins, and destroyed six hundred barrels of corn. Henry was determined, more than ever, to block the river's frequent rises, so he went into Jackson looking for powerful men who could move tons of dirt day after day. It would take quite a few to do the job; he estimated at least twenty.

Northampton County was a small world. Everyone knew Henry and his intentions. The other planters wouldn't hire out their hands for such back-breaking work, and the free blacks wanted high prices, rates that Henry refused to pay. He went back to Hillside with one boy that year, a teenager who would replace Scipio as the hog driver. The previous summer Scipio had died of brain fever, which he'd caught, as Henry had described, by drinking water that was too cold when he was overheated.

The New Year's feast was at Hillside in 1848. Most of the Burgwyns were there: Henry, Anna, and the five children, and the bachelors, John Fanning and Thomas. The McRaes made an appearance with their two children, John and Kate. Julia had actually given birth to five children, but three had died as infants. Also visiting were the Doanes from Boston who were distant cousins of Anna's and long-time friends of the Greenoughs.

The evening's dinner conversation centered around Henry's and Thomas' labor plights. They needed dikes: long, high, wide ones, but they didn't have the labor to build them. Their own hands were needed to work the fields, and to add construction to their work load would be too hard on them, would risk injuries, sickness, and death. The day's hiring attempts showed that no work force could be gathered from the surrounding countryside. So the Burgwyns appeared resigned now. They would have to live with the freshets. Perhaps they would have to let their best land go to timber. Maybe they could use it for soiling, but that, too, was labor intensive. Mr. Doane was quick with a suggestion.

"Why not hire the Irish? Scores of them are in Boston's streets looking for work, desperate for work. Ships are bringing more every week. They'll work cheap, and with proper management, would be much more efficient than your Negroes."

The suggestion hit a chord.

"But will they come South?" asked Thomas.

"These men are begging for work. They're hungry, starving. They'll come if you pay their passage."

"But will they work?" asked Henry.

"They'll give you an honest day, the right ones. Some aren't worth the rags they wear, but most, I've heard, will work hard. Bet they'll give you a third better work than your blacks."

Henry had doubts. "The heat, the bad air, can they stand up to it?"

But Thomas was sold on the idea. "We'll hire them for five months, before the heat comes. About fifty should do it, wouldn't you say? Fifty could finish the work in five months."

"Four months," said Henry. "It'll take a month to hire and bring them here."

"I'll get them to you," said Doane. "I'll make all the arrangements, the hiring, the passage. I'll have them here by February."

"Price?" asked Thomas.

"Well, let's see. If you pay their passage, then house and feed them. Hmmm. Two dollars each. That's one hundred dollars a month for fifty. That's fair, I'd say."

Fair! The Burgwyns couldn't believe it. That was a tiny fraction of what they paid free Negroes. Henry had just paid Sweeney Cameron two hundred and fifty-two dollars for his fourteen-year-old boy for the year. Twenty-one dollars a month, for a boy. The price convinced them. Henry and Thomas decided to give the Irish a try.

The next day they escorted Mr. Doane down to the dam sites. Henry had drawn up a plan which showed just how elaborate and heavy the work would be. Doane wasn't intimidated. Possessing some experience in such things, he agreed to supervise the work for a prearranged fee. He also suggested that they wheel the earth in, haul it up on high towers and platforms, then drop it down into thick trunks. The Burgwyns agreed to provide the necessary beams and planks from their own sawmills.

During the afternoon of January third, Mr. Doane and his family set off for Boston. He had the authority, with certain restrictions, to engage the employment of fifty Irishmen and bring them to Carolina.

THE SCHOONER *PYRETUS* CAME UP IN A WINTER STORM and deposited its Irish cargo at Occoneechee Wigwam's wharf. Nineteen laborers, four carpenters, one mason, six women, and three children wobbled off with sea legs, drenched, frozen, their tattered baggage hanging on sore backs. Thomas had prepared some makeshift shelters, some tents, but most would be huddled into his lowland barns. The Irish experiment was off to a bad beginning.

The cold rains continued to fall off and on, and a freshet rose and covered the low grounds. The Irish couldn't work. Thomas took the opportunity to go out of town on business, while Mr. Doane started back for Boston to gather a second contingent. The first group was to work for Thomas, and in his and Doane's absence, a foreman was appointed among the Irish to supervise the work. John Fanning was also asked to keep an eye on them. But the weather remained too wet to work, weeks passed, and by the third week of February, no progress had been made.

HE RODE A MUDDY LANE BENEATH SILENT, February clouds, as damp winds carried the muted sounds of woodpeckers deep within the swamp. Dead trunks loomed in the pale light. The ditches along the lane were saturated with still, dark water, and the murky bogs ran right up to the top of the dikes. Henry sniffled and coughed from a lingering cold. There was little confidence in his movements, a frown of worry on his lips. His mind was preoccupied, and he was ignorant of the young colt he was riding. His treasured little girl, the youngest, was sick with a high fever. Anna was home nursing her, and his thoughts were there beside them.

He drifted out of the moody swamp, passed a pile of stark, twisted brush, and veered around a sandy bend. Ahead was John Fanning's Alveston Plantation, which the road bisected on its way to Occoneechee, Henry's destination. The colt, one of Roxanna's, had been broken the previous fall, but hadn't been ridden much since. The youngster seemed to sense the rider's indifference and used this to its advantage. An unexpected forward jerk got Henry off balance, a sudden stop had him wavering, and a final quick buck and rear had him in the mud. Henry landed safely on his rump. He cursed the animal as it kicked up the lane, stupid and ornery as its high-breed mother.

Henry pulled himself out of the goo, wiped the sticky mud off his hands, and sighed a deep, tired breath that brought on a wheezing cough. He looked up questioningly into the sad clouds, and for reasons unknown to him, sensed the gods were aligned against him.

He walked the lonely road, passed barren fields with numerous, small ponds of standing water, then turned down the soggy lane to Alveston. Simon, John Fanning's coachman and stable hand, met him there. The colt had run straight for the stables and was now munching from a trough of oats. Henry walked to his father's house, a large frame dwelling, rather plain, but comfortable. Within, Henry found his father in a depressed mood. Often, when left alone for long periods, John Fanning despaired of his dead first wife and his dead children, the infants, Collinson. His girls, he thought at times, had forsaken him; they hardly ever came around. Only Henry and Thomas remained close. Of the two, Thomas was his favorite, and when his younger son was away, even for short periods, John Fanning's depression would become acute. Henry usually avoided his father when he was in one of these moods, but today, he had little choice; he didn't trust to go out on the colt again while the animal's recent victory was fresh in its tiny brain.

Their conversation was short, tight, strained. Henry asked about the Irish, and John Fanning said they had been in an ill humor of late, but that he had pacified them with fresh mutton. Henry asked if they had been working, and the father responded with a grunt. Sick little Annie was the next topic of discussion. The news depressed John Fanning all the more, he responded with a moan of agony, then retired to sleep, a long, sad, winter nap. Henry retreated to the library, read away the afternoon, retired early, and was up before his father. He had the colt saddled, and was off to Occoneechee to see about the Irish.

The weather had turned, the sun was shining, and already its rays were soaking up the moisture. Henry kept a tight rein on the colt as they negotiated the sloppy roads. He crossed over the creek bridge, waved a languid hello to some of Thomas's hands cutting timber, and stopped at the saw mill to talk to Stallworth, Occoneechee's overseer. Stallworth directed him to the Irish encampment, warning Henry he wouldn't get much of a reception.

"Can't do a thing with them folks. Worse than Niggers! I ain't got much respect for folks happy on their backsides."

Henry took the warning in stride. This was Thomas' group; he wasn't responsible for them, but he'd get them working.

Another quarter mile, up a rise, then through the house lot, and he could see the curling smoke of the encampment down in a grove near the big barn in the low grounds. The colt trotted down to the bottoms, across the flats, and as Henry drew near, he immediately noticed the squalid conditions. A half dozen canvas tents were pitched in the dark of the trees, near a creek, somewhat sheltered from the wind and recent rains. An old slave shack at the edge of the grove had been refurbished to an extent. About fifty yards off, down toward the river, the barn stood, and some of the Irish were lounging on its porch. It was a warm, sunny morning for February, about fifty degrees, the best day of the year so far, yet the Irish were giving no evidence of industry, and seemed satisfied to sit in their ragged camp. Henry noticed three women squatting by a fire outside the shack. He rode toward them, the object of their complacent stares.

Women and children were not a part of the bargain struck up with Mr. Doane, but evidently some of the men wouldn't come without their families, and once they were there, Thomas was trapped into keeping them. Henry looked down on the pitiful waifs by the smoldering fire, their faces stained with grime, black from smoke. Somewhere under the dirt was that fair Celtic complexion, the gold freckles, but those lovely features were indistinguishable now.

McCall was the name of the man appointed as foreman. Henry asked the women where he was. One woman stood up and answered him.

"And who is it that might be askin' for 'im?" she asked defiantly, in a thick brogue. She looked at Henry like an urchin might look at an English gentleman on a Dublin street.

"Henry Burgwyn," he answered sternly. "Your employer's brother."

"Aye, the answer to me prayers," she said with a twinge of sarcasm as she turned to the other women.

They giggled softly.

"And he'll be wantin' to have a word with you, no doubt," she redirected to Henry. Then she gestured to one of the women who immediately scampered toward the tents in the grove. Henry thanked her. She didn't respond, her fists on her hips and a rude, smug expression on her face.

Henry waited patiently, as he eyed the dingy camp. He noticed the remains of a devoured goat half buried in the sandy loam, and noted that the fire was fueled by planks cut from Thomas's mill. He looked over toward the barn at a stack of planks that had obviously been sifted through. A small rage began to rise.

The Irishmen gathered under the dark of the trees, then made their way toward the visitor, a large party of them. One fellow appeared to be leading the way, a strapping man with a thick, unkempt red beard. They slowly emerged, walked purposefully. Henry eyed them with care. Many sizes, most looked sturdy, all were filthy. To Henry's right, another party made their way from the barn, then they were all gathered around him, the whole contingent, men, women, and children, thirty-three sets of eyes all focused on the lone rider. The man with the red beard spoke first.

"Mornin'," McCall said laconically.

Henry removed his hat, and all the Irish who were wearing hats followed his example.

"Are you Mr. McCall?" asked Henry.

"That be me," the red-bearded man answered.

Henry nodded, said nothing, slowly guided his eyes over the pitiful group.

"I'm Henry Burgwyn, your employer's brother."

McCall nodded, also said nothing. There was awkward silence for a moment.

"And what can we be doin' for you?" asked McCall.

"I've come to see what progress has been made in my brother's absence, but I see there's been no work at all."

"And there won't be any!" came a loud, angry voice from Henry's left. It startled him, and McCall glared at the man to shut him up, then looked up at Henry.

"We have no settlement," said the Irishman calmly. "And we won't work 'til we have one."

Henry was shocked, disbelieving. Doane had made those arrangements before they ever left Boston.

"You were paid one month's wages before you embarked. We paid your passage. You are to work for the same wage for four months."

"Liar!" yelled the same angry voice as before.

"Shut your mouth, Brenner!" screamed McCall. "We'll have none of that!" Then he looked at Henry and spoke calmly again.

"Is that what Mr. Doane told you?"

"Yes."

"He's mistaken."

The doubt was on Henry's face. McCall read it.

"The passage was paid, yes, but we were paid no wages, and were told to make our settlement with your brother when we arrived. Your brother left before that could be done."

Again, Henry found what McCall said hard to believe, but it did explain their idleness. We'll settle this right here, he thought.

"The terms as we agreed with Mr. Doane are..." Henry paused briefly," ...we are to pay your passage, house and feed you, and each man is to work for two dollars a month for four months."

Immediately his words sparked a reaction among the gathering. They jabbered among themselves, moved restlessly, began to yell, some at their appointed spokesman. McCall raised his voice over the crowd.

"You've wasted your money bringing us here! We'll not work for that!"

The volume of the shouts increased, thundered; fists shook over heads. The young colt jumped and twitched under Henry; he held the reins tightly, and maintained control as he looked at the seething, dirty faces. McCall stepped forward, turned and faced his countrymen. He raised his hands over his head and showed the flats of his palms to them. They hushed, but the tension remained.

"We'll not work for a pittance," said McCall again as he turned and faced the southerner.

Henry felt a shiver of guilt. He knew the wage was low, very low, and these people were in a sorry state. They probably had been gouged before. The colt's ears were back, but it was still now. Henry sat up, spoke.

"I have no authority to negotiate for my brother, but if you make a proposal, I will relay it to him straight away."

McCall looked over his shoulder for assurance, but he knew the rate they had all agreed upon.

"Six dollars a month. The other terms are acceptable," said McCall.

Henry felt a wave of release, began to relax inside. He was comfortable with that rate, knew Thomas would be too. Almost felt he could speak for Thomas and accept it.

"Reasonable," said Henry. "I'm sure we can reach an agreement. My brother is in Petersburg. I'll send your proposal to him today. In the meantime, I would be personally grateful if you began work."

McCall shook his head. "No settlement, no work."

"I see. Very well, we'll have your settlement as quickly as possible."

The tension began to fade, and the Irish seemed relax. A woman cleared her throat, looked at McCall, with an expression that said he had forgotten something. McCall saw, remembered.

"Oh, we have a grievance, one grievance. If you would be passing it to your brother?"

"Yes?"

"God in heaven. Don't know what you feed your blackies. God only knows how it may sustain them. As for us, we good Irishmen, as sure as the sun will rise and fall, we'll all be perishin' if you insist we survive on the miserable fare your brother is offerin'."

Henry twitched, and felt the touch of guilt again. Thomas had not done enough preparation for these people. He shouldn't have left, shouldn't have relied on John Fanning to take care of them.

"We're doing the best we can under the circumstances," answered Henry. "But I'll personally see to it. I'll get you better food and more of it."

He eyed the tents in the grove. "I'll have a word with Mr. Stallworth, too, and ask him about building your people some proper shelters."

McCall looked satisfied, peered over his shoulder and saw that his whole group seemed sated.

"We'll be much obliged to you," he said.

Henry put his hat on, walked the colt a few feet forward, reached down and offered Mr. McCall his hand. The Irishman took it, shook it vigorously.

"If I supply you with the proper tools, axes and saws, to gather your own fuel, will your people quit burning the planks meant for the dikes?" Henry asked politely.

McCall frowned, then winked and grinned.

"Is your brother as reasonable a man as yourself?"

Henry smiled. "Yes, I assure you, he is."

"Then we'll be doin' good work for 'im."

"Very well, I'll be off to see Mr. Stallworth then." Henry tipped his hat to the Irish, turned the colt, and trotted away over the flats. The thought of his sick little girl quickly jumped back into his head as he rode. He felt a weight, a burden. He hurried along, looked up into the cloudless blue sky and wondered what he had done to displease his Lord.

THE HOUSEHOLD WAS FRANTIC when Henry arrived back at Hillside. Little Annie's condition had worsened. The other children were removed to the east wing at the far end of the house. They were noticeably frightened.

Madie and the housemaids were doing their best to keep them occupied.

Anna was panicked. The child's fever had risen higher; she could not break it. She didn't know what the sickness was, couldn't be bilious as they had at first supposed. Henry ordered York to saddle a fresh, more reliable horse, and he was soon off for Jackson to bring Dr. Barrow.

A week passed, Annie's condition didn't change. Her fever persisted, the doctor unable to identify the cause. The whole house was under a constant siege of stress.

The Irish also remained idle. Henry had sent their proposal to Thomas with a recommendation he accept it, but had heard nothing from him. The weather had held up, warm and clear, and was being wasted. A month had passed since the Irish had arrived; and the season was drawing late.

Henry decided to take matters into his own hands. He set off for Occoneechee with a month's pay in his bags, and told the Irish everything was settled. Six dollars a head it would be, and here were their first wages. It was time for work. The Irish were perfectly satisfied, and promised to set to it immediately.

Two days later, Stallworth turned up at Hillside, with news that the Irish had quit working, actually hadn't ever started. They weren't helping with the new shelters, and would stand around watching Occoneechee's carpenters do the work. They had a new grievance. The married men thought they should get eight dollars a month, and the others agreed. They refused to work until the grievance was met.

Henry set off once more, met their demands again, but this time put the agreement to paper.

> *"This is to say that there is now no further difficulty or disputes between us & the Mr. Burgwyns. All matters being adjusted to our entire satisfaction & we will now proceed to work faithfully for 4 months on the terms agreed upon viz eight dollars per month & board."*
>
> *Anthony Kemp, John Crafter, James Murphy, Thomas McCall.*

Henry carefully printed each man's name, and had Stallworth witness their marks. Then he watched them set off for work.

Little time had passed before one of Occoneechee's boys showed up at Hillside, a messenger from Mr. Stallworth. He reported that only a handful of Irish were working, the rest being sick, or mostly drunk. A gang had set off for Halifax with their advanced pay the night before, and had had a grand time. As a result, they were too incapacitated to work.

Henry's anger bubbled over and he decided to wash his hands of this group. He had heard from his brother, knew he would be home soon, and he told the boy to tell Stallworth to do nothing until Thomas arrived. He was not to be consulted about the Irish from hence forward.

Another steamer carrying Mr. Doane and the second Irish contingent arrived at Hillside. Henry was prepared for them, had shelters ready, and an agreement drawn up in advance, ready to be signed. The Irish accepted it, and the work commenced.

Meanwhile, Annie's fever had broken, but she remained bedridden, and despite Anna's nursing and constant attention, was growing weaker. Henry sent letters off to several doctors describing the symptoms and asking for a diagnosis and treatment. He received a different answer from each. One doctored called it Eresipelas Erratic or Black Tongue. Dr. Beckwith diagnosed it Typhoid Fever, and another physician thought it The Plague.

Henry took a two-week trip away from Hillside to consult personally with the doctors. The venture paid no appreciable dividends, and when he returned, little Annie was fading.

A ride to the dam sites showed that little work had been done, the scaffolding and towers weren't complete, the trunks not even started. Doane was told the Irish must work faster. The spring rains would be upon them soon, and with them, the threat of a freshet.

THE FIRST BREATH OF SPRING ROLLED into the Roanoke Valley—warm winds, flowers, flocks of birds, and fresh, fragrant mornings. One such morning, Henry sat with his wife at his daughter's bedside. The child was pale and silent, her breathing labored. They were doing all they could for her, and had tried all they knew, but she continued to slide slowly away. She was in God's hands now, and it seemed He was taking his time. A difficult decision, whether to take a sweet little girl.

Henry was smothered with helpless feelings; they'd been suffocating him for weeks, and he could not stand to wait and watch anymore. He kissed Anna's sad cheek, rubbed a shoulder, and left the room, to pray for an elusive blessing.

He visited the stables, chatted with York, and tried to get a word from his shy little boy, Kinchen. He then saddled a gelding and went out into the glowing fields to watch the planting. The weather had been prime for plowing and sowing, the rich soil a perfect texture. He thought, perhaps, the women had sowed the wheat a bit too thickly in the Orchard Field, but it didn't really bother him. He was feeling a little apathetic about it all.

He had not been down to see the Irish and dikes lately. He'd been letting Doane take care of it. The work was going so slowly, a snail's pace, and visits usually brought on the same helpless feelings that haunted him within his own house, within the sorrowful shadows of his daughter's room. The new dikes offered no escape, no distraction, but today he thought he had better go down and see them.

The trees were pale green along the river, fresh tiny leaves, soft and delicate, swirling in a gentle breeze. They reminded Henry of little girls dancing. Everything reminded him of healthy little girls these days. He rode along the edge of the fields, cool shadows to his left, warmth from a blazing sun to his right. A slow gait took him around the bend in the river, and ahead he could see a mound of dirt, a small, finished dike, the only dike completed. Three of his Negroes were throwing grass seed on the raw dirt. He stopped and talked with them a while, then continued on his way.

The main dam site was empty, tools and equipment scattered around, but otherwise there was not a soul in sight. The anger bubbled up within him, he tried to control it, but his tolerance was down, and he set off for the settlement with a red, grimacing face. He found the Irish lounging among the shelters, and rode in among them; he stopped in the middle of the village, and looked at them with disgust. He could see the guilt within some. They glanced away, wouldn't look at Henry's face. Some scampered off, out of sight. One fellow, Flaherty, didn't shy away. He watched Henry boldly, then got up from the molasses barrel he was perched on, and made his way toward him. Henry recognized him as one of three or four troublemakers, unofficial and self-appointed leaders of the group. Tyrants actually, they were violent men who ruled the others with their fists. They were outnumbered, but the others did not seem to have the backbone to gather and face up to them. Henry watched Flaherty draw near.

"Where is Mr. Doane?" Henry asked.

"He's at your brother's place," said Flaherty casually.

Henry squinted down at him with angry eyes, and red, puffy cheeks. "Why are you not working?"

The Irishman looked up into the sun, wiped a sleeve across a sweatless brow. "Hot day—Doane, he gave us a holiday. Been working good for you of late."

A bold-faced lie, thought Henry. Sunday was the only holiday, it was Thursday, and Doane had strict instructions to work every day, rain or shine. They were behind schedule, and he would not give them a day.

"Doane would not do that," said Henry.

"Oh, but wouldn't he?" asked another Irishman moving from the shaded interior of his hut.

"Your friend, Mr. Doane; he's cheatin' you."

Henry looked at him queerly. His name was Rourke, another of the tyrants, the ring leader.

"He's stallin'. Draggin' out the work, he's squeezin' you for money."

Henry pointed an angry finger. "Not another word from you."

Rourke stopped in his tracks.

"He has nothing to gain from those tactics. We have agreed on a set fee. You are a liar."

"Doane is a bloody scoundrel!" Rourke yelled back. "He intends drawing out this work through the summer, and is countin' on you payin' him to finish."

"You will curb your language when speaking to me, Mr. Rourke, and you shall not speak of Mr. Doane in those terms."

"The hell I won't," said Rourke in defiance.

"Enough!" There was silence as others gathered.

Henry settled the argument. "You were hired for four months, and four months only. At that time, if not before, you will be leaving here, whether the dikes are complete or not. This, I have already decided, and Mr. Doane was informed of my decision weeks ago."

Rourke and Flaherty looked at each other; they had nothing to say.

"Now, I am ordering you to gather all your men and earn your pay."

"We certainly will not," hissed Rourke. "We will not be working in this heat."

"Heat!" taunted Henry. "This is not heat. The thermometer was at seventy degrees this morning. Oh, if you could only feel the heat, but you will not get the chance, not from me. You, and all of your backsliders will be off my plantation tomorrow."

"Damn!" yelled Flaherty to Rourke. "He's firing us!"

"I certainly am. You will be gone from here tomorrow."

"All of us?" asked one Irishman from the gathered crowd.

"All of you," said Henry.

He rode to where the Irish were laboring at Occoneechee. The work was moving along there, but still far from finished. Thomas and John Fanning were at the far end of a long dike, but Henry spied Doane supervising high on some scaffolding nearby, and he made his way toward him. Doane saw him coming, waved.

"Good morning, Henry."

Henry was too angry for pleasantries. "I've fired my Irish," he yelled.

Doane wasn't sure he heard right. "What's that?"

"I've fired my Irish."

The men working nearby heard, stopped their work, looked at Henry. Doane was surprised, shocked.

"I found them lying around the village. They lied to me, said you had given them a holiday. They refused to work. We had words. I fired them."

"Damn them," said Doane.

"Yes," said Henry.

Doane climbed down, off the scaffolding, while Henry waited.

"What are we going to do with them?"

"I told them I wanted them off the plantation tomorrow. Spoke a little quickly I'm afraid. You can bring them over here, if Thomas will take them. If not, I'll send them off on the next steamer."

Thomas and John Fanning came riding up. "Good morning, Henry!" yelled Thomas. "How's little Annie?"

"No better," said Henry curtly.

"Oh, sorry to hear that."

"Henry has fired his Irish," said Doane.

Thomas winced, "I see."

"They are a worthless lot. I can do better with blacks."

"Probably can," said Thomas diplomatically. John Fanning didn't agree. "It's just a handful that are troublemakers. You should keep them for the term, Henry, it's just a bit over a month longer. Get rid of the troublemakers, and keep the good ones, raise their wages."

"Thomas can do that if he wishes, but I can do better with blacks," Henry repeated.

"Henry was wondering if you would take them on?" Doane asked Thomas. "He'll just ship them off, if you don't."

Thomas pondered a moment. "Suppose I will, but I have no place to put them. Will you let them stay in your village?"

Henry buried his forehead into a hand, considered for a long moment. "Yes, they're far enough away not to bother me, but if they destroy any of my property, I'll prosecute."

"Understood."

Thomas now made a proposal to Henry that he'd been considering for some time.

"You know, these dikes I'm building will benefit your land down river. Since I'm taking on your Irish, don't you think you should share in my expenses?"

Henry frowned. "Have you forgotten that I paid your group's first month's wages?"

"No, but now I'm taking on your group for the last month and half."

John Fanning sensed a battle. Always the peacemaker, he interjected. "Now, now, we can discuss this some other time when tempers aren't so testy."

Henry huffed. "I'll send them off on the next steamer," and he rode away.

"These damned Irish," said Doane. "Wish I had never made the suggestion."

HENRY BURGWYN'S EXPERIMENT WITH IMMIGRANT labor came to an end at a loss of thousands of dollars. Shortly after he fired the Irish that April, Henry hired eighteen free blacks, and they finished the project that summer. Thomas didn't keep his Irish beyond the original term. Almost all of them returned to Boston. Thomas also hired free blacks to finish the job.

A dispute over compensation for the Irish simmered between the brothers. It was finally settled when Henry paid Thomas an amount both agreed was fair. The building and improvement of dikes and dams continued at both plantations, as long as the Burgwyn brothers owned them. White labor, on a large scale, was never again employed.

On May 15th, 1848, Henry made an entry in his journal.

"*Our dearly loved little daughter Annie left us this morning for her final home, at 2 o'clock, 8 minutes. She died without pain & in the utmost quiet. We have been with her constantly— her mother, for 8 weeks, has been ever by her bedside. It is a sad, sad loss, which none but our God can know; she was eminently lovely & beautiful. She has been a precious loan from Heaven too valuable to be suffered to be long away.*"

Dr. Barrow performed an autopsy, and found that Annie's little heart was four times its normal size, a classic symptom of rheumatic fever. Sad days followed; Henry took Anna out into the air as much as possible, her own health having broken down by the stress. Finally they placed their little daughter in her last receptacle and traveled to Jamaica Plains where they buried her by her little brother, her aunt, and her grandfather and grandmother in the Greenough family vault.

Upon their return, Bishop Ives, the Episcopal Bishop of North Carolina, paid a visit to Hillside to console them. While there, he baptized little Pollok, one year old, and also confirmed Anna into the Episcopal faith.

ALL THE FAMILY WAS VISITING UP NORTH in Cohasset when it happened. It was likely the fire started in the chimney, but nobody really knew for sure. During, or his wife Rachel might have had something to do with it. They were sold shortly thereafter. There was a time during the house's construction that the bricklayers had been called off on another job, and Henry, in his rush to complete the work, had used his inexperienced hands to build the eastern stack. If the fire had started there, it quickly spread to the roof, then steadily downward. The fact that the house was brick didn't help; the fire got so hot the mortar simply melted away. By nightfall, it was a glowing, smoldering pile of rubble. On September 1st, 1849, the elegant manor house at Hillside Plantation, burned to the ground.

Henry kept a roster of births and deaths at Hillside. Probably not by coincidence, two new names were entered in the death ledger with the same date as the fire: Nan and York.

⁂ 9 ⁂

THORNBURY

THERE WAS A COOL CRISPNESS to the dawn air, a certain freshness, as dry breezes blew the autumn scent of changing leaves. Above, the sky was crystal clear, the stars still showing brightly within its varying colors, black to midnight blue. He rode hurriedly, could feel the anticipation, the alert excitement. He had to be in place, be at that perfect place at the right time, before the morning's first light lured them from their roost.

He saw the dike rising up out of the dark, veered toward it, climbed to its spine and followed it, cutting through the swamps. The live oaks and cypress closed in, surrounding the mound, forming a low tunnel. He slid down the horse's back, his face just beside the laboring neck, looking ahead, eyes watchful, searching for the place. It always seemed to be a bit further than he remembered.

Then he heard them clearly, whistling wings, just over the tops of the trees, just above him. The anxiety surged through him, and he looked up through the trees into the dark, trying to catch a glimpse. But they were gone.

"C'mon, c'mon, they're already moving," Harry called back to Kinchen while keeping his voice down.

"Comin'," answered Kinchen impatiently while evading the low branches.

Harry squinted into the dimness, "Can't be much further, just ahead!"

Then they were there at the break in the trees, between the swamps and the millpond, where the ducks traded back and forth, from their resting place to the harvested cornfields. Harry spurred his horse to the other side of the break, jumped off, tethered his mount quickly, then pulled the gun from the saddle holster and loaded it. He scanned the changing sky. Kinchen pulled up behind him, also dismounted, but pushed his mount to the edge of the dike under the dark of the trees. There, he stood in silence, holding the bridle loosely. Harry also sank into the shadows, his eyes shifting, his ears alert for the whistle of wings.

Kinchen watched him, the soft light on Harry's face, an expression of pure concentration. He was very intense about everything he did. Kinchen admired that, wished he was more like him, but was equally thankful for his own relaxed ways. It was comforting to lay back and watch, no pressure, no burning need to excel. He was good at some things, very good, but the things he wasn't good at, well, he just didn't worry about it. Harry, on the other hand, young Harry had to be the master of all.

Harry jerked a finger into the air, smiling as he glanced over his shoulder at Kinchen. A flock of mallards flew high over the swamps, their dark silhouettes barely detectable. Kinchen ducked his head out of the shadows, watching their deliberate flight. They zoomed over the dike, their wings barely patting the air. Over the pond they went, over a bordering stand of pines, where they began to mill around. Their cackling and chuckling hit the still air, and reverberated over the water. It was the call to feed, and the sound sent goose pimples up Harry's back. He watched them circling, cackling, until their wings set and they dropped below the trees and into the corn to feed on stray ears and kernels.

The hunter turned and looked into the reddening sky over the swamps, watching for dark clumps of erratic flyers. The mallards usually flew high, and Harry rarely got a shot at them, but the summerducks, or wood ducks, often screamed low over the trees and through the break, and if he was quick and a good shot, he could pluck them out of the air.

Big flocks of green heads continued to cruise over, and Kinchen and Harry could see flashes of white from their wings and bellies. But they were still much too high, well out of range. The sky grew significantly brighter and Harry began to fear the summerducks had already moved, could already be feeding. Perhaps the group he had heard earlier, while making his way up the dike, had been the last.

Kinchen heard a faint whistle behind him, over the pond. He turned, and saw a flash of color; the woodies burst unexpectedly through the break from behind. In one quick motion Harry had the gun at his shoulder, trailed the birds as they passed over the swamp, and fired a rushed shot. The terrific boom broke the morning's stillness, but no ducks fell. The woodies screeched a call of alarm, climbed higher, and Kinchen watched them until they dipped down into the swamp.

"Didn't lead 'nough, you were behinds 'em," Kinchen advised.

"I know, I know," said Harry angrily. He was already reloading.

"Didn't count on 'em comin' from over the pond, did yuh?" Kinchen asked teasingly.

Harry ignored the jab. "What do you make of that? Do you think they fed last night and are moving back to the swamps?"

"Umm-hmm," Kinchen answered languidly.

"Did you see them? Where'd they go?"

"Went down in da swamp. Sure 'nough. They'll bring more, yuh know."

Harry shifted his vigil to the west, to the dark skies over the pond and the distant cornfields.

Kinchen saw movement, just a glimpse of the birds over the trees before they dipped into the darkness below them. "Dey's comin," he said.

"I see them."

Harry watched the flying silhouettes draw nearer. He held the gun loosely, at the ready. When he heard the first whistles, he stepped into the open. The ducks reacted instantly, flared, veered upward to the right, and the rising sun caught their dashing colors. Harry aimed at the lead bird, led him perfectly.

K-boom!

The woodie folded up, rolled through the air, tumbled down through the trees, his momentum carrying him into the swamp. Instantly, Kinchen was mounted, spurring the horse down off the dike and into the shallow waters, splashing through the brush. Feathers weaved through the air. He saw the duck floating, reached low from the saddle and grabbed its neck. In one fluid motion he turned the horse, while holding the prize high over his head.

"Kilt dead!" he yelled.

Harry looked on with a satisfied grin.

Before a red sun was in full view over the swamps, Harry had shot two more summerducks. But with the new light, the morning flights came to an end and the hunter's ardor seeped away. Harry climbed a huge live oak, and shuffled carefully over a wide, thick limb that reached out over the pond. Kinchen followed. The view was sublime, peaceful, the sky displaying glorious colors. A graceful flight of Canada geese made its way up the Roanoke, their placid honks growing steadily weaker as they drifted away. Harry admired.

"Isn't it grand!"

Kinchen scanned the horizon, black eyes soaking up the color. He nodded, but the view didn't have the same affect on him as it did on Harry. He hadn't been away up north to school, and now home for just a visit. The sights were familiar to him, commonplace.

"Every night I'm away, every night when I go to bed, I think of home. I remember the mornings most of all. The mornings just like this."

Kinchen couldn't relate. This was all he knew. He hadn't been more than ten miles from the plantation all his life. Garysburg, which the new railroad passed through on its way north, was the furthest he'd been, and there just wasn't much difference that he could see between it, Jackson, or Halifax.

"Wha' it like up Noth?" he asked.

Harry looked at him, a gentle look, then peered off at the sky again.

"Busy," he said, then paused.

"Lots of people, sprawling cities, big buildings that block out the sky. Oh, it's got countryside, pretty countryside, but it's not the same." He paused again. "It's different."

Kinchen couldn't form a mental picture; he tried, but failed. Harry's description meant nothing to him. There was just a huge void in his mind when anybody spoke of any place other than Thornbury and Northampton.

"C'mon, getting hungry," said Harry with a sigh.

They scampered off the limb, jumped down on to the dike. Harry unloaded and holstered his gun. Kinchen tied a leather strap around the ducks' feet, then draped them over his horse. They walked quietly through the tunnel of trees, leading their horses, and after they reached the end of the dike, mounted and rode for home.

"Sure am hungry," said Kinchen patting his rumbling stomach.

"Ruthy will have something for us, don't you think?" Harry countered.

"Oh yeah, she treats us hunters good 'cause we brings her good dings ta cook up."

Harry grinned, swished his tongue over his lips. "Good eating tonight. She's going to make a feast of these summerducks."

"Yep. Gotta watch her dough. Eats half what she cooks."

"Sure does. Says she testing when you catch her."

"She da testin'est cook I's ev'a seen," said Kinchen. They both laughed.

"What do you think she's got for us this morning?"

"Tatta cakes and flap jacks and butta'."

"Bacon?"

"Umm-hmm."

Harry felt a sharp pang of hunger. He spurred the horse, suddenly with an urge for a race. Racing was an old rivalry between them, ever since the two had first set out together on horseback, when they were little boys. Harry had never won though. Kinchen was two years older, but more importantly, he was a natural. He rode a horse as if he had been born for it. Occasionally, Harry resorted to trickery. He would make sure he had the faster horse, or set off ahead without a warning, to give himself a head start. These ploys never worked, and Kinchen would always catch him. But Harry never ceased trying.

Harry glanced at Kinchen, careful not to catch his eyes. Then he suddenly slapped down on Glasgow's rump.

"Hahh!" He vaulted out ahead, through the trees and quickly into a meadow. Kinchen was caught flat-footed, completely surprised. His eyes went big; he frowned, then smiled, and clamped down on Judy's sides jumping after him. Glasgow galloped through the yellow broom sage, as Harry looked over his shoulder, laughing, heading for a narrow path through a thick grove; Kinchen on Judy was closing fast. Harry had a good lead entering the grove, the path too skinny for passing. Glasgow jumped a brook, staggered, and Judy made up the time. Kinchen was right behind them when they broke into the open again, a flat field. They cut for the plantation road at a fast run, Harry buried in the saddle, Kinchen riding high like a jock, his weight pushed forward. Judy passed Glasgow quickly, easily, adding to her advantage as she made for the road and the gate beyond. Harry had one chance: a short-cut, off the road, straight for the stables with a jump over a low rail-fence.

Kinchen was on the road; he saw Harry making for the fence to his left.

"Go Suga', fly!" Kinchen slapped Judy's shoulder, one quick snap. The mare dug harder, dirt and rocks flying. They passed through the gate, rounded a stand of trees, and Kinchen glanced again to his left. He saw Glasgow out ahead, riderless.

He pulled the mare to a jarring halt, looked back towards the fence, and spied Harry sprawled out on the ground at its base. Kinchen felt a moment of panic, and spurred Judy to a gallop. The white boy was up on one knee now, squeezing an ankle. He got to his feet, hopped, limped. Kinchen rushed up, halted.

"Sit down!" he hollered. "Might have sump'n broke."

Harry hobbled. "I'm fine." He tried to put weight on the ankle, winced, staggered, and almost fell.

"Sit down!" insisted Kinchen, as he hopped off Judy. He strode to Harry's side, steadied him and helped him to sit down.

"Never can beat you," said Harry with evidence of pain in his voice. Kinchen didn't answer. He was on his knees, feeling gingerly about the swelling ankle.

"Glasgow's bigger, stronger than Judy."

"He an old man," said Kinchen, still looking down at the ankle.

"Judy's old."

"Yep, but she still gots the lightness in her feets... Nothing broke here."

"See, told you I was fine."

"Ain't gonna be walkin' fo' a spell."

"Sure am. I'll be walking home here directly."

Kinchen shook his head. "You just rest here a spell."

Harry leaned back on his hands, looked at the sore ankle, rotated the foot with a glint of pain in his eyes. Kinchen checked back at Judy who was cropping grass, but he didn't see Glasgow.

"We Burgwyns just can't stay on a horse," said Harry trying to be amusing.

Kinchen blinked, looked back at the boy, and suppressed a smile. The Burgwyns couldn't stay on a horse. It was the standing joke around Thornbury and Northampton. Harry's Great Uncle George Pollok, and his Uncle Collinson had died from falls. That wasn't funny, but Master Henry couldn't stay on a horse either, and his brother Thomas had had quite a few falls as well. John Fanning seemed to stick pretty well to a horse, but he was an old man now, who puttered about mostly. Mistress Anna had become quite a graceful rider.

"Why is that?" asked Harry.

Kinchen scratched the back of his neck. "I supposes it's on account dat y'all Burgwyns are a bit top heavy, a little large about da should'as, a bit light about da legs and hips."

Harry wasn't expecting such a scientific answer, smiled, surprised.

"Never thought of that. Suppose you're right."

"Yep, dat be it."

Kinchen strolled over to Judy, removed the ducks draped over her, and placed them around his shoulders, then he led her over to where Harry lay. He helped Harry up on one leg, pushed him up on Judy, then grabbed the bridle and led the mare toward the stables.

Daniel, the woodcarver, was standing near the paddocks with hands on hips, watching the boys walking in. Glasgow was standing nearby, neck bent, pulling grass.

"Heard y'all shootin' early dis mornin'," Daniel yelled. Daniel was a boisterous Negro, jolly, and looked at the light side of everything. He saw the dead ducks hanging from Kinchen's shoulders.

"Gots some, I see."

Kinchen nodded. He wasn't in the mood for Daniel's foolishness. He stopped, whispered to Judy, walked over to Glasgow, and pulled him over by the reins.

"Y'all been racin' again?" asked Daniel loudly, looking up at Harry. Harry put a finger to his mouth, and cut his eyes around the stable yard.

"Hurt bad?" asked Daniel softly. Harry shook his head.

"When ya'll gonna learn?"

Harry shrugged, grinned, and looked at Kinchen who just led Glasgow over beside Judy, and then led both horses towards the paddock gate. Daniel whispered to Kinchen as he passed.

"Like father, like son," referring to the Burgwyns' inability to stay on a horse.

Kinchen wasn't amused. He whipped his head around, frowned, and shook his head at Daniel, defending Harry with his gestures.

The woodcarver chuckled. He slapped a hand on a thigh, folded his arms around his chest, and watched the boys slide by with a wide grin.

"Going to stay on and beat you some day," said Harry.

"We'll see."

"I will."

Kinchen didn't answer; there was a silent pause.

"Guess you have to groom the horses now, and clean the gun and birds," asked Harry with a tone of guilt.

"Umm-hmm."

Another pause.

"Won't be able to sneak in without Mother knowing, will we?"

"Nope."

Harry felt bad for the trouble he'd caused. He looked down at Kinchen, at the back of his head, wanted to say something, to apologize, but knew he really didn't have to. The slave would already know he was sorry, the gesture unnecessary. Harry smiled, comfortable, a sudden flow of warmth inside. He kept looking at Kinchen, and the cozy feeling quickly passed unacknowledged. The young slave led their mounts to the big frame house, passed Harry over to Polly's care, then tramped back to the stables for his chores before breakfast.

THE YEAR WAS 1855, and much had changed in the lives of the Burgwyns during the six years since the burning of Hillside. Promptly after the disaster, when Henry returned to the South with his family, he rented another house in Jackson. He had no immediate plans to build a new manor house, and the old routine of the early Forties returned. During the following summer, Anna gave birth to another child, a boy, John Alveston, whom they called Allie.

Prosperity slowly grabbed hold during the early Fifties. Minnie and Harry were sent away to school, while the younger boys were tutored at home by Madie and a seminary student. Eventually Will and Pollok would also go north to study. Henry and Anna became active in the Episcopal Church during this time, and were instrumental in the founding of "The Church of the Savior" in Jackson. It was consecrated by Bishop Ives in April, 1851. Henry also designed and helped in the construction of a new Court House at the county seat which was considered the most beautiful and stately in Carolina at the time. As a planter, he continued to take great strides and saw his reputation as a successful innovator grow. He wrote articles, began to attract national attention, and served a term as Vice President of the American Agricultural Society.

Despite all the successes and rewards, Henry didn't seem quite satisfied with his situation. Late in the summer of 1851, he started a four-month trip to Europe. Oddly, he went alone. He wrote home frequently though, and always ended his epistles with pleas to his wife to remind new little Allie constantly of his father. The reason behind Henry's trip remains a mystery. He might have gone for reasons of health, although some have said he went to observe European farming methods. His letters seem to indicate that it was merely a sightseeing tour. But when he arrived in Florence, a destination he seemed to have greatly anticipated, at least a partial nature of the trip is revealed. Anna had distant relatives in Florence, a contingent of Greenoughs, and it appears that Henry was seriously considering the beautiful Italian city as a permanent home for his family, a far off compromise between America's North and South. The expanding sectional differences back home may have had him gravely concerned.

He thoroughly checked the prices of dwellings, visited potential schools for his children, even went so far as to examine the cost and quality of food. He found these basic necessities satisfactory, but otherwise, thought Italy undesirable. All the men were either soldiers or priests. He found evidence of oppression by the government and the Catholic Church everywhere. At street corners, there were fat, greasy monks begging food, compelling Henry to turn away in disgust. The peasants were ill clad, worse off, it seemed, than his Negroes back home. He saw women doing work he would never have asked his strongest hands to consider, and the merchants he met cheated and lied. A permanent move to Florence was quickly dismissed.

Henry became extremely homesick during his stay. He had nightmares where he woke up weeping, and frequent dreams of kissing his wife and children. On the return leg he stopped in Paris and wrote Anna: *"This city has no charm in comparison to Jackson with you there."*

Henry returned home in December, and immediately made plans for building a new home on his plantation. By spring, the work was under way. In April, 1852, nine months to the day Henry left for Europe, Anna gave birth to her eighth and final child, yet another boy, Collinson Pierrepont Edwards, or Collie.

The grand new house was completed in 1853. It didn't stand on Hillside's original sight, a bluff overlooking the Roanoke, but was moved to even higher ground, further away from the river, a healthier location. In design it was very similar to Henry's original home, but larger. It had two stories over an English basement with sprawling wings, at least two piazzas, and an elegant observatory situated high on its roof. Except for the foundation, chimneys and stoops, it was void of bricks. The burning of Hillside had proved them no guarantee against fire. Besides, the making of brick was hard, slow work, and the kiln was greatly depleted. The new structure was assembled completely with lumber cut at Henry's own sawmill. Painted white, facing north, sitting at the end of a mile-long lane that bisected the main road between Jackson and Halifax, it stood as majestic evidence of the Burgwyns' new wealth. At the home's completion, the plantation was renamed "Thornbury," after the village in England where John Fanning had been born and reared.

For the next decade Thornbury thrived, a model plantation. It included a growing number of barns and outbuildings, several mills, a hospital and a chapel. There was even a small railway with a steam engine that carried crops and supplies to and from the wharf on the river. In 1854, it was the site of another reaper competition, this one on a much larger scale, and one that would draw international attention. The rivalry between Cyrus McCormick and Obed Hussey had heated up and would continue for several more years. This time, McCormick brought an improved machine that stood up to Hussey's mower, and after this demonstration, Henry would become less committed to the Baltimore manufacturer.

Henry's journal claimed his black family remained reasonably healthy and content. There were the occasional epidemics that filled the hospital, and doctors were called in when needed, but the nursing was mostly performed by Anna, Madie, and several governesses, who also looked after Allie and Collie. Five slave deaths was the average rate per year on the plantation, mostly of infants. The birth rate must have surpassed the deaths, because Henry traded in slaves sparingly. Great emphasis was placed in Christianizing his people. The new rector of the Church of the Savior resided at Thornbury and held services in the chapel every third Sunday. Bishop Ives, when he visited Thornbury, commended Henry and Anna on their work. He thought the Negroes attentive and inspired. But baptizing and confirming slaves was not necessarily a matter of saving souls. Back in 1831, and just twenty miles to the north in Southampton County, Virginia, Nat Turner had led his famous insurrection where sixty whites and even more blacks had perished in worthless violence. There were over two hundred slaves on Thornbury, Alveston, and Occoneechee, and few whites to control them. The Burgwyns would be sadly exposed, if there was a rebellion, and religion served to hypnotize and pacify. No hint of an insurrection ever arose at Thornbury though. Henry's worst problem was the clandestine drunkenness in the barns at night. For a long period, a local free black snuck on to Thornbury and traded whiskey with the hands, until he was finally caught and run out of the county.

The year 1855 was a happy one at Thornbury. There had been only three deaths on the plantation, and the Burgwyn children were healthy and active. Even old John Fanning, who suffered from chronic pessimism, confided in his diary that it appeared his sons had finally overcome the maze of difficulties that confronted anyone who attempted large scale planting in the South.

HE SAT ALONE IN A SPARSELY furnished room, the newly plastered walls stark white. Outside, visible through a bare, frosty window, puffy white flakes were falling, the first heavy snow of the season. John Fanning wrinkled his nose, squinted against the room's brightness, and wished he could paper the walls. The contractor had advised him to wait until spring, after the plaster had fully dried.

A terrible feeling of loneliness engulfed him. Except for a cook and several servants, the grand four-story brick house at number 694 Spruce Street in Philadelphia was empty. He had helped his youngest daughter, Sarah Emily, purchase the house back in October, warning her that both the price and the house were too big for her, but she had insisted. Em had hardly been there since. She was visiting in New York with friends, and had left her sickly father behind to knock around the cavernous new house alone.

A coal-burning stove accompanied John Fanning in his isolation. He was buried in a large chair near it, old bones absorbing its warmth. A thumb flipped through a stack of envelopes lying on a table. Only a few of them were addressed to him, and none were from his children. There was a telegram from Henry though, requesting that he accompany young Harry home for Christmas. Harry, or Hal, which was John Fanning's nickname for his oldest grandson, was attending a prep school at nearby Burlington in New Jersey.

The thought of Hal brightened his gray face. The boy had recently passed through Philadelphia, just after Thanksgiving, on his way back to school from Carolina. He remembered the look on Hal's face when he greeted him, sincere pleasure at seeing his grandfather, a look that was absent from most of his family, with the possible exception of his son Thomas, on occasion.

John Fanning's thoughts turned to his son. Thomas was in his early forties now, but had suffered an attack of paralysis the previous year, and his recovery had been slow. His right arm and hand were still troubling him during his last visit, and he could hardly write.

My dear Tom—I parted with him last July—he has had a narrow escape with his life. In twenty years we have not been so long separated—I must now rely on him as my prop and support—he is alone and so am I—God's will be done.

John Fanning obsessed a while, but finally turned the worrisome thoughts away, to cheerful Hal.

Such a lively, fearless boy. Oh, the joys of youth!

He recalled the boy's slight limp, a healing ankle he had sprained after a fall from his horse during a recent hunting expedition. He had begged Hal to be more careful, reminding him of his Uncle Collinson, and Hal had promised. But he knew the oath was empty. A boy of fourteen had no real concept of danger or death.

The first evening of his visit he had taken Hal to the circus. The boy had been enthralled, not so much with the clowns and colors, but with the animals, particularly the sturdy ponies with strong, lovely women riding bareback. The next morning, Sunday, they had gone to St. Mark's for prayer, then spent a quiet day in Em's spacious abode. That afternoon, John Fanning escorted Hal to the depot, and waved him off, but that night his dreams were full of worry. Just the week before, there had been a terrible accident on the tracks near Burlington, and as many as twenty-five had been killed, and fifty wounded; some of the injured had been dear friends.

Their faces passed through his mind.

John Fanning felt a skipping thump in his chest, a sudden burst of frightening activity, then a quick return to a normal beat. He rubbed the area with a flat palm, held it there, took a deep breath, sighed, one big sigh.

I am seventy-two years old, have always been reasonably healthy for my age, thank God.

He searched back to the previous summer, the first spasms at Old Point Comfort while visiting with Anna and Henry. A trifling thing at first, but the pain had become severe. It was this that had prompted his retreat to the cooler air of Philadelphia, and the home of his baby daughter. She had shown little concern.

He coughed, glanced out of the frosty window at the falling snow, more flakes joining those that had preceded them.

Em had brushed his illness aside, and had distracted him with her desires for the house, which he had diligently pursued. He had helped her move in, as much help as a sick old man could give, but as soon as one of Em's desire was satisfied, it seemed another arose. She left him for New York.

"You're fine, Papa. Nothing a trip abroad won't cure. Shall we go to Europe next season? Oh yes, let's do!"

Her departing words swirled in his head. He had supposed that he would receive kindness and affection from her, but her inattention had only reminded him of a lesson he should have learned long ago. Never apply too much weight to expectations.

"*God forgive them, for they do not know what they do.*"

Allowances must be made for infirmity of temper and over indulgence at an early age, which begets selfishness, or rather, a want of consideration to the gratifications of others. "Vixen" has never suffered from self-denial.

"To err is human—to forgive divine." Alas, but for divine forgiveness what would become of us? His mind rattled on, bored, isolated.

He was feeling better though, weeks of Dr. Emerson's administerings had taken away the fretful pain and weakness. The cooler weather had brought on an attack of rheumatism, but even that was better now. He was ready to go out into the world, to rise up from his dormancy.

Misters Hubbard and Boyd were to pay a visit today. Both were members of the Philadelphia Club, and were to deliver news of John Fanning's acceptance as a nonresident member. He had hoped that they would go on an outing together. But the snow had started early that morning, thick, heavy flakes, and they were piling up and threatening to be deep.

Hubbard and Boyd will not come, and I must pass another day alone.

A thin stream of sunlight cut through the window and rested on his arm. He noticed it, rubbed its warmth into his elbow, looked up, out of the window again; the snow had changed to flurries. Struggling to his feet and using the chair for balance, he reached for the sill, and placed his weight on it. He could see a dim sun through thin clouds. John Fanning touched the window gently, tracing the frost with a finger. He followed a melting drip, as a bird sung cheerful notes in the holly just outside.

"Lord be praised."

The sun burnt away the dull morning, strong rays pouring down and melting the snow. A large covered carriage pulled up at the front of the house on Spruce Street. John Fanning had his visitors.

The three old men ate a hastily prepared meal, enjoyed some sherry, then took a carriage ride that would last three hours. They made several social calls at Washington Square, then headed down Broad, around by the Gas Works to Grays Ferry and West Philadelphia. The snow was receding quickly, the day glorious. John Fanning felt that he was coming awake, as if he had been asleep for a long, long time in some far away land. Even when engaged in conversation, he reacquainted himself to familiar objects passing outside the carriage window. Sunshine bathed everything. He felt a ripple of joy, even giddiness, and smiled inwardly. So refreshing, the ride, the companionship. He felt different in his outlook, and in his body, much stronger.

When the mind suffers, the body cries out.

He made a silent resolution: *I shall endeavor to keep an active and healthy mind.*

The carriage skipped over Falls Bridge then turned for Laurel Hill Cemetery, where Mr. Boyd was considering purchasing a large plot for his family. They climbed a winding road, passed through stone gates, and came to a halt near the site. The three took a pleasant stroll on a gravel walk-way and came to the large lot, a quiet, peaceful place. John Fanning made polite comments on the plot's attractive appearance, then fell silent and excused himself.

He walked slowly, purposely, his carved cane guiding the way through a grove of naked hardwoods. He toiled through rising fog, melting snow, the smoking earth, then paused in the cold grayness under the trees to gather his bearings. Turning slightly to his left, he entered a rounded field with many monuments, climbed upward to the low summit, his eyes scanning the gray marble as he passed. He stopped in front of a new stone, rather plain, but handsome enough he supposed. John Fanning removed his hat, white hair flicking in a chilly breeze, then bowed slightly, stiffly, as if addressing an old acquaintance.

The name on the stone was Julia Burgwyn McRae. Born Wilmington, North Carolina, 1810. Died Philadelphia, 1853. Around her were several smaller stones, more McRaes, Julia's dead infants. The Reverend had accepted a new congregation in Philadelphia some years back, and Julia had not lived long at her new home. After his wife's death, the Reverend had transferred the babies from Carolina to be buried near her. The interments had been recent, and all the monuments were new.

He blinked, swayed, squinted upward to the heavens. Dry, cracked lips whispered a prayer.

Poor Julia, my oldest and sweetest child. Why must the best suffer so?

He had outlived five of his children, his wife, and many of his grandchildren. Thomas, his favorite son, would be next, he feared.

He allowed the self-pity to swell up within, powerless to prevent it; he asked his Lord why he was being punished. A tear rolled down a wrinkled cheek and a trembling hand rubbed his left arm. He dropped his hat, bent over, picked it up. Sparks of light in his eyes, dizziness, and he steadied himself with the cane. Alone again, very alone, he did not feel the warm ray of sun that touched his face.

Emmy came home for the Christmas holidays, catching John Fanning quite by surprise, for she had not announced her intentions. She appeared pale and weak he thought, but was looking more and more like her mother. To gaze at her was to bring on vivid memories of a woman who had lost her life shortly after giving birth to this precious girl. The Lord had traded one life for another, not allowing the father to enjoy the simultaneous love of both. He had not resented or blamed little Em, but instead, had spoiled her.

The next day they met Hal at the depot, he having just come over from Burlington. They took him Christmas shopping and bought gifts for everyone at Thornbury. John Fanning also shopped for the hands at Alveston. The next day, Em and Hal went shopping again, while the patriarch stayed home and supervised the packing of the trunks.

They took the cars to Baltimore that afternoon, Em sending her father and nephew off alone. John Fanning had begged her to come, thinking it strange that she would prefer spending Christmas by herself in a city of strangers to going south to be with her loving family. But Vixen could not be moved. She had washed her hands of Carolina, and had sold all her land and slave interests to her brothers. It was the place of her birth, yet she refused to live there, and would only visit on rare occasions. Philadelphia was her home now, and she admired its sophistication.

Harry and John Fanning detrained at Baltimore in a storm, and boarded a steamer that evening in gloomy fog. They feared a long night of rocky seas, but the storm soon passed, and the Chesapeake smoothed out like glass. In Norfolk the following morning, they took the cars on a new rail line that stretched directly to Garysburg. The carriage roads were rough, but at 2:30 that afternoon, the trunks were being unloaded at Alveston. They had traveled from Philadelphia to John Fanning's Alveston Plantation in a little more than twenty-four hours; they marveled at the time.

Thornbury was but a short trip, Harry choosing to ride John Fanning's favorite horse, while his grandfather rode a carriage driven by London, Alveston's coachman. They took the Cornwallis road and soon passed through a handsome new gate where the old Hoburn Gate to Bull Hill had once stood. When they cleared a slight rise where a barren maple stood, John Fanning asked London to stop. Holding his gaze was the grand new house sitting alone within a great expanse of cleared fields spanning for miles. Old eyes soaked up the sight, studying, admiring, considering Henry's many sacrifices and heartbreaks. Harry also gazed at his father's accomplishments, but reveled only in the end result.

A flock of curly-haired boys tumbled off the piazza and greeted the newcomers. A tall red-headed girl followed behind them. Minnie was sixteen now, a young woman. There was joyous laughter and a great cheer went up as the boys pulled their brother from his mount and their grandfather from his carriage. Minnie greeted them with kisses, and led them to a contingent of adults standing on the piazza: Henry, Anna, Madie, and the pastor of the Church of the Savior, the reverend Mr. Lightbourne. The large family filed through a wide foyer and into the drawing room decked for Christmas. Over the mantel was a glowing portrait in Italian style of the Madonna and the infant Savior, displaying evidence that the family claimed a closeness to their Lord. The servants moved in with tea and cakes, playing their role, and interacting as affectionate members of the household. The boys constantly tugged on Harry and fawned over John Fanning, who beamed from the attention. Eventually, the children flew to the lawn, it being a mild day, and the grandfather rocked on the piazza, observed, drew from their excitement and energy, until the clouds rolled in and issued their chilling sprinkles.

Christmas Eve was dreary, cold, and wet, yet nothing could lay a blot on the spirit of the season. Thomas came over from Occoneechee, looking much better since his attack. The healthier color on his long face was a great relief to his father, who now only wished for the presence of Vixen. He still wondered why she had preferred to be away from a family he knew she adored.

Exuberant anticipation for the arrival of Saint Claus filled the house, casting an infectious spell, and the day could not have passed soon enough for the children. Discipline was loosely enforced, John Fanning's lap being the only calming influence. After a fine evening meal, all gathered by the warmth of a great fire in the drawing room where the tree was displayed. It was a time for reading and for prayer. Finally, the children's eyes grew heavy, and Grandpa kissed the soft cheeks, wishing pleasant dreams. Once they were tucked away, Anna called for Polly, told her to find London and Kinchen and send them for the trunks of gifts at Alveston, where they had been kept safely away from prying eyes and fingers.

The old man dozed on the couch near the fire, occasionally opening one eye to watch Anna flitting around the room as she wrapped presents and filled the stockings. She was full of Christmas spirit, preparing for a special morning, and John Fanning watched her admiringly.

A woman with a wonderful attitude, he thought.

Never looked too deeply into the past or too far into the future, lived for the present whether it was good times or bad. She had suffered her share of pain, had lost many dear ones, and despite her desperate struggles to keep them, she always picked herself up and moved on. Such wonderful children she had raised, what support she had lent Henry during his labors. Anna was the purest, the best of women. Hers was a happy, healthy family now, the Lord was showing His favor, and Anna's good heart deserved His praise.

A tiny, contented grin came to his lips as both eyes closed. Anna hummed a holiday tune, and the old man drifted off, his mind weightless.

Before a weak sun could penetrate the thick gray clouds, little Pollok was down in the drawing room under the tree. Harry caught him digging in the stockings. After grabbing Pollok's ear, Harry sent him off to wake the others. The oldest boy made an attempt to police his siblings; no packages should be opened until all were gathered, but Harry's heart went soft when he saw the torture the little boys suffered, and he gave in. Still in his bed clothes, John Fanning was the last to arrive, in the nick of time to witness the rapture. He had never witnessed such flailing about, the determination, the squeaky voices, the wide young eyes. It was perfect anarchy. The last gift presented was from Henry to Harry. John Fanning watching intently as the boy opened the elegant box. It was a handsome gold watch on a chain, a very expensive watch. He saw the flush of pride on Harry's face when Henry told him he was now responsible enough to take care of such a gift. The boy fingered the ornament nervously, opened the locket and examined the beautiful face, the delicate hands. A better gift was unimaginable. So grateful, Harry could not look his father in the eyes when he thanked him.

After a filling breakfast and a change into their Sunday best, the family rode the carriages over muddy roads to the chapel where all the hands and the overseers' families were gathered. It was a tight fit; there was standing room only on this special occasion when whites and blacks mixed. The Reverend Lightbourne spoke a simple sermon, extolling the virtues of obeying your Lord, a message with a double meaning. After hymns, the congregation filed out for the traditional handing out of gifts and rewards. Wagons and carts were brought up. Henry made a quick speech in the drizzle, and the ceremony passed rapidly, the hands now free to enjoy their holiday.

New Year's Eve opened clear and blustery; the thermometer at Anna's bedroom window showed twenty-nine degrees. Kinchen and London had two large carriages in the circle in front of the house, and were loading one with large, heavy trunks. The Burgwyn family was about to split again. Uncle Thomas had already escorted Minnie back to her school in Raleigh. Now, Henry, Anna, and John Fanning were taking Harry and Sumner to Burlington. The family said their goodbyes on the piazza, Grandpa making a final protest.

"Sumner is much too young to be sent away from home!"

His objections were in vain. Harry was sent off at a similar age, and no exception would be made with the next boy.

The household waved farewell as the carriages rolled away for Garysburg, Kinchen and London driving. John Fanning's mood remained sour. After they delivered the boys, Henry and Anna would return south, and he would go back to Em's in Philadelphia, an undesirable destination. He would miss the children, and would be away from Thomas again. He knew Em would neglect him. His other grandchildren in the city, Kate and John McRae, would be little consolation. They were in school and their infrequent visits would offer him none of the joy of Thornbury.

As he boarded the cars and heard the whistle blow, John Fanning had a depressing vision: he was wrapped in a shawl in the freshly plastered room that needed paper, buried in the big chair by the coal-burning stove, looking out that plain, cold window. He was searching for buds, and praying for the first tokens of spring.

❧ 10 ❧

LETTERS HOME

West Point, N.Y.
Buttermilk Hall
Nov. 30th, 1856

My Dear Mother,

I received your most agreeable letter today & to prove how much I appreciate it, I seat myself a few hours after its reception to endeavor to answer it. You have doubtless ere this, received the poor apology for a letter that I sent you last week & will, I hope, excuse all its imperfections.

Last night we had quite a snowstorm & it is quite cool tonight, but I suppose it is almost warm to what it will be. Yesterday, I took tea with Captain Foster, my tutor, who with his wife, have been very attentive & kind to me.

I received letters from both Sumner and Maria today. Tupps tells me some of his adventures at Burlington—he did not seem to like the boys as much as he did the studying & the eating part of the place. Maria's letter has a good deal of French about it. For instance, instead of spelling the word "companions" as I have written it—she spelled it "campagnons," which is wrongly spelt both in French & English—the French being compagnions & the English as I wrote it first.

The place where I board, about two miles from the Point itself, is almost entirely a German settlement and, in walking about, almost everybody you meet is of that persuasion. The village is named for the nearby falls, and today I paid them a visit. They are about 40 or 50 ft. high, & the water was some 20 ft. wide & rushing over rocks & stones at a tremendous rate. The whole mass of water was one white sheet of foam & when it would strike a rock, would leap up in large bodies to a distance of several feet & then rush onward as if impatient of the check it had received. It was really a magnificent sight, as it rolled along irresistibly—reminding a person of Mae Bailey's poem, "Horatius at the Bridge." It was singular in beauty & could only be surpassed by the sight of it tomorrow, as it will undoubtedly be surrounded by glistening snow.

Unfortunately, there was an old woman drowned there yesterday & was picked out a few hours afterwards.

The dress parade, as it is called, of the cadets is a very fine sight & they have probably the finest brass band in America. It consists of 40 odd men, all Germans, & the music, I am afraid, beats Father's Italian Opera. The band major wears a hat almost as large as himself, & has a large sceptre with which he regulates the movements of his attendants. I admire their parade whenever the opportunity presents itself.

One cadet of the Academy is now in what is called the "Black Hole," & has for his food bread & water, a miserable diet to be sure.

You caution me about the use of Tobacco. I do not think there is much danger of my falling into its use, for of my three companions here, there is not one who chews & although they smoke, they look upon chewing with as much disgust as I do. As for smoking— I have firmly resolved not to smoke until I am 25 years old if I do then, & I hope I shall not.

I was introduced to Major Delafield who is the superintendent of the post & is heartily detested by the cadets, but that is to be expected. He has, without exception, the largest nose I ever saw.

The next time you write please send me an account of the plantation work at Thornbury & Alveston, if it is not too much trouble. I want to send it to Grandpa—must I address him then as you wrote me? Or to Paris, or some other place?

I am very sorry indeed Mr. Phillips is dead, poor fellow, he leaves a wife & children, does he not, & also in indigent circumstances, unless I am mistaken? Did you say Rhody's William is dead?

You say Mr. Patterson has undertaken to superintend the great ditch. What ditch is it you refer to? Does Father still continue with his magnanimous resolution to boldly defy allurements & enticing arts of Sommers, & like a second Don Quixote with his squire— well exemplified in the shape of his upholder M. David le Docteur a la toe— to venture forth and boldly defy mortal combat against his witty antagonist, Vent et Froid, so with all his forces?

I am glad you intend writing me every Sunday, & I will endeavor to do the same for you. Please ask Father to write me once a fortnight, but do not on that account stop writing me yourself the week Father writes, for that would be robbing Peter to pay Paul. If you can find the time, I would like you to write me twice a week, but always once a week.

The hour is late & I have yet to reply to Sumner and Maria. Give Skiggs & Lilliepod my love & tell them if they don't behave better I will put them both in royal chancery with the punishment attached. Please give my best love to Father and Madie. I am ever your most affectionate Son,

H. K. Burgwyn, Jr.

West Point, N.Y.
Jan. 2nd, 1857

My Dear Mother,

This is the first opportunity that has offered itself to me for writing you, & I hasten to embrace it, well knowing you would be glad to hear from me, as I from you.

Night before last we had the coldest weather that has been experienced here in the last century—the thermometer reached 24 degrees below zero—the night previous it was 16 below & I had my ears frozen, but they thawed out in a few minutes. I pitied the poor sappers who stood guard that night from the bottom of my heart. They had to be relieved every quarter-hour & ever most frozen. We have had it cold enough to skate, & I bought a pair of skates. I have not had but one sleigh ride since I have been here, & that was from the Point here on a wood-getting concern, which was not the best or fastest riding in the world.

You have no idea how dreary this place is—nothing in the world to enliven a person except the few letters I receive. The snow almost blinds me as I walk up to the Point. The other day, as I was coming out of church, I fell down twice before all the people—who gave me a kind giggle, which made me so angry & ashamed that I almost vowed I never would go to the church again, but luckily, almost, was the maximum to which my indignation reached. There are three churches in town— a Pres., a Metho. & an Episcopalian, but of course I go to the latter & intend to make it an invariable rule whenever the weather will permit. I commenced reading the Bible yesterday, it being New Year's Day, & intend diligently to read two chapters a day.

A letter I received from Pollok can hardly be said to be perfectly free from mistakes and blots. It is two pages in length & I have counted 30 blots on it. Sumner's letters have quite an opposite comparison. How do Allie & Collie progress in their studies under the tuition of Madie? I have just finished a letter to Pollok in which I gave him some advice about studying & about his badness, which judging from Sumner's letter, is considerable. I ended by entreating him not to allow us to consider him a disgrace, & not an honor to us, using language which, if any, I think would be calculated to make him change for the better. I have no doubt but that his next monthly report will exhibit a great improvement in both his studies & in his conduct, either & both of which would give me great satisfaction. I expect to study very hard this winter and spring & in fact now I study 8 hours & a half a day. I always study until 11 o'clock PM & generally till half past.

Please tell Father that, if I were he, I would not press my appointment to the Academy (West Point), next June for two reasons— first, when I enter I am compelled to state my age, & secondly, by June a year hence I will be very well prepared indeed, & he can get the appointment in June, 1858.

You mentioned in your last letter that you thought you would go to Old

Point & spend the summer there. I am particularly anxious to come home in June, so that I may help Father in the harvest, after which, I would very much like to accompany you and Maria. I want Maria to teach me French, which will improve hers as well as mine. I want to teach her algebra. I expect to do a great deal of studying at the "Summer Seat." Will you buy me a new straw hat?

My current wardrobe is in a rather dilapidated condition. The new shirts you sent me have proved of poor quality. The plaits in the breast came apart & now they— to use a mathematical or classical language—exist only in the remembrance of the things that were, or in things which are no longer. I still have the old shooting coat Father gave me, & if I possibly can find room in my trunk, I intend to bring it home to demonstrate to any & everybody how many large & terrific tears a piece of cloth can sustain. I think if I were to dress myself in it & go in New York begging alms, no one could have the hardness of heart to refuse me.

What is the plantation news? I am very glad indeed to hear Father has become so smart & active. I am afraid my employment of the term "smart" will lead you to suppose that I have become Yankeefied during my stay at the North, but I assure you, I am as good a Southerner as ever.

I was very surprised to hear that Father, on his own accord, is ordering breakfast an hour earlier than usual. I am very anxious to see the plantation & view the improvements with which you & Father doubtless intend to astonish me. I am prepared to expect anything within the bounds of possibility & if necessary without. I was glad to learn he sold so many turkeys & I suppose he will sell a good deal of butter. You say he is planning many improvements to Cypress Plantation. I suppose he will put the cleared portion in corn, will he not? Does he plan to keep all his carriage horses or work some of them to the plough? Will he run Squire at Belfield this spring? Does Kinchen still make a capital jock?

I am afraid you will hardly be able to recognize me for I have grown about $3/4$ of an inch since I came here. I am sure you will be glad to hear that I am to take a bath tonight— as a general thing, I take a bath about once a week.

Tippikitupps writes me that you do not favor jambonies. My only request of you is to try jambone (for I don't expect you can do it yet a while), but try to learn how to play a jambone— let jambonies alone for the present & also bones jambones, but do try to understand jambone. I believe I shall write a treaties on the subject.

I have written you a nice long letter, and now I must close. Please give my best to Father, Madie, Allie, & Collie— wishing them all a happy New Year. I am ever your most affectionate son,

                                            H. K. Burgwyn, Jr.

Chapel Hill, N.C.
Sept. 15th, 1857

My Dearest Mother,

According to my promise, I seat myself to write you about your promising son— hoping that it will be an agreeable theme to you, & if you would like to see the aforesaid individual, just picture a Chapel Hillian sitting on a shuck chair writing with his desk covered with books & papers & pencils, & you will have his ambiotype exactly. If you were to stand outside in our dismal backyard and look north at this dilapidated structure, sometimes fictitiously called a house, whose nearest side rejoices in having four windows in the form of a cross. In one of these are three pillows, twisted about, & which, I suppose, are intended to keep out the wind. If your imagination is strong enough to keep this view before your mind, you will have the chief attraction as far as the scenery of my domicile. The weather also conspires to add some little gloominess to the scene, for the sun does not permit himself to be seen, & the clouds which serve to shield it from our gaze, send forth a strong wind which, howling dismally through the open cracks of the edifice, prove most forcibly the near approach of autumn.

I hope you reached the plantation before the Equinoctial storm which is now raging here in all its fury— for if you were to catch a cold upon your already severe one, I am afraid that you would not recover from its effects for a much longer period than usual. So be very careful about going or being out late at night or early in the morning, & let everything go to racket rather than go in the pantry before breakfast, or rather make old Ruthy do it for you. What is the loss of a few pounds of sugar or coffee, which she may appropriate to herself, compared to the loss of your health? Oh, by the by, do you still prescribe in your intuition to cover over the portion of the piazza between Father's room and the spare room & make it a place for the guns? And speaking of guns, please put Father again in mind of sending those guns & sparks I placed in the right-hand-side of the gun case. I am very impatient to come home again & try my luck at shooting the hapless squirrels who may chance to come within my range. By the by, please ask Tippikitupps to have Driver Jim bait one or two places in the Flodden Field for Turkeys and to make blinds for them at the baits. Ask Tupps to write me how many coons he has sent to navigate & explore the dark waters of the sluggard Cocytus, & ask him if the guns had returned & in what order the others were.

I was very glad to hear you were ever so well satisfied with Shocco Springs. I don't like this place half so much as West Point, but I liked the Academy very much. I think this place is fast improving in point of dissipation— the faculty is trying to put it down as much as possible. I hear that they caught twenty students last night either drunk or with liquor in their possession. I *should think that if the trustees would make it incumbent on the faculty to expel every student who was caught in that state & have it carried out, they would soon have this college equal if not superior to the University of Virginia, which stands second only to West Point.*

You must tell me whether Wilkins Power was as devoted to Maria at Shocco as at Weldon. He has a brother in the Soph. class here & in my section, but the latter is as fat as the goddess of mischief before the fall of man, when she had nothing to do but sit down.

I suppose that you feel much more comfortable & fixed now that you have your big "Cherubs" around you. When do you expect Madie home? I suppose you are very much in want of her.

I don't suppose I told you how acceptable the box I brought with me was to my famished, hardworking college friends. It was an occasion for joy & general gratification & lastly, & by no means leastly, for some of the tallest eating I ever saw, excepting that of Tupps when you get him right hungry & give him a fair showing. The jar of preserves especially was voted to be first-rate &, had you seen the rapidity with which it disappeared, you would have said that in this case the votes were the true indices of their sentiment & were not influenced by bribery or janning or treating or anything else.

So there is to be a new overseer? What is his name & where is he from? I am very glad his manners are so much better than those of his commanding hosifers. How did Father raise him?

As I told Father in my previous letter— I do not trust my watch to the express, but please keep it home until I return. I think on my return often, yet, sadly, it will not be until Nov. 25th. I shall continue to write weekly and trust you will do the same. Give my love to all, I am ever your most affectionate son,

H. K. Burgwyn, Jr.

P.S. Remember not to go into the pantry before breakfast or after supper. Have Ruthy go instead!

Chapel Hill, N. C.
March 10th, 1858

My Dear Mother,

I have not either time or brain enough to write in French, Latin, or even English for I have had for the last few days the supreme felicity of one of the, if not the, very worst colds that has ever visited a poor mortal.

I have again looked in my trunk for the celebrated flannel undershirt, but sad to say could not discover anything of it, & am afraid that if it ever was in my trunk, something I am greatly inclined to doubt, it must have fallen prey to the thieving propensities of some waiter in old Yarborough's hotel. Believing this to have been its fate, the following eulogy is hereby requested to be sung in solemn chorus for its untimely fate by Isabella, Madie & Mrs. Freeman to the line "Hail Columbia" or "Good Old Moses."

> A foreign shore & distant land.
> A small hotel & thieving hand.
> It left a name at which your son grew warm,
> for it was given me by mother, my kind dear marm.

A few flourishes by Pollok would greatly enhance the solemnity of the occasion.

It is sleeting and has for the greater part since Monday. Now the trees are covered with frozen rain, & their limbs & twigs, crusted with transparent ice, present one of the most beautiful appearances I ever saw. In Professor Hilliard's yard there are several large willows whose slender & drooping limbs receive with muteness continued drops of frozen rain. While it clothes them with enchanting but perfidious beauty, it also threatens their destruction. Reminds one irresistibly of the description we used to read of the fairy realms of the Ice King. The dark foliage of the cedars & the glistening particles of the ice afford a beautiful, & you might also say, an allegorical contrast to each other—the one representing the dark shades of a man's character, or the passions, & the other, the light, or the results when his good parts gain the advantage over his evil & shame. The latter, though brighter, are less numerous than the former where carrying out the simile—the good deeds of man are fewer & more seldom to bear with than the bad.

I dreamt last night that all of us were on the Central America & that you insisted on going on deck, & in spite of all my protestations & endeavors to keep you out of the cold wind, you accomplished your purpose. And just as you were about to be swept off by the approaching waves, the bell (usually regarded as productive of nothing but discomfort) luckily woke me. So do you see what affect your habit of going into the pantry during the dark, cold hours has on me?

I am very sorry indeed to hear that Father has decided to employ Wilkins again. I suspected he would, as soon as I heard that he was remaining at Thornbury from day to day. I despair now of ever seeing him go away. He will stay with Father until he loses him $4 or $5000, & then for the next three or four years there will be a great hue & cry versus that miserable scoundrel Wilkins, as there was before against the villain Reid, the treacherous Sterling, the drinking Fairgrove & that miserable fellow Boyce. I would not be at all surprised if next year Wilkins were head overseer, & then there would be no telling where it would stop. My heart sinks within, though I try to hope for the best.

You mention that you have invited two or three pretty young girls to visit this spring. What are their names & where do they come from? I expect to have a good deal of pleasure this Easter.

I am very glad to hear that Aunt Emmie is to return soon and take her leave of the Adriatic. She will arrive, I understand, about the time I am ready to leave for home. How much joy it will give us to see her once again. Where do you suppose she will live?

The hour grows late, and I must put away my pen. Give love to all. In haste, ever your most affectionate son,

                                  H. K. Burgwyn, Jr.

Chapel Hill, N.C.
March 6th, 1859

My Dear Mother,

Another week has passed & I am again at my post as everyone should be who adopts "Semper Fidelis" as their motto.

I think you have treated me shabbily lately in the letter department.

I have not received so much as a line for 10 days. Also, my letters, though only about two pages & a half long will nevertheless occupy about 4 or 5 pages of yours. In fact, according to an approximating calculation, my letters equal 5 pages of yours, but if we take into consideration the number of lines in our letters & the space lost on each line as well as the closeness of my writing, mine possibly equal from 6 to 7 pages of your letters.

I received a missive from Tupps yesterday. He appears rather pleased with Georgetown, but does not speak in as high terms as I expected. I suppose, however, he has still a slight feeling of homesickness, which undoubtedly will wear off. He likewise says that they do not give him quite enough to eat, but you who know Tupps' habits are fully aware that after expunging the fare at home, nothing less than a ducal repast would suit his delicate palato.

Do you know whether Maria will come to my commencement? I engaged Chuck Bruce's room for her, or rather asked Chuck to let me have it for a lady. He promised it to me and then came to me the other day & asked if I still wanted it. I told him yes. He then said that Mrs. Levain had tried to get it for President Buchanan, but that old Buck could not get it. So, I will cut the President out of his room, even if he cuts me out of my appointment at West Point.

I received last Tuesday a catalogue of the Virginia Military Institute. It does not say anything about how old or how young a person must be to enter. I am still very much in hopes that I may get the appointment to West Point. Has Congressman Clingman answered Uncle Tom's letter yet, and if so, to what effect?

I am very glad to hear that Father made you a present of a sewing machine. Now you will be able to spend a good deal of time very pleasantly sewing with that.

There is very little of interest to pass, but just arrived here is a young lady— Miss Delia Haywood— from Raleigh. She is staying with Miss Hubbard &, as I am duty bound, I called on her, but was not very much pleased. However, tonight, another young man has engaged to carry her & Miss Hubbard to Church. He is to take the latter while I am to devote myself to Miss Haywood. We are to wait until the 11th hour before asking to be allowed to have the pleasure, as well as honor, of escorting them to Church, in hopes that somebody else may ask before us &, pardon the expression, we in consequence "Save our Muttons." If, however, we should be so unfortunate as to get cornered and swung, then I for one determine resolutely to shoulder my burden & appear in a perfect ecstasy of joy at being allowed to conduct the Raleigh delegate to Church.

I am afraid if the weather continues as warm as it has been the fruit trees at home will put out & then a frost will come & kill them all.

I must apologize for the brevity of this epistle, but there is simply little to tell. Please pass my devoted expression of love to Father and Madie, and the boys. Ever your most affectionate son,

H. K. Burgwyn, Jr.

P.S. I hope you will make your Bashi Bazouks do some studying. You never will make that boy Collinson behave unless you punish him oftener.

Chapel Hill, N.C.
June 10th, 1859

My Dear Sister,

I am compelled to devote the greater portion of my spare time to preparation for the approaching final examinations, but I cannot help myself from snatching a few moments to answer your very welcome letter of the 4th instant.

First let me say that I was very glad to see that this letter, unlike your previous, was neither open for want of sufficient gum arabic, nor was the direction mistaken by reason of the chirography, nor yet, was the postmark so much later than the heading as usual. This time it was only one day behind time. Generally it is not less than two or three, & unless I am mistaken, I have known as much as four days to have intervened between the postmark & the marginal date. However, I don't wish to open a discussion on the matter, less it would be found out that both my chirography & everything else is at least equally as bad as yours, & saying that, with all due respect to your instructor in the art of penmanship, abominable.

So what is your opinion of Mother & Father renting a house in Raleigh? I am sure you are delighted, what with the greater availability of suitors. I only wish I were with you to witness Mother's unfeigned joy at having to fix up a whole house without asking help from anyone. How much enjoyment she will take in putting up this & pulling down that, in sweeping a cobweb out of one place & into another, only to remove them again for it is too much pleasure to be enjoyed all at once. If I ever become a rich man, I intend to import a cargo of spiders & buy Mother a couple of hundred brooms of all kinds, long & short handled, just so that the spiders may spin their webs, so that Mother may sweep them away. What rapture she displays with her strokes, like a High Judge striking at injustice, like a Saint conquering the wicked. I hope too that Mother may not cause a rise in the price of gravel around Raleigh in order to have everything, as Jack-a-Dandy would say, "Spandy, Spry, Neat & Clean." I am very much in anticipation of getting a long letter from her this week telling me whether the reality equals the anticipation.

I am very pleased indeed that you will attend my commencement, and am so very much looking forward to your arrival. We shall have grand times. I know Father will be too engaged with the harvest to attend, & this is sad enough, but as you are aware, Mother has also yet to make a commitment to attend. Would you not put in a kind word for your favorite brother? Tell her that, likely, I will stand first in the class. Give my best to all, ever your most affectionate brother,

H. K. Burgwyn, Jr.

⁂ 11 ⁂

WHITE SULPHUR SPRINGS

THE TAVERN KEEPER HAD TOLD HARRY that the road had once been an Indian trail, and if he looked closely, he might spy worn markers on grand trees set by tomahawks. Harry had yet to see any faded chops, but given the way the dusty, orange pike rolled straight over hills instead of skirting around them, the road's original designers couldn't have meant it for wheeled traffic.

Female chatter and laughter overlapped the sound of beating hooves. The coachman slapped the horses' rippled hind-quarters, as spinning wheels struggled against deep ruts in the hard-packed lane. Minnie's crackling voice shattered the soft mountain air; Kate muffled her giggles. John McRae sat motionless with a blank expression, trying to ignore his sister and cousin. Harry, too, had grown tired of the feminine prattle, and gazed off at the mountains, their purple hue faint behind the summer haze. He wondered how the scenery had changed since the arrival of Europeans; it must have been a wild, enchanting world.

The four were on a sojourn to "The Springs," a ritual for the South's elite, a recently adopted habit for the Burgwyns. For years the family had escaped the marshy lowlands and stagnant air of eastern Carolina during the hot season. New England and the delightful beaches near Nantucket had been the initial destinations of their annual pilgrimages, but as sectional differences grew, and the company of self-righteous northerners became intolerable, Henry shifted his family's migration to the seaside at Point Comfort, near Hampton, Virginia. Recent yellow fever epidemics across the water in Norfolk had alarmed them though, so the Burgwyns sought higher ground. Ever since, they had visited White Sulphur Springs, a resort nestled within the gentle peaks of western Virginia.

Henry, Anna, and the children had preceded the young adults to the mountains that summer. Harry, at just seventeen, had recently graduated from the University of North Carolina, first in the class of 1859. The speaker at the commencement exercises had been President James Buchanan, a man for whom Harry had little affinity. Buchanan had cut him out of a cadetship at West Point, a bitter disappointment. As an alternative, Harry had enrolled at the

Virginia Military Institute in Lexington, a village he had just passed through on his way to the Springs. After his short holiday, and in the first week of August, Harry would take up residence at the school.

Minnie was attending St. Mary's, a girl's school in Raleigh, and had stayed after classes to attend Harry's commencement. First cousins Kate and John had been visiting in Carolina, and were stopping at the Springs for a short spell before making their way back home to Philadelphia.

Trains and coaches had carried them from Raleigh to Lexington, but given the cool mountain air and sunny skies, John and Harry had been persuaded to rent an open carriage and Negro driver for the remainder of the journey. Last night, they had crammed into a wayside tavern, and today, they would easily cover the remaining twenty miles to White Sulphur Springs.

The road grew steep, weaving snake-like up Virginia's ancient Alleghanies. At the summit were marvelous views of green heights, some crowned with jagged outcrops of gray boulders. Below were striking vistas of patchwork valleys, sleepy, sparsely settled, but the rich soil thoroughly cultivated. Down they went on a windy, shady road, red dust clinging to cool, dark ferns fringing the pike. They were surrounded by black forests as thick as jungles, flourishing from heavy rains captured by the peaks. Harry could feel the crisp air on his face, could smell its freshness. The girls sighed in delight as John finally stirred and let loose a smile.

Gradually the road leveled off and straightened out. A lovely stream rolled in and flowed beside it, gurgling, applauding. Beyond it were lush pastures, dairy cows, and wild flowers—all pleasing to the eye, stimulating to the nose.

A flood of memories whirled in Harry's head. Images of last year's trip, pleasant, most of them, but some were awkward and painful. Last summer he had experienced his first infatuation with Miss Rebecca Mayo, a Richmond beauty. Her face and figure had haunted his dreams since their first introduction. Intoxicating, green eyes. Deep, rich auburn hair. A gentle, fair complexion surrounding a turned up nose and a perfect smile. Bare shoulders, smooth and round. The arousing cleft in her chest flowing down to full bosoms hidden in lace. Just the sight of her made his palms perspire. When she was in close proximity, he stammered, and made clumsy gestures. When away, he felt both anguish and relief. He'd never felt such emotions, had always been a master of his passion, but found himself tossing and turning in bed at night, keeping Sumner awake. Miss Mayo was two years older, and had a mature, melodious voice that revealed her confidence. She attracted many suitors, and all much older than he. But Harry had been too shy for advances, too inexperienced for romance. This year would be different. He was a college graduate now, had grown five inches, was six feet tall, a little gangly, but handsome. He was much more mature, confident. How impressed she would be with the change!

All four were anticipating their arrival at the famous refuge of the Southern Aristocracy. Prominent people, some from as far away as Texas and Florida, migrated there each year to drink and bathe in the hot, luxuriant, and health-reviving waters. The resort could accommodate over fifteen hundred guests, and for decades had brought relief to those suffering from the tedious boredom of the plantation. To its visitors, "The Springs" was the year's liveliest social event. The men smoked their cigars and sought stimulating conversation that usually centered around politics, farming, and business. The women busied themselves chaperoning their children, and occasionally, arranging marriages. Life-long friendships developed and were nurtured there. White Sulphur Springs, a place where the influential bonded. More importantly, given the impending constitutional crisis, the alliances formed there played no small role in unifying the fledgling country that would emerge in the not too distant future.

Their carriage turned into a grove of towering chestnuts, and rattled up a graveled, but well-worn lane. Ahead, breaking through the trees, was the majestic hotel building. White-framed with immense columns supporting wide roofs and shading verandahs that ran its length, the hotel resembled an oversized Georgian Mansion. The grounds were perfectly manicured, a rich lawn with ample shade trees sprawled before rows of white-washed cottages with pretty little porticoes smothered in vines. The resort oozed with affluence.

Children of all ages played Blind Man's Bluff in the blue-green grass, while Negro servants, dressed in fine cotton, attended their every need. The adults lounged on the massive porch, chatting, drinking the tangy water. Others were down at the stables preparing for an afternoon ride over lovely hills on handsome, well-bred horses. Still more were immersed in the warm springs that purged their bodies of the year's accumulated impurities.

Upon their arrival, Harry, Minnie, and the McRaes realized they had missed afternoon supper and found the guests passing the afternoon in relaxation. Three of the Burgwyn boys had noticed the slow approach of the newly-arriving carriage, and they tumbled over the lawn, racing to greet them. Eleven-year-old Pollok was the first to bound up, grabbing the tiny door before the carriage came to a full stop. Little Collie, the youngest, followed screaming "Sister, Sister!" Nearly fourteen, Sumner gracefully brought up the rear, thinking himself too mature and dignified to show too much enthusiasm. One boy, Allie, was conspicuously missing.

There were hugs and laughter, and little childish stories. Collie attached himself to Minnie, then pulling her hand, led her toward their family's cottage, while proclaiming his knowledge of every nook and cranny of the place. Harry and Sumner, who had squabbled incessantly last year, now clasped hands and expressed how they had missed each other. Pollok and Kate, arm in arm, followed Collie and Minnie as John McRae gave directions to the driver and rode with him to deliver the baggage.

The procession rolled over the lawn, passed the first row of cottages, then turned right and came to the third cottage from the end, a yellow miniature of the hotel, columns, verandah, and all. Henry, always restless, was off on a gallop, but Anna's nurse Madie greeted them, and there was Allie, sitting on the portico pouting, noticeably pale, obviously sick. Anna was napping inside and Madie put a finger to her lips to calm and hush the parade, then smiled and opened her arms to embrace the clan.

A yellow sun dropped behind the hills and wide shadows fell on the resort, casting their spill on the summer evening. The Burgwyns, reunited, took advantage of the cool air by crowding the small portico. There were pleasant conversations, some smiles, but universal concern; Allie was very ill, and Anna could not relax. Only frequent naps relieved her anxiety. The trip from Carolina had been hard on the frail little boy, and then he had over exerted himself upon their arrival. Ever since, a strange weakness had come over him, accompanied by wheezing and shortness of breath. A doctor from Montgomery, there on holiday, had found nothing obviously wrong. There was no fever, no runny nose, just a little nausea. The doctor said to keep him quiet, a difficult assignment given the many adventurous temptations about. Allie's brothers and sister fawned over him, but the attention was not always welcome.

The dinner bell sounded, invading the peaceful valley with its call for action. Henry took Anna by the arm, guided her down three wooden steps, and set off toward the grand hotel. Madie followed with Allie carefully in hand, the others trailing behind. Dressed in evening finery, hundreds of guests converged on the huge steps that climbed to the verandah and the hotel's main entrance. Then, after passing through the towering main doors, they entered a high-ceilinged parlor with shining, hardwood floors. On both sides of the wide hall were brilliant staircases ascending to the second level, but passing these, and continuing down the long foyer, the throng flowed through delicate French doors and into the grand dining room. A servant greeted each family and escorted them to an assigned table decorated with linen cloths, imported china, and fine silver. Overhead were spectacular chandeliers, their candles burning, and crystal pendants reflecting the soft, yellow light. White Sulphur Springs was a fitting symbol of the Old South's famous refine.

After a dinner worthy of the atmosphere, the guests spilled out into several parlors that adjoined the dining room. Henry, filling his pipe with tobacco as he strolled, was accompanied by his two oldest boys to the far end of the verandah. Their father wanted to have a little talk, and had sought a private place from which to deliver a lecture. Harry and Sumner knew what was coming. Their bickering of the year before had caused turmoil for the entire family, and with Allie sick and Anna worried, Henry now called on them to curb their tempers, pleading for consideration. The boys put him at ease, sighting that a year of separation and maturity had deepened a mutual fondness. Henry was skeptical, but pleased with the response.

Other guests began to stream onto the wide porch, while Harry kept careful vigilance. Then Miss Mayo appeared. He caught just a glimpse of her, a fleeting peek at her deep, green eyes. She was surrounded by an escort of five, a young couple, a short, chunky, balding man, and a middle-aged couple whom Harry recognized as her parents. They stopped just on the other side of the wide steps, and he spied, trying to see her face, but cautious not to stare. His view was blocked; she was facing him, but obscured by her father. He leaned back against the rail, folded his arms across his chest, and nonchalantly turned his head. This time a white column concealed her. Harry turned away, rubbed his nose, grinned. She was here! He looked again, not able to resist. Still no success, but at least she was here. He would make his approach at the proper time.

Servants lighted dozens of lamps. Small children fussed and cried as they were carried off to bed. An announcement was made. It was time for the nightly tradition, "The Treadmill," a great promenade. Guests lined both walls of the long, main parlor, and the day's new arrivals, usually four abreast, were announced and paraded through. Each would stop along the way, chat, renew acquaintances, and make introductions. At the end of the hall, the visitors would find that all the tables had been removed from the dining room, discovering the massive chamber had been converted into a ballroom. A piano, and a full ensemble of fiddlers and drummers were set for a night of dancing.

Harry, Minnie, John, and Kate opened the march, gliding gracefully through the hotel's main entrance, smiling and bowing as their names were announced. They rolled into the spacious hall, a slight echo falling from the high ceiling. It was beautifully lighted, and decorated by the guests dressed in their finest. Harry and Minnie peeled away to the right, making their way down the line, shaking hands, exchanging pleasantries. Harry glanced ahead, saw that Rebecca Mayo was in his line. How fortunate! Suddenly he felt a lovely thrill. He led the procession, he would be the first young man introduced, and would ask her the honor of the first dance. His stomach fluttered, and he tensed in anticipation as he made his approach. Harry bowed slightly to Miss Mayo's mother, and clasped the hand of her father, James Mayo, a banker. They spoke briefly of Harry's studies; he told him he planned to be an engineer.

"You've met my daughter, I believe."

It was time to be passed along. Harry stood tall, reached for Rebecca's delicate hand, smiled confidently. Mr. Mayo made an introduction.

"May I present Dr. and Mrs. Peyton Armstrong."

Harry couldn't believe his ears. Mrs. Peyton Armstrong? He hadn't even noticed the man beside her, that chunky, unattractive, balding man... her husband. Harry struggled for composure. The smile disappeared, but, with difficulty, he brought it back.

"Newlyweds," Mr. Mayo added.

"Wonderful," was Harry's forced response, "Is this your honeymoon?"

Rebecca nodded, smiled adorably, revealing those perfect white teeth. She commented on how dashing Harry looked, but also marveled at how much he had grown, making him feel like a school boy. Rebecca held her hand out flat, chest high, looked at her new husband.

"I knew him when he was this high," she giggled.

Harry swallowed the compliment like a sharp fish bone. He made his congratulations to Dr. Armstrong, introduced Minnie, then moved on. Dazed, he went through the motions down the line, as he digested his disappointment, maintained his good manners, but otherwise showed little interest in the remaining guests. He was the first to reach the ballroom, but he found it empty except for the musicians and servants. Looking back down the line, he noticed he'd rudely left his sister far behind. He stood awkwardly, waiting.

Strings and keys released a melody and the ballroom filled quickly. The dancers whirled then alternated a variety of slow and fast steps—the Fox-trot. Kate was a veteran and superb dancer. Harry's coordination was a little off; he struggled to keep up with his new long legs. Finally, the opening prance was over. Polite bows. Clapping hands rose then faded. Harry escorted his cousin from the floor, shared some refreshments, then lost her to a tall Kentuckian. Looking about the ball, he spied Sumner surrounded by a coterie of young girls. A cute boy, his brother, and an impossible charmer.

To Sumner's left the older girls had gathered against the wall, some sitting on sofas. Harry sighed, looked them over, but the new Mrs. Armstrong had snatched away the thrill of the hunt. He brooded as the others frolicked, then finally made his way toward a large parlor where he thought Henry would be found. No doubt, his father would be in deep conversation, comparing new farming practices. Dull, but male association suited his mood at the moment.

The room reeked of tobacco. Clusters of old portly men in gray suits filled the parlor with their low ramblings, all vigorously trying to make their points, letting their mouths do what their arms and legs could do no longer. Debate, a favorite pastime among southerners. Harry peered into the nondescript old blue-bloods, moved unnoticed among the cliques, but didn't find Henry amidst. He left the parlor, made his way down a narrow hallway, and entered another, even smaller parlor. Within, an elderly man sat alone. Harry turned his feet as if to depart, but his eyes stayed focused. What an extraordinary looking old gentleman, he thought.

He was sitting at the very edge of a wide-winged chair, erect, alert, a cane propped on the floor, both hands resting at its top. He was staring at a burning candle on the window sill, blinking, obviously concentrating. But it was the old man's hair that had caught Harry's attention. Silvery white, thrown back to fall into long, free strands, cascading down beyond his shoulders. Its whiteness was so bright, it seemed to glow. The face also bore a strange attractiveness—a high, rounded forehead, deep-set, gray eyes, a heavy brow. The nose, sharp, well-formed. A large mouth, firm, perfectly straight. Harry thought it the face of a very wise man, one who bore his awareness like a medal. He was small, rather fragile, but there was no mistaking a certain strength and determination about him. Harry wondered why he was sitting alone. Could he be one of those eccentric, hateful old souls? He tried to read his thoughts, but the expression was blank, indiscernible. The gentleman slowly turned his head, gazed at Harry with a certain shyness, and blinked repeatedly. Harry squirmed, realizing he was being disrespectful. The time had long passed to excuse or introduce himself. He chose the latter.

"Pardon me, sir," Harry stammered. He stepped forward, extending his hand.

"Permit me to introduce myself."

The old man blinked again.

"I'm Henry King Burgwyn, Jr.," he said, hoping the name would strike some recognition. The old man lifted his right hand and gave Harry's a weak clasp, then looked at him with vague eyes as if coming back from another world. Harry could almost see his mind clicking, until the straight mouth curved into a timid smile.

"Ahh, young Harry Burgwyn, I know of you," the old man said wistfully. "Was speaking with your father a moment ago. Tells me you've just completed your studies at Chapel Hill. Very proud of you, he is."

Harry blushed, bent awkwardly, still clasping the old man's hand, as he listened to the words jump randomly from the large mouth. The gentleman had the advantage.

"Now you're off for the Virginia Military Institute, fine school. I think you'll find it most challenging."

Harry nodded, smiled nervously. The old man's grip grew stronger.

"I've been to your Thornbury, in the autumn, two years ago. No, pardon me, three years ago. Lovely place. Your father's a fine planter, innovative. Very pleased with his operations. Good soil there along the Roanoke, but a problem with flooding, if I remember. Has a sophisticated system of dikes and ditches, doesn't it? Met some of your little brothers while I was there, Pollok, Alveston, and... I've forgotten the other little boy's name."

"Collinson," Harry interjected while trying to keep up with the tide.

"Yes, yes, Collinson. All your brothers appear very bright and lively. Believe you were away at school at the time, so we haven't had the pleasure. And there's another boy isn't there?"

"Yes sir, Sumner, and a sister, Maria, the oldest," Harry added.

"Ahh yes, Sumner and Maria, haven't met them either. But if Maria is anything like your mother Anna, it will be a great pleasure."

Harry beamed with pride, thanked him for the compliment, and waited patiently for him to reveal his name. The gentleman acted nervous, controlling the conversation, as if afraid to reveal a giant flaw. Yet he seemed most dignified and learned, obviously a planter himself, undoubtedly an aristocrat. Finally he let go of Harry's hand, and placed his again at the top of his cane. He fell silent, turned his eyes back toward the burning candle, and returned to his previous self-absorbed gaze. Harry straightened, regained his composure, but was surprised with the sudden, almost rude silence.

"My name is Edmund Ruffin," the old man said suddenly, while quickly refocusing on Harry's face, as if in hopes of catching the boy's initial unguarded expression. But Harry just blinked and disclosed an uneasy smile.

"Very pleased to make your acquaintance, sir," he said politely.

Harry had heard the name, probably from his father, but it bore no significance to him.

"You've not heard of me?"

"Yes sir, my father's spoken of you, I believe." Harry was surprised and a little taken aback with such a question.

"You know nothing of me?"

Again, Harry found the question discomforting. "Pardon me, sir, but since you know my father and family, and evidently have visited Thornbury, then I assume you are a planter."

"You're correct in your assumption." Ruffin smiled, satisfied that the boy knew nothing of his reputation.

"Please, son, have a seat." Ruffin pointed to a twin chair situated on the opposite side of the window. "That is, if you prefer the company of a teetering old man over the beauties that abound in the ballroom." Ruffin sighed, "My days with the ladies are long over. Nothing so foolish looking than an old man with a young girl."

Harry ignored Ruffin's attempt at humor, hedged anxiously, his legs spread apart, his hands clasped behind his back. "Thank you sir, but I'm looking for my father. You mentioned you just spoke with him?"

"Oh yes, he went searching for you, intended introducing us. I thought he may have sent you ahead."

"No," Harry said, briefly perplexed. "A coincidence, sir. I disturbed you while looking for him." Harry felt a sudden unexplainable need to escape, but realized he was committed.

"I see," Ruffin looked down for an instant, then pointed an open palm toward the empty chair. "Your father should return momentarily."

"Yes," Harry admitted. He glided to the chair. The old man scooted up even further, barely hanging at the edge of the chair, broadened his stance as if to do battle from a sitting posture. The room fell awkwardly silent. Ruffin stared like a spider.

"So, do you plan to pursue a military career? Is that why you've entered the Institute?"

"Perhaps," Harry nodded. "But I plan to study engineering."

"Ahh, like your father," Ruffin grinned. "And then a planter."

"Perhaps, but not straight off," Harry answered noncommittally.

"A noble profession, planting. A higher order, we are," a slight pause. "The guardians of virtue. Your father is among those of us who carry a great burden of responsibility."

"Oh!" Harry exclaimed.

"Oh yes. It is the duty of those more fortunate, the intelligent, the educated, the refined, to protect and further our civilization. It has been the way for centuries. Without us, the driving and stabilizing force of the planters, man would have remained as savages."

Ruffin spoke in a self-righteous tone. Harry noted it, watched the old man's eyes turn upward as the words poured from his mouth. He was formal, sounded as if he'd said the words before, many times, rehearsed them even.

Ruffin's eyes rolled downward, refocused on Harry. "Because of your birth, your father's profession, your family, you bear the same responsibility."

Harry twitched slightly, folded his hands together. "I've always considered my station honorable sir, and what is honor without responsibility?"

Ruffin nodded, smiled.

Henry suddenly appeared at the doorway of the parlor, paused. "Well, I see you've found each other."

Harry quickly rose, while Ruffin remained seated, a true patrician.

"Yes, yes, we were just discussing honor and responsibility. You have a fine son, Henry."

Henry gave Harry a knowing grin. "I'm afraid my son doesn't know your reputation, Mr. Ruffin. I'm sure you did not properly introduce yourself. Harry, there before you is the most prominent agronomist of our age."

Ruffin beamed, he did not blush. He knew his accomplishments, felt that most had slighted them, and was not ashamed of compliments.

"A great reformer, Harry. He single-handedly developed a way to bring fertility back to Virginia's tired soil, then promoted his methods through articles and visits to plantations. He made a trip to Thornbury a ways back." Henry turned to Ruffin. "If I remember, it met with your approval, did it not?"

Ruffin nodded. "With a few exceptions."

"I've borrowed his use of marl and manure," Henry said to his son. "And my yields are up considerably. I've shown you the figures."

"Yes sir," Harry agreed, taking his seat again.

"Mr. Ruffin had to force-feed his peers to an extent. Stubborn, weren't they?"

"Still are," Ruffin said.

"The farms in eastern Virginia were on the verge of collapse. Many were abandoned, the planters were moving west to more fertile ground, but the ones who stayed, the ones who listened to Mr. Ruffin here, well, they've had a rebirth. And not just in Virginia, but all along the southern coast. Why, some newspapers are calling him the Savior of the South."

With chin high, Ruffin merely blinked. Harry noticed his prideful air.

"Well, I believe that was a proper enough introduction, wouldn't you say, Edmund?"

The old man smiled, then slowly turned and looked at Harry.

"You see, young man, I was serious when I said it is our responsibility, your father's and mine and others like us, to maintain and promote our culture. My home, Virginia, was in dire need. Many didn't know what the problems were, much less the solutions. Enriching my own lands wasn't enough. I had to pass on my methods, so my home, my neighbors would recover. Otherwise, we would have sunk into oblivion, or worse, become a state of shopkeepers, like our neighbors to the north."

Henry cleared his throat, "Ah, Mr. Ruffin has some interesting political ideas as well."

Ruffin immediately sat back in his chair, making no effort to cover his disapproval of the condescending sound of Henry's statement. Harry looked questionably at his father.

"Pardon me, Edmund," Henry said. "May I?"

Ruffin turned his face slightly, looked away, but lifted one finger from his cane, a gesture for Henry to proceed.

"Mr. Ruffin is a Southern Nationalist, a Secessionist. He believes the North and South incompatible and that both sections would be better off separate. The differences are—"

"Logical," Ruffin interrupted. "Completely logical. The North can keep their tariffs, which are nothing but a tax on us to promote their industry. They can keep making their brass buttons with their immigrant, wage-slaves, and their states can surrender their rights to the Federal government. We'll be rid of their bigoted, religious zealots, their despotic politicians, and their selfish, materialistic vices. Those silly, but dangerous abolitionists will finally be quieted, so we can keep our Negroes satisfied and peaceful, which is in their nature anyway. The South will be free to pursue our own interests, agriculture, direct trade with Europe, and we can use the resources that otherwise go to tariff to spread our culture west. There's no reason why the two countries can't cooperate. We can continue to trade, we can be military allies. Secession will promote friendly competition and we'll be free of their corruptible values. Some fool up in New England will have no say in what we can do down here in Virginia or Carolina. Secession is the perfect solution, the only solution."

Harry listened attentively. The man definitely had his opinions, and he seemed quite bitter against the North. He had personally known no other southerner who was quite so resentful. His words were rather coarse, indignant, and showed a far different side than the reserved, almost shy old man he had met just a few moments before. The issue seemed to disturb him, provoke him. Nevertheless, there was a degree of logic in his views. Secession appeared a reasonable solution to the problems that had plagued the country for decades. He wondered if his father agreed, and asked him.

"I have to agree with many of Mr. Ruffin's points," Henry said. "But I don't believe secession is the best solution. Excuse me, Edmund, but your views are not among the majority in the South, nor is there a preponderance of crusaders in New England. We've always been able to compromise in the past."

"Compromise!" Ruffin interrupted again. "Compromising with fanatics won't pacify fanaticism. Has it shut up the abolitionists? It won't. They will continue to bark and scream until there's a blood bath. They won't be satisfied until all the Negroes are free or all the slave-holders are dead. They, who stand on their soap boxes and preach their eulogies of virtue, while children are chained to looms across the block. They have no grasp of the truth, no historical conscience. Slavery is as old as man. It is the very ladder with which we have climbed from barbarism to civilization. Without it we would have remained in heathen ignorance. Men have always consumed other men; it is inherent in our character, the very core of our love for independence and ease. It is our lot, the intelligent, the industrious, and the artistic not to toil like stupid beasts, but to cultivate and nurture our civilization so that the toilers will benefit from our accomplishments."

Ruffin paused, looked at his tiny audience. Henry and Harry sat, speechless, in no position to respond. They didn't altogether disagree. Harry marveled. Here was a completely logical man. Obviously, he had spent his life in observation and study and had found the truth. He admired the confidence that came from knowing the truth, and desired to have it himself. Ruffin noticed he had their ears.

"The Negro is an inferior race, would you not agree, Henry?"

Henry paused, then nodded timidly. Ruffin looked at Harry.

"They show no capacity for moving forward alone. Look at our free blacks here in the South, and, I should add, they are no better in the North. They live in squalor, they are susceptible to vice, have an aversion to regular labor, can't care for themselves. Look at Liberia, a perfectly fertile land, yet the freedmen who have migrated there are unable to survive without our subsidies, taxes we pay to keep them alive. As free men, the Negroes are a drain on our resources, retarding our own progress. As slaves, they are productive contributors, benefiting from our Christianizing influence. They gain from our association; we provide them with comfort and pleasure. They are healthy and content. The northern idealists claim we own their souls, that we abuse them. We, as masters, know we don't have complete power over servants. We have a right only to their labor, nothing more. Some few of us, unfortunately, attempt to exercise more power than we have. Some men abuse or neglect their property. Some men brutalize their wives. Should the entire institution of marriage be condemned for the abuse of a few? Overall, a Negro child born in the South can depend on a degree of comfort and happiness unattainable to free blacks in the North. Even their relations in Africa might envy their development. Our system benefits servant and master, yet the abolitionists plan to pull down the Negro by freeing him. It just doesn't stand to reason, but I need not defend slavery to you, do I, son?"

"No sir," Harry answered. Henry fidgeted.

"The abolitionists will not be content with compromise. You should know that, Henry. Mark my words, the coming election, the northerners will elect Fremont or some other radical. The abolitionists will agitate, agitate, and agitate. And then you will holler for secession. The radicals will hold court in Washington, and there will be no room for compromise. You know well that abolition would be a scourge on the South, a disaster."

"Well," Henry stood. "I wanted you to meet Mr. Ruffin, Harry. He's been such a great influence on me and my development of Thornbury. As you can well see, he possesses a sharp and cultivated mind, and most stimulating ideas."

Harry sensed that his father didn't totally agree with Mr. Ruffin.

He had found his words quite stimulating, wanted to hear more, but obviously Henry was maneuvering for Harry's departure.

"The music sounds delightful, does it not?" Henry was giving his son a cue, and finally made himself clear. "Mr. Ruffin and I have some business to discuss."

Harry stood.

"Yes, yes, go kick up your heels, my boy. There are some perfectly marvelous young girls out there. You'll get your fill of politics as the years go by, but there are just so many young ladies to conquer." Ruffin gestured toward the door with his cane.

Harry bowed slightly, offered his hand. "A pleasure, Mr. Ruffin. I would very much like to speak with you again."

"Yes, in good time, my boy. We'll surely speak again."

THE WEAKNESS WAS SUBTLE AT FIRST, then came over her in waves. She was terribly warm, perspiring; she shouldn't have danced the last dance, but could not resist the tall Kentuckian who had been waltzing with Kate. They were talking right next to her, but she was so light-headed, their words dwindled to distant echoes. The music was disorienting, buzzing in her mind. Little stars were shooting from the corners of her eyes in frightening little sparks. She made out Harry through the haze; he was just entering the ballroom.

Good little brother, he'll escort me to the cottage.

Her legs and feet were heavy; it was like walking through knee-deep water, and she tried to make her way. The air left her head, the room swirled, spinning colors, and then all was black.

Minnie collapsed in a heap.

The dancers closed around her. The music stopped. The Kentuckian knelt over her, placed her head on his knee and spoke to her gently. She didn't respond. Harry pushed through the crowd, quickly knelt beside his sister.

"I was just dancing with her. She seemed perfectly fine," said the Kentuckian over the jabbering, milling spectators.

"She's been traveling, exhausted I suspect," Harry responded. He placed a hand on her forehead and felt the wet perspiration.

"She's burning up. Here, help me take her to the sofa."

The two lifted her by the arms and shoulders, the crowd parted, and they carefully carried her to a smooth, velvet couch.

"A wet towel!" Harry yelled. "Someone, please bring me a cool, wet towel!"

He put the back of his hand against her cheek and felt the penetrating heat. Minnie whispered, inaudibly. Kate moved in, stroked her hair, and exchanged a concerned glance with Harry.

"Sumner, where's Sumner?"

"Here," said Harry's younger brother.

"Go get Father, quickly!"

"Where is he?"

Harry pointed toward the side door, while still staring at Minnie's bloodless face. "In the small parlor, down the hallway from the larger one!"

The Kentuckian spread his long arms, and begged the crowd to move back. A Negro servant appeared with a towel, and handed it to Harry.

He dabbed Minnie's forehead, and spoke to her. Eyes shut, she was perfectly still and quiet.

"Come sister, wake now." She didn't respond to the cool moisture. "She's burning with fever," Harry whispered to Kate. Kate began to cry.

Henry broke through the crowd, placed a hand on Harry's shoulder, and moved him aside. He felt the damp heat on Minnie's face, the simmering flesh. He pushed an eyelid open, and the eye rolled back.

"Bilious," he murmured.

With that, Henry scooped Minnie up in his arms and swung for the exit. The crowd tumbled back like dominoes. Out of the ballroom, down the hallway, he carried her with Harry, Sumner, and Kate just behind him.

"A doctor, Harry!" Henry yelled. "Get a doctor! And quinine, we'll need quinine!" Harry dropped back.

Effortlessly, Henry carried Minnie down the wide steps, across the lawn and toward their cottage. Anna was knitting in a chair, Pollok reading to Collie, and Madie, with little Allie sleeping on her lap, hummed in a rocker. Henry burst through the doorway.

"Bilious," he panted.

He placed Minnie on the closest bed, and Anna and Madie were on her like cats, stripping off her dress and undergarments.

"Wet towels, Henry, hurry!" Anna shrieked.

Allie was startled by the excitement, he cried and rubbed his eyes. Kate grabbed his hand and led him to another bed. Sumner was sent for more water. Trying to get the fever down, the women rubbed the wet towels over Minnie's naked body. Henry set off to beg for more towels, as Harry appeared with the doctor. Motionless, unconscious, Minnie's condition made it impossible for the doctor to administer any medicines. All anyone could do was work to break the fever, but, all night, it raged. In the morning, the chills came. They wrapped her in blankets, until the sweat came again, and then the chills, and then the sweat once more. By next evening, Minnie still had not awakened.

Gloom hung over the Burgwyns. Anna had lost her sister Jane to bilious fever, actually malaria. No one knew where the sickness came from, only that it struck suddenly, often in the spring or late summer. Sometimes it was mild and passed quickly; on occasion, strong and dangerous, it proved fatal. Jane Greenough had been just a little younger than Minnie when it took her away. She had been staying at Hillside, near the swamps that bred the undiscovered carrier, the female anopheles mosquito.

The days trudged by with no improvement. Minnie's fever still raged, and she had yet to regain consciousness. All her family could do was hope and pray, as she lay in a trance-like sleep. Every morning, Madie and Sumner would take the younger boys away and try to keep them entertained, while Henry and Harry lounged on the portico, too depressed to enjoy themselves. Anna would not leave Minnie's room.

RUMORS SPREAD THROUGH THE RESORT that the Burgwyn girl was dying of fever. Many guests stopped by the cottage to pay their respects and good wishes, among them, old Edmund Ruffin. White hair shining gloriously in the afternoon sun, he came teetering up with his cane and a Negro servant for support. Henry, of course, invited him to sit a while and rest, and Ruffin gladly accepted the invitation. The servant helped him into a ladderback chair, then slipped into the yard, hands in pockets, standing within earshot of his master. Ruffin immediately expressed his concern for Minnie, and prayed that a merciful Father would preserve her. Then there was silence, broken only by the nervous creak of Henry's rocker. Some peculiar laughter broke out, a ways to the right, toward the hotel. Henry excused himself.

"Anna hasn't eaten all day," he said. "I must insist that she eat."

Totally preoccupied, Henry rose and entered the cottage without a word of good-bye or thank you to Mr. Ruffin. Harry noticed the indiscretion.

"You must pardon my Father. He is not himself."

"Oh, of course," countered Ruffin, then murmured, "I have lost children myself, a terrible ordeal. Fathers should not have to watch their children suffer. A true mystery of the Lord's ways."

Harry nodded solemnly.

"I must depart momentarily," Ruffin said, as he leaned forward and reached for the porch rail. The alert servant noticed and stepped toward him, but Ruffin waved the cane in his other hand, and the Negro stopped, instantly returning to a casual stance. Ruffin spread his hand out on top of the rail, stretched his fingers in the sunlight. They were so stiff and sore; the warm rays always seemed to make them feel better.

Harry was thinking of the conversation of the other evening. He wanted very much to continue it, but wondered if the time was appropriate. He might never have the opportunity again. He realized that a man of such caliber rarely came so close. Finally, he followed his instincts.

"I find your ideas on secession very stimulating, sir," Harry said abruptly.

Ruffin couldn't have been more pleased with the boy's initiative. He wrote articles, wandered to plantations, and took trips to the Springs for the very purpose of spreading his views and winning converts. He would never pass on an opportunity.

"Oh. Very good. Few boys your age take an interest in such things, or should I say young men."

"I'm particularly interested in what would become of the South if there were abolition," Harry added. "I was unable to ask you to expand on that."

Ruffin raised his hand from the rail, stretched his fingers again, then leaned back as he rubbed the hand over a frail leg.

"Catastrophe. And not just in the South," he said quite seriously. "You see, this globe on which we now stand is actually very small indeed. The markets, the great cities, they are all very delicately connected. If there were abolition without compensation, it would financially wreck the planters. What would become of Thornbury and other plantations without the slaves? Production of cotton and staples would dry up. The mills and markets in the North and Europe would soon feel the effect. Gradually, they would shut down. Abolition would spark a chain of disasters. Bankruptcy would become almost universal, and would spread as far as distant China. Perfectly catastrophic, abolition is a dangerous ideal."

"I see," Harry pondered. "But what if there were compensation?"

"Ha, you'll never see it," Ruffin grunted cynically. "Where would the money come from? The government, the taxpayers? Compensation would be a drain on the country's resources, would also set off a financial crisis, a little different, but ultimately with the same effect. And these are just the financial repercussions. Abolition would also set off social and political calamity. Where would the Negroes go, what would they do? They have no education, no skills in demand other than their labor. Would they have political rights? I shudder to think. The chaos of Africa reborn! Everything we've accomplished in the South would come tumbling down. No government, no law, no order, utter anarchy. Abolition would set off a wave of misery."

"So abolition is quite impossible," Harry mused.

"Ahh, seems impossible to you and me, but what of people ruled by ideals, those bumbling, unrealistic do-gooders who want their government ruled by lofty concepts? 'All men are created equal.' Ha, no such thing, an idea, the crutch of lazy, talentless men, not the truth. No man has ever been born free, and no two men ever born equal. Some men come in this world with brawn, others with brains, some with neither. There's nothing fair or equal about the nature of things, but with their twisted reasoning, the idealists would somehow like to see men with great minds toiling in the fields beside those with lesser capacities. We are dealing with short-sighted, ignorant people who have no concept of the stagnation that would result if that came about. Where go the masses, the rabble, without learned men to guide them?"

Secession would prevent the disaster, Harry thought. Shut out the abolitionists, so southern culture, a centuries-old culture, could continue to grow and prosper.

Ruffin watched the boy's face, sensed the mind working, and could almost see the logic clicking and grabbing hold. If only the older men could see it as clearly.

"War," Harry said. "Whenever there's talk of secession, there is also talk of war."

Ruffin corrected him. "Coercion is what you mean. It's perfectly within a state's right to secede from the Union. If the northerners used force to bring us back, it would be illegal coercion, unconstitutional."

Legality, coercion, constitutionality, it didn't matter, war was war, Harry reasoned. Ruffin looked the boy over, noticed he wasn't quite satisfied.

"The North won't fight for the Negro," Ruffin said loudly without a thought that his servant might hear. "They're too practical for that. They'll not spend money and blood for the concept of Negro freedom. They'll bluster and bluff, but they won't fight." Ruffin paused to see the effect, then continued.

"Greed and profit are their motivation. Base demagogues rule the North, men who almost exclusively seek self interest. Immoral. They are hostile to the planter, envious of our wealth and virtue. They try to cover and compensate for their inadequacy with talk of emancipation, enhancing their reputation with a seemingly noble mind. But will they sacrifice their life and fortune for that cause? Definitely not! They will fan the flames of slave rebellion, but will they pick up a gun and join the mob? Shallow to the point of emptiness, corrupt and deceitful, grasping and vile, that's the character of the northern businessman, the by-product of profiteering enterprise. A warrior is willing to sacrifice himself for a noble cause. Our tormentors to the North lack such fiber."

Harry didn't believe secession would be so easy. Men didn't fight just for profit, or the lack of it.

"What of pride, Mr. Ruffin? Is secession not like a slave running from his master? Is it not like a wife fleeing from an unappreciative husband? What of honor? Will they not fight for honor?"

Ruffin had few followers, and even this boy would not agree with him. He found it very irksome. The sharp old mind was growing dull from resistance. Neat, tidy, straight and logical, it locked up. The emotional argument was always so muddling and tiresome. You couldn't argue against emotion; it had no clear foundation. The North would not fight. Why didn't the boy just accept it? Ruffin scrabbled up to leave, motioned to his servant.

"No!" the old man barked at Harry. "There will be no war."

OUT SHE CAME ON A STRETCHER, PALE AND SILENT. Other

than a few spasmodic fits, Minnie had not awakened. The fever still soared. The doctor had recommended moving her where she could get better care. It was risky, but she was not improving at the Springs.

Harry watched them lay the stretcher across a carriage. Sumner and his mother and father squeezed in to accompany Minnie on the ride over the mountains. Harry, Madie, frail little Allie, Pollok and little Collie piled into two other carriages.

Two days later, at Lexington, the rest of the family boarded the cars, while Harry and Henry stood alone at the depot. The weight of a coming tragedy hung over them, and they exchanged a strong handshake as Henry passed two envelopes to his son. One was addressed to Colonel Smith, the commandant of Harry's new school, and was not to be opened. The other contained money.

Hope absent from his face, the father boarded the chugging train, as it started its eastward trek. Harry watched until the smoke disappeared and the mournful whistle could be heard no more. He then turned and looked up at the distant hill where a white fortress stood, his new home.

Tall and lanky, the handsome boy stood before the Colonel's desk as the envelope was opened and perused.

"This will be handed you by my son, Henry K. Burgwyn, who joins your Corps of Cadets & will, I trust, avail himself of the many advantages offered by your institution. Being but lately arrived from low country, I dare say the drill will bear heavily on him at first, but I trust to his perseverance to overcome this difficulty. It is only the first few months that I fear.

Harry has always been a hard working student & I trust will continue so. But I well know the effect of association. I will esteem it a favour if you will see that he is made acquainted with some of those you esteem most highly. He has always eschewed low & vulgar companions, & being somewhat reserved in his manner is not likely to seek companionship unless he is thrown into it. His college life has brought on indolence of body, which has been increased by his rapid growth, being only 17 yrs., he is six feet high."

August 12th, 1859, Harry was formally admitted to the Virginia Military Institute. Two days later, he was absent without leave. A telegram had arrived from Petersburg, a message from Anna. It said that Minnie would not survive twenty-four hours. Harry was on the first train.

Anna made an entry in her diary on August 15th, "My darling Maria mysteriously woke from a death sleep today. She will make a full recovery. May God be praised."

A week later, trim and dapper, Harry Burgwyn was back in Lexington drilling with the cadets.

⚜ 12 ⚜

A Fool's Dream

It takes an enlightened man to envision a world that is just and fair and good, an idealistic man to dream such a world could be, and a foolish man to try to make it so. There is nothing more dangerous than a fool.

IT HAD RAINED FOR DAYS, BIG DRENCHING rains that stained and flooded the creeks as they tumbled down to the brown Potomac. That morning, the downpours had finally stopped, leaving behind a thin veil of October fog. The change in weather had a young man up and ready for a long awaited stroll to town. His name was Henry Kyd Douglas and he resided at Ferry Hill Place, a modest home which stood on a low bluff, on the Maryland side of the river. Within sight of his home, in Virginia, and just a short trek over a nondescript little bridge, was Shepherdstown, where the lad had plans to spend some gift money just received for his recent nineteenth birthday. But before young Douglas would reach his destination, he would have a chance encounter.

As he passed over the bridge and through the lifting fog, Douglas spied an overloaded wagon stuck quick in the mud on the River Road, just downstream and on the Virginia side. Pulling on the reins of two straining horses was a tall, lanky old fellow trying vainly to free the vehicle, and Douglas wondered who might be driving a heavy wagon on that notorious road after the recent deluges. Certainly it couldn't be a local man.

The boy paused at the head of the bridge, peered through the mist and watched the old man repeatedly switch off from tugging, bawling, and slapping his horses' rumps. It was obvious to Douglas that the wagon was hopelessly stuck, the horses spent, the load too heavy. Yet the old man seemed frantic in his determination to be free. Curious about the man's identity and why he was there, the boy quietly circled off the bridge and up the muddy lane, until he arrived unnoticed twenty feet from the mired wagon. He studied the preoccupied old fellow, his height, the crooked bend in his back, the huge hands and feet, and the wild, wavy hair streaked with gray. With arms folded, leaning back hard on one leg, Douglas finally made his presence known.

"'Fraid you're stuck tight, stranger."

The words alarmed the old man. He jumped, then quickly turned and displayed a flowing, gray beard and frightening blue eyes. The man was too startled, much too startled, and he stood as if ready for combat. Douglas took notice, a flash of suspicion, but the old man straightened up and relaxed.

"You're right about that, son," he said with a contrived little laugh. The boy moved closer.

"'Fraid you got no choice but to unload your wagon." Douglas reached for the canvas tarp that covered the load in an effort to look at what was underneath. The old man frowned, and reached to intercept, his long fingers beating the boy's to the tarp.

"Mining tools," he said. "Very heavy, sure don't want to unload them."

The boy suddenly realized who the old man was. "You must be the fellow who moved into the Kennedy Farm, across the river, down a ways."

"You're right, son, Isaac Smith's the name." He reached out with his massive hand and swallowed one of the boy's, shaking it profusely.

"Father said somebody had moved into the old place. You're mining the hills near the iron works, aren't you? Henry Douglas's my name. Live just across the river there. Right there, near the bridge."

"Well, that makes us neighbors, doesn't it?"

"Yes, sir."

The two looked at each other awkwardly for a moment, then Douglas reminded Mr. Smith of his troubles.

"Don't know how you're gonna move that wagon without unloading it."

"Well, that's just not an option, son. You know anybody in town there that owns a good team?"

"We've got a team."

The old man's sparkling eyes turned wide. "Do you think you'd be a kind neighbor and give me some help? I'd be much obliged. Would include you in all my prayers to our Heavenly Father."

Douglas strolled around the wagon, sizing up the situation. "My father's away right now, but I don't think he'd mind if I helped you."

"Would you, son? Would you? I'd be much obliged."

"Yes sir, I think our team with yours will get you outta that mud. Would you care to come with me, Mr. Smith, and rest up at the house?"

"No, son. No, I'll wait here, but I sure would like your help. Hurry, you go on. I'll wait here. Hurry back now."

Henry Douglas was back in half an hour with his father's carriage horses and his Negro coachman. Isaac Smith was very excited when the two boys hooked up the team, and seemed overly pleased when the four horses easily pulled the heavy wagon from the pasty mud. Douglas thought it best that the two teams carry the load over the bridge, and over a series of hills on the

Maryland side. Mr. Smith was very grateful.

Kyd Douglas thought Smith a simple, pleasant man, but also rather foolish. There were no valuable minerals in those hills. The old man was just wasting his time and money. Over the next week, Douglas asked around, but nobody knew much about Isaac Smith. He kept to himself, but had many visitors to his rented farm, all strangers. Apparently, his only permanent company was a rather hideous old mulatto woman. Douglas concluded that, in addition to being simple, Smith was a kind, reverent man, and an eccentric old hermit.

Kyd Douglas could not have known of the insanity that ran in the old man's family. He couldn't have known that his mother had committed suicide in a fit of depression, or that Smith's grandmother had suffered from the same malady and had died young, or that he had a mad aunt who had three sons condemned to asylums, or that two sons of an uncle had been judged mentally ill, as were two of Smith's own sons. Douglas couldn't have been aware of the murders Smith had committed, of his conspiracy that was now under way, or of his fanatical abolitionism. He couldn't have known that the old man's real name was John Brown, and that he was the most dangerous man in America.

John Brown was a bitter man with a troubled past. He was the oldest son of a pious, domineering farmer who had operated a stop on the underground railroad, but who also had helped drive his first wife to a manic suicide. Brown emerged from his father's yoke with feelings of inferiority, and typical of folks with such feelings, tried to suffocate them with ambition. He failed miserably at everything he tried. After two wives and a large brood of dysfunctional children, he came to closely resemble his despotic father. Now sick, and possibly deranged, Brown was twisting his ambition from business to crusading. He had never been to the South, but being resentful of the decadent southern planters whom he perceived were leisurely getting rich off the scarred backs of downtrodden slaves, he was now setting out on God's mission and a glorious fate. It wasn't mining tools that had snarled and bogged down Brown's wagon that foggy October morning near Shepherdstown, but old pikes sent to him by rail from New England, pikes that Brown planned to pass among the slaves he freed. Just a few short weeks after receiving unwitting aid from young Henry Kyd Douglas, he would raid the Federal Armory at Harper's Ferry with a tiny army of boys who had fallen under his dictatorial spell.

The raid on Harper's Ferry was a fiasco. After renting the Kennedy Farm in Maryland, Brown gathered his insurrectionists and led them into the town. They killed five townspeople, including an innocent free black who was the baggage master at the train depot. After gathering hostages, including a great-grandnephew of George Washington, the raiders waited for rebellious slaves to join them, but when none arrived, they boarded themselves up in the U.S. Armory. Two days later it was stormed by a company of marines led by Robert E. Lee and Jeb Stuart. Ten of Brown's followers were killed, most of the rest captured.

Washington's relative escaped unhurt. No slaves ever rallied to Brown's call.

There's a thin line between brilliance and insanity. During John Brown's imprisonment, trial, and right up to his execution, he evidently carried himself very well. He won the respect and support of many with his pious dignity. He was also a great prophesier, believing only blood, and lots of it, would cleanse the sin of slavery. He was an idealistic and obsessed crusader, and once his plans failed, he willingly gave himself up as a martyr. Southerners labeled him mad. Emerson and Thoreau compared him to Christ.

Henry Kyd Douglas would witness John Brown's capture at Harper's Ferry on October 18th, 1859, and would also be nearby when Brown and six of his followers were hanged for treason in early December at Charlestown, Virginia. He would always regret his assistance to Brown, but like hundreds of thousands of Americans, the raid would alter Douglas' life forever. For John Brown's desire to fill a void in his soul with a crusade for justice would lead directly to war.

Reaction to the raid in the South was one of frantic alarm. To southerners, there was no worse crime than conspiring to inflame slaves to rebellion. It drove thousands of white men to join militia units. One year later, Abraham Lincoln's election would bring the country to the brink. Lincoln harbored some slight sympathy for Brown, which went a long way to feeding the South's paranoid mistrust of northern intentions.

Henry Kyd Douglas would later join the Confederate cause and would become the youngest officer on Stonewall Jackson's staff. He was wounded six times during the war, the most severe at Gettysburg, where he was also captured. Later exchanged, he was commanding a brigade when the Rebels surrendered at Appomattox. Later, he would write a book about his adventures with the famous Jackson.

Thomas J. Jackson also played a role in the John Brown affair. The insurrectionist was considered so dangerous that a heavy guard was sent to Charlestown before the execution to help keep the peace. A part of that guard was a contingent of cadets from the Virginia Military Institute commanded by the future Confederate hero.

IT WAS THE BEST NEWS OF his long life, an answer to prayers. The devilish raid would convince more southerners of the dangerous motives harbored by northern fanatics than his agitation and pen could ever do. Edmund Ruffin saw Brown's fiasco as a tremendous opportunity that would finally awaken docile and submissive southerners to action. He wasted little time, went to work straight off drawing up a petition he titled "The Harper's Ferry Memorial." A propaganda piece, it was used by Ruffin to admonish northerners who applauded the treasonous murderer, stirring the public mind to distrust countrymen who rejoiced at attempted insurrection. It was time for the South to seek its independence and cut the malignant fanatics out of their lives.

After securing publication of his petition in several Virginia newspapers, Ruffin was on the first available train to the site of the disturbance.

Harper's Ferry was a picturesque little village nestled within towering foothills at the confluence of the Shenandoah and Potomac Rivers. Yet, at the time of Ruffin's arrival, it was an armed camp of over fifteen hundred militiamen who guarded every pike for suspected insurrectionists. The town was whirling with rumors and visitors, aroused and electrified with tension. There was the scarred armory building with its broken windows and doors pocked with bullet wounds. Witnesses and participants of the affair were at every street corner fanning heated emotions with their grizzly accounts. The little old man joined them, agitated, and proudly proclaimed that the raid proved, without a doubt, the natural subservience and loyalty of the Negro slave who had not rallied to Brown. Frightened, he had merely clung closer to his master. Ruffin was able to acquire a number of Brown's pikes—six-foot poles with long Bowie knives fastened at the tops, which had been shaped in a Connecticut blacksmith's shop. He carried them as he agitated, having tied a note to one that read: "A sample of the favors designed for us by our Northern Brethren."

Brown and his surviving associates were being held at nearby Charlestown, and as the day of execution drew nearer, Ruffin learned that only the military guard would be allowed to witness the punishment. Witnessing the villain's hanging was the main motive for his trip, and Ruffin followed the advice of a friend and sought membership with the militia. He begged and was able to persuade the VMI cadets to allow him to join the Corps, and soon he was wearing the bright red tunic and white crossed belts of the student soldiers. Slight of height with stooped shoulders, the old man thought himself foolish, as he tripped over his long gray coat while drilling with the color-guard. Eventually, memories of drill while serving in the army during the War of 1812 got him in step and in good standing with the cadets. Never shy with his opinions, he was soon sharing his radical views with the boys. They listened to Ruffin's call to brutally crush any attempt by misguided northerners to rescue John Brown.

THERE WERE DRUM BEATS AND BUGLES and all the drill, and he'd gotten used to them; the young naturally adjust quickly. The discipline, and the structure, had made him stronger. He could feel it, and he liked it. And now he was sleeping in the open air of Jefferson County, the moist, drizzly, cold air of December. Gray smoke from countless wild fires drifted within it, carrying a sooty scent that penetrated his clothes, his blanket, his pack, everything. The fires were set by angry Negroes who were rampaging at fool Brown's desperate failure. That was the talk. There was lots of talk, and Harry didn't believe a fraction of it.

For one with a very sensible outlook, these were annoying times, and he had suddenly found himself at the center of the annoyance. It all seemed simple enough on the surface. An unbalanced fellow had gone off to Kansas and hacked up five pilgrims with broad swords, then had run off to Canada where he had dreamed up a conspiracy of rebellion. The attempt was made, considerable blood was shed, he was caught, and now he was to be punished. Men often run wild. There must be laws to check them, and when they are broken, there must be justice and punishment. Simple enough. Yet, for fear that this wretched lawbreaker might be saved by those who were sympathetic to his rebellion, it was now necessary for hundreds of militiamen and soldiers to guard him. Harry was one of the guards, the assignment normally an honorable duty. Yet, something was gnawing at him; subtle tugs at his sensibilities. The rebellion had been financed by prominent New Englanders. There was a general outcry of sympathy and compliance from the northern papers. Not so much for Mr. Brown's methods, but certainly for his cause. On the other hand, there was Mr. Ruffin, an associate of his father's, a previously feeble old man who was now virile and alive with excitement. He had joined the ranks, was drilling with them, was laughing like a schoolboy, basking in the situation. It was all very disturbing.

He had been born in the North, had spent nearly half his life there, and he had not known that abolitionism ran so strong that northerners would condone or finance murder for its sake. Harry had written his mother and father, asking their views. Anna had responded, but her note made no mention of Mr. Brown, nor did it acknowledge that her oldest son was guarding him. He was anxiously waiting for a letter from Henry. Surely he could tie the situation into a tight little ball. But no note had arrived and the day of execution was quickly closing.

The duty was monotonous, and he daydreamed. He saw a clear image of John Brown at the head of a thousand angry slaves spilling through the gates at Thornbury. How would their hands react? They wouldn't join him, surely not. They would flee. Some would fight and defend the place. None would join the insurrection. He wondered if that was wishful thinking, but the more he thought of it, the more he arrived at the same conclusion. They would flee or fight. Their people would never raise a hand against his father.

He had a solution for all of this, a very simple solution. Gather up all the leading abolitionists, load them on trains and bring them to Thornbury. They could spend time there, all the time they'd like, and when they left, their minds would have changed and this hubbub would dissolve. Harry was certain of this, as sure as sunrise.

The morning of execution arrived. He woke as before, damp, a numbness in his toes and fingers. There was a change though; no rain pelted the clinging dead leaves. The smoke still wove through the trees, just as thick. His nostrils were black with it.

They marched through a vacant Charlestown, the inhabitants having been cleared away, not even a stray newspaperman about. They followed a cobblestone road out of the place, came to a clear pasture with frostbitten grass, the scaffold situated in its center. Major Jackson positioned their battery of brass cannon. The cadets formed a long, straight line. They waited. More soldiers filtered into the pasture until there were over one thousand. The day was pale and threatening, a cold wind, an occasional splash of sun, but mostly it was gray.

The pasture was jammed; the last column arrived, Brown's escort led by cavalry. The condemned sat on the lid of his coffin in a plain open wagon, the sheriff and the jailer accompanying him. He was wearing a coat, pants, and floppy hat, all black. Oddly, his feet were adorned with red slippers. The wagon bumped to a halt at the foot of the scaffold, and Brown quickly vaulted to the ground with no apparent sign of fear in his movements. Harry studied his features. The beard was gone, though the face was still grizzled. Lines like deep rivers flowed from sunken eyes. It was an extraordinary face.

Quickly, almost eagerly, Brown ascended the steps to the scaffold deck. Harry was not alone in his opinion; this man wanted to die. Brown handed the jailer his hat, then shook his hand. Words were exchanged. Harry couldn't hear them.

All were expecting a speech from the fanatic, a last pathetic defense of his actions and his cause, but Brown paid no notice of the army that surrounded him. The jailer pinned a pillow case over his head. Wrists and ankles were securely tied, the noose placed around his neck. The jailer spoke to Brown; he gave a muffled response, then was positioned over the trap. All was ready, yet the show was prolonged as the Richmond Grays maneuvered closely around the scaffold. Brown waited impatiently, protested the delay.

An officer of militia cried ready from below, said it again louder. The Sheriff said something to Brown who nodded, then the Sheriff and jailer descended the steps together. Harry didn't see the arm that swung the hatchet that released the trap, but he heard the screeching hinges. The body fell heavy, like a bale from a barn loft window. A brief spasm; death was swift.

He dangled, and there were no hurrahs; not a single elevated word of disrespect from the witnesses. Even Edmund Ruffin was moved. Like most, Harry felt a sense of closure, speculated that this man would soon be forgotten. Ruffin vowed to let no one forget. He aimed to make Brown the spark of southern independence. In his mind, glorious times were approaching.

⁘ 13 ⁘

A Peculiar Situation

THERE WAS A HISSING FROM THE STOVE, dying red coals surrounded by gray ash. A frosty windowpane melting, drips streaking against the gray light. Icicles, clear and wet, dribbling, bap, bap into a wooden bucket. The thaw at last.

He looked up from his bed, a sack of hay on raised boards, and watched an old brown cobweb waving in the draft, the remnants of a half-devoured beetle hanging, gently whirling. The spider was long dead, he thought, or curled up in some dark, dingy corner. Where do spiders go in the winter?

The room grew brighter, an orange tint to the light. A sunny day was coming.

"Goin' ta town, Massa Henry got a speech ta'day."

Kinchen swung out of bed, bare feet on cold planks, between which the light found forgotten ground under the shack. Bent over, muscles tight against the chill, he poked a stick into the stove, and the coals crackled. In went two dry logs, then he hopped under the covers again until the warmth grew.

"Goin' ta town, Massa Henry got a speech ta'day. Missas Anna goin' too. Got's ta shine up the buggy, groom da bays, oil da traces. Goin' ta town ta'day."

Bare feet on cold planks again. He raised his night shirt, bent toward the stove, red heat on a black fanny.

"Ehhh, eh, dat feels good."

He found woolen socks rolled up under the bed, his britches draped over the chair, a red vest on a hook by the window. He looked out and saw pale blue sky, some wispy clouds.

"Gonna be a fine day. Goin' ta Jackson." His mood was cheery, and he began to whistle while he prepared for the day.

His best boots hung from the ceiling on hide cords. He pulled them down, took a dirty handkerchief to them, some spit. A long, heavy great-coat was draped behind the door, a gray scarf, his derby hat. He stepped outside into the glorious light, cool fresh air up wide nostrils.

"Glory ta God in da highest."

Making for the woodshed, he scooped up an armful of seasoned logs, then turned for the kitchen.

Old gray Ruthy, fat, with heavy, drooping cheeks, was rocking in her chair. With swollen ankles, and her legs too weak to stand for more than a few minutes, she reached over the stove, stirring the sizzling bacon. The smell filled the room. Kinchen clamored in.

"Mornin' Ruthy, mornin'." He laid the wood on a dwindling pile by the door. Ruthy ignored him. He pranced over to her, kissed her on the forehead. She grunted.

"Goin' ta town ta'day. Needs anyt'ing?"

"Not'n, not'n in the wurl."

"Wha' we eatin'?"

"Eggs if'n you goes and gets 'em."

Little Sam, his eyes dull and sleepy, slipped into the kitchen with a basket of eggs.

"Ha, good ding, got's work ta do. Goin' ta Jackson ta'day," Kinchen said so the boy would hear him and be envious. Little Sam just sat on a bench and looked at him. He smacked his lips, bored.

"You say yuh goin' ta town?" asked Ruthy.

"Yes'sem."

"My, yuh 'ad betta' do sump'n with dat face. Filthy!"

"Yes'sem."

With a clean face and a full stomach, Kinchen headed for the stables.

"Baaa-bee, baaa-bee lambs!"

The bay geldings tumbled from the stalls and loped across the paddock, completely subservient to their master, Kinchen. He chuckled, rubbed their noses, pulled their ears, then passed through the gate. They bobbed their heads behind him as he led them to be groomed.

The black buggy shone in the brilliant sun—the bays sleek with their painted hooves and freshly brushed manes and tails. There was a slight scent of freshly oiled leather. Stationed at the end of the cul-de-sac, Kinchen stood among the oyster shells, straight and proper, his gloved hands clasped to his front. The air was still and crisp, not a cloud in the sky, white ice turning to clear water. The grand doors opened, and Henry stepped to the piazza, Anna's hand firmly in his. Kinchen quickly brushed his coat, took off his derby, looked it over, placed it neatly on his head again, grinned. Henry guided Anna down the long steps, and the slave eyed her kind, familiar face, high cheek-bones, flashing blue eyes.

"Good morning Kinchen, a beautiful morning," she said with that marvelously clear voice.

"Yes'sem, praise God for a glorious day," he whispered as he bowed, tipping the derby. Then he quickly moved to the head of the horses, steadying them, as Henry helped the mistress in.

"The geldings look good," Henry said. He strolled around the buggy to mount on the other side. "Very healthy."

"Oh, yeah suh, dey's got da appetite, suh."

Kinchen mounted the driver's seat, took hold of the reins, his back as straight as a flagstaff. "Ready, suh?"

"Watch the mud today," Henry warned.

"Yeah, suh." Henry needn't have cautioned him. Kinchen was always slow and steady through the mud.

The buggy snapped over the oyster shells until they hit the mile-long plantation road. It was thawing sand from there to the gate. Little pot-holes obstructed the way, the spinning wheels fracturing the thin ice, sending out a cracking sound like breaking glass. They gently bounced along, as Henry watched the passing fields, his hands grubbing within them. Anna looked vainly for buds on barren trees. The couple did not talk, but casually observed the yellow sunshine, a welcome stranger.

Henry had been anticipating this day. Events had moved swiftly since John Brown's raid. No sooner had the stir somewhat subsided, than the election had come, and it had all started fresh. Somehow, Lincoln was in Washington, South Carolina had seceded, and now there was more than just talk of a North Carolina Convention. It was time for Henry to air his views.

They passed the gate, and Henry's head turned.

"The gate needs painting, Kinchen," his voice rising over the bouncing buggy. Kinchen nodded as he concentrated, squinting against the crisp air. The main road was rough, squishy. There were sharp turns, patches of mud, then hard, frozen dirt where the early light hadn't penetrated the trees. The bridges were still slick, but Kinchen guided them through, giving no appearance of great effort.

The bells could be heard from quite a ways off. Seemed all of Northampton County had come awake and made an appearance. Jackson's streets were jammed with carriages, buggies and horses. Kinchen bit at his lip, and he brought the bays to a slow but steady walk, expertly directed them through the maze. The obstacles seemed to part. A sharp left turn, then by White's Hotel, he brought the buggy to a gentle halt before a throng at the courthouse steps. Kinchen leaped into the deep mud, settled the bays with his comforting whispers, then helped his mistress to high ground. Henry followed, stepping gingerly in his fine black suit. Stark, pale faces within the crowd watched them approach, their mood, strange and serious. Sheriff Peasley came forward and shook Henry's hand. Anna greeted him with a nervous smile. Peasley turned, glared at the crowd. They made room. Kinchen backed away, went to the buggy, and tied feed bags to the bays.

There was standing room only. The crowd had been well behaved, polite, but a series of speakers had solved nothing. They were as confused and frustrated as before. South Carolina's secession had split her sister state to the north down the middle, and Northampton was similarly at odds. Two speakers had been adamant for preserving the Union, one had raved for immediate secession, the remaining had spoken for compromise or had taken a wait-and-see attitude. Sheriff Peasley introduced the last speaker, Henry K. Burgwyn.

He squeezed Anna's hand. All the concerned faces turned to him, as he made his way down the crowded aisle. Here was the richest planter in the county. His stock had risen sharply over the past decade. He had played an active role in community affairs. He and Anna had been instrumental in the founding of the Episcopal church in Jackson. Henry had designed the very building they now occupied, the most beautiful courthouse in Carolina. Always driven, he was well educated, was considered level-headed, and a man with plenty of common sense. His opinion would carry considerable weight.

On what side of the coin would he fall? His beliefs were a mystery. Never impassioned with politics, he'd always been rather reserved on that score. The crowd sat up in their seats. The ones standing tipped on their toes and stretched their necks.

Henry put on his spectacles as he shyly turned to his peers. He removed a folded piece of paper from his coat, cleared his throat, looked again at the quiet faces.

"The unfortunate death of my Uncle Thomas Pollok brought me and my family among you some twenty years ago," he paused and looked at the paper.

"As you all know, since that time my energies have been directed at the building of my estate. Other than the weight of my single vote, I've played no part in lawmaking. In affairs of national importance, in the Presidential and Congressional elections, I have always embraced the Whig platform. I have followed the career of the eminent Mr. Clay, and have adhered to his views. Mine has always been a spirit of compromise."

The air went out of the crowd, disappointed that yet another speaker had joined the ranks of the uncommitted. Henry eyed them, then refocused on the paper.

"For those of you who know nothing of my personal life, my views and beliefs, in the past, have sprung from necessity. Although a southerner by heritage, I was born and educated in the North, and resided there for seven years. I married a New England wife, and have since been constantly visiting there. I have an estate in New England as large as that in the South. Therefore, self-interest alone should make me a Union man."

Henry sensed restlessness in the gallery and a trembling about his knees. His arms dropped, and he let the paper fall to his side. He looked about the room, spoke forcefully.

"However, these are not days for men to be motivated purely by self-interest. North Carolina is suffering from shocks received from two extremes of our Union. New England on the one side, and South Carolina on the other.

Small in numbers, the extremists perhaps weld more influence than they deserve. But the abolitionists of the North, through organization, perseverance, industry, and with no inconsiderable support from the pulpit, have grown very strong indeed. The 'Black Republicans' have allied with the Garrison, Wright, Douglas, and Sumner abolitionists, and as the recent election has shown, through their assiduous cooperation, they now hold reign in Washington."

"The Fire-Eaters of Charleston, the Barnwell Rhett faction and the Mercury, have long hated the Union, and have chosen to remove themselves from a government they find repugnant. They have wasted years of wind and words in the Capitol, and because of their neglect to organize, and their failure to call upon the churches of the South, their raging passions have caused them to cut the bonds of our Union. They have called to their sister states in the south to join them, and some undoubtedly will go. Now North Carolina is thrown into the unenviable position of choosing sides. But choose sides we must and, gentlemen, ladies, I have come today to tell you that I have chosen my course."

The crowd now hung on his words, in deathly quiet. Henry took a deep breath, sighed.

"Or perhaps the course has been chosen for me, for I cannot call brothers those who have willfully financed and armed a crazed fanatic whose sole purpose was to murder innocent men, women, and children. That treacherous Mr. Brown made my decision, he, and the hideous stubbornness of the puritan mind."

The heightened energy in the room ached for release. The uproar came spontaneously, but it was brief and quickly returned to a simmer. Henry stood patiently until there was quiet.

"For years I have visited the North, nearly every summer. At first I observed impartially, not really aware of the great distances between us. Gradually I came to know the stubborn character of the puritan mind. The present generation has been literally nursed and educated in abolitionism. Abolitionism has been the great theme of their newspapers and lectures, the literary portion of their almanacs, the foundation of their school books, and the illustrations of their annuals. I doubt that you will disagree; there is a great distance between them and us."

The crowd was silently watching him. Henry was satisfied that he had the room's complete attention. Most knew little of the North, had nothing to draw from. They were learning from one of their own who had lived there.

"The New Englander is ignorant of the peculiar situation of our people. Almost exclusively agricultural, residing in a sparsely settled country, families of wives and children surrounded by ignorant and credulous Negroes who, if left alone and unseduced by designing men, are content to follow their duties and occupations throughout their lives to their final rest, and satisfied to receive from God the reward of using the talent given them. But they are easily misled, and when excited by liquor, which is always the first thing they aim at when in insurrection, the Negro can perpetrate the most horrid atrocities upon women and children such as would revolt the minds of the most rabid abolitionist. Witness the account of every servile insurrection on record. This position of the southern people, our people, is not, and cannot be realized by those who have never been so placed. Nothing can so rouse the mind of man to madness as the conviction that his wife and family may be subjected to the horrors of another Southampton insurrection. And this, too, excited by those who should be our friends and brothers."

Henry glanced at Anna, but could not see her face or read her thoughts. He raised the paper, and a compelling tide of words flowed.

"The abolitionists will not, and cannot be made to understand our situation. I have made this sad conclusion. Our glorious and noble Union, the hope of liberty throughout the world, the great labor and result of the combined wisdom and patriotism of the wisest and most patriotic body the world ever saw, will be shattered to pieces because a set of stubborn men insist on forcing an abstraction upon us, that slavery is a great civil and moral evil."

Whispers spread throughout the gallery, a general nodding of heads.

"The question remains, will North Carolina secede? For me, it is not a question of will, but when. Our situation dictates that we cannot remain with the North. We must rid ourselves of puritanical fanaticism, which, in its blind pursuit of its own vain images, would destroy a paradise, would substitute for the mild precepts of our Holy Religion, a 'higher law,' an antislavery bible, and an antislavery God. They would hurl the blessed Savior of mankind from his throne in Heaven, and place John Brown, the cheat, the horse thief, and the midnight murderer, in his stead."

The murmurs from the gallery rose to chatter. Henry searched for Anna's eyes, made sure he caught them.

"There are those among us who cling to a hope that the northern conservatives will flex their muscles, that somehow they will suffocate the fanatics, and preserve our Union. Unfortunately, this is nothing more than a dream. They've had decades to quiet them, but the abolitionists have only grown stronger. Common sense has surrendered to fanaticism. The conservatives are now powerless to prevent the tragedy of disunion. I only hope that they can prevent a war, for surely the Black Republicans will not tolerate South Carolina's transgression. Pray that the conservatives rise up and prevent war, for if ever the two sections of this country engage in a trail of battle, neither France in its bloodiest days, nor England in its convulsions, nor yet Rome in its decline, could show a parallel."

The room was solemn.

"But I will talk no more of war. Talk encourages the act. It will not be our choice just the same. If the North attempts to coerce, then the South Carolinians will only defend themselves, and if such is the case, the deep South and the middle tier of slave states will see the injustice and join South Carolina's cause. But I see no reason why a Southern Confederacy cannot live peacefully, side by side with our northern neighbors. Let us pray that it will be so."

Henry paused, geared up for his conclusion.

"Our words today will accomplish nothing, solve nothing. Future events will dictate our course of action. There will be a convention, I am sure. We cannot be neutral, and when the time comes to vote for Union or secession, remember our peculiar situation, the helplessness of our women and children, and remember the contemptible stubbornness of the puritan mind."

There was loud and universal applause, Henry bowed slightly. Sheriff Peasley grabbed his hand, shook it vigorously, patted his shoulder. Suddenly, there was a loud hoot from the back of the room, then a great commotion of yelling and prancing. Anna looked over her shoulder, alarmed. She was surprised that the greatest praise was coming from the county's poorest sorts. She looked back at Henry. He'd disappeared, swallowed up by the admiring herd.

THE DAY HAD TURNED WARM. Water had risen in puddles in the muddy street, releasing earthy smells, manure. Jackson was quiet, nearly barren, no sounds penetrating the thick masonry of the courthouse. Kinchen strolled along the plank walk, socialized a little with the other waiting servants, exchanged plantation news: the births, the sickness, the deaths. He drifted back to the carriage and team, stationed himself there for the long wait, killing time, letting it pass as easily as air through lungs.

A buzz came from the courthouse, slight at first, then growing. Servants lifted their heads, curiously. Suddenly, the large double doors flung open, a jumbled crowd of white folks spilled out, loud, excited. The servants sprung to their feet, startled. The throng began to gang and mill about on the steps and planks, turning anxious faces back to the doorway. Henry, with Anna tight at his side, cut his way through, nodding at his peers, smiling nervously. Anna delicately blinking. The couple pushed their way through waving arms, suffering the intensity of the crowd. Kinchen felt the swarm move toward him, fought off an urge to flee, and held his ground. He came up, took his mistress by an arm, and whisked her to safety. Henry followed, barking instructions.

"I'll be dining and staying at Spruill's tonight!"

Kinchen nodded from the driver's seat.

"Drive safely on the roads! Don't suffer the horses!"

"Yeah suh!"

"I'll expect you at half past eight in the morning."

"Yeah suh." And the bays pulled off slowly. Anna turned to catch her husband's eyes, but they had turned to his admirers, and the fine black suit vanished into the crowd.

There was tightness in her shoulders, a trembling in her hands, and she didn't sit back in the carriage, until they were beyond the outskirts of town.

"My, was dat Massa Henry's speech dat caused such a ruckus?" asked

Kinchen with thrill in his voice.

"Yes, Kinchen, it was," said Anna plainly.

"My-my!"

And for a tiny instant he wanted to ask what his master had said, but, as was his habit, he let the impulse pass. Not his business, nor his place to know, that is unless Missas Anna volunteered the information. He hoped and listened for her voice, but her thoughts were not with his. They were mixed, shooting randomly, and she struggled to bring them to place; she had a vision of an untidy room that she desperately wanted to clean. It would be so simple just to take a broom to it, sweep it all away.

But the differences were too vast, the problems too entrenched; she knew there were no simple solutions. Still, she hoped that the great minds of the day might salvage some sort of compromise. Henry was not so hopeful. He had accepted that a split was inevitable, and this she could not imagine: Jamaica Plains, a foreign land.

She stared off into sleepy fields, her mind trying to grasp the concept of two nations and of the war that was likely to be fought between them. No matter how convincing Henry's argument, she could not dismiss the possibility of a contest. She knew men's pride, and she knew their fear, and both were terribly combustible.

A sharp gust turned her face, she shielded her eyes, and settled back deeper in her seat. The sun had grown weaker, and she pulled her wrap closer to her chin. The spinning carriage wheels caught her attention, she watched them for a moment, then looked at Kinchen, his mud-spattered coat, the gray scarf loose around his neck, the tilted derby. She imagined his face, alert, mindful of the road, creamy brown. Some white blood in his ancestry she wondered. She had thought about this previously. His mother had been very dark, but York had been light-skinned, Kinchen's a similar tint.

Her mind continued on this track. It had been there many times before, the core of the problems surrounding them, she believed. The skin and hair were different, yes, and the physique and other features generally so, but there was something else that she had never been able to put her finger on. She had heard various opinions. Most whites thought them deficient mentally, but she rejected that. She had known some clever ones during her twenty years among them, and she had known some very dull whites. Another common belief was that they were meant for labor, being physically large and strong, but this was undoubtedly false. Many were quite frail and small. Look at Kinchen. He was no Apollo.

There were as many opinions as there were people. They were bantered about quite freely, and she had heard them all: the lack of morals, ambition, discipline. She could go on and on, but none to her rang true. Still, there was something. Something she could not identify, despite years of conscious effort, and so she had concluded that the differences were beyond her personal intellect, and since she believed her intellect to be good, she perceived the differences were beyond just about anyone's intellect. And this, in her opinion, put it in God's realm. It was He who had thrown them together and for a purpose only known to Him. Could it be a test? No mortal on earth would ever solve His riddles. She was sure of that, and it was best not to dwell too long on it.

Once again, she reminded herself that she was powerless. She had concluded this a hundred times, but her conclusion had not prevented her mind from wandering back. Her deduction did not soothe the fear. Two extremes were pulling the country apart. Her birthplace was at the center of one, and her home the center of the other. The slaves were in the middle, the match head. She could clearly see a crevasse, black and frightening, and Henry had just pushed them closer to the edge. She shifted nervously in the carriage seat, reached and clasped an iron handle, squeezed it tightly.

"Nearly home, Missas," said Kinchen over the rattling carriage. They had closed on the Hoburn Gate, the entrance to Thornbury.

Anna didn't answer, but she felt some relief. She would be safe among the familiar. And she looked to the fields, to the burning stumps and the hands tending them. She smelled the smoke. It reminded her of burning leaves in New England, and she longed again for that simpler life, the same life she had wanted twenty years before. Keeping a nice tidy house in Boston. Oh, how different it would be.

14

THE BOY COLONEL

April 16, 1861

The Honorable Leroy P. Walker, Secretary of War,
Confederate States of America

Sir—

The object of this letter is to recommend Cadet H. K. Burgwyn, of North Carolina, for a commission in the Artillery of the Southern Confederacy. Mr. B. is not only a high-tone Southern gentleman, but, in consequence of the highly practical as well as scientific character of his mind, he possesses qualities well calculated to make him an ornament, not only to artillery, but to any branch of the military service.

       Thomas J. Jackson
       Prof. Nat. Phil. and Instr. Va.M.I.

May 20, 1861

Captain H. K. Burgwyn,
Camp Ellis, Raleigh, N.C.

Sir—

I hope this letter finds you well and not overly burdened in your important duties. By unanimous sentiment, and in expressing our appreciation of the benefits received, and from the very excellent lessons in drill given us during our sojourn at Camp Ellis, the Company, as further evidence of our respect and esteem, have resolved to present you this inscribed dress sword. We sincerely hope it meets with your approval and expectations.

Respectfully, Your Obedient Servant,

Captain Marshall Featherston Tompkins
Lafayette Light Infantry

JOURNAL OF EVENTS
H. K. BURGWYN, JR.
Lt. Col. 26th Regmt. N.C.V.

S T R I C T L Y

P R I V A T E

The 27th day of August, 1861
I was today elected Lt. Colonel of the 26th Regiment, North Carolina Troops. I am now 19 years, 9 months, & 27 days old & probably the youngest Lt. Colonel in the Confederate or U.S. Service. I mark the occasion by commencing my journal, and hope to have the time and energy to attend to it religiously. The command of the Camp of Instruction was given me on the 5th July, & after being disappointed in the organization of the 12th Regiment, I have been elected to a position in this the 26th. May Almighty God lend me His aid in discharging my duty to Him & to my country.

The Regiment is commanded by Colonel Zebulon B. Vance, a mountaineer and former Congressman from Buncombe County. A more devoted man to our Cause could not be found. He has the golden tongue of a statesman, speaks with great clarity, and the men receive great inspiration from his words. He has the uncommon ability to quickly win affection and friends, which, unfortunately, is not necessarily a good trait for a commander of a regiment. I fear he lacks knowledge in the military arts, and is not duly qualified for his rank and position.

We have, in all, 10 full companies. Most are farm boys from the Piedmont Counties, but we also have some mountain men. Fine specimens, a hardier, stronger set I have not seen. They take to discipline slowly, but once they see and understand its necessity, they embrace it wholeheartedly.

I will now allot some space for events since the opening of hostilities. The tidings of Mr. Lincoln's call for volunteers reached me while still at the Institute. The news sparked quite a commotion, and for me, I must admit, considerable turmoil. I knew not what to do, as Virginia and my native North Carolina had not yet seceded. The question on what to do, however, was soon answered, when

Colonel Smith ordered the Corps to pack up and march for Richmond. After an arduous trip, we were surprised with the level of excitement in the state capital and were soon infected by the war fever that prevailed within. There was little doubt that Virginia would go the way of her sisters to the south, and surely my Carolina would follow. That would prove exactly the case, but at the time these facts had not yet transpired.

The Corps was immediately instructed in its duties about the city, which soon became routine and rather tedious. The prevalent fear among the Cadets was that our talents would be wasted together as a unit, instead of being dispersed to new organizations where our expertise could be passed to new recruits and volunteers. Our fears were unjustified, & slowly & surely as the passing of time, the Cadets scattered to the four winds. At the time, I was very disappointed in not receiving a commission in the artillery as I had a letter of recommendation from Professor Jackson to the Secretary of War. Old Professor Jackson, since that time, has acquired the distinguished and martial name of "Stonewall," which he duly won for his heroics at our great victory at Manassas. If General Jackson's name had then carried the weight of fame that it now bears, I surely would be in the artillery.

On 30th April, & due in part to my Father's tireless efforts, I received a commission as Captain in the Provisional Army of North Carolina, & was instructed to report at Camp Ellis immediately. After some weeks of drilling volunteers, I yearned for the command of my own company & volunteered to recruit one hundred men from the wilds of Ashe County. A perfectly delightful trip, which will forever be stamped in my memory. I took the cars to Statesville via Salisbury, then hired a buggy for the remaining 70 miles to Jefferson. The foothill country reminded me very much of Occoneechee Neck, except that ours is richer & has the appearance of low bottom lands, while that of the prior has more the appearance of high table country. When I crossed the Yadkin near Wilkesboro I saw a very fine mountain cottage & some very fine level bottom land. It was a very pretty place & the land was very fine. If I had any money to invest, I could not think of any better way, I believe, to spend it than to purchase a farm of one or two hundred acres in those mountains somewhere & raise some stock. After this war is over, I intend to get a pair of saddle bags & go to that part of the state, buy a good horse, and travel all over it.

At Jefferson, I found the people to be good-natured, easy, with not a superfluity of energy, & rather disposed to take the world as it is. If I had gone there to recruit one-year volunteers, I would have had my quota in a fortnight. But as I was going in search of regulars, soldiers who would serve for the war's duration, my recruiting sojourn proved to be a miserable failure, & not due to the lack of effort on my part, I should add. I endeavored to see as many persons as possible, & attended public meetings, which were called for the sole purpose of getting volunteers. At each I made public speeches & private explanations. The sum total of my efforts equaled two names who were actually from Virginia, and as it turned out, would probably not have joined the company. Given the exhausting and discouraging situation, it was no wonder that I was enticed back to Raleigh with a promise of promotion to Major and the command of the Camp of Instruction at Crabtree. That appointment, of course, led to my current position with the 26th.

There has been a state of war for nearly five months, but I have yet to hear a shot fired in anger. That, I believe, will soon change. The enemy has taken Hatteras Island & our destination will not be Virginia as we had supposed. Orders are just received to get ready to leave as soon as possible. We are bound for Fort Macon on the Carolina Coast. All are ready to start & anxious for a brush with the Yankees.

The 1st day of September, 1861

Today we arrived in New Berne where I met my Father. He was sent by Governor Ellis to take possession of some small arms, which are supposed to be on board an English vessel now laying off Beaufort. Our reunion was brief, as Father was in earnest. Before parting, he left to my charge a second horse, Waverly, and Kinchen, an old friend. I protested the appointment, sighting that both were too valuable to risk. Father was perfectly insistent, & my arguments were in vain. I must say though, that I am pleased with the appointments, & Kinchen seems very well disposed to his new title, "A Colonel's Gentleman."

The 3rd day of September, 1861

Tonight the regiment arrived at Morehead City. I gave the men permission to sleep in the cars, while I, with Kinchen, went in search of a suitable billet for both me and the horses. Nothing could be found due to the late hour, so I now write with the aid of a candle while resting at the foot of a weeping willow.

The 6th day of September, 1861

Yesterday the regiment arrived here, Bogue Banks, and I am very pleased to see that the camp we now occupy is named for Father—Camp Burgwyn. Spent last night in an old fisherman's cabin, & I must say, that of all the nights I ever spent in the neighborhood of mosquitoes, last night was the worst. No sleep visited my weary eyes until very late & oh the mosquitoes, how they did trouble me with their constant buzzing and biting. Kinchen had the perfect solution, tobacco and his pipe. The smoke kept the bloodthirsty fairly at bay. I was tempted to lend aid, but remembered my vow to Mother not to smoke until the age of twenty-five.

When the time came for sleep & the pipe extinguished, the pests returned. Kinchen slept soundly, seemingly undisturbed, but I, after a few short hours of fitful slumber, woke & found myself nearly devoured.

The 17th day of September, 1861

I am field officer of the day with only 25 men under me. An unnecessary waste of rank it appears to me. I greatly lament that I have been unable to excite more attention to the necessity of aiding nature by art & rendering our security perfect. Making rifle pits from sand dunes seems to satisfy the local strategists. I've been insisting that we build bomb proof shelters for the men, so as to render the enemy cannon harmless, but my pleas fall on deaf ears.

The sight of these poor free Negroes who have been hired to aid in the building of fortifications both alarms and depresses me. They have scarcely any clothes, and are starved to the bone. I am told that their wages are months past due, & they have no money for food or other pressing necessities. Sadness overcomes me at the sight of these poor creatures. Despite the good service, their needs must be fulfilled, or they must be sent home. I will write Father about the matter forthwith.

The 22nd day of September, 1861, Bogue Island, 9 PM
This morning I was informed that Yankees had landed 2 miles below our camp. Took 4 companies, about 350 men, & investigated. It proved a false alarm.

The 28th day of September, 1861
My diet of late has been almost exclusively fresh fish, which is both abundant and cheap. Kinchen has proved a miserable cook. I fear I must suffer from his attempts for quite some time, as I do not expect a furlough before Christmas. But, at my first opportunity, at my next visit to Thornbury, I shall earnestly put Aunt Ruthy to work with lessons.

The 4th day of October, 1861
If we could get some efficient officers, particularly a Colonel who knew something of the management of a regiment, the 26th could be a very fine regiment.

The 9th day of October, 1861
I am troubled with my efforts of late to acquaint Kinchen with the duties of his new position. I have been forced to use a heavy hand at times, & I've been quite stern. I am afraid I've deeply hurt his feelings on several occasions, & this is a shame for he tries very hard. I will endeavor to curb my anger, but he simply must improve.

The 11th day of October, 1861, Camp near Fort Macon
Colonel Vance has located our new camp on clay soil, where the drainage is very poor. I suggested that we relocate, but he replied that the men had already built chimneys to their tents & don't want to move. He himself is now quite unwell from the unhealthiness of the location.

The 15th day of October, 1861
I went to bed about 9 o'clock last night, & about eleven there came up the

most furious storm which we have ever had, I think. My large tent, which was already pretty nearly destroyed, had its destruction completed by the night's winds. We are still in the same mud hole, and I have remonstrated with Vance time & again. Yesterday, the Colonel of a nearby regiment told him if he remained here all his men would be sick. Vance knows nothing, and is perfectly ignorant of the machinations of a regiment.

The 18th day of October, 1861

Received today a brief missive from A.L.D. A ray of joy that shines on these dark days in camp.

The 26th day of December, 1861

A great many deaths in my regiment, much sickness still, & the discipline wretched. Since the events in the previous pages, I have been very sick with typhoid fever. While still at Fort Macon, dear Kinchen tried his best to nurse me back to health, but the fever would not release its heavy grip. I left Camp Wilkes on the 24th October & remained a few days at Carolina City Hospital, where I was continually dosed with Calomel by a drunken doctor that, I must admit, I myself had recommended as surgeon to the regiment. Father came down & removed me to New Berne where, under the care of Dr. Hughes, I gradually grew better until the fever left me. During this time, the great Federal Armada, which was commanded by Commodore DuPont passed south & was exposed to a very severe gale. The crew, some 80 odd of the steamer Union, which went ashore off Bogue Banks, were captured by my regiment and sent to Raleigh. I myself went to Raleigh & after remaining a week or ten days, went to Thornbury and stayed there another week, but on my return from there, I commenced to have chills, which so reduced me & weakened my strength as to detain me till the 23rd December. I arrived here the next day, & on Christmas Day reported for duty. Hereafter I will be, I hope, more punctual in attending to the journal.

While in Raleigh, I was very much honored by daily visits from A.L.D. who nursed my nearly broken spirits. I must say, I miss her company very much.

The 3rd day of January, 1862, Camp Vance

Good health has returned and my time has been very well occupied, what with being in command, drilling 4 hours a day, hearing & giving recitations on tactics, attending to improving the winter quarters, and a score of whatever else may come up on any particular day.

I attended a party on New Year's Eve in Beaufort & there saw all the beauties of the burg. Alas poor Yorick, to the eye of so accomplished a judge, all exhibited failings, & out of 60 or 70 there was not one really pretty. Of course, none could compare to my A.L.D.

The 4th day of February, 1862

None of our regiments are so efficient as they should be. My own is the best &, if it had a good Colonel, would be a most capital regiment. Colonel Vance is a man without any system or regularity whatsoever, & has so little of an engineering mind as to say that the Croatan entrenchments are worthless, unless the enemy lands & attacks us there. His abilities appear to me to be more overrated than those of any other person I know. As an instance of his procrastinating habits: the regiment has been in service since 27th August &, until today, we have not had a color bearer of general guides appointed. If I have mentioned the matter to Vance once I have done so 20 times. Some of his officers are exceedingly inefficient in tactics, & could they only be got rid of, the regiment would be much improved. I am exceedingly disgusted with my present position. Vance is totally unsuitable in my opinion & I am heartily tired of being under his command. As for discipline, not the faintest idea of it has ever entered his head. One or two things of late occurrence I will mention. I reported 27 officers absent from a reveille, & he did not even ask them all why they did not go. I reported two or three absent from drill. Not a syllable did he say to them concerning it to my knowledge. Oh, if only I could get a Colonelcy of my own regiment.

The 8th day of February, 1862, Camp Branch

The regiment arrived at our new quarters near New Berne yesterday. Today I took a tour of three forts along the Neuse below the town. Fort Thompson, 5 miles downstream, is the strongest and mounts ten guns. Fort Ellis is next and mounts nine. Fort Lane is closest to the town, and is the smallest of the three. It mounts but 4 guns. The last two forts, I believe, are designed very poorly. All the guns are directed downstream, are not casemated, and thus, can be easily enfiladed by any vessel after passing them, without the possibility of a reply from a single gun. Since both forts occupy bluffs on high ridges with slopes on the river and land sides, a better design would be to cut embrasures through the top of the crest, the guns be planted under a brick arch three feet thick, & the whole be covered with ten feet of earth. These could serve as a counter-battery to enfilading fire.

Tomorrow there will be a review of all the troops defending New Berne. This evening we had some extra drill to insure a good show.

The 10th day of February, 1862

In reading the New Berne Progress, I saw an article supposing to be a passage from a Philadelphia newspaper. It said that Burnside lost 40 to 50 vessels in the late storm. While riding out the gale, the General chose to remain on deck, despite the protestations of his staff. He made a brave reply, "I am in the hands of God." A few more storms as this & if he don't mind, I'll say he will be in the hands of the Devil.

The 11th day of February, 1862

Kinchen, who just arrived from an errand from town, has passed me a rumor that Burnside has taken Roanoke Island, a disaster if true. It is the key to all of eastern North Carolina.

The 15th day of February, 1862

Today we learned that Elizabeth City, Edenton, and Plymouth have fallen to Burnside. Predictable occurrences, given the fall of Roanoke Island. I have written Father & told him that no navigable stretch of the Roanoke is safe, and recommended that he remove all his cotton, even if he has to haul it. Also advised him to make preparations to remove his Negroes.

We may expect disaster and defeat just so long as we expose small detachments, unsupported by any convenient troops, to attack by the enemy. My conviction that we had better withdraw all our troops from Washington & Hyde & concentrate them at the most important point grows stronger each day. If New Berne is the most important, concentrate them here, or at Weldon, or the Blackwater. Exposing 4,000 men to 15,000 of the enemy & expecting the minority to conquer is the extreme of bad judgment.

The 27th day of February, 1862

Tidings are that Burnside has returned to Hatteras & will attack us here shortly. My candid opinion is that when he does, New Berne will fall just as Roanoke Island did, saving that we will not be taken prisoners. It is a very great mistake, it appears to me, to divide our troops, so as to expose the detachments to a certain defeat. I am not giving up. My spirit rises with each of our disasters. Not a particle of yielding is within me, but I do wish to see better generalship, so that a fair show can be given to our men.

The 3rd day of March, 1862

Took a patrol downstream & saw many new improvements to the forts. They are casemated now, & several new, smaller batteries have been added, so to scatter the fire of the enemy. A few charred logs are to be added as well, so to addle their brains.

The 12th day of March, 1862

Intelligence deemed to be very reliable has been received to the effect that the enemy is close at hand & preparing to attack us. Fifteen steamers are only 7 miles below us & probably will attack on the morrow, or certainly the next day. The news was received by our men with no cheering, no undue exultation, no efforts to keep their spirits up with noisy demonstrations, but every eye brightened, every arm grew nervous, & the most deadly determination is on all. The enemy may rely upon a hard fight, but God's Providence is over us all. Though having His omnipotence constantly before me lately, I am much more impressed with it now, & I am sure He will order all for the best. I am in the best spirits *imaginable. I used to think the night before a battle I would be anxious for my own fate & that of the day. Now, if I had my wish exclusive of the fact that our defenses may be improved with delay, I would not postpone the fight a day. May God's will be done.*

⚜ 15 ⚜

A FALSE CHRISTENING

IT WAS A MELANCHOLY MARCH afternoon. The rain had stopped, but a chilly mist prevailed. Staring into the campfire lost in thought, Kinchen poked at the coals, while the smoke curled upward, spreading into a thin veil, reluctant to mix with the mist. He was sitting on Harry's black trunk, wet, shining in the pale light. Inside were all his master's effects: an extra uniform, socks, a stack of letters, his journal. Behind him was Harry's new white tent fly, and behind that, Waverly was snoozing in an old tumble-down shed.

The camp was alive with soldiers in gray strutting here and there. They seemed on some earnest mission, but were doing nothing much at all. There was a sense of nervous excitement about, but it hadn't infected Kinchen. The Yankees were at hand, they all said, but the slave doubted it; he'd heard such rumors before.

Now and then his eyes would roll up from the fire, and he'd watch the proud, gray roosters swagger. He'd crack a tiny smile, laugh inside. They thought this was the center of the universe; that both of the Lord's eyes were upon them, and His angels had all gathered in tribute. "Vanity, a wicked curse on humanity," was one of Missas Anna's favorite sayings, he recalled.

Three crows cawed in a nearby swamp, an obnoxious racket. Kinchen watched them flap awkwardly among the stunted pines and scraggly brush. An ugly guttural noise escaped from deep within their throats, then one would caw and another would strive to outdo him. It went on and on, they wouldn't leave. Evil birds, guardians of the camp's trash.

Kinchen spied an unusual sight, a white man not in uniform. He was walking up the muddy path from the brickyard, which was about five hundred yards from the camp and near the works. The man wore spattered black riding boots, thigh-high, very fine. A slick cape was thrown over his shoulders. A brown felt hat dangled from a cord around his neck. He was dressed as a gentleman, walked like one, slow and steady, but his cheeks were dented and scarred, and his nose long and bent, with a hump in the middle. His features showed poor breeding, and Kinchen sensed he wasn't a gentleman at all.

Nobody else seemed to notice him. When he reached the camp, he veered to the right, toward the swamp, and walked between it and the tents. Now and then he would stop and look about. Unlike everyone else, he didn't seem to be in a hurry to get anywhere, didn't appear to be looking for anyone in particular. What was he doing in camp? Kinchen watched him turn toward the swamp, speeding the crows on their way, as he made his approach. He stopped at the edge, emitted a dry cough, then turned and looked back at the camp again. The white man's eyes panned around the tents, caught the Negro looking at him, but ignored him. It was queer, this man. Kinchen seldom saw white men around camp not in uniform, at least not accompanied by an officer, especially one slinking around like this fellow.

The muffled sound of many voices distracted him. It came from off to his left, and Kinchen turned to check its source. A tangled mass of men was walking down the County Road from New Berne. They were carrying guns, but there was no formation to their ranks. There were hundreds of them, but not one wearing a uniform. Kinchen spied a soldier with two stripes on his arm, head down, trudging through the camp mud toward him. Kinchen stood up.

"Soldier, suh."

The Corporal stopped, looked up.

"Yeah."

Kinchen pointed to the mass of marching men. "Who's dem?"

The Corporal peered to the left. "They's militia. Come here to help us fight the Yankees."

Kinchen nodded. "Who's him?" and he pointed toward the mysterious man by the swamp. The Corporal turned and squinted through the mist, then looked back at Kinchen.

"Who?"

"Him." Kinchen kept pointing, then looked at the swamp. The white man in gentleman's clothing had disappeared.

TWO GRAY SHADOWS, EACH LEADING A HORSE, moved noiselessly through the dim pines. The wet forest glistened in the wintry dusk, and the figures' slight movements released a cold shower from every needle, twig, and branch. The officers paused and listened. Both were shivering, but more from excitement than from the cold and damp. Other than the steady drippings on the forest floor, the evening was still and solemn. Then came the echo of axes striking soft pine.

"They're cutting a road along the rails," Harry whispered to Graham, an old mate from college days at the University of North Carolina, now a lieutenant in the Second North Carolina Cavalry. Graham nodded.

"Moving up their guns. They'll attack in the morning."

Graham nodded again.

Harry held a hand near Turk's steaming nose, and just stood and listened. The chopping grew heavier, louder.

Graham smirked, "Did you ever imagine we'd be here back at Chapel Hill?"

Harry didn't hear him, hypnotized by the chopping.

"Where are your pickets?" Harry whispered.

"Back there, to the right, about three hundred yards."

"You'll have to pull them in after dark."

Graham looked up into the rapidly fading light. "It's almost dark now."

"We'll go back in a moment," Harry replied.

Graham looked at the young Lt. Colonel as he peered into the forest, his face heavy with concentration.

"Will they attack us on the right? Will they work around our flank?" Graham asked.

"Your company's up against the creek, right?"

"That's right."

"There's no bridge below Weathersby's, and there's none on our flank. No, they have to attack our front."

"We're mighty weak out there, just our two companies and a section from Captain Brem's battery."

"I'll be there in the morning," Harry assured him. "Vance is sending me over with four companies to take command of the flank."

Suddenly, they heard a shout about a hundred yards to their left, then murmuring voices, much closer. Harry motioned Graham to withdraw. They crept back through the thick stand of pines, then arrived at a clearing where they mounted. A slow walk through the dark brought them to one of Graham's pickets, where sign and countersign were exchanged. They ordered the pickets to the redoubts, then made for Bryce's Creek and Weathersby's Road, which they followed to the battery. Harry took his leave of Graham there and followed a path to the swamp. Guiding his buckskin gelding, he waded the belly-deep bog and came out to the right of the redoubts occupied by his regiment. He made a report to Colonel Vance, then invited J. J. Young, the regimental quartermaster, to dine with him. The two trotted down the line of trenches, crossed the railroad, entered the brickyard now occupied by some militia, then turned left and followed the muddy path to the far end of the camp.

Kinchen was huddled by the fire beside Harry's tent fly, cooking some not-so-fresh fish, soupy corn meal, and scorched coffee.

Harry and Captain Young paid little notice of the slave who served them. Instead, they sat near the fire and talked excitedly of tomorrow's prospects.

Kinchen took Turk back to the shed, removed the saddle and bridle, cleaned off the mud, dried him, covered him with a blanket, then fed him.

"We'll hold them. The works are strong, the boys are ready for a squall, and we have reinforcements coming, a whole brigade," Young claimed optimistically.

Harry didn't share his confidence. The Confederate line was over two miles long, from Fort Thompson on the Neuse River up across the County

Road, over the railroad, through the brickyard, and then a full mile to Bryce's Creek. Only four thousand men were available to man the works and three-quarters of these were between the fort and the railroad. Only the Twenty-sixth and two companies of dismounted cavalry held the right. There was hardly any reserve, just one infantry regiment and the rest of the Second Cavalry, and they were up the County Road, far away from the right wing. Burnside and fifteen thousand Federals were out there in the woods. If they were to attack the right in force and break the Twenty-sixth, they could turn and crush the rest of the Rebels against the river bank. Reinforcements wouldn't be up until tomorrow afternoon at the earliest, and Harry was sure the Yankees would attack in the morning.

"General Branch has left us fairly defenseless," was Harry's claim.

After the poor fare, Harry ordered Young to go back to the regiment and bring companies B, E, F, and K back to camp. He was to take the companies to the other side of the swamp, on the far right, so they would be in proper position at dawn.

Harry went to his trunk, removed a pen, an ink-well, and his journal, then went to his fly. After lighting a candle, he opened his diary and made the day's entry, then finished the ritual with a silent prayer. Ready or not, he was excited about the prospects of his first baptism of war.

He closed the journal, blew out the candle, and left the fly. He placed everything back in the trunk, and looked about for his servant.

"Kinchen?"

A subdued response came from the shed, and Harry found him quietly brushing the horses, as they ate from a small pile of fodder.

"I've been ordered to take four companies to the far right."

"Yeah suh." Kinchen didn't look up from his work. He wasn't his usual contented self. Hadn't been for weeks. His reunion with Harry had come off nicely at first, but it hadn't taken long for his new master to express and enforce his dominance. He was no longer Kinchen's childhood friend who happened to be the master's son. Years of schooling and the army had changed all that. Harry was a perfectionist, wanted things done his way, had become more and more intolerant of Kinchen's little imperfections, like his cooking. Harry had lost his temper on several occasions, and still hadn't appeared at all satisfied with his body servant.

"The horses and you will remain here at camp."

"Yeah, suh."

This pouty mood irked Harry. If it had been anyone else but Kinchen, he would have asked his father to replace him long ago.

"It'll be safe here."

Kinchen still had that wounded look, like an injured deer. He didn't answer, and Harry shifted his feet.

"But if there's any sign of trouble, any at all, you bring the horses and the trunk through the swamp. I'll be on the other side. Understand?"

"Yeah suh."

"If I have any trouble, I'll send for you, and you come right away."

"Yeah suh. I'll come."

Damn, if he doesn't snap out of this soon, I'll have to send him home, Harry thought.

"Well, I'll be leaving now."

Kinchen continued at his work, but then remembered his promise to Massa Henry and Missas Anna.

"Now yuh take care, suh. Don't yuh go needlessly exposing your person. Your Mamma, your Papa, they'd never forgive me."

"No Kinchen, I'll be careful."

Kinchen's pitiful expression hadn't changed. Harry wished he could say something to make him smile, but nothing came to mind. Perhaps Mother and Father have coddled him too much. No. He was hard worker, the best damn stable hand and coachman they'd ever had.

Harry reached out and touched his servant's shoulder. "Supper was good."

Kinchen looked up with black, saucer eyes. He knew Harry was just being polite.

"Um-hmm."

Harry stepped back. Nothing he said did any good. He'd dented the only thing Kinchen really had, his pride.

"Good-bye."

Not long after Harry had left, Kinchen remembered the mysterious white man who had been in camp, the man dressed as a gentleman.

"Lawdy, I's forgot ta tell 'im 'bout it."

BECAUSE THE SWAMP WAS THICK AND DEEP from the late winter rains, Harry led the four companies up the railroad toward New Berne until they came to an old wagon track. The track, which was really nothing but a couple of ruts crowded by the piney woods, skirted above the swamp and met Weathersby's Road. A left turn would eventually bring them to the battery and the far right wing of the Confederate line.

It was so dark two men were sent ahead with lanterns, and more soldiers carrying lanterns were interspersed within the column. If the companies lost contact with one another, they wouldn't wander blindly into the woods. The cloudy night, moist air, and thick forest allowed no natural light to penetrate the evergreen canopy. Each man could hardly see the fellow marching ahead of him, and they marched so tightly, that if one man stopped, it would start a chain reaction of bumping, tripping, and cursing. Finally, they reached the wider and well-traveled Weathersby's Road, where there was no canopy and the column could loosen up.

From the black came a chorus of snorting horses, hundreds of them. The eerie medley was unnerving, but they all knew this miserable blind walk in the dark would soon be over. The two companies of cavalry occupied this part of the line, and the snorting came from their mounts.

Around the bend came the glow of campfires. The column stopped, and Harry went in search of an area to bivouac. About a hundred yards behind the redoubts was another pine grove so thick, that if the men raked away the top layer of brown needles, the ones beneath would be dry. A perfect place. Soon, three hundred and fifty men filtered in, and the grove became illuminated by many fires, the smooth scent of burning pine filling the night air.

Beside his companies from the Twenty-sixth and the cavalry, Harry was to take under his command the section of artillery. He called in the commanders of each unit, and was apprised of the ground and defenses. He gave out instructions for the morning. Harry's infantry was to hold the redoubts between the swamp and Weathersby Road. The battery of two guns lay astride the road, and the dismounted cavalry was to defend the broken ground between it and Bryce's Creek. The stream was wide and deep, so there was little risk of a flank attack, but just in case, mounted vedettes were sent up the road to cross a bridge upstream. They were to work down the opposite bank and provide advance warning of any enemy attempt to reach their flank or rear. Later that night, an independent company of infantry arrived to give the line additional strength. Harry positioned them in the rear as a reserve.

After all dispositions were complete and all orders given and understood, Harry made a prearranged visit to his old college mate Lieutenant Graham's tent. He was invited to spend the night there, but neither man had much sleep. They talked until late, a little about school days, but mostly about how many Yankees they would slay in the morning. Long after the fires had smoldered down, and all candles had been extinguished, Harry tossed and turned. Excitement, fear, and anticipation held his mind alert. It would not shut off.

After tomorrow, he thought, some full, young lives would be no more.

DAWN ROLLED IN GLOOMY AND GRAY. The mist was gone, replaced by a thick fog. Harry thought this a terrible disadvantage. The lack of visibility would hamper their defense.

Before there was any light, he had his entire command at their posts with orders to remain perfectly quiet and listen. The men were shivering in the trenches, looking into the gray haze, their hands gripping their rifles so firmly that knuckles stood out white. Harry stood perfectly still; he yawned repeatedly. His orderly thought this peculiar, what with everyone else's nerves stretched and tingling. But the Lieutenant Colonel had made a pact with himself during his sleepless night. He would endeavor to remain and appear perfectly calm, so as to inspire his men.

The peace was broken by the solitary report of a cannon, away to the left, probably down at Fort Thompson. Harry thought the shot had the sound of a Parrot gun. He grabbed the cord hanging from his neck and pulled his gold watch from under his shirt. It was just after seven o'clock. More shots rang out, and the enemy began answering, slowly at first, then steadily, becoming incessant. Gradually, the cannonade moved down the line from left to right, growing ever louder. Some of the firing seemed to come from across the swamp, but it was hard to tell; fog distorted the sounds. Then came the sharp crackle of rifle volleys, also from far down the line. It rose, then faded, then rose again to a crescendo mingling with the roar of artillery. The men shifted around in the trenches. Harry concentrated on his front. Visibility was less than twenty-five yards, and if the Yankees moved out of the woods and crossed the cut-over area before their trenches, the Confederates would not see them. Harry moved to the front of a trench, leaned over the parapet, and looked into the white soup. How could they be fighting down the line? How could they see what they were firing at? He realized if the enemy advanced, they could rush his redoubts before a volley could be fired to stop them. He had to be prepared. The order went down the line.

"Fix bayonets!"

KINCHEN WAS BUILDING A FIRE WHEN the first sharp blast of the Parrot gun ripped through the still morning. It surprised him. He dropped an armful of firewood, but then it was quiet again. He continued at his chores. Then came more shots, then more. They grew louder, closer. The horses were moving around in the shed, frightened. He went back to calm them.

The sound of battle roared through the camp. Kinchen remained in the shed and listened to the horrible racket. He talked to Waverly and Turk, and rubbed them anxiously. The scent of burning powder drifted in and out occasionally, and it caused him to peer out. The fog had thinned some, but it was still too thick to see beyond the tents. Time seemed to be standing still. The crackle of rifles, the boom of artillery, how long would it last? He thought he'd been in the shed for hours.

Gradually, the faint yelling of men mixed with the ceaseless roar of guns. He heard the scamper of footsteps, and caught a glimpse of a man running by the shed. Kinchen looked out, saw the silhouettes of a handful of men loping through the haze, some twenty, then forty, scurrying through the camp. He stepped just outside the door, called out to the closest moving body.

"Whar' yuh goin'?"

The body paused, pointed behind him. "There's Yankees in the brickyard!" he yelled, then continued his flight. Kinchen noticed he wasn't wearing the gray. He was one of those militia.

A whole tide of men came streaming through the camp, running over and through the tents, trampling them. He could see their faces now, pale and panicked, like rabbits running from a burning field of broom sage. An officer came bellowing from the left, his sword waving.

"Rally, men! Stop here! Rally!"

Most of the fleeing militia just glanced at him and kept running. Some paused for a moment only to start up again, when they saw most of their friends and comrades still heading for the woods. An older fellow with a bushy white beard wasn't running, but came ambling through the camp at a fast gait. The officer directed his pleas at him.

"Stop here, help me stop your boys."

The old man ignored him, and the officer screamed an oath, deciding to try humiliation.

"Think of the papers; they'll be full of what cowards you are."

The old man paused, glared at the officer. "I'd rather fill a hundred newspapers than one damned grave." He resumed his hurried pace. The last of the militia bolted through the camp. The officer looked down at the mud, his sword lowered at his side.

Standing by the fire he had not been able to start, Kinchen looked at the discouraged soldier, a little bewildered.

"What's goin' on?" Kinchen yelled.

The officer looked up, saw the black face through the white vapors, but said nothing. Kinchen could see the lines of concentration on the pale flesh. The eyes were sad and dull, but slowly grew wider, as if they had just been alerted to danger. The officer sheathed his sword and ran back to the left.

Kinchen didn't quite know what to make of this. There were Yankees in the brickyard. What did it mean? The firing was still just as heavy, even heavier, up and down the line. The camp was quiet though, not a soul in it. He had no idea the center of the Confederate line had cracked wide open.

What had Massa Harry said? "Come to me at the slightest sign of trouble." Kinchen figured this was trouble and time to saddle the horses.

He pulled off the blankets, and folded them hurriedly. He was heaving a saddle onto Waverly when a spattering of shots cracked over the roar at the front, close. He went to the door. Sunlight cut through the fog. There was a flash, like the reflection off a metal gun barrel. Three figures were hunched over in the camp, fiddling with the tents. Kinchen eyed them suspiciously. A patch of fog drifted between the shed and the tents, and he lost sight of the pilferers. When the cloud passed the sun shone bright. Kinchen saw blue. Blue uniforms! He instinctively ducked behind the door.

"Yankees!" he hissed, "Yankees in the camp!"

His mind raced. What to do? If he tried to saddle the horses, they might hear him. If he tried to steal out with them, they would surely see him. He stood perfectly still, clutching the cold planked wall, his heart beating heavy in his chest.

His ears strained to listen, tuning out the roar of guns, trying to hear any footsteps approaching.

There came a loud shout, behind him, behind the shed, up in the woods. Kinchen sensed a lot of men up there, a lot of men. Then came an incredible crack, a whining sound, rap, rap, bap against the wood. Balls were hitting the shed. He fell to the dirt floor, into the hay and dung. The horses kicked and whinnied, their hooves dancing around his head, knocking off his derby. Kinchen grabbed it and rolled clear; he got to his knees. He heard another shout, then yelling, cheering. A wave passed the shed. He crawled to the door, saw the backs of men, a long line of men. They were running through the camp, toward the brickyard. They wore the gray.

COLONEL VANCE RODE AT THE EDGE of the grove, up and down the line. An unceasing flood of words bellowed from his mouth. He had not shut it since the guns had begun their work.

Three times the Yankees had rushed the redoubts, and three times they had been easily repulsed. There had to be two hundred of them dead and dying among the stumps, the Colonel thought,

The enemy was firing high. Even mounted, Vance had bullets whizzing above him all morning.

"Keep it up, boys! They can't break you! Let 'em keep trying, we'll lay 'em to waste!"

He paused for a moment. A deafening racket rose on the left, thick sounds of fighting. He hadn't heard anything from the right, across the swamp.

J. J. Young came panting up, frosty breath puffing from his mouth. "Beg-begging to report—Colonel, sir."

"Go on, Captain," said Vance, looking down from his horse.

"Maj- Major Carmichael—dead sir—shot through the head."

Vance sank in his saddle. Carmichael, third ranking officer in the regiment, a fine soldier, dead. He took a moment to reflect on that.

"What's goin' on over there, Captain?"

"We're in a bad way, sir." Young had caught his breath. "That damned militia ran, sir, cowards. They just up and ran and left a hole right in the center of our line around the brickyard, but the Thirty-third came up from reserve and plugged it. Did a fine job of it, I should say. They're on our left now."

"So we're holding them," Vance interjected.

"Yes sir, but the Yanks attacked again, sir. Right at the brickyard. A whole brigade, I think. They seem to know our weakest point. Very strange."

Vance pulled at his chin. "Are you implying treachery in our ranks?"

Young stammered. "Well, yes—yes, sir—treachery—or—or—a paid Yankee spy."

"Don't think on that, Captain," Vance said sourly. "So a brigade attacked again. Are we holding them?"

"Yes sir, we are, and the Thirty-third is holding, but the Thirty-fifth, you know, Colonel Sinclair's regiment?"

Vance nodded.

"Well, they up and ran too, and the Yanks poured through. I saw Yankee flags on the parapets. Our whole line, right down to Fort Thompson, is retreating back to New Berne, sir. We and the Thirty-third, and Colonel Burgwyn on the right—we're the only ones left on the field. Enemy's working up the County Road, moving toward the railroad. They'll cut us off."

Vance stood up in his stirrups, looked down the line to his left. The sun had burned away the fog, but a cloud of smoke obscured his view. The crackle of rifle fire was at its height. Still, there were no orders no news from General Branch.

"Are you sure about that, Captain?"

"Oh yes, sir. Was over there myself, behind the Thirty-third. Colonel Hoke had to pull three companies out of line to guard his flank. Some Yankees were behind him, firing into his rear."

His boys were doing well, and he hated to pull out. But Young was right. If they didn't rush up the railroad immediately, the only escape route would be through the swamp and up Weathersby's Road to the bridges over Bryce's Creek.

"Very well, Captain. Go to Hoke and tell him to withdraw up the railroad. We'll be right behind him."

"Yes, sir." Young saluted and trotted off toward the smoke.

"Orderly!" Vance screamed.

"Yes, sir!"

"Go through the swamp to Colonel Burgwyn and tell him to withdraw. Tell him the left and center are defeated and are retreating to New Berne."

Vance then called for his adjutant, told him to pull the troops out of the redoubts. They would go double quick to the railroad.

AFTER THE THIRTY-THIRD PASSED through the camp, sweeping the Yankees before them, Kinchen finished saddling the horses. He then broke down Harry's tent fly and packed everything into the black trunk. He looked over the wreck of the camp. What would come of those things, he wondered.

Beside the consistent clatter at the front, everything else had quieted again at camp. The trouble was gone. Kinchen decided not to leave quite yet. He sat on the trunk instead, smoking his pipe, and listening. His stomach gurgled; he hadn't had a bite to eat all morning and it was getting close to noon.

A long double line of Confederates came jogging up the path from the brickyard. Kinchen stood up and watched their approach. They ran right through the camp, passed him, then up the little incline into the woods.

"What reg'ment ya'll be?" Kinchen yelled.

"The Thirty-third," someone answered.

The long line slithered past like a frightened snake. An officer came trotting up beside his men, his sword tucked tight against his arm. He spied Kinchen watching the procession.

"You better get out of here, boy!" he shouted as he passed.

Another soldier yelled advice: "Get outta here, Yankees right behind us!"

Kinchen quickly knocked his burning pipe against the bottom of his boot and stuffed it in his coat pocket, then pulled his derby tight on his head. He was reaching down to pick up the trunk when bullets whistled in from the direction of the County Road. The line of Rebels near him recoiled and crouched, then went to their knees and returned fire. Kinchen squatted behind the trunk. Another sharp volley rolled down from the woods behind them. A Yankee flag was waving through the bare trees. They were cut off.

Some of the gray soldiers dropped their guns and ran for the swamp. Kinchen jumped on Waverly and grabbed for Turk's hanging reins. He realized he'd been too hasty. The trunk. He looked back at it. Another volley came whistling in, buzzing his head. Couldn't get it. He put his heels to Waverly's side as the rest of the Rebels bolted. Leading Turk, Kinchen galloped ahead and splashed into the swamp.

"ARE YOU SURE HE SAID WITHDRAW TOWARD New Berne?" Harry asked Vance's orderly who had just waded the swamp.

"Well, no sir. Ah, I mean, yes sir. Colonel Vance said the left and center were defeated and retreating to New Berne."

Harry shook his head in frustration. "Where is the enemy?"

The orderly shrugged, "Not sure, sir. I think they're on the County Road."

"So the Colonel is retiring up the railroad?"

The orderly's eye's flashed, "Yes, yes, he's retiring up the railroad."

"Very good, we'll try to catch up with them there," Harry finally surmised.

The two companies of cavalry were already mounted and poised on Weathersby's Road. The section of artillery was limbering up. Harry ordered his infantry to form behind them and put Captain John Lane in charge of the rear guard. He then ordered the cavalry to strike on ahead and use the old wagon track that intersected the railroad. Once they arrived at the rails, they were to find Colonel Vance.

They hadn't fired a shot. Harry had heard the terrible fighting down the line all morning, but not a single Yankee had shown himself on their front. That was disappointing, but not as disheartening as the news just arrived. Now they had to make a mad dash for New Berne to avoid being cut off and captured.

There was Kinchen, sitting on the side of Weathersby Road, soaking wet, shivering, Waverly and Turk tied to a sapling behind him. He'd brushed against a tree and fallen into the swamp during his harried flight, then had to chase down the horses. Limping, working his way through the piney woods, he'd come upon the road, but hadn't been sure which direction to go. Then the cavalry galloped up and told him Colonel Burgwyn and the infantry were right behind them. Kinchen sat, and waited.

Harry had been troubled as to Kinchen's fate, but the confusion had prevented any effort on his part to find him. The sight of him by the road was a great relief. Here he was, a little out of sorts, but safe.

"Yankees! Colonel Harry, hundreds!"

"Where?"

"Back dare," Kinchen thrust a thumb over his shoulder.

"Did you see them? Had they reached the railroad?"

"Don't know for sho', didn't really see 'em, but saw dare bullets. No, didn't really see da bullets, felt 'em."

Harry suppressed a grin, untied the horses and handed the servant Waverly's reins. "That's fine, Kinchen. Glad you came through all right, saved the horses. Very good."

Harry didn't see his trunk. "Where's the trunk?"

Kinchen glanced downward. "Couldn't get it, suh."

Harry frowned. All his personal effects, gone. He imagined dirty Yankee hands fingering through his journal. The look hit Kinchen like a dagger.

"Well, couldn't be helped I suppose," Harry said resignedly. Kinchen didn't answer.

"Are you up for a ride? Got to catch up with the cavalry," Harry said as he mounted Turk.

"Yeah, suh."

The mounted companies were halted, crowding the narrow wagon track. The Boy Colonel and his servant drove through and around them, ducking and pushing away the sappy pine branches. They found Captain Hays, a neat, dandy little fellow who commanded A Company, at the head of the column, near the tracks.

"No sir, didn't find Colonel Vance, but my flankers came up on a straggler from your regiment. The Twenty-sixth cut through the woods up ahead, toward the bridges over the creek. They're in a bad way, I'm afraid, stampeded."

Aha, Harry thought, now Vance will see the value of discipline.

"Have you located the enemy?"

The Captain sat up, brushed his chin against a shoulder. "Ah, yes sir. Bad news. They're down the line, not far, coming this way. And they're on the County Road in great numbers. Ah, they'll beat you to New Berne. You're cut off sir, unless you go over the creek. I suppose that's why Colonel Vance went that way."

Harry puffed, concentrated. "Can your cavalry get through?"

"Yes sir, if we hurry."

"The artillery?"

"Yes, if we leave now."

"Go, go now!" Harry urged, waving an arm.

"What about you? Will you head for the bridges?"

"Yes, yes," Harry yelled impatiently. "Go! Save yourselves!"

Captain Hays yelled the command, looked at Harry. "Hurry sir. Good luck."

Harry and Kinchen pulled their horses back and watched the one hundred and fifty cavalrymen file out of the narrow road and gallop up the side of the tracks, the artillery and caissons bouncing at their rear. The two then turned, sliced into the woods, and came upon the independent, infantry company already on the track. Harry ordered them to turn around.

Two of his companies were also on the track, and the other two were still on Weathersby's Road. Harry galloped to the intersection to direct traffic. One company still on Weathersby's, was ordered to continue up the road toward the bridges. Captain Lane's company was instructed to hold up and stay as the rear guard, while the remaining three filed off the track in front of Lane. There were strict orders for all to stay in ranks, in columns of four.

Harry sprinted to the head of the column, found a lieutenant, dismounted Turk, and ordered the young officer to mount him.

"Go up ahead, check the bridges, see if they're clear," Harry barked. The Lieutenant saluted briskly and galloped around a bend.

THEY STREAMED THROUGH THE SOGGY FOREST like a flock of frightened sheep; fear had spread through them like a contagious disease. Yet, not a Yankee was within a mile of Vance's men.

They broke out of the woods, came to the creek, and dove in. Most, feeling the ice-cold water and sensing its depth, flopped back to shore. A handful made the seventy-five yards across. Three drowned.

Colonel Vance charged out of the woods, loudly exhorting his men to swim. His horse splashed into the creek, faulted, and Vance tumbled over his head and disappeared into the dark depths. Captain Horton jumped in and fished him out. Another soldier quickly fixed his bayonet to his rifle and poked the Colonel's hat, before it floated away.

Nearly four hundred men were milling along the bank, some heaving their rifles into the creek. Horton, having just beached Colonel Vance, couldn't believe his eyes. Soaked, shivering, teeth chattering, he flew into a rage.

"What in hell are y'all doin'?"

"The Yanks will not have my gun," a Private spoke up defiantly.

"The Yanks ain't gettin' any of our guns, and none of us! If I see anyone throw his gun in, he's swimmin' in and retrievin' it!" Horton yelled, eyes bulging. He stood, puffed, and watched for a reaction. The men settled down.

Vance got up, tried to wipe off the mud, and looked about.

"We've got to get across. No prison for me." The threat circled around in his head.

He saw a small boat lying upside down on the other bank. He called to a handful of his men huddled together.

"One of you, get that boat and row it across!" He turned to his adjutant, "Pick out some boys, send them up and down the creek: find boats!"

Fifteen minutes later no other craft had been found, and the little row boat was half way through its maiden voyage, full compliment, three men and a rower. A Private did some figuring, whispered in his mate's ear.

"Prepare your mouth for some Yankee pie, it'll be three weeks 'fore we all get across." His friend chuckled and passed the word.

Vance paced, swung his arms around, blustering. Finally he lost patience.

"Captain Horton."

"Yeah, sir."

"I'm going across to find more boats. You're in charge here. I recommend you have the men sit down, keep them quiet, no fires."

"Yeah, sir."

"I'll be back as soon as I find more boats."

Vance mounted, tucked his hat tight on his head, led his shiny black to the creek, and slowly guided the animal in. All the men gathered at the edge, and watched, yelling encouragement. The horse lost the bottom, pumped against the current, and was swept downstream as Vance clung desperately to the mane. Some of the soldiers kept yelling. The Colonel hung on, the horse's head and nose barely above the water. They finally found the shallows about a hundred yards down, and splashed to the bank. They climbed a rise, and Vance turned, waved. The men cheered, waved back with arms high. The sound of their cheers echoed over the water, reverberated through the trees. Vance removed his hat with a flourish, reared the black, then galloped away, full speed.

"Politicians." Horton mumbled with disgust. He turned to the men, "Shut up, sit down! Shut up, boys!"

THE SMOKE BILLOWED UP OVER THE PINES, far ahead. Harry thought the worst. The Lieutenant soon trotted up and confirmed the sad intelligence.

"The bridges are burning, sir."

"Yankees?"

"No, didn't see any. I believe they were set by our own men."

Harry rubbed a hand over his forehead, and turned away.

"But I found the rest of the regiment." Harry looked back. "Heard some cheering when I was working my way back, down by the river. I made a look-see. They're stacked up by the creek, trapped. One small skiff ferrying them across. The Colonel swam over to find more."

"How far?" Harry asked.

"Just up the road a ways and through the woods, less than a mile. They look pretty sorry, sir. Captain Horton's got them settled down, but they're disorganized and jumpy. Some boys drowned when they tried to swim for it."

"Very well, Lieutenant, dismount, but stay here at the front and lead the way."

"Yes, sir."

Harry mounted Turk and worked his way down the column, informing his officers of the situation. He urged them to keep discipline, to keep the men calm and in ranks. After the Lieutenant turned the column into the woods, Harry worked ahead and located Vance's six companies. He was livid. They hadn't even posted pickets.

Harry's column was ordered to halt a hundred yards shy of the creek, but the men were to stay in line. Captain Lane was put in charge and pickets were spread out with orders not to fire unless spied by the enemy. Harry then returned to the creek and found Captain Horton.

"This is silly, Colonel. We'll neva' get across like this. Vance just has to find some boats."

Harry ignored Horton; he looked disgustedly at the rabble lounging by the creek.

"Yes, yes, Captain, but in the mean time we must prepare. Most of your men don't have guns. Where are their guns?"

"They threw them in the creek," Horton growled. "I couldn't stop 'em in time."

Harry winced. "We must have discipline, Captain. Designate some officers to reorganize your men into companies and form them in a column along the creek."

Sitting by the bank, a Private pointed across the creek, yelled.

"There's a Nigga' over there." The men got on their feet, milled about.

"Halloo! Halloooo!" The Negro had a hand cupped to his mouth, was pointing downstream with the other. "Dey's boats! Dey's boats!"

Three men who had already swum across spied him, ran toward him and pounced, scaring him half to death. After conferring with the Negro, one of the soldiers yelled back across the creek.

"He says there's a big boat down stream, and Colonel Vance is bringing more. We're to follow him."

"Good, tell him to wait 'til we're ready," Harry yelled back. Then he turned to Horton. "Form the men in columns of two along the creek, by company. Inform me when you're ready."

Firing broke out behind Harry's columns as they made their way downstream, but the sound came from a distance. Horton's men remained restless, while Captain Lane's four companies and the independent company kept perfect calm, as they marched parallel in the woods. Lane's column came to a wide swamp, and the Captain ordered the men through the waist-deep muck.

Horton's men had an easier crossing, and they were first to spy the boat landing downstream with the Negro and the three soldiers. They broke ranks, fighting, and kicking in a mad rush. They overfilled the craft, tossing the Negro out. Harry came up with a bound, furious.

"Out of the boat! Every one of you, out!"

The soldiers froze.

"Everyone out or I'll have you shot for mutiny!"

They slowly complied, all but three. Harry threatened, fingering the handle of his sword.

"Out!"

Two of the three jumped, but one stubbornly remained. Harry drew the sword, pointed it at him, and glared. The last man scowled back, but got out. Captain Horton ran up.

"Back in line, back in line, all of you!" he screamed.

"Sorry, Colonel. They're just plain whipped."

Harry went right to the business at hand. "Follow me, Captain. Draw your sword."

He walked to the head of the line of men, stood at one side, placed his sword across the first man's chest, and told Horton to stand on the other side and do the same.

Harry spoke up so all could hear. "Now—we're going to fill this boat like Confederate soldiers. First man who pushes goes to the end of the line. Understood?"

"You there." Harry looked at the Negro. "What's your name?"

"Alfred, suh," he said sheepishly.

"Is that your boat?"

"No, suh."

"Well, Alfred, tell me when you think it's full." The Negro nodded.

"Two at a time, Captain," Harry said to Horton. "Two," and they lowered the swords so the first two men could pass, then raised them again.

"Four."

At eighteen the Negro called out. "Dat's 'nough."

Ten minutes later the boat was back for a new load. The process was repeated, and then Harry called in another officer to replace him at the head of the line. Firing could still be heard in the distance, so he checked on the placement of the pickets, to make sure they were out far and thick. By the time he came back, Vance had arrived with three more boats, each capable of carrying at least twelve men. The little skiff was brought down too, so there were five boats running.

The sun was falling into thickening clouds. Several hours had passed since the retreat. Harry couldn't believe the Yankees weren't all over them, so he decided to form little scouting parties and try to locate the enemy, without bringing attention to their vulnerable condition. Over an hour later, all of Horton's men were across the creek, and the first of the scouting parties made their report.

"They're up by the bridges, sir," a Sergeant reported. "Close to a thousand, I'd say. I think they know we're down here. Waitin' on us. They don't think we can get across, and reckon they have us bottled up snug. A mounted patrol just passed on the road, and looked to be headin' for Weathersby's."

There was really nothing they could do but keep ferrying across and hope the Yankees stayed put, but Harry decided to form Lane's company into a battle line to protect their rear.

While he helped with the dispositions, Harry spied Kinchen standing quiet in the woods by Waverly and Turk. He told his servant to hold the horses' reins and swim them across the next time the little skiff came over, and to get a soldier to help him.

The minutes passed, no Yankees appeared, and all was quiet. Only two companies and the pickets were left to ford. Harry spied Kinchen again. He hadn't budged since he'd spoken to him.

"I thought I told you to go over on the next skiff."

"Yeah, suh."

"Well."

"'Cided ta wait and go wid you."

"I'll be in the last boat over. Don't want you to wait. Look, here it comes now. Go!"

Kinchen slowly led the horses down to the creek bank, but the skiff was full before he arrived. He stopped and lounged, waiting for it to come back. It came back, filled again. Kinchen made no move to climb aboard. Harry noticed.

"I'm ordering you to go over," Harry snapped.

"No, suh," Kinchen answered. "I'm a goin' wid you."

"No, you're not. I'm ordering you to go now."

"I'm not one a' yo' soldy'as, Massa."

"No, you're my servant, and we're not arguing. You're going over."

"Yeah, suh. I's your servant, but your Papa, he owns me, and he says if there's any danger, any danger a t'all, stay wid Massa Harry."

Harry scowled at him, then shook his head.

"Suit yourself."

The sun was covered, its light fading. The last of the pickets had trickled in and filled the big boat. All that was left were two privates, Captain Lane, Harry, Kinchen, and the two horses. One of the middle-sized boats was halfway across to pick them up.

A soldier on the far bank sounded the alarm.

"Look out, Yankees!" he howled, and pointed upstream.

A handful of blue scouts were a hundred yards away, leveling their rifles at the last of the regiment. Some Confederates on the far shore shot first, causing the small band to waver. Then they fired. The bullets whistled down the creek, passed high. Harry looked at Lane, and the two privates.

"Can you swim?" All three nodded. "Swim for the boat!"

Harry jumped on Waverly. Kinchen was already mounted.

"Ready for another swim?"

"Ain't dried yet from da first," Kinchen replied, referring to his earlier fall in the swamp.

They plunged into the ice-cold creek, going under, then popping up. More Yankees appeared and fired on the swimmers. The bullets splashed around them. Lane and the privates reached the boat, and held on to its sides as the rowers ducked and pushed it quickly down stream.

The frigid water had stolen their breath, but Kinchen and Harry held the manes tight in their hands. The horses struggled, snorted, kicked. The Yankees fired again, narrowly missing.

Both riders had lost their stirrups in the plunge. Attempts to regain them were in vain. They desperately tried to wrap their legs tight to the massive bellies, but the strong kicking of the animals' hind legs prevented it. Only their grip on the manes kept the riders attached. The horses finally found the bottom, and struggled to get their feet. The riders hugged their necks, kicked their sides, and screamed in their ears. Waverly and Turk staggered to the shore and rumbled up the steep bank.

Finally, Lane's Rebels formed and delivered a heavy volley at the enemy skirmishers, scattering them.

Dozens of soldiers instantly gathered around Harry and Kinchen, cheering, patting the horses, reaching up and shaking the riders' hands. Kinchen looked down at all the chuckling faces. Chills shot through him, his jaw was vibrating, his mind spinning with excitement, his body twitching as it absorbed the attention. Then came a flash of warmth. His heart skipped, swelling his chest, and he howled. Howled with laughter.

THEY WERE LED THROUGH A FALLOW FIELD TO A GROVE where there were fires. Naked men stood around them, roasting their wet uniforms on sticks. Harry and Kinchen stripped and hovered over the flames as orderlies rung out their clothes. Captain Lane and the two privates soon joined them.

Harry slapped Kinchen's bare back. "Believe that's the first time I've beaten you in a fair horse race," he declared.

"Fair?" Kinchen replied. "Yeah, it took bullets now, didn't it."

They both laughed.

It began to sleet, and Harry's face turned pensive as he watched his men scurrying for shelter. They were ragged, tired to the bone, had no food, no provisions, no tents, and it was a two-day march to Kinston before they would find relief. The crisis was far from over.

He looked back at Kinchen who was shivering, while marching in place.

Why in heaven's name had he waited until the very end to cross? What purpose did it serve?

Kinchen noticed Harry was watching him, turned and looked into his master's face.

"Believe I's gettin' ta like dis soldrin'," he said with a smile.

Harry looked at the big white teeth. Kinchen was smiling, beaming. He hadn't seen those teeth in weeks.

The fire spat at them, the sleet growing heavy, and they sat down near the heat and covered themselves with soggy blankets.

❧ 16 ❦

RICHES AMONG THE DEAD

"Harry"

Go my own beloved Harry,
Now the country calls for thee,
Where so'er its need is greatest,
There I wish my boy to be.

He, who felt mid this dark passion,
The pangs that rent a Mother's heart,
He alone, who knoweth all things,
Knows how dear to me thou art.

But if I knew the shaft would hit thee,
I could not, would not, bid thee stay,
When duty points the path so clearly,
I would not wish my boy away.

Go to this dread field of carnage,
Win for thyself an honored name,
For who would ever wish to cherish
Life with a Stanley's tarnished fame.

Press forward then, where dangers thicken,
Fear not ill will thee betide,
Though the sired hosts are 'round thee,
Thy guardian angel's at thy side.

Storm the redoubt, drive back the phalanx,
Fear no sharp-shooter from the wall,
Thy mother's tear the spark will dampen,
That would have sped the fatal ball.

Lead on the columns, never waver,
Though shells are bursting all around,
Thy Mother's prayers are hovering near thee,
To ward off every fatal round.

But when victory crown's thy banner,
Lay aside thy heart of steel,
Let the captive and the wounded,
Naught but thy compassion feel.

Bring me back a heart unhardened
By the cruelties of war,
A heart alive to every kindness,
As in the peaceful days of yore.

                      Anna G. Burgwyn— June 20th, 1862

IT WAS LATE JUNE, and the first hot days of summer were upon them. Gray figures shimmered in heat waves rising from steel rails. Ransom's Brigade was stacked up near the depot in Petersburg. Anticipated orders had come. They were off for Richmond where the Yankees were within sight of the city's gates. Harry's regiment had been ordered to leave at half past three, but the locomotive that was to carry them had not yet arrived. Two other regiments from Ransom's Brigade were at the station, and they too were to embark on their short journey. Their trains were also late.

    Kinchen was with the regiment's six horses; he had them in the shade of a lean-to aside newly constructed army stables. The heat was stifling, no breeze, the steamy moisture like a suffocating blanket. The still air smelled of fresh-cut pine, and the horses' tails cut a steady rhythm as they swished away the flies. Sitting on a rickety old stool, Kinchen synchronized the tapping of his bare foot to the waving tails, was whistling an ancient melody while his knife cut into a sappy stick. The tack was clean. The horses were fed and watered and long since groomed, so now he sank into meandering daydreams as time slowly ticked away.

    The hours passed. The sun fell. The soldiers managed to cook some rations, and the food had long been digested when a whistle finally pierced the distance. A derelict train pulled in at nine PM. Eleven splintered old cars. How were nine hundred men, six horses, and a Negro servant to fit into just eleven cars? After much pushing and shoving, they filled the cars, and the straining engine chugged out of the depot. The slave sat alone in the horses' car, his ears full of the grating click-clack of rusty wheels on iron, as the train crawled north at its slow pace of ten miles per hour. The horses slept, and Kinchen, with knees to his chin, drifted in and out of disjointed dreams. The rumblings and bumps kept him in a miserable state. Teeth rattled in his mouth, and he thought only his closed lids would keep his eyes in his head. The cars squeaked into Richmond at one AM.

The regiment spilled out and quickly formed on a cobbled street.

Kinchen had little trouble unloading the horses alone. Soon the officers had mounted, without a word of thanks.

The Carolinians were led through dark streets. Harry, riding at the column's front, felt a sense of doom within the city. Richmond was not yet under siege, but all feared it would be soon. The Yankee guns to the east had been plainly audible for days.

The regiment quietly made its way out of town and finally bivouacked in a huge, open field not far from the city's fairgrounds. Harry knew he would not see a bed for some time, and decided to treat himself. He rode Turk back into town, and checked in at the Exchange Hotel on Franklin Street.

Kinchen stayed in the camp, gathered the remaining horses and staked them out, then rolled into a blanket near them and fell instantly asleep.

A clean bed wasn't Harry's only motive for going back into town. He knew his father was staying at the hotel, had received a telegram from him the day before yesterday while in Petersburg. Henry was in Richmond on urgent business. He'd been appointed a military aid to Governor Clark and lately had been shuttling back and forth between Raleigh and the Confederate capital. The Federal pressure on Richmond had sucked in all but a handful of the Confederate troops defending eastern Carolina, and Henry was there to lobby for their return. It was a lost cause. The Union army was less than ten miles away, and the Richmond defense force could spare no troops. Eastern Carolina had been neglected by the Rebel government from the war's beginning, although it was a vital part of the Confederacy, particularly the railroads coming up from Wilmington and further south. However, nothing took precedence over Richmond, so once again the tarheels would have to make due with what they had.

The Exchange was full, but Harry was able to convince the clerk to allow him to double up with his father. He crept into the hot and unbearably stuffy room. Henry didn't stir, and the feather bed drew his son in beside him.

Harry slept late. The bright sunlight streaming through the windows finally pried his eyes open and pulled him from the soft folds and sour sheets. Henry was gone, but a folded note by the wash-stand mentioned a series of early appointments at the Capital, and invited his son to join him for a mid-day meal.

Harry was drawn to the window; its clear glass panes, despite rippled imperfections, revealed a city in crisis. The boulevards were overflowing with marching troops and wagons. Funneling, black clouds were rolling from every chimney and smokestack. The factories were churning out war materials, the private homes, bread. Richmond had once been a town of less than forty thousand people, but now its numbers were untold. Government and factory workers had its dwellings overflowing, not to mention the tens of thousands of soldiers camped in and around the city.

Harry observed with the naive eyes of a youth; he saw the townspeople gathering and yelling encouragement to the new troops. They were not jubilant crowds throwing flowers and waving kerchiefs though. The mood in Richmond was much too sober for that. The Battle of Seven Pines of a few weeks back had cured the city's excitement for war. Over five thousand wounded had been carted into Richmond during the days that followed the battle, and the suffering masses quickly filled its hospitals and other medical facilities. Private homes took care of the remaining, and the city's women suddenly found themselves as nurses. Feelings in Richmond were serious and concerned, but not yet panicked. Harry thought the view from his window inspiring. He could sense the city's earnestness, a young country working feverishly to maintain its existence. An incredibly historic time he thought, and now he would be a part of it. Exciting, absolutely exciting.

A shock greeted him just outside the hotel's doors: swarming crowds, the indescribable noise, and the air noxious with the overpowering smell of sweat and horse dung. The crushing masses pulled him from the doorway and carried him along, until he reached the slopes of Capital Hill, where it finally thinned and allowed him a full stride. It was then that the faint rumble of artillery rolled into town. It had an instant and hypnotic effect on the crowd. Suddenly, all was quiet; movement stopped, everyone listened. When the vibrations finally faded, the commotion returned, this time louder.

Harry heard his name over the clamor. Somehow, Colonel Vance's adjutant had found him. He had new orders. Ransom's Brigade had been directed to the front immediately.

Harry was surprised with the news, but still contemplated a quick dash to see his father. Standing in the west square with Washington's huge statue looming overhead, he studied the mounted figure while he debated. The impatient frown on the waiting adjutant was playing an unwanted influence. There was the imposing Washington, the great American, now considered a great Virginian, and he too was beckoning him to the front. He made his decision. As Harry turned away from Henry and the tall white columns of the Confederacy's seat, a thought passed quickly, a nervous speculation. He didn't know when he might see his father again.

EAST OF RICHMOND AND MOSTLY ALONG THE JAMES RIVER was a land of traditional southern plantations. Tobacco had fueled the wealth, but by 1862, it had also exhausted the soil. Now the area was sparsely settled. Three-quarters of the coastal plain was in timber. Narrow lanes, bottomless when wet, rambled through and around hundreds of creeks and swamps that lazily drifted to nearby rivers. The Chickahominy was nothing more than a wooded marsh that teemed with mosquitoes. It also acted as an impenetrable barrier to the approaching Yankees. Numerous deep ravines that housed blackened streams also served in that regard, along with scrubby pine thickets, honeysuckle, and underbrush. Old mansions with sublime vistas, grand hardwood forests interspersed with evergreen hollies, and rolling fields of grain reminded the soldiers of Virginia's old colonial splendor. This was the landscape where Harry and Kinchen found themselves. This was the ground on which the armies would duel.

George McClellan, with the largest army yet assembled on the western hemisphere, landed on the Virginia coast earlier in April, and using his heavy guns as a wedge, methodically drove the Rebels up the narrow peninsula between the York and James Rivers. Joe Johnston commanded the Confederates. Never a gambler, and comfortable with defensive tactics, he offered token resistance. A small pitched battle was waged around Williamsburg, and only after the Rebel government in Richmond leveled heavy pressure, did Johnston lash out at Seven Pines. A drawn fight, it did not stop the Federals. Fortunately for the Confederacy, Johnston was wounded and temporarily incapacitated. Henceforth, Rebel tactics would change. Robert E. Lee would be in charge.

The Confederate commander needed to know Federal dispositions, so the southern cavalry, under the dashing Jeb Stuart, was sent on a glory-filled ride around the Union army. The raid disclosed that the Federals were vulnerable. McClellan's right wing was separated from the rest of his army by the swampy and bankless Chickahominy River. Lee's first thought was to attack the isolated wing, and he developed a bold scheme. Two divisions would remain at McClellan's front as a covering force, and with his other divisions, Lee would set out for the Union right flank. He would be joined there by Stonewall Jackson, fresh from his miraculous victories in the Shenandoah Valley. The battles would last seven days.

Ransom's Brigade, with Harry and the Twenty-sixth North Carolina, would be part of the covering force. They would be directly to McClellan's front, heavily outnumbered, and in a precarious position if the Yankee general read Lee's bluff.

PRESSING TURK, HARRY OVERTOOK HIS REGIMENT marching east on the Williamsburg Road. No wagons bounced at the Carolinians' rear. All their baggage had been left in Petersburg and would only be brought up when the transportation could be spared. Kinchen alone, and clomping along on Waverly, was hovering within the dust at the regiment's heels. Harry found him fresh and full of smiles.

"How'd yuh sleep in dat bed, Massa Harry?"

"Just fine, Kinchen, thank you."

"Did yuh find Massa Henry?"

"No, he was up early and at the Capital. In meetings."

Kinchen nodded, "Dat's fine, you'll see 'im soon 'nough."

Harry placed his gloved hand on Kinchen's arm, spoke in earnest.

"I need you to go back to town. Go to the hotel, the Exchange Hotel, and tell Father that my regiment has arrived, and that our brigade has been attached to General Huger's Division."

Harry reached into his coat pocket and pulled out his billfold, and handed his servant some money, then produced a sheaf of paper from his saddle pouch, a pencil, and began to scribble a note, a pass.

"Tell him the division will be along the Williamsburg Road near the field of Seven Pines. I'm hoping he'll make a trip to see me."

Harry's father was not entirely a stranger to a battlefield. Although he had never graduated from West Point, Henry had recently tried to get a vacant command of North Carolina troops. As an aid to the Governor, it was also within his function to observe any military action, so it wasn't an unusual request that Harry should ask his father to come to the front.

"You understand? That's General Huger's Division on the Williamsburg Road."

"Yeah, suh. Gen'ral Huga's Division on da Williamsburg Road."

"Right."

Harry finished the pass that all slaves were required to carry, if not with their master or a white, then handed it to Kinchen.

"How's Waverly?"

"Just fine, suh. Limpin' a bit, but can make town. He healin' up."

"Good, you take him to the hotel and take care of him. Come out with Father, if he can come. Tell him to write you a pass to come back to me, if he can't. He forgets these things you know."

"Yeah suh."

"Don't come out if Waverly's still got that limp though."

"Yeah suh."

"Good, well, safe trip."

Kinchen's marbled, black eyes were bright and cheerful. He showed no concern as a white-toothed grin escaped from behind thick lips.

"Now yuh stay away from dem Yankee balls and bullets, Massa, yuh hear?"

Kinchen's grin spread wider, he chuckled, then tipped his derby and spurred Waverly.

The heat was torturous. The sun reflected off his cheeks and into his squinting eyes. He could feel perspiration through his shirt, dripping down his sides from his armpits. Another drop hung from his nose. He brushed it away, but another soon appeared. It dripped upon his lips. He licked them and tasted the salt. Harry halted Turk, dismounted, then positioned himself in the shadow of the animal, as he began to walk. Company B marched beside him.

There was not the usual talking and laughing in ranks. The rolling thunder of artillery fire had the soldiers' attention. It was growing louder, sharper.

There was a commotion ahead, soldiers were scurrying from the road, as the regiment parted to avoid a passing ambulance. Harry noticed pale, dirty hands and feet poking from its bed. Muffled groans reminded him that he was nearing a real battle. The slight scent of death on the wind punctuated the thought.

The regiment settled back into its marching rhythm. Harry looked down, closed his eyes, and let his feet carry him. He tried to let his mind drift, but it would not let go of the anticipated battle. The sound of the guns beat the air like violent surf on a beach, constant, unyielding. The thought of death was always within some dark cavity of the brain, unrelenting as the ocean.

He sensed someone was watching him, opened his eyes slightly, turned his head, and focused on marching feet kicking up dust. He looked up and met a pair of gray eyes with brown specks, the pupils nearly nonexistent. They were calling to him from the shade of a wide-brimmed hat, looking for answers. The face was tanned with black and white stubble on the chin. Wrinkles slanted downward from the eyes. It was the face of a father.

"How far are them guns, Colonel?"

Harry's eyes let go of the soldier's face and looked up into the sun's brightness, then he closed them and let his ears do the work.

"Four miles, I'd say. Less than an hour's march."

How far until his children were orphaned, Harry thought. That's what he was asking. He wondered if the men were ready for this. They had never been in a real fight. Was he ready? All he had was schooling, no more experience than they had.

The front was now a good mile away, and Ransom's Brigade was going in reserve, filing off the road into an old pasture. Dried-out cow dung covered the field. There were patches of high weeds and thistle, but otherwise the grass was eaten to the nub. Harry noticed it was overgrazed, and thought the grass would die in the hot sun. But war had made an unpleasant visit; the cows were gone. The field would get a rest and a chance to recover. If the blue rains came, it may live. Strange, war might save it. War brings life as well as it takes it away.

The fighting had lulled at their immediate front. No sounds of battle came from the east, but to the north a much heavier cannonade could be heard, a great pounding on the earth. It was some distance off, yet the horizon was dark and smoky, and the rumbling guns moved toward them like an approaching thunderstorm. Even the faint rattle of musketry could be heard. General Lee was turning McClellan's right, and the menacing mass of Federals to the east was now quiet, perhaps confused. Harry didn't know Lee's strategy; he had no idea that his old professor, Jackson, was up that way, but he took the sound as a positive sign and assumed his army was on the attack. Harry sat in the hot sun, among the dung, and listened to the storm for better than an hour.

They were on the road again, marching hurried steps. Two of Ransom's regiments were filing into trenches, as great balls of solid shot flew over and bounced dangerously near the gray columns. Harry was on Turk, oblivious to the danger, as he watched a battery of six guns unlimber nearby. The Twenty-sixth turned off the road and into another field of parched, trodden-over grass. The regiment was being held out of the trenches, in reserve, but exposed to the bouncing black balls. They deployed for battle, and Harry, still mounted, continued to observe the six guns to his left. Their fire added to the den, a hellish sound that drowned the senses. A hot ball plowed into a team of mules hurling flesh, blood, and limbs through the air. The survivors, tangled in the traces, lay on the ground kicking, convulsing, until they finally settled, dead from shock.

Ears back, hooves thumping, Turk pulled and pranced. The Colonel's legs wrapped to the horse's side firmly; he held the bit tight in the mouth. A dozen men dove to the ground in front of Harry. He saw them and instinctively ducked. A ball bounded between them and leaped three feet over his head. With Turk's sweat smeared on his face, he watched it roll harmlessly behind him.

"Can't stay here! Useless casualties, if we do!"

Harry galloped for Colonel Vance, found him buried in his saddle, his hands nervously clutching reins, strangely silent. Harry had never seen Vance awake without a tide of words from his mouth. Stunned, he had never imagined such a cannonade.

Harry yelled over the roaring guns. "Can't stay here, Colonel!" He angrily pointed to the rear. "Got to move to that line of trees!"

Four quick nods of his head was Vance's only response.

"Quickly, Colonel, got to move quickly! Shall I give the orders?"

Vance's face seemed vacant, but he nodded repeatedly. Harry didn't waste time, screamed at the Colonel's adjutant.

"File right, quickstep, to the grove!"

The regiment lay down in the woods until the day drew late. Projectiles flew harmlessly overhead. Not a man was lost. The Yankees never attacked, but just to the north, at Gaines Mill, the Rebels hurled themselves at the Federal V Corps in uncoordinated and costly assaults.

They broke the Union line, but Jackson was conspicuously late and failed to cut off the Yankees' retreat. McClellan's right wing managed to reach the south side of the Chickahominy. One day was over, there were six to go.

After dark, the Twenty-sixth was rousted and ordered to go on picket. Two hundred yards beyond the trenches was a thick stand of pines, and two hundred yards within the woods was a regiment of Georgians. The Carolinians were to relieve them. Colonel Vance took six companies to the right, and Harry took four to the left.

The ground dropped off considerably. In the forest, Harry couldn't see ten paces before him, had no idea where they were going. The woods thickened with bamboo, briars and every serpent and flying bug known to God. The ground seemed to slither underfoot, and mosquitoes frenzied on the fresh blood of four hundred men spread out and lost.

They'd gone at least two hundred yards, but no Georgians. Harry's foot sank into a swamp. He stopped, listened; the croaking frogs and buzzing bugs were deafening.

Damn! There couldn't be a regiment posted in that mess. Just couldn't. He called Lieutenant Jordan.

"Here, Colonel, right here." The two reached for each other blindly.

"A swamp to our front, Lieutenant, can't go further. Pass the word. We're turning left."

They went fifty yards, fighting through bamboo the entire way. Another swamp. Harry felt like a victim of a cruel joke. He was in a vacuum, lost, and the pressure bore down on him like a heavy weight. He looked up at the moon, a sliver of light. He wished he had seen it before they entered the woods. Now it was useless to him. The word was sent down the line again.

"About face!"

The companies were spread out and disoriented when they finally broke out of the bamboo. It took an hour to regroup the flung-out troops. Harry led the way again. He came to another swamp on his left, perhaps the first one. He turned right. Another swamp there too. Harry halted his command, and with Lieutenant Jordan in toe, followed a narrow neck of high ground between the pools of mire. The neck soon gave out, so he checked the position of the moon, then waded in, plowing through the thigh-deep muck, and scrambling over rotten logs. There was slime everywhere, a stench filled his nostrils with suffocating moisture. Vacant darkness. A crooked moon was his only guide.

Voices. They came from ahead, but whose were they? Was it Vance? The Georgians maybe, or were they Yankees? No way of knowing. He had no choice. Harry called out.

"Hello there!"

No reply.

"Hello there!" again, louder. An eerie quiet. The silence told him to go no further. Harry turned back to the neck. When he reached the companies, he deployed them where they were. Then he set out alone in search of Vance.

He found a private from Company E, one of Vance's companies, dozing by a twisted pine. Harry jabbed a boot into his leg. The Private jumped, startled, scrambled for his gun.

"Take me to Colonel Vance."

The soldier found his feet, saluted, "Yeah sir."

He then scampered through the woods like a scared rabbit, and Harry had to jog to keep up. They hadn't gone thirty yards, before Harry heard spattering musketry to his rear. His pickets were firing.

"Hold up there, Private!" Harry yelled.

The soldier doubled back, while Harry listened. The shooting didn't die away, but grew stronger, wider.

"You know where the Colonel is?" Harry asked.

"Yeah, sir, I can find him."

"Take him a message. In case he doesn't hear, tell him my pickets are engaged. We're a thousand yards to the left of your picket post. Tell him to join us. Got that?"

The boy nodded.

"Good, go." And the Private leaped away.

The firing had spread out ahead of him, to his front, to his right, and even to his left. He was half way back when it broke out to his rear.

Vance was also engaged. He, too, had gotten lost, and had placed some of his pickets along a fence row with Yankees just on the other side. They had poked their guns through the rails and fired. Most of the Twenty-sixth had wandered into enemy lines, and some of the Federals were actually behind them.

So this would be their first fight, Harry thought. The men spread out, lost in the dark, in the woods, in the swamps, where an officer had no control. He pushed on into the confusion, and reached his men. Yankees were all around them, the Rebels firing every which way, perhaps even at themselves. Who could tell in the murky darkness? Pulling in his officers, he called for a cease fire, then ordered the companies to put the moon to their backs and advance toward high ground, back from where they had come.

It was after midnight when they finally reached safety. Vance had used the same tactics, and the regiment came together at the edge of the forest. Word was sent back to General Ransom that they had been driven in. A ridiculous command came back.

"Retake the ground you have lost."

Infuriating! Harry thought. What ground? Ransom had never given a clear description of the position they were to initially hold. Where were the Georgians? Ransom should at least send an aid to place them where they belonged, but the General really didn't know.

The Twenty-sixth, in mass, advanced back into the jungle, Harry near its front, never really knowing when they might come face to face with a foe. Ahead lay a dark void with shadowy phantoms gliding in the black. Death would take but an instant. A flash of powder in the dark, a bayonet slashing from behind a tree. It was a horrible feeling, like millipedes crawling up his spine.

Firing broke out a ways off, but the balls clipped through the leaves overhead. The regiment grabbed the forest floor, some of the boys returning fire. Harry listened, watched the gun-flashes. He detected a body of troops firing in the other direction, ahead, a little to the left. They couldn't be part of his regiment. Perhaps they were the Georgians. They, no doubt, knew the enemy's position. He ordered his men to cease fire on fear that they might hit friends, and they continued to hug the damp ground through a sleepless night.

Finally the puzzling darkness disappeared. A hundred yards to the left was the Georgia regiment. How could he have missed them?

Later that day, Harry found time to write in his new journal, and finished the brief entry with a declaration.

"Couldn't have found my post in the dark to save myself from the gallows."

FLAPS AND STRINGS FROM STARK WHITE TENTS waved in a gentle breeze. Campfires sputtered smoke. Stained and bent playing cards, discarded tin cans, a fork, and bits of clothing littered the camp. Over there, a wagon laid with cracked and broken wheels. Beside it were the putrid remains of a horse. Canteens, rifles, axes, spades, bayonets, knapsacks, all were heaped into indiscriminate piles. The Yankees had abandoned their camps in a hurry, leaving evidence of their character behind. A promiscuous, slovenly, filthy lot, Harry thought.

Two days and a night had passed since the episode in the swamps. Two days of short advances, while the guns roared to the northeast. Thousands of men were dying up that way, splintered to pieces under the cannonades, riddled by the musketry. The Twenty-sixth had seen little action, had suffered no casualties, and had inflicted only one. A Yankee picket had wandered too close to their lines the day before, and Private Thurston, a husky man with a squeaky voice, had picked him off from one hundred and fifty yards. The dead Federal was a stringy-haired blond with a turned up nose. Harry had gone through his uniform, and had found letters written in German, useless as far as intelligence went. He gave the boy's equipment to his killer, who shared it among his mates. The boots were the grandest trophy, but they wouldn't fit Thurston's big, insensitive feet. He reluctantly gave them to little Johnny Webb, who greeted the gift with wide eyes and a toothy grin. That was yesterday, and today the blue soldiers were in full retreat, running for the James and the cover of their gunboats.

Harry kept the men in formation, as they marched through the abandoned camps. He would allow no pilfering: bad for morale. There would be plenty of rewards when final victory came, and only victory should serve as their motivation.

The regiment prowled narrow roads with unknown names. Everywhere were signs of a dispirited foe; equipment of every description lined the canopied lanes. Occasionally, dead bodies in blue met his gaze. He wished Lincoln and his cabinet could see the misery. If they were truly men, they would reconsider their course, he thought. Only wallowing devils were unmoved by cruelty.

The roads curled through the swamps and forests. Trees, severed by exploding balls, clogged the way. They crept on, and to the north, the firing continued. Not for an instant did it cease; instead, terribly distinct and hideously foreboding, it seemed to increase.

Another night came. With taxed limbs and an exhausted mind, Harry posted his lead pickets. The want of sleep was overpowering, his body tingled. He stumbled for the rear, fixed up a pile of dry pine straw and fell in. He began to dream, visions of home. He was in the parlor, in Raleigh, his family all around. His cousin Kate, with a sagging mouth, sat beside him and listened to the war stories rolling from his tongue. The boys were spellbound. Collie sucked his thumb, Allie didn't blink, Pollok leaned against that old green chair and smiled. The parlor door opened abruptly and Kinchen walked in, his eyes on Harry possessing a knowing glint. He had an announcement; Miss Annie Devereux had come a callin' with her mother. Harry sat up, the boys moaned, and the shots rang out. Three of them, along the picket line. Their intrusion broke the vision and woke the dreamer. He wiped his eyes, managed to stand, staggered in the direction from where the shots had come. He walked ten paces, heard nothing, then turned around and went back to his bed of pine tags. He promised himself, only general firing would pry him loose again.

The pines loomed overhead. He listened to them sway and creak in the wind. The green needles were whispering with the breeze, telling him that blessed peace, if lasting but a moment, should be cherished still. Away with painful thoughts. Away with wretched visions of blood and slaughter. Let the heart pump slow. Let the verve revive. Dreams, let them come.

JULY FIRST, THE SEVENTH DAY, and still the Twenty-sixth had seen little action. Yesterday, however, their eyes had glimpsed a bit of horror's aftermath. At four PM, they had bivouacked at White Oak Swamp, and nearby, on the field of Glendale, part of Longstreet's Division had stormed several batteries. The ruin exceeded anything yet beheld. Yankee bodies, raked into stacks, were broiling in the afternoon sun. An orgy of flies buzzed unmercifully around their prey, laying eggs within the dead tissue. The wounded, still in the field, sprayed their mournful cries into the sickening odor. The sights, smells, and sounds conspired to fill Harry's memory forever.

At dawn, the regiment was up and marching down the Charles City Road. By noon they were stalled. Ahead, General John Magruder's Division turned down the wrong road, belatedly realized their mistake, and turned back. Part of Huger's Division slipped in front and separated themselves from Ransom's Brigade. Magruder bulled his way into the gap, snarling the thin passageway and cutting Ransom off from the rest of his division.

Vibrating through the trees, making the leaves flutter and shake, came the now familiar sound of an artillery battle, but much closer than usual, and directly to the east. Harry's regiment plodded closer to the din and, by late afternoon, was posted in a fallow field, guarding Magruder's right flank. Just through the trees, the battle raged. The cannon fire was unrivaled, but its effects were obscured by the thick grove. Harry sent a private up a tree to reconnoiter, but the high perch revealed little, only a gentle, sloping field planted in corn and clover. The top of the hill was engulfed in smoke and flying debris. Harry had no clue to what was transpiring.

Six days of maneuver and fighting had sent the Federals reeling from the gates of Richmond. The jubilant Rebels were hot after them, and Lee had hopes of destroying his opponent. The opportunities had been there, but his plans of turning and encircling the Federals had all fallen short. Difficult ground had made McClellan elusive, and inexperienced Rebel officers and troops had compounded the problems. Even Jackson's brilliance had been mysteriously absent. Although on formidable ground, the Yankees were now cornered, and Lee had one more chance to pinch them off, before they reached the James and the protection of their gunboats. Cloaked in smoke, it was McClellan's rear guard that Harry's scout had failed to see atop that otherwise gentle hilltop. Thirty-two guns and thousands of infantry were blocking Lee's designs. The Yankees had picked their ground well, and the Rebels had found it puzzling. The open slope provided an excellent field of fire for the stacked Federal guns. To the left and right of the hill, which was really a plateau, were shallow valleys, their sharp ravines rising to the batteries. Creeks, gullies, and broken, wooded hills made turning the stronghold difficult. Stretched out behind the hill was the bulk of the Army of the Potomac. It had but a short march to go before reaching its supply base at Harrison's Landing. McClellan's Headquarters was at the southern edge of the eminence. It was situated in the red-brick Malvern House, a seventeenth-century structure that had come to give the plateau its name, Malvern Hill.

General Ransom directed his brigade into tight battle formations. A foolish deployment, Harry thought, with enemy shells shrieking overhead. Needless exposure. The regiments stood in the sweltering July heat for hours. Only a merciful God prevented any casualties.

General Lee had given up on maneuver; the enemy flanks were too strong. Instead, he positioned his artillery into grand batteries that would place Malvern Hill in a crossfire. If effective, a frontal assault by his massed divisions would win the day. The result was an afternoon of deafening barrages, yet the day was melting away, and the Federals were holding. The Rebel guns were beaten back and silenced. At that point, an infantry assault would have been murderously foolish. Somehow, despite efforts to stop them, the Confederates charged. A General intoxicated with opium. Hurt feelings. Two overly zealous regiments. Confusing orders that were garbled by distance and misinterpretation. False reports. Misguided units sucking others into the fray. A combination of unlikely events brought on the assaults. Everything had to have gone just right for things to have gone so wrong.

A strange silence hung over the battlefield for a time. Harry thought it ominous, like a momentary catching of breath between furious convulsions. A familiar refrain followed the lull, however. Weak at first, it slowly gained momentum. A high-pitched sound that brought both fear and joyous excitement. A shriek, away to the left, careening through the forest, ghostly and unnatural, wicked. The sound of a Confederate charge: the Rebel yell. Harry listened to it drift ahead, up the slope, rolling like an irresistible tide. Then came a massive discharge from the Federal batteries, once more the pounding on the earth. He imagined figures in gray being crushed and spattered under the barrage. The high-pitched screams deviated into dull moans, then started up again. Still to the left, but further away, fresh troops were charging the hill. The cannonade was continuous, drowning out the yells. Wave after wave of Rebels tried the hill, only to be swept away. Harry could tell that each successive attack was getting a little closer though; the crackle of musketry was mixing with the thunder. But the sound of death and mayhem made him shudder. He paced, clasped his hands together, wrung them, and repeatedly smacked his palm with a closed fist. The gruesome clamor lasted for over an hour.

Long shadows from the grove reached into the field and touched the gray line. A red sun was making its decent. Seven PM, Ransom's Brigade was ordered to advance. Harry said a prayer, and ordered his soldiers forward. The regiment stepped off grandly, but the skillful order wouldn't last. Thin layers of smoke hung in the forest, like high cirrus clouds that had fallen from the sky. The setting sun displayed a soft, warm, glow, almost peaceful, but the forest was dark and shadowy. The smoke burned the eyes and blinded. Roaring guns befuddled the mind. Spherical case shot saturated the woods and plucked at green leaves and tense nerves. The regiments drifted apart. The Twenty-sixth floated to the left, and the Twenty-fourth North Carolina to the right. Harry felt the vacancy, but he was helpless to prevent the gap. Suddenly, they were alone. The sounds of battle drew them deeper, but the noise was confusing. Echoes, reverberations, where exactly was it? The regiment wandered through the grove, shifting to the right, then back to the left, losing cohesion. Fleeing soldiers in gray filtered through. They loped through the woods like frightened deer. Harry called to them, but panic made them deaf. Then came a cloud of runners, skulkers from all states. They were men without senses: blind, deaf, and dumb. Harry grabbed at them as they rushed past, finally had one by a thin, bony arm, and asked him where the battle lay. The boy, gap-toothed, sweaty, gave him a blank stare.

"My regiment's cut to pieces, to pieces," he stammered.

Harry could get nothing more from him. He let him go. The Carolinians slowly felt their way through the smoke, choked and confounded. Harry saw a nap of curly brown hair just on the other side of a large log. He peered over. A fuzzy-faced boy was on his knees, eyes closed, lips moving, his hands clasped under his chin. He was praying as if at an altar. Harry unsheathed his sword, grabbed the boy by the collar and violently shoved his head against the log. The sword poked at the neck, making a small indentation in the soft, smooth flesh.

"You're taking us to the battle," Harry said, his eyes wide with anger. The boy responded with a blink and a feeble nod. Harry took a deep breath, blew hot air from flaring nostrils, then stood the boy up.

"Lead on, I'm right behind you."

A solid black ball sliced through the trees, cutting off a huge limb overhead, and sending it spiraling downward. The fuzzy-faced boy, a Louisianian, ducked, but was otherwise unperturbed. He quickly gathered his bearings then led the Carolinians a little to the right. Hatless, the boy's head bobbed through the woods, his curly locks weaved in maze-like tangles, his body lean and taut, his legs angly, but purposeful. Harry felt a sharp pang of guilt, sorry for his impulsive anger toward the boy.

Just ahead, the brilliant light of dusk shone through the trees. The boy stopped, pointed. Harry squinted into the reddening sky. At the edge of the forest was a rail fence; beyond, a field of oats, and beyond that, a steep, cliff-like rise. The Yankee guns were plainly silhouetted against the crimson sunset. Malvern Hill, the eastern side—the boy had led them to the enemy's flank. Harry looked back at him and caught his strained eyes. The face had a pale sickness to it. Sweat bubbled, and a wet lock of hair was glued to a furrowless forehead. Some just weren't cut out for this, Harry thought. A sheltered boy, son of a devout and idealistic preacher, he guessed. Harry said nothing, but displayed a grateful face. The Louisianian blinked in shame, directed his eyes to the ground, then slithered away.

Harry barked out orders for his companies to form behind a low swell aside the fence. Vance's companies and Harry's had separated in the forest, but Vance had also found his way to the battlefield and was a hundred yards to the left. Harry ordered Company D to reach over and join them.

In the gaining darkness, the combatants still howled, the cannonade at a deafening pitch. To Harry's front and left, shattered regiments in gray lay on the slopes like writhing snakes.

The Twenty-sixth pitched over the fence with a yell, then paused briefly to reform. They surged forward again and punctured the oat field. Unchallenged, they charged. No guns were directed at them, no volleys came from the hill. They seemed like ghosts, unseen in the gray drifting smoke.

Shocked, exuberant, they pressed on as if the hand of God protected them. The oat field gave way to another rail fence. The momentum of the charge broke it and trampled it under foot. A mound of black dirt rose ahead, then a wide shallow ditch. It was there that the missiles began to fly. So thick, Harry thought them as numerous as grains of wheat from a reaper. Grape shot and minie balls ripped and tore at dusty gray uniforms. Carolinians began to fall, but still they reached the base of the slope and struggled upward. Burning knees, hoarse cries, scrambling feet, heads tilted as if fighting a high wind, they charged.

Several companies responded to Harry's grating calls. He ordered them to stop and prepare for volley fire. Then came a surprise. Tattered, gray figures with waving arms emerged from the smoke and the waning light. They pleaded for the Carolinians to hold their fire. Friends were ahead. Between the Twenty-sixth and the Yankee batteries was the Second Louisiana. Harry was in a quandary. He couldn't go back and waste the assault with nothing gained. He couldn't fire on friends, and couldn't press on through the blinding smoke. The enemy fusillades persisted, as balls hummed through the ranks. Standing in the open would be suicidal. Harry and Colonel Vance had no choice but to order the regiment to the ground.

The anger boiled hot in his brain. Blinding thoughts flooded the senses. He searched for someone to blame, but couldn't concentrate. Finally, he let his mind flow, cool and liquid, then let the anger go.

The canister and grape buzzed overhead like a swarm of maddened hornets. Sprawled on the hillside, chin in the dirt, lips parched, throat sore, his eyes stinging from sweat, he strained to look up the slope, and saw a cluster of grape plow into the dirt and careen overhead. A foot, six inches perhaps, the distance between life and death. The Yankee guns didn't have the range. Twenty more yards though, and the deadly clumps of iron would shred the regiment to bloody tatters. He heard the guns belch, and raised his arms over his head as if to block; he buried his face into the cool soil and heard another set of missiles whistle overhead. He could almost feel the wind. Harry looked up, down the line, saw dirty, grimacing faces anticipating pain. Some were crying. Some were hit. There was blood spattered across a boy's cheek, his eyes open, dull and lifeless.

All the Confederates still alive on that wrecked hillside were singular in mind. They prayed to their one God, and to his son, Jesus Christ. They pleaded and begged their Lord to take away the last, lingering light of day. Make the guns blind. Make the light flee, so the Yankees will stop their harvest.

Other Rebels were still fighting. One of Harry's own companies had missed the order to lay down, and were still charging up the hill. He caught sight of them, to his right, a row of black shadows against a rose colored sky. Then came a volley and a barrage and they went down. They had charged within fifteen feet from the guns, fifteen feet.

The Twenty-fourth North Carolina also made an attempt at the massed guns. Even further to the right, they stormed up the ravine, and Harry could barely make them out in the growing darkness. On they went, yelping like wounded dogs, then stopping and firing a vengeful volley. He could not see its destruction, but the Twenty-fourth went no further. A barrage of double canister took its toll. The regiment wavered, returned fire, then grabbed the hillside.

Harry buried his head in his arms, and felt a powerful, shameful guilt roll over him. He despised himself for hugging the earth, and tried to block out the sights. But his ears still heard the sounds, a chorus of horror: the vomiting guns spitting death, rattling musketry, the whicker of shells flying overhead, calls of desperate men in fruitless charges, the howls of the wounded and suffering, that ceaseless cry for water. He felt naked, vulnerable, like a screaming newborn, red and purple, with tiny fingers and toes clinched in fury. He wanted to crawl in a hole, and disappear into the womb.

Darkness made its descent. The only lights came from the flares and flames of the guns still firing. They cast an eerie glow over the ruin. Harry suffered from thirst; his lips cracked, his tongue thick and stuck tight in his mouth. Some of the boys were passing canteens, but Harry ignored them, refusing any offers as if in search of punishment. He shut off his instincts and wondered what next.

The earth grew cool beneath him, but the guns still fired. The moon rose, and the chills came. His perspiration began to evaporate. He thought of the wounded, warm blood flowing over goose-pimpled flesh. How they must suffer. His mind continued to work as his body lay still. For three tormenting hours he lay there with his regiment. At ten PM the guns finally halted. Shortly after, the Twenty-sixth received orders to silently leave the field.

A COOL, FRESH BRANCH, SWEET-TASTING WATER. His raging thirst had drawn him to the brook, and he could almost feel the fluid pumping into his arteries and strengthening his numb limbs. There was still much work to be done, but he would have been useless without water.

The regiment was scattered about in the dark, confused, disoriented. He had to gather them up and bed them down. Harry had detached thirty or forty men to bear the wounded off before they left the slope, but he had yet to make arrangements for their care. There was his horse, Turk. He had hobbled him somewhere out there in the dark. He sent a lieutenant to find him.

The night had turned unusually cool. He shivered beneath damp clothing. Teeth chattered, his shoulder muscles were clamped tight against the chills, and his socks, soaked from perspiration, made his feet feel frozen despite the summer season.

The first of the wounded came in. Harry had found a grassy fold in the earth, where he had ordered fires made. He had shown the bearers where to lay the hurt. Then he saw that they had water. Soft groans came from ten men as he ambled among them speaking words of encouragement. He suddenly felt a dizzy weakness, an enormous need for sleep. He realized he was babbling, shut his mouth, bent down, took the cold hand of a filthy, barrel-chested soldier, and began to rub warmth into it. The soldier lay motionless. Only labored breathing showed he was still in this world.

Fifty yards off, huge flames leaped near a big barn. What looked like slinking, dark shadows danced near the fires. Curious, Harry wandered over. Heard sobbing, childlike, as he made his way through the brush. He saw bearers rushing in and out of the barn, and wounded soldiers, on litters, strewn all around. He made his way through the maze of bodies and felt the warmth of the flames; he shivered as his own body adjusted to the change in temperature. A stream of light poured from the barn's wide doors and mixed with the flickering light of the flames. He waited for the traffic around the door to wane, then peered in. There were black-haired men in blood-spattered shirts with rolled up sleeves. They were bending over tables of moaning men, jamming crude metal instruments into them. Surgeons, men with blank expressions, looking like hands butchering hogs. Careless, unrestrained, seemingly unaware that men with families, boys with mothers, were at the end of their jagged saws. Harry was surprised that their victims weren't screaming in agony. Drugged, they must be drugged.

He felt a hand on his shoulder, then was pushed against the barn door.

"You're in the way there! Get out of the way!" a corporal bawled.

An officer on a blood-soaked litter was whisked inside. His hands and face were black, his foot dark red and mangled with white, broken bones that were splintered and exposed. Harry stepped back, his eyes still glued to the butchering. He finally blinked, closed his eyes, felt that dizzy weakness again. No need to see this, he thought. Don't need these memories.

Lieutenant Jordan was back with the regiment's horses. He had them tethered on a painted fence not far from the wounded. Harry found Turk quiet, asleep.

"Found him, I see." Harry said as he gave Turk's shoulder a light stroke.

"Yes, sir, just where we left him. Private Matheny took good care of him." There was pride in Jordan's voice. He had an uncanny sense of direction, Harry remembered. His own was good, but he never would have found his mount in this darkness. He stripped off his damp jacket, folded it carefully, then pulled a spare from a saddlebag on Turk. He was still cold, so he put on his India rubber coat as well.

"Orders, sir?" Jordan asked with a strange cheer in his voice.

"Go to sleep."

"Gladly, sir."

Harry turned toward the wounded, wandered over. Captain Cummings was standing among them, a tall, dignified man, competent.

"How many?" Harry asked.

"All in, sir. Fifty-eight here, and, ah, over by that barn there." Cummings pointed to the illuminated barn by the fires.

"Head wounds, most of them grazes. Bleed a lot, but not serious. Most will be back with us soon, sir."

Harry nodded in approval.

"We'll lose some, sir. Ten maybe. Bad shoulder wounds." Cummings looked over toward the barn again.

"The dead?" Harry asked.

"Not all that bad, sir. We left fifteen on the hill."

"Fifteen too many, Captain," Harry said with angered remorse.

Cummings gulped, a little embarrassed. "Yes, sir."

Seventy-three casualties, Harry thought, seventy-three and nothing to show for them. They hadn't even fired a shot. Useless waste. Harry turned and looked at the survivors. Dozens of fires were flickering. All was quiet.

"Officers?" Harry asked.

"One," Cummings said. "Lieutenant Mayhew, Company E. Ah, probably won't make it, sir."

Harry glanced down, nodded, then walked among the stricken. All were asleep, peaceful.

"Ah, Colonel Vance came by looking for you sir," Cummings said softly. "Said he'd see you in the morning. Perfectly exhausted. Went to sleep."

"Have you seen Captain Jones?" Harry responded.

"No, sir, haven't seen him since we went in," Cummings said in a tone that conveyed concern. Harry knew Jones was fine; he had ordered him to gather the strays. He was to report back, but evidently hadn't returned. Harry suddenly felt the overpowering weakness again. His eyelids yearned to close. He walked toward the painted fence.

"Make these men comfortable, Captain. Then get some rest. We'll need to bury those men on the hill in the morning. That is, if the Yankees have left."

"Yes, sir."

Harry was sure the Federals would be gone in the morning. They had made their stand. They'd run for the river now. All the Rebels had done today was give them satisfaction.

"If you see Captain Jones, tell him I'm up by the fence. Beyond the horses. Going to sleep."

"Yes, sir, sleep well, sir."

He drifted toward the horses, felt a desire to socialize with Turk, but staggered past him. His legs wobbled, his arms hung flimsy by his sides. But his mind was clear, was definitely stimulated by the day's events. He wanted to go over the battle again, make some sense out of it. He followed a cow-path that ran along the fence and came to a sturdy post, felt his legs burn as he squatted, then leaned against the post so it would bear the pressure. He sat in silent pain, listening for a moment while his head rested against the rigid wood. There were soft murmurs among the crackling fires, nothing more. No guns, no screams, only stillness, and he soothed himself with the comfort of tiredness. He decided not to ruin the moment with thoughts of battle. His eyelids tugged. He let them fall, felt a burning dryness in his eyes, but his muscles began to relax. His mind was still alert though, and almost too tired to sleep.

A memory spilled in. An image of a ragged gray fox he'd come across years ago, prostrate in the forest at Thornbury. He had thought the fox was dead at first, it being rare to see a live fox in daytime that wasn't rabid. He had gently touched the pads of one hind paw with his boot, and the fox had bolted, as if shot from a gun, a gray streak. It stopped fifty feet away, looked back, its long, red tongue panting, the wide, bushy tail limp. Its ears were pointed upward, alert, but its gray eyes showed exhaustion. Hounds had been running it all day.

The fox stared at him, and Harry had stared back. An understanding had been reached after a meeting of the eyes. Harry would do him no harm.

Sensing that, the fox scampered into nearby thickets, rolled up, and went to sleep, too exhausted to fear its vulnerability. Now, Harry felt the same. He was sure the fox had been as stimulated as he was right now. Glad to be alive, eager to be restored, anxious to run another day.

Voices came from the camp; irritated voices of men just awakened. Harry opened his left eye. A lantern was waving among small mounds of sleeping soldiers, spraying a pale light, moving toward him. He closed his eye, pulled the rubber coat tight against his throat. He wanted no visitors, wanted no responsibility at that moment. But the light drew nearer.

"Massa, Harry? Is dat you?"

That smooth, gentle, drawl. Familiar. Comforting. He was surprised to hear it, but he welcomed the sound. A visit from Kinchen, that was different.

"Yes, Kinchen, it's me. Why on earth are you here?"

"Oh lawdy, I's found yuh! Found yuh! I's been wanderin' through dese woods and fields fo' I don't know how long. But I's found yuh!"

Harry couldn't help a grin, but kept his eyes closed. "Yes, you've found me. Now, why are you here?"

"Massa Henry. He sent me a lookin'. He worried sick. Just a pacin', and..."

Harry cut him off, managed to sit up. "Father, here?"

"No Massa, he a ways off." Kinchen looked up and peered into the darkness, pointed. "He over dat way. A good ways off, I say. He wid all da Gen'rals."

Harry leaned back, closed his eyes again. He thought of his worried father who had probably observed the battle, seen the slaughter.

"You awlright, Massa?" Kinchen noticed Harry's closed eyes.

"Fine, just fine, but lucky to have a merciful God. Did Father see the battle?"

"Oh yeah, suh. Now dat was sump'n to see. All dat clatter. All dat smoke. All dose sold'yas. Ya'll whipped again, den yuh?"

Harry didn't answer, squirmed against the post, kept his eyes closed.

"Massa, I's sure glad you awlright... Massa, you sure you awlright? Your eyes..."

"Fine, I'm fine. Just tired. Very tired."

"Lawdy, I's say yuh are. Me too." Kinchen sat down and propped himself against the boards of the fence, thoughtlessly continued to talk.

"Lawd, what my eyes have seen ta'day, ta'night." He scratched his tight curls.

"All dem sold'yas. Tired, they are. Hurt, lots of 'em. Saw dead men, Massa, dead as a cow struck by da lightnin'. All stiff and swollen."

Kinchen chimed on, and Harry just listened. He loved to hear the liquid words slowly roll off his tongue, so warm, almost hypnotizing.

Lovely accent. He didn't have it. Had spent too much time up north, and didn't think he had an accent at all. Maybe, he did. Maybe not as strong, and he could simply turn it off. Kinchen couldn't.

"And da dark. Pitch black. Blacker dan me," Kinchen mused. And Harry drifted off to sleep.

A hundred feet away, Captain John Lane was sitting on a stump. His company was balled into a knot close by. All his boys were accounted for, four wounded and two dead. He thought of the missing boys, the letters he would have to write. One would go to a neighbor, Percival.

He suddenly remembered something, stuck his hand under his jacket, and squeezed a pocket. Empty! He squeezed the pocket again, jerked up, patted all over himself. The envelope, the company's pay, where was it? He looked all over the ground and among the sleeping men, panicked, eyes searching. His mind trembled. He'd had it before the charge. Had felt it plainly, tight and safe in his pocket. Hadn't checked since, and forgot about it in the excitement. It must have fallen out. How? Where? Where did he bend over? Where did he lie down? The hill! The slope! It's on the battlefield. No, the bearers would have found it. He went to check with Captain Cummings.

Cummings was still up, still tending the wounded. Polite, a gentleman, he hadn't seen the envelope, nor had any of his boys. They would have turned it in. All of them, all of them were honest boys, and wouldn't steal another company's pay. It had to be on the battlefield, hundreds of dollars, laying out there somewhere between the camp and Malvern Hill.

It would be there in the morning. No, he thought, there'll be scavengers all over that field, combing the bodies. He had no choice, he had to go search. Lane looked at the painted fence, saw the lantern on the ground, and the dim figures of Kinchen and Harry.

Kinchen was not yet asleep. He was thinking of Henry, worried, and wondering if he should go back and tell him Harry was safe and well. A shadow appeared over him, startled him.

"Kinchen?"

He jumped, felt his heart throb, clasped his chest, but instinctively answered, "Yeah, suh."

"Colonel Burgwyn, is he asleep?"

Kinchen reached for the lantern, raised it, caught Lane's face in the light. A little fellow with a scraggly beard of a youth, sunken eyes and high cheekbones, a small mouth with pert, red lips shining through the silky hair. Kinchen recognized him, then looked at Harry. A handsome, peaceful face, his mouth hanging open.

"Yeah, suh, he asleep."

"I have to wake him."

"Um hmm." Kinchen clasped Harry's arm, shook it. His master grunted, closed his mouth.

"Colonel Burgwyn?" Lane asked.

Harry opened his bleary eyes, grunted again, blinked.

"Colonel Burgwyn, please pardon me for waking you."

"Captain, Captain Jones?" Harry said, expecting a report on stragglers.

"No sir, Captain Lane, sir."

"Is there a problem?" Harry mumbled.

"Yes, sir," Lane stammered. "I've lost my company's pay."

"Lost?"

"Yes, sir. I had it before the charge this evenin'. Now it's gone. Not in my pocket. It's on the field, sir, I believe."

Harry paused for moment, tried to brush out the cobwebs and gather his thoughts.

"The bearers may have seen it," he finally replied. "Did you check with Cummings?"

"Yes, sir. None has seen it. None has turned it in. Request permission to go search, sir."

"Request denied. Go to sleep, Captain. It will be there in the morning."

"Begging your pardon sir, but there'll be scavengers all over that hill tomorrow." Lane's voice became more frantic. "Just can't face the boys in the morning. And the families of the dead, sir, no sons, and no pay."

Harry said nothing, but he knew Lane was right. He had to at least try. Had to soothe Lane. A good officer; it wasn't his fault. He pulled out his watch. It was almost two AM. Lane watched, anticipating.

"I know it's late, sir. We all need sleep, but I just won't sleep knowing that the pay is lying out there and ripe for the picking."

Harry slowly got to his feet, brushed off the dust. Kinchen stood too.

"Well, Captain, when did you last see it?" Harry asked.

"Before the charge, sir. Felt it in my jacket pocket."

"Before we entered the woods, or before we advanced into the oat field?"

"The field, sir, checked it right after we climbed that fence."

Harry reached down for the lantern, but Kinchen's hand beat him to it. "Gonna need help, Massa."

Harry shook his head. "Prefer you stay here."

"Know yuh do, but I's a' goin'," the slave said defiantly.

"Won't be pleasant."

Kinchen nodded, "I know."

"Suit yourself," Harry said, apathetically. He was cranky, knew it, but he couldn't help it. Nobody's fault, but he sure needed his sleep. The sun would be up early, and there would be plenty of work tomorrow.

Captain Lane sprung ahead, stopped, turned, thanked Harry, then pointed the way to Malvern Hill.

There were long slivers of splintered branches, and crippled trees pockmarked by minie balls, shrapnel, and canister. Green leaves littered the forest floor. Yesterday morning the leaves were sucking in the sun light, helping to nourish their host. Now they were curling, drying, dead. Kinchen was holding the lantern high, shifting it from hand to hand as each arm tired. Lane walked beside him, pupils wide and black. Harry walked five feet behind them, thinking of tomorrow, making lists in his head. The shredded forest guided them toward the oat field, to the now fallen fence. The three stopped, peered into the open dark. Clouds had rolled in. There were no stars, no moon, but Malvern Hill was aglow with Yankee fires.

"Still up there, Colonel," Lane said to Harry.

"Packing up, I suspect," he responded. "Is this where we came out?"

"Can't tell, sir." Both officers looked about, trying to find a familiar landmark. Kinchen's eyes were trained on the glowing hill.

"Won't dey see da light, Massa? Won't dey see da light and shoot?"

"No," Harry said as he ventured into the field. "They'll think we're gathering wounded. Won't shoot at bearers unless we get too close."

Somewhat relieved, Kinchen apprehensively stepped over the fallen rails and into the field, still holding the lantern.

"Do you think you dropped it in the field, Captain? If you did, we'll never find it in these trampled oats."

"Don't know, sir. Suspect it fell out on the slope."

The three ranged into the field, slowly, heads down, searching. Kinchen waved the light. Harry and Lane were still not certain this was the same ground they had advanced over. Harry was sure the search was hopeless. Lane prayed for luck. Kinchen noticed his own nervous excitement, looked at his shaking hands.

They reached the second fence, also fallen, and looked upon the dark slope, a vacant, black area between the light of the lantern and the glare of the fires above.

"Raise the lantern high," Harry instructed Kinchen. The slave raised it high over his head, illuminating a small part of the hillside. The officers hunted for bodies, the dead from their own regiment.

"Over this way." The three moved further to the right, and walked fifty yards down the shallow gully at the base of the hill. Kinchen raised the lantern every ten paces or so. Finally they spied a corpse, and climbed twenty feet up the slope.

Sprawled out, head downhill, his chest ripped apart and rib cage exposed, his entrails flopped out like a ball of giant worms. A grisly sight, and the man unidentifiable. An overpowering stench suddenly filled the air. All three pulled out handkerchiefs and covered their noses and mouths, kept them there. Lane felt he might gag. Harry pointed to the right, and they walked further along the hillside. Now they were able to remove the kerchiefs, the stench only slight. Lane was coughing. Kinchen heard a wail, stopped in his tracks. Over to his left, further up the hill, a faint groan came out of the dark, then a desperate call.

"Second Louisiana, come bear me off!" A wounded Rebel had seen their light, and had thought they were bearers. Harry and Lane also stopped. More pitiful pleas came from the black.

"Water, water!"

Kinchen shivered.

"Please God. Come bear me off!"

The whole hillside began to moan. Dozens of wounded were still on the slope. Harry's heart twitched; he wasn't prepared for this. Why hadn't that regiment bore off their wounded? There was nothing they could do, they had not brought water. Harry looked at Kinchen, saw his sad, round eyes, shook his head, then gestured further to the right. They walked on.

The air began to stir. A slight breeze at first, then a hard gust like the type that preceded a storm. They could hear the wind blowing through distant trees, a sound like an applauding crowd, eerie in the dark. Kinchen breathed the air in. A fresh smell, moist and clean, that cleared away the scent of decaying flesh. Sprinkles rolled in. A fine mist like ocean spray spattered cool on their faces. Lightning flashed, a far away thud in the sky, spooky, and its light allowed a momentary glimpse of knotty corpses. The search for the missing pay seemed more hopeless than ever.

They came upon more dead bodies. Harry and Lane recognized some of them. The three moved forward in a clump, shielding their eyes from the mist, ever looking downward. Lane saw a single corpse, darted ahead, bent over it, waved for Kinchen to bring the light closer.

"This is Simpkins, Colonel. I was close to him in line. It's near. The pay's got to be near here." The three spread out, searching, eyes peeled.

Minutes passed. The search grew wider, further away from the body of Private Simpkins. Nothing, no envelope. Harry stopped looking, put his hands on his hips, then pulled his hat tight on his head. Lane wouldn't quit, his eyes trance-like and focused on the ground.

Ten feet from Simpkins was a tangle of three dead Confederates with faces down. Kinchen moved toward them, placed the lantern on the ground and cast his eyes over the bodies. He didn't really know what he was looking for, but didn't see anything irregular. He squatted next to one of the corpses, placed his hands on an arm and leg, and pulled. The body flipped over. He looked at the face, pasty, bloodless, with an expression of agony. He moved to the next body, turned it over too, the face like a bloody rag. He turned over the last corpse, peered underneath, saw a pale package wrapped in string. Kinchen squinted at it, stood up, waved.

"Colonel Harry, Colonel Harry, come quick!" He raised his voice over the blowing wind and pointed downward at the envelope. Harry hurried over, Lane right behind him.

"That's it!" Lane exclaimed. He quickly grabbed the package, and a sense of relief shot through his body. He smiled, delighted, thanked Kinchen profusely. The slave returned the smile, beamed triumphantly.

Harry grinned at Kinchen and looked him over. He had known him all his life. Had never thought on it, perhaps even had taken him for granted, but here he was, in the middle of a battlefield, had come looking for him in the dark, a dangerous trek. Somehow, he had found him, and had volunteered to come look for the missing money. Didn't have to, had insisted on it. He had poked around the corpses, and had found it. Truly amazing. Harry looked at the black face, shining, wet from the rain. He looked at the proud, black eyes and the bright teeth. There, in the dim light, he was grinning. Standing there among the dead. For an instant, unmindful of the dead, just smiling.

THE PURPLE CLOUDS BILLOWED IN, and the cleansing rains came in torrents. The Confederate camps were drenched. There was little sleep in the night, and in the morning, after a meager breakfast, Kinchen was sent to Henry with word of Harry's safe return from the battle. The young Lieutenant Colonel went about reorganizing his regiment, and found the boys unfit for combat. He also learned that Ransom's Brigade had been shattered, suffering more casualties than any other Rebel brigade. Three of the five Colonels were wounded, and one Lieutenant Colonel dead, his leg blown off by a Federal shell. The Twenty-sixth had come through the fight quite well in comparison to other regiments of the brigade.

The Federals abandoned Malvern Hill, just as Harry had predicted, and he expected orders at any moment to prepare for a pursuit of the retreating enemy. Due to casualties and a dearth of officers throughout the brigade, Harry found himself in charge of the Twenty-sixth. Vance was needed elsewhere, being one of only two healthy Colonels left in the brigade. The soldiers had to be gathered up, fed, and reformed into companies. Shelters for the wounded had to be built to protect them from the persistent rain. He had to ensure that ambulances transported those who could be moved. Ammunition and weapons had to be inspected. No time for rest, Harry was pressed with duty until late in the afternoon.

The expected orders never came. Except for harassing the withdrawing Unionists with artillery, General Lee wanted no repeat of Malvern Hill. Any attacks would have the added disadvantage of having to endure the Federal gunboats' massive one hundred-and-eighty-pound shells. Lee was satisfied with bottling McClellan up at Harrison's Landing, where the Yankees sat until recalled by President Lincoln. Richmond had been saved.

That evening, Harry found time to compose a letter to his mother. Within the note he thanked a merciful Providence for his healthy condition, and described in some detail his close encounters with death. He described the confused fighting, the poor generalship, and the horrible condition of his brigade. He also revealed what was probably the prevalent attitude among the Rebel soldiers, delight at having relieved Richmond, and disappointment at having failed to destroy McClellan. He closed with an apology for the briefness of his correspondence, and with an expression of hope that the letter would relieve her anxiety.

Later that evening, the regiment's baggage train arrived after its long trek from Petersburg. Harry would have a change of dry clothes and a comfortable tent. Kinchen also came with the wagons. He bore a note from Henry expressing relief for Harry's healthy condition and begging him to be more prudent.

THE MORNING OF JULY THIRD OPENED FAIR, BUT BALMY, one of those humid Virginia mornings that spared no clues that the day would be uncomfortable. Harry again expected a movement toward the enemy, but word soon came that it would be another day of rest and refitting. After Kinchen prepared breakfast, Harry asked his servant to prepare Turk for a ride. He was going to make a survey of the battlefield at Malvern Hill. The slave saddled Turk and Waverly and expressed a desire to accompany him. Harry showed no enthusiasm for companionship, but did not object. Kinchen noticed the aloofness. He had seen it before in Harry, many times, but he didn't let it discourage him. Kinchen followed a short distance behind his master, and did not engage him in conversation. Harry was in a serious mood, almost brooding. He was riding to the battlefield in search of answers.

Burial parties dotted the slopes. They were mostly free blacks who had been hired by the Confederates to root out trenches, and dig graves. Bodies in gray were lined in neat rows, hundreds of them, if not thousands. Buzzards circled overhead, attracted by the stench that was still present, despite the previous day's rains. As the sun rose, and the air grew hotter, the smell would become overpowering. Harry had never seen so much human wreckage. The bodies pulverized into the soil and the rubbish strewn about seemed more the result of a tornado than of human design. Kinchen was somber, quietly horrified. Harry did not pause among his own dead though. Instead, he steered Turk toward the hilltop, toward the Yankee dead.

The Negroes had not worked their way to the corpses in blue yet. By the looks of things, the Yankees had prepared their own dead for burial, but then had hurriedly left. The corpses were stacked in neat piles. The largest, Harry guessed, contained eight hundred bodies, the size of a large regiment. He rode near the piles, Turk at a slow walk, Kinchen, on Waverly, right behind him. Harry seemed to be on some grotesque pilgrimage, looking over the bodies, but saying nothing. Kinchen thought him far away, as if contemplating. Harry gave Turk's reins a slight tug, brought the gelding to a halt, then removed his hat. He casually took a handkerchief from his pocket and wiped his brow, replaced the hat, then stared vacantly off to the east.

"Why did they come?" he murmured. Kinchen heard him, but did not respond. He sensed Harry was talking to himself.

Why did the northerners come, he thought. For freedom? He looked at Kinchen. For them? He continued to hold his eyes on his servant. If that was it, freedom, then they really didn't understand us. Didn't understand Negroes.

Kinchen felt Harry's gaze. His eyes seemed distant, as if in another world. It made him uncomfortable, and he squirmed in his saddle. Harry realized he was staring and looked away.

The Yankees didn't even understand themselves. They say they're fighting for freedom, and some may even think so. But no, it's not that. They need us, and they're envious. They hate our wealth, and they want it. They want it back. They've always thought us possessions. Stars on their flag. They want no sister to the south, no competitor for empire. We are ruining their vision, their dream.

Kinchen watched his master. Saw that his mind was working, churning. He wondered what he was thinking.

Harry spied a small stack of five dead soldiers twenty yards away. He gave Turk a little squeeze, steered him toward the pile, and stopped him just short. He looked down on them, barefoot, all five, and filthy. He noticed four of the five men were shot in the head, the result of the Rebels attacking up hill, he reasoned. He looked at the waxy faces, pale, dark shadows under the eyes. They looked familiar. Not familiar in the sense that he had somehow known them, but he knew he had seen faces like these before. Immigrants, Irish or Germans probably. Perhaps one was a Pole or a Scandinavian. He'd seen thousands of them up north, in Boston, in Philadelphia, New York, and even in Baltimore. Filthy, ignorant souls who clung to some kind of false hope. They were men with no future. Sumner, his brother, had called them poor men with bad teeth. He had picked it up from a school chum, no doubt. The immigrants had come to America looking for a better life. Instead, they had found slums and no jobs. Valueless, someone had called them. Who was it? Who had said that? A cadet at West Point. He couldn't remember the cadet's name, but recalled the face. He never forgot a face. He was a northerner, a New Yorker. Terrible thing to label someone valueless. He had told him so, but the New Yorker explained, and it made sense, he recollected. He said immigrants were like fire logs. When a mill burned one up, they just reached into the slums for another. Too many of them. Easily replaced. The mill owners, the foremen, they went through them hand-over-fist. Didn't take care of them, didn't care if they got sick, or even killed. They just reached and grabbed some more. They were men without value, worse than slaves.

Harry turned in his saddle and looked at his servant. Kinchen hadn't followed him, was twenty yards away, looking at him with a bewildered face. Valueless? Kinchen? He thought not. Definitely not. Hard to replace someone like Kinchen, yet these immigrants were fighting for him. Why? For freedom? For a word with an obscure meaning? Why, the immigrants were hardly free themselves. Perhaps some of them were here for a cause. Some of these Yankees were honorable, noble men. Noble, but misguided. Some, though, were here for money, for plunder, or perhaps just for their monthly pay. Others, the others were here, he thought, because they had more stature as soldiers than as lowly laborers.

He sat back in the saddle, sighed. It was getting terribly hot, sweat dripped into his eyes, stinging them. Turk began to paw at the dirt, complaining, thirsty. Kinchen, too, was getting restless. The putrid air was making him woozy. He was tired of the sight of decaying bodies, and brought his hand to his face. He covered his mouth and nose, looked at Harry and finally guided Waverly toward him.

Harry noticed Kinchen's approach. He wasn't ready to leave, wasn't yet satisfied with the answers to his questions. Hard to figure. Why men went to war. Especially hard to grasp why these Yankees were dying down here in Virginia. He wanted to stay a little longer, search a little further. The answers had to be up here among their dead.

He noticed a reflection in the dirt. Something shiny was next to the five dead soldiers. A coin, perhaps. He dismounted, reached down, picked it up. No, it was a brass button with U.S. boldly stamped in the middle. He studied it, then strolled away from the dead, leading Turk, his back to Kinchen. He flipped the button in his fingers and wondered who had made it. A factory up north? Likely. A factory that employed immigrants? Probably. Harry looked up and swept his eyes over the barren plateau, the ground the Yankees had held so well. Debris from the battle was scattered everywhere. The wasted implements of war: muskets, bayonets, caissons, wagons, clothing, and unused ammunition. A virtual fortune.

A realization flashed in his mind. Someone was getting rich on this war. A vision popped in his head, a fat man wearing a starched white shirt and a splendid woolen suit. He was riding a fashionable carriage drawn by a well-groomed horse. A shady lane and fine homes surrounded him. A man with influence, a man with political friends, a man who placed money before honor, and who was comfortably at home getting rich. Only there wasn't just one. There were hundreds. Owners of mines, factories, mills, ships, railroads, and newspapers. Powerful men who usually got their way. It was they who wanted this war, wanted to keep the southern states as possessions, wanted to put down the wealthy men of the South once and for all. They were hiding, hiding behind a noble cause of Union and freedom. Had convinced the noble youths, the naive farmers, and the ignorant immigrants that the war was necessary. Told them the worst about slavery, and the people believed the worst was the norm. Judged without the truth. Rich men had manipulated them. Despots behind the scenes. Subtle tyrants.

Harry shook his head. Oh, the hypocrisy of the northern cause!

The anger bubbled in him, so angry he felt he might cry. He clutched the button tight in his fist, then slowly turned and looked again upon the corpses. He saw the dead men in blue in a new light. Good men they were, all of them. Fighting for a cause they thought right, were told was right. Their perception was noble. But nobility is not all knowing. They were unaware of the hidden manipulators, the subtle tyrants, knew nothing of their greedy motives. Harry closed his eyes, then slapped his fist into his palm. Kinchen noticed.

"Massa... You awlright?"

His eyes popped open, focused on Kinchen, saw the puzzled black face. He realized he'd been acting strangely. He sensed a twinge of embarrassment. Wanted to explain. But it was hot, had gotten very hot. He loosened the top button of his tunic, took out his handkerchief and wiped the sweat from his neck, then dabbed his forehead. Would Kinchen understand?

Harry mounted Turk, sighed, then noticed the button again, a shiny brass sphere. He held it up for Kinchen to see.

"Riches among the dead," he proclaimed sarcastically, a hazy clue to his private conclusion. Kinchen grinned uneasily, squinted at the button, and like Harry at first, thought it was a coin. Harry held it between his thumb and forefinger, then dropped it in the dirt. It landed by the cool, bloodless feet of the five dead immigrants. Harry then gave Turk a gentle kick and the gelding started a slow walk. Kinchen let them pass, stared at the shiny object by the corpses, and finally realized what it was.

"Riches among da dead?" Kinchen mumbled.

Harry heard the mumbles, but ignored them. He was too tired to explain further, too angry, and he spurred Turk to a trot, but paused and motioned for Kinchen to follow him. He looked back at the dead one last time, the rows of virtuous dead. He had his answer now. It was something he had already sensed, but it had lain vague and hidden in his brain. His pilgrimage had brought it back to the fore, and he would not forget it again. It passed through his mind slowly, and he said it silently to himself for emphasis.

There is always a little evil among the good, and some good among the evil. Always.

❧ 17 ❧

> # A.L.D.

Headquarters, 26th Reg. N. C.
Troops Camp near Chaffin's Bluff,
4 miles below Richmond, Aug. 22nd, 1862

Colonel H. K. Burgwyn, Jr.
Raleigh, N.C.

Sir—

I send this note as a friend & have composed it with hopes that you will act on it promptly. Colonel Vance, or should I say Governor-elect Vance, will leave here in a day or two or at least this week & as a friend I advise you to return to the regiment. General Ransom says that he should not recommend you for Colonel on account of your age. He said he did not intend having any boys commanding regiments in his Brigade. I have spoken to several of our officers & they will not submit to have anyone else. They swear they will not stay under an officer appointed over them.

We thought that Ransom may have said this in one of his frets without meaning, but he has since made it clear he is very serious.

The Regiment will stick up for you without a doubt. A committee was formed with the purpose of recommending officers to fill vacancies due to Vance's resignation. Yesterday they waited on Gen. Ransom to know if he would approve them. He emphatically denied to approve your recommendation & subsequently the committee recommended no one for Colonel. He is now maneuvering to have Colonel Ruffin in your stead. This, of course, he cannot do legally unless a court finds you incompetent. Ransom will find no evidence to support any such claim, but, please, come to us as soon as you can. I wish for you to resist to the last this usurpation of power. I am too angry to act. I shall resign, if you are not allowed to be elected.

I have the utmost confidence that you can defeat Gen. Ransom's machinations, but for God's sake, please come. I pass this information as a friend and trust *you will treat it with strict confidence. I do not fear for myself, but for you and the regiment. I cannot imagine us commanded by anyone else. I am, sir, your most obedient servant,*

> Captain J. J. Young
> Quartermaster, 26th Reg. N.C.T.

THE ROAD WAS NICELY SHADED, AND THE land had a little roll that broke up the monotony of an otherwise empty lane. Elms were the predominant trees, big towering hardwoods whose long shadows blocked the morning's glare and cooled those passing under the reach of their full limbs. Beyond the treeline were a few swaying fields of timothy ripening in the strong August sun. Echoing out of darkened hollows came the braying of cows enticing their calves to water and shelter from the heat. The comforting sound reached up to the road where a gray rider sat upright on a smoky horse. The rider's thoughts at the moment were far away, but the earnest moos broke the spell and brought him back to the peaceful lane where distant troubles had no place. He halted the horse for a moment, took in the air, and let the scenery flood his senses.

It was a pleasant ride from Raleigh to Will's Forest. Harry had covered the five miles on many occasions while he commanded the camp of instruction at Crabtree the year previous, and again during his current furlough. Will's Forest was the estate of Major John Devereux, Harry's third cousin and the son of the same Thomas Devereux who had fought the heated legal wars with Henry two decades back. Those ill times were nearly forgotten now, Thomas Devereux was long dead, and the two families had drawn tight once again.

The Major usually wasn't the object of Harry's visits. Rather, it was his lovely eighteen-year-old daughter, Annie Lane, who lured him to the sprawling estate. The romance had begun nearly a year before, had started as a youthful infatuation, but had grown and taken on more mature characteristics. Harry had plans for a union, intended a proposal for a wedding following the war. He had every intention of executing proper etiquette before his plea, although all his attempts to consult with the Major so far had been frustrated. Annie's father was the quartermaster general for state troops and had been away at Wilmington on important business for the past month. His return to Raleigh had been repeatedly postponed, delaying Harry's strategy until his own furlough was about up. Fortunately, Harry had been advised that Major Devereux had returned to Will's Forest yesterday, and not too soon, for a train bound for Richmond that was to carry Harry back to duty was leaving the Raleigh depot early the next morning.

He let the horse step at a lazy gait, there being no specific hour for the appointment. The leisurely pace suited him. His troubles back with the brigade in Richmond at the hands of General Ransom had him tied in knots, testing his emotions for weeks. What could have fueled the General's prejudice towards him? Was it really his age, was that the reason for his lack of confidence, or did he have a favorite he wished to appoint? Couldn't Ransom see that it was he who had trained the regiment, it was he whom the troops admired, not Vance. The command of the Twenty-sixth was his just due, and it was the law, yet Ransom could not be budged despite having absolutely no grounds on which to prove incompetence.

What little respect Harry had for the General was evaporating like a puddle after a summer shower. He had already considered that it might be necessary to go over Ransom's head to the War Department, a ploy he was being forced into and did not relish. There was one alternative though, he had a plan, and it was the intricate aspects of this solution that kept flowing in and out of his head, dominating his consciousness and attitude.

But it was time to let it go. Nothing could be done until he arrived in Richmond and consulted with Ransom himself. He had a fateful appointment now, was about to ask a father to let him have his oldest daughter forever. He wasn't nervous about the appointment with the Major, had no doubts about his decision, could not have been more confident that he had found his mate for eternity. But the troubles with Ransom kept crowding his mind, distracting him from his present mission. That's why he kept the pace slow, to let the pretty countryside and pleasant thoughts of Annie clear away the agonizing pain of rejection by his commander, an old neighbor, and a long-time friend of the family.

The line of elms came to an end, the road now exposed to a burning sun. He paused at the edge of the shade, spoke to Equinox, his father's slate-colored gelding, having left Waverly and Cora back at Chaffin's Bluff with Kinchen.

"Just a minute here, boy."

He gathered his thoughts, rehearsed his request one last time, then looked down into a shallow valley with a shaded creek, where black cows stood lazily. The view brought on an urge for easier times, for an era without war, without tension. It compelled him to wonder why his generation had been cursed by so many powerful men with conflicting ideals.

Harry spurred Equinox, and they trotted into the fiery sunlight.

THE HOUSE WAS TUCKED AWAY DEEP within a twelve-acre grove, the lane cutting through cool woods. Harry rounded a bend, caught sight of the giant white columns, four of them, each so large that two men could wrap their arms around them and barely touch fingers. The home seemed to rise up out of the trees as he approached, massive, resembling a Greek palace. He slowed Equinox to a walk, circled around toward a wide stairway of fifteen steps that climbed to the columns and a high porch. A Negro was perched at the top, waved at Harry before he started his descent.

"Good morning, Richard."

"Mornin' suh," the slave said as he took the reins. Harry dismounted.

"The Major's expecting me," said Harry as he made for the steps.

"No, suh."

The Colonel stopped, looked over his shoulder at the gray little man. "No?"

"No suh, the Major's gone. Called away quick, late in da night."

Perplexed. "Is he in town?"

"No suh, took a special train out."

"Where?"

"Weldon, I believes."

He was lost for words. Wanted to ask why he wasn't told, but he figured it rude, and that the Negro wouldn't know. Harry stood there awkwardly, trying to collect himself.

"The others are here, suh. Missas Margaret, Miss Annie, the chilluns," said Richard attempting to comfort him.

"Yes, yes. Thank you, Richard." The servant led Equinox away, and Harry climbed the stairs slowly.

The door opened when he reached the top. It was Nadie, a rather protective old servant.

"Good morning, Nadie."

"Mornin' suh," she said in a cool tone.

"Will you inform Mrs. Devereux and Miss Annie that I'm here?"

Nadie didn't move, simply cleared her throat. She was strict in matters of protocol. Harry gave her a displeasured eye, but pulled out his card and gave it to her. She took it and closed the door.

He spun around slowly, removed his hat, and peered into the surrounding forest for a moment. He didn't acknowledge the almost deafening sound of a million buzzing insects, but instead, began to pace up and down the long stone porch.

Must be some kind of an emergency at Weldon, he thought. It had sure fouled things up. He couldn't possibly talk with him anytime soon, probably months. Couldn't do it by letter. No, it had to be proper, face to face.

He finally leaned against a column, looked out into the forest again, heard the insects now, their sound, overpowering. He had heard the clicking clamor countless times before, yet rarely had he ever acknowledged it and truly listened. A completely different world, he thought. They have no idea of the turmoil we weave around them, and we are just as unaware of their struggles, the savage ethics of the forest.

Suddenly he was very tired of the war, the way it intruded, engulfed, the way it pulled people down to another level. It made him realize humans had not really come very far.

For all our accomplishments, for all our boasting, we are still just like them, the creatures of the forest. All a part of God's plan, I suppose. We are merely frightened beasts.

Nadie stepped out on the porch.

"Colonel Burgwyn?" Harry peered around the column.

"Suh—Miss Annie Lane Devereux."

Nadie stepped aside, and there she was, a marvelous girl, and the sound of the insects no longer registered.

Dark curls, big brown eyes, smooth rosy cheeks, and a disposition to match her radiance, she was a southerner both in blood and sentiment. She stood with a proud shyness, her hands clasped in front, a timid smile. Yet Harry sensed the hidden disappointment. He moved toward her, took her hands, kissed her tenderly on a cheek, while Nadie watched with a curled lip. The servant took a seat by the door and the couple walked hand in hand to a shaded bench at the far end of the porch.

The words didn't come easily. Annie knew of Harry's appointment with her father, and was aware of its purpose, for the couple had already talked of marriage. Harry had expected to see her only after he had spoken to the Major, and had planned to formally propose in the garden that very afternoon.

"I had supposed you would have called later, after receiving father's message," she finally opened.

"An oversight produced by haste, I believe," said Harry, "I never received it."

A hand rushed to her chest. "Oh dear, he has treated you badly."

"No, no, I'm sure he was in a great rush, the train."

Annie looked away, slightly ashamed. "That can be his only excuse. I'm sure he admires you and approves—if I had known I would have sent Richard myself."

"But you couldn't have known—don't think on it. It's a passed event, nothing we can do, it's useless to fret."

"We don't know when he'll return," she said with fading hopes.

"Makes no difference, I must report tomorrow."

Annie propped herself up to cover her despair. She knew it would be months before another furlough. She wanted to suggest Harry write him, but that would be too assertive, an unattractive gesture.

Harry felt the burden of her disappointment, and searched for something to brighten the situation.

"If my plan follows through, I may be able to snatch another visit very soon."

"Plan?"

"I've told you."

She perked up. "Please tell again."

Harry paused a moment, took a breath. "Since General Ransom, in his misguided opinion, refuses to consider me the rightful Colonel of the Twenty-sixth, I shall submit a proposal that we be allowed to trade my regiment for another in General Pettigrew's Brigade."

"Oh yes," she remembered.

"I'm confident General Pettigrew will approve, and if the transfer is made, I will be very close, and perhaps can get a short leave to see your father."

"But doesn't General Ransom have a say in the matter?"

"Undoubtedly, and he will not be inclined to accept it, the Twenty-sixth being larger and in better order than any of Pettigrew's regiments. But if he refuses, he will have a regular hornet's nest on his hands."

"How so?"

Harry was momentarily distracted by Nadie feverishly fanning herself from the heat, as she rocked at the far end of the porch. "Nearly all my officers will resign if Ransom attempts to appoint a new Colonel over them. Quite embarrassing and a terrible inconvenience. Also, I will appeal to the War Department, if he makes such an attempt. His actions are clearly unlawful."

"Is your father not in Richmond now with such an appeal?"

"Yes, but I've wired instructions for him to wait, until I've made my proposal to General Ransom."

It was all very tidy, prospects were promising, and Ransom's were not.

"General Pettigrew has just taken command of his brigade at Petersburg, and I've been assured that he will remain south of the James. I spoke with General Martin just yesterday, and he informed me that portions of my brigade have already left to join Stonewall and General Lee. So you see, if the transfer is made, I shall remain close for a long time to come, and perhaps will even be moved to Weldon or Goldsboro."

It was all very complicated, but Annie was satisfied, and very hopeful that Harry would not go off to join Stonewall.

Mrs. Devereux stepped out on the porch, whispered to Nadie, and the servant rose and went back inside. Harry got to his feet quickly.

Mrs. Devereux was the charming daughter of a respected physician. She still had her youthful good looks, and appeared much too young to have grown children. She shared Annie's large, pretty eyes.

The mistress greeted the Colonel politely, and was very complimentary. They spoke briefly of the unfortunate missed appointment, and she apologized for her husband's oversight and omission. Harry was quite forgiving.

"A very warm day," said the mistress.

"Yes ma'am, but cooler here at the Forest." Harry replied.

"I've asked Nadie to deliver some refreshments to the veranda. Won't you join me?"

The veranda was just above them, shaded by the same roof as the porch, but higher, cooler, more exposed to the rare breezes. They retreated there, and Mrs. Devereux didn't stay long, excusing herself after one cool drink. She instructed Nadie to accompany her, leaving the couple alone, a compliment to Harry.

And the lovers remained there while the morning moved to noon and beyond. A lazy, sultry day together in the shadows. The words flowed freely, there was laughter, then silent comfort. Harry twirled his fingers slowly in

Annie's curls, his favorite flirtation. He was tempted to propose right there, during this peaceful escape, but suppressed the urge. The sun fell below the trees and sent its last rays to clear away the shadows under the veranda, a signal for the coming departure. Harry would spend his last evening at the rented home in Raleigh with his family, but before the parting, he would leave Annie with the greatest confidence of his devotion to her, his glittering eyes clear evidence of his sincerity.

Richard brought Equinox. Harry kissed Annie's hand, turned reluctantly and descended the steps. He mounted the handsome gray, waved sadly, and guided the horse toward the lane. Annie watched him draw away, disappearing into the forest. She listened to the hoof beats, until they were smothered by the unyielding sound of clicking insects.

18

THIS VALLEY LEADS TO FREEDOM

May 6th, 1863
Bivouac, South Anna Bridges
Near Hanover Junction, Va.

My Dear Mother,

Shad brought me your letter of the 25th instant, and I am very glad to hear from you. Due to ceaseless activity, I regret I was unable to answer until this evening. I suppose you have heard of our great victory at Chancellorsville. Today saw 2,000 Yankee prisoners pass by for Richmond. Good uniforms, stout men, but lacking in spirit. I regret to be the bearer of dreadful intelligence however. Our great Stonewall was badly wounded. Can't bear the thought of losing him. May God spare the old professor to lead us into victory once again. Otherwise our affairs in the east are everywhere in the most prosperous condition— ain't it a wonder. In the west, affairs are not so tidy. Much talk of Vicksburg around camp, but in my opinion, old Grant will find the swamps, fever, and Bronze John the worthiest of opponents.

I will endeavor to catch you up on events since my last effort. Last Saturday, as you have surely heard by now, we took the cars from Goldsboro & all went right till near Halifax where the train containing the right wing of my Regiment was stopped to pass the mail train, & the one in which I was stopped, was some three hundred yards behind it. While thus stationary, the train with the 11th North Carolina ran into us, killing one man, mortally wounding another & severely injuring 8 or 9 more. A disgusting affair, born from neglect. We were then detached to Halifax and remained until 2 PM. Reached Petersburg at 11 PM & marched rapidly through the town & took the cars for Richmond. Reached Richmond 5 AM & were sent to the North Anna Bridges & at Hanover Junction received intelligence that Yankees were at Ashland & expected to raid the junction. Camped now along the Telegraph Road near the South Anna.

There is great excitement in Richmond about the Yankee cavalry raid, and we hear that Stoneman's Corps is at nearby Louisa C. H.

Yesterday I visited Walter Russell, an old friend from the Institute—you may recall my mentioning him on several occasions. Well, he is in a hospital tent here and nearly the whole of his thigh was carried away by a shell. The wound is very serious but his spirit good. Today, General Pettigrew ordered me to send Companies A & B to Polecat Bridge, as there is a rumor that more Yankee cavalry are in King & Queen. I suppose the whole regiment will be sent, if they are not soon cleared out.

Tell Father that I am not discharging Kinchen, but only giving him a furlough. I sent him with many misgivings, as Shad is & always will be worthless as a cook or valet. I do not think that I can spare Kinchen for more than a fortnight. Please have Father arrange it so as to let me have him again at the soonest opportunity. If you recall, I sent by him a New York paper for Father & a Yankee canteen. Did you give Miss Annie Devereux the box of sardines with my compliments? Has Kinchen been instructed on how to fricassee turkey or chicken? Your letter makes no mention of this.

Please tell Father not to send that miserable Turk. Send my Hawkeye instead. He is such a big, strong horse and will weather the coming campaigns just fine, I believe. I have the black mare Cora & shall keep her, but I will sell Waverly at the earliest convenience. It will be a sad parting, but he has grown too weak for active service. We are given but 10 lbs. corn and 5 of hay a day & graze them 4 hours a day when possible. I know Pollok will be disappointed to lose Hawkeye, but I believe Turk will suit his purposes just fine.

To give you an idea of what Kinchen is worth in camp as a cook—I was offered $20 a month for his services before he left. As I have told you, these attacks of the flux come on quite suddenly & last a week, more or less. They have seen fit to come forth again, & now I am regulated to a buggy, most disagreeable. When these attacks come on, I try to have my food carefully prepared, which no one but Kinchen can do. Along with Hawkeye, if possible, please send by Kinchen one blank book for journal, handkerchiefs & summer clothes. Have him bring some butter & a bag of hominy from the plantation, & also please have him bring my rifled pistol for I intend shooting frogs and terrapins to add variation to my diet.

Can't tell you how much I've wanted Father's opera glass. My little telescope greatly fatigues my eyes and is useless while on horseback, very difficult to catch an object. Tell him I promise to return it, if he can send it by Kinchen.

Rumors abound & I tend to think them more than probable. General Lee will call in all his troops from South Carolina, North Carolina & Southern Virginia, except for a few garrisons, & try the invasion game again. I do not hesitate to say that all are ready & willing & are confident of success. I am proud to say that at our last muster day, my Regiment numbered 936 officers and men present. I dare say the largest regiment in the army. No doubt General Petti-

grew's Brigade will be permanently attached to General Lee soon, & I believe we will make a fine addition.

So you see I have written you a long letter & hope it will inspire a like response from you. I know you suffer from little news around Raleigh, but your words bring me such pleasant joy, even though they be trifling. I do not know where specifically you should address your letters as the future movements of my Regiment are uncertain. If you send them to Richmond in care of General Pettigrew's Brigade, they should find their intended. Please remind Father that any letter to you is also meant for him. Give my love to all, and give my regards to Miss Annie Devereux if by chance you see her. Ever Your Most Affectionate Son,

> Henry K. Burgwyn, Jr.
> Colonel, 26th Reg. N.C.T.

P.S. Since my Regiment may be going to the front at any moment, I fear if Kinchen is not sent to me soon the opportunity will be lost & I stuck with Shad. Please send him as soon as practical. I know Father finds him indispensable, but would he prefer sick stock, or a feeble son?

GENERAL PETTIGREW HELD A REVIEW OF his brigade one May morning in a fallow field near the tracks below the South Anna trestles. Major General George Pickett's Division was camped just over a rise, and the Virginian, with two of his brigadier generals and their staffs, rode over to view the affair. Pettigrew's Brigade of Carolinians was new to Lee's army, pulled in and added to A. P. Hill's new Corps just before the second invasion of the North. Even though his division was part of Longstreet's Corps, Pickett was curious about the quality of the newcomers.

Four Carolina regiments made up the large brigade, the Fifty-second, Forty-seventh, Twenty-sixth and Eleventh. It was larger than most in the rebel army, due in part to Harry's Twenty-sixth, which was twice the size of a normal regiment. Spread out in a cool, fresh morning, glittering in the soft light, the brigade, formed in line of battle, made an impressive sight. Veteran and well-drilled, it maneuvered professionally, proving itself ready to be a part of the famed Army of Northern Virginia.

Always the perfectionist, Harry was not at all satisfied with appearances. His regiment's drill was good, probably the best in the brigade, but his soldiers' uniforms were atrocious. They were tattered and patched, varied in color or style, and he couldn't sight one man in twenty wearing a similar hat. Boxes of new uniforms were sitting in warehouses at the depot back in Weldon, and Harry had recently detailed one of his officers to retrieve them. He hadn't returned yet. So the Twenty-sixth gave off the appearance of bedraggled farm boys.

Mounted on black Cora, Harry was within earshot of General Pickett when Captain McCreery of Pettigrew's staff asked the General his opinion of the brigade's performance.

"Singular," was Pickett's one word response. Evidently he did not share Harry's prejudice of the men's attire.

After the brigade was paraded and dismissed, Pettigrew paid his respects to Pickett, formally introducing himself. The two had little in common. Pettigrew was a scholar, an aristocrat, not a professional soldier. Pickett's origins were far humbler, and he had graduated from West Point, although he had ranked last in his class. Little did the two know that in a few short weeks they would be thrown together, along with another unlikely General by the name of Trimble, into one of the most desperate assaults in history.

A train pulled up to Hanover Junction that very afternoon. On board was the new issue of clothing for the Twenty-sixth. Harry's boys made a brief march, then were soon rifling through the boxes. They were disappointed in finding no trousers. The tunics however, were of good quality and generally dyed in the same shade of gray. The troops refused to wear the new standard forage caps, preferring the shelter of their stained, wide-brim hats, although they were not above keeping the caps on hand as possible trading material. Of particular concern was the lack of shoes; they had last been issued to the regiment six months before and were getting rather worn. Several more hard marches and the soles would be paper thin.

Much to the relief of Harry's bowels, Kinchen was also on the cars. With him came a box of food from Thornbury, the Colonel's summer clothes, a delicate pair of opera glasses belonging to Henry, and lastly, Hawkeye, the big chestnut gelding.

"What's for suppa, boy?"

"Ham an' hominy!"

THEY WERE ON THE FRINGE OF SUMMER, the brigade marching north on the Richmond Stage Road below Fredericksburg. From the distance came a yammering sound of artillery, a light cannonade. The Yankees had been threatening battle along the Rappahannock the past several days, but there was little prospect that the skirmishes would escalate into a full scale engagement. Most of Lee's army had moved off to the west: somewhere around Culpeper Court House. All that remained on the heights below Fredericksburg was Lee's rear guard, portions of A. P. Hill's Corps, which Pettigrew's troops were now marching to join.

It was closing in on dusk when the brigade filed into the old works below Hamilton's Crossing, the same ground where Stonewall Jackson's boys had repulsed a heavy attack during a cold December morning almost six months prior. All was quiet now; the artillery fire had long died off. The troops slept in the trenches that night, ready for battle, the officers a bit tense, for they knew their long thin line was all that lay between Richmond and over one hundred thousand Yankees on the other side of the river.

Harry's regiment was poised to receive an attack the next morning. The men were awake and alert when the first artillery salvos whistled through the air, but the fire was sporadic and gave no indication that it would pick up, so they settled back into the trenches and relaxed. They peeked out now and again, when the volume increased for brief intervals.

Around mid-morning, Harry and Colonel Marshall visited the forward pickets who were sparring with enemy sharpshooters. Harry borrowed a rifle and tried his hand, laughing when his rounds gave no sign of being near their mark. With the new little opera glass, he spied at the enemy troops who had crossed the river a few days before, confirming that they were less than a division and in too small numbers to be a threat to the Rebel lines. He returned to his works satisfied that the Yankees were just making a show.

The next day the enemy division recrossed the Rappahannock and removed the pontoon bridges. In response, Pettigrew's Brigade was pulled out of the trenches and sent downstream toward Port Royal, to block any plans the Federals may have had for turning their flank. The Twenty-sixth camped near the river, the pickets posted along its tree-lined bank, while the enemy sentries occupied the other side. For the better part of a week, Harry's boys would be entertained each morning and evening by the enemy drums, so loud and numerous in fact, that Harry teasingly poked to his men that two-thirds of the Yankee army must be drummers.

A state of curious suspense hung over the Rebels around Fredericksburg. They all knew an important campaign had begun, but no one was sure of General Lee's plans. Most believed in the invasion rumor, and thought Lee was taking them back to Maryland or perhaps even Pennsylvania. A minority believed he was just maneuvering the Federals away from Fredericksburg, attempting to get in their rear and threaten Washington. There might be a third battle around Manassas before the summer was through. News of a big cavalry fight over at Brandy Station found its way back to the rear guard, but it neither confirmed nor denied anyone's guess as to Lee's motives. About the only thing everyone could agree on was that the Yankee General Hooker was in for a surprise.

On June 15th, the regiment woke to a strange stillness; no drums, no bugles, no bands playing over the Rappahannock; the Yankee army was gone. They had moved off because a disaster had visited a small Federal army guarding the Shenandoah Valley. Part of General Ewell's Second Corps had nearly destroyed it at Winchester the previous day. Perhaps the bad news had spurred Hooker into finally turning his back on the Rebels at Fredericksburg, to pursue those advancing north. The now empty Union camps removed all pressure from A. P. Hill's Corps; Pettigrew's Brigade flung into activity, as all the regiments prepared to march.

Harry pried himself from his duties, and he and Kinchen went into Fredericksburg, which was now safe from the rows of heavy guns that had once shelled the town from the heights across the river. The town was a mere shell, but rubble and burned-out buildings still held a few stubborn townsfolk. They had to be living in poverty, yet Harry somehow managed to sell Waverly. Certainly there was a need for horses in the town, even an old lame one, but the price could not have been good. Harry had little bargaining power; he couldn't take the horse with him, and couldn't leave it behind.

He managed to write his father a brief note before the regiment set off at three PM. The Twenty-sixth marched nine miles during the hottest day of the year, passed through the ravaged ground near Chancellorsville, and camped several miles beyond.

Harry had a bad dream in the night, and he didn't really remember it when he woke the next morning, yet as the regiment marched another eighteen miles under a broiling sun, its impressions hovered just below his consciousness. The Carolinians marched in good spirits despite the heat; in fact, the whole army moved with an undefeatable aura. The Colonel's mood was much more solemn. Something was troubling him, but he didn't know exactly what. He'd been anxiously looking forward to this movement, thrilled to be a part of a campaign that might end the war, but once the march began, once he realized the boldness of the move, feelings of doubt seeped in. Or could it have been the dream that was bothering him? Perhaps the sudden meditations came from a concern for self preservation.

Far back in the long dusty column, Kinchen was riding light and high in his saddle aside the brigade's wagon train. When they neared Raccoon Ford on a pretty little river called the Rapidan, the low country slave saw his first real hill, a huge green hump in the earth. He stared at it for a while, pondering. Very pleasing to the eye, beautiful in fact, and even though he had never seen such a sight, the hill brought on unexpected feelings of nostalgia, as if perhaps, he had seen it long, long ago in his distant youth. He struggled with his memory, but the bulge bore no real familiarity. Still, it held his gaze for a long while. Finally, he guided Cora over toward a wagon, called out to the driver as he pointed at the hill.

"Sergeant suh, is dat a mountain?"

The Sergeant lazily turned his head and with heavy eyelids looked off to his left. He spat, rolled some tobacco in his mouth.

"Nope," was his only reply.

The answer caught Kinchen off guard; he had been positive it was a mountain; it was so big. He looked at the Sergeant queerly, but the soldier only spat again, then closed his eyes against the dust and heat. Kinchen kept staring at the mound, even after the column had passed it by, occasionally peering admiringly over his shoulder. He didn't have to wait long before another large foothill came into view. The brigade passed through Stevensburg and bivouacked in the shadows of Mount Pony, southeast of Culpeper.

Kinchen rejoined the Colonel, pitched his tent and prepared his dinner. After he staked out the horses for the night, he moved away from the camp's light. He liked to sit in the darkness each evening, watching the stars, passing the time silently before sleep. That evening, instead, he studied the black silhouette of Mount Pony looming above him. Its shape brought on the same mysterious feelings as the other hill, wistful. Confused, he sat, searching. No answer came to him, and he couldn't explain the coolness that ran down his spine. The hill was titillating; it made him feel good, but he couldn't quite grasp that simple conclusion.

Harry had the same bad dream in the night. It woke him around midnight, and in the morning, he remembered it vaguely.

That day the brigade marched through Culpeper, bands blaring. Many of the boys had fallen out the day before; the heat and eighteen miles being too much. But they continued west, the wagons full of those who could not keep up. General Pettigrew cut the day's march down to twelve miles and ordered a bivouac within sight of the hazy Blue Ridge.

Kinchen now understood the difference between a foothill and a mountain.

That evening, Harry wrote home:

June 17th, 1863
Bivouac, Hazel River, near Culpeper, Va.

My Dear Mother,

I am resting comfortably from the day's tramp & expect another of the same duration tomorrow. We have had three separate marches, since I wrote Father last from Fredericksburg. The day we left, an order came round for every single trunk to be sent to the rear. Mine had to go with the rest. I sent it to Richmond by my sutler, with instructions to express it to Raleigh. My name was on the cover in the largest sort of letters, so please look out for it.

Today another order has come round for a rigid inspection of baggage, which is to be reduced to the minimum prescribed by law. We are ordered to have 3 days cooked rations in haversacks, & 3 days more in the wagons. I suppose the division supply train will carry one or two days more. All this preparation means, in my opinion, a movement upon the largest scale. This should carry us to Winchester and beyond, and it is possible that General Lee may be able to get 10,000 more troops in the Valley, which would give us a very large army of effective troops, & no Yankee army can whip such a mass when handled by Lee. He has completely deceived Hooker thus far, & is certainly making a very bold movement, but I think we will strike a tremendous & a successful blow.

After we leave here, I suppose that the difficulty of getting letters to the rear will prevent my writing except at long intervals. I shall have to be very guarded in my language lest some Yankee might get hold of my letter. Heaven only knows how or when I will hear from you. The irregularity of the mail now is a constant & just reproach to our authorities. Direct your letters to Richmond & put Pettigrew's Brigade–Heth's Division–Hill's Corps. I suppose once & a while I may be able to get a letter from you. I wish I could give you more news, but you have no idea how difficult it is to hear anything definite & to get reliable information. Troops are continually passing in every direction & going, it appears, in the most opposite directions, & yet they all have one common aim, one common destination.

I lie down tonight upon a single blanket having sent my fly to the rear today. Kinchen has made me a biscuit or two & one piece of ham. Hardly enough to hold back the pangs.

And now I must bid you farewell. What will be the result of this movement now afoot, God alone can tell. I hope to be able to do my duty to the best of my ability & leave the result to His infinite wisdom & justice. What ever may be my own fate, I hope to be able to feel & believe that all will turn out for the best. With love to all I am ever your Most Affectionate Son,

H. K. Burgwyn, Jr.
Colonel, 26th Reg. N.C.T.

P.S. Kinchen sends regards to his Mistress & little Masters. Says the fat he received from Ruthy's cooking has long since vanished.

WITH EXCITEMENT ON HIS BLACK FACE, he began the long climb. Dark green mountains filled his view, glistening, still wet from a sudden, but brief shower. There was a fresh scent in the air; he had never smelled anything like it. He sucked in his breath then let it out slowly. Troops crowded the narrow winding track, but he paid no attention to them, his face lifted upward, his eyes refusing to blink. Higher and higher he went, damp air, cooler. The sun shone through a thin veil of clouds, hurrying along the rising mist. Cora began to labor; a flat-country horse, she had never climbed a mountain. Kinchen pushed her, anxious to reach the top and look down on the soft green folds.

Head bobbing, straining to look over the wagons, he rounded the summit, and felt he had reached the sky. There was a distinct line of clouds overhead; beyond, clear blue vastness, below, to the west, another ridge of high mountains. The passing clouds pelted him with big wet drops, and a breeze rolled up, delightful. The column didn't pause, so he pulled Cora over to the side of the road and stopped. A wagoneer saw him trapped in wonderment, caught

Kinchen's eye, smiled, and nodded, acknowledging the beauty. Kinchen felt delivered. He grinned timidly, respectfully at the power that surrounded him.

Dizzied by the sights, he reluctantly started the slow plunge into a yellow valley. Below, he could see a white river reflecting sunlight, colored squares of ripening crops, dark specks that were houses. He was falling into another domain, a mysterious kingdom, a world where everything was new. His senses took it all in, the sights, the smells, and he felt a boy again, that innocent freedom of youth.

The road leveled off and straightened out when they reached the valley floor. It quickly went to dust, the gray column smothered. They soon marched into the enthusiastic town of Front Royal, with jubilant townsfolk lining the streets. The regimental bands played. Pretty girls ran up with flowers, pinning them to dirty tunics, decorating the horses, sometimes treating a soldier with a kiss. A Negro boy was hanging from a tree limb, reaching out and tapping the barrels of shouldered rifles as they passed. The men marched proudly, but not too fast. They sang, waved back to the crowd, paused when the girls approached. It was a scene of gaiety, and even though no petals hung from Cora's neck or traces, Kinchen couldn't help but be wrapped up in the mood. He felt honored to be a part of this army, proud to march with it, to serve it, to attend one of its commanders. Riding alongside the soldiers gave him a sense of duty, a function, importance. The troops liked him, perhaps even respected him, because they could see that he did his job well, and to the Colonel's satisfaction. These boys were not city fellows, nor sons of plantation owners. They were from the land of Carolina's small farms, had never owned a slave, and some had never seen one before the war. How hard a man worked, hunted, and fought was their measure. Kinchen's horsemanship had shocked them, and they had been stunned to learn that he had once been a jockey. Curiosity spurred many visits. They observed the slave's good manners and composure, and enjoyed his sense of humor. Teasing him was one of the men's favorite pastimes, and Kinchen took it good-naturedly, knew the toying was a sign of their affection, for he had endured such playfulness at the hands of Harry and his little brothers all his life. So even though he knew no drills and carried no arms, he felt a part of this army. He ate the same food, marched the same miles, suffered the same hardships, and enjoyed the same celebration, as they passed from town to town.

The brigade filed through Front Royal, crossed the South Fork of the Shenandoah River, then the North Fork, and marched two more miles before encamping near Cedarville. Kinchen followed his routine, moved up to the Twenty-sixth's bivouac and cooked the day's supper ration for the Colonel. Harry took the plate, but didn't touch the food.

Each morning when the regiment left its camp, Harry ordered the band to play "The Girl I Left Behind Me," and every evening when they filed into a new camp, he directed them to strike up "The Campbells Are Coming." This remained a ritual throughout the great march north.

Pettigrew's Brigade followed the Shenandoah River down the valley with the Blue Ridge to their right and the Alleghanies to their left. On June 21st, they stopped at Berryville and remained there through the 22nd. Jeb Stuart's cavalry brigades were engaged in delaying actions east of the mountains around Middleburg and Upperville, and were being pressed back to Ashby's Gap. In case the enemy broke through, Heth's Division, with Pettigrew's Brigade, remained within supporting distance of two of Longstreet's divisions that were guarding the gaps. The enemy threat disappeared the following day, and the Twenty-sixth's trek north continued.

They passed through rich country, and Kinchen was impressed with the great fields of wheat. Rocks and boulders were prevalent, made him wonder how the planters plowed. There were handsome little farms and the occasional plantation, and he never tired of the constant view of majestic mountains. The rolling pasture land convinced him it was good horse country, and during the brief rests he grazed Cora in clover. The officers did a good job of preventing the men from foraging, but they couldn't stop all the flankers. Kinchen set off on some expeditions of his own, searching for little tidbits that might spice up the Colonel's table. His yield was disappointing, a few mush melons and the like. Most of Lee's army had preceded him, and what Kinchen found Harry rarely ate. The Colonel's lack of appetite provoked concern. In all their years together, Kinchen had never seen him fail to empty a plate. He wasn't sick, wasn't suffering from the flux. Harry just wasn't hungry.

The Colonel usually rode at the head of the regiment, and various officers accompanied him depending on which company was on the point. Lieutenant Colonel Lane and Captain Young were frequent companions. At times Harry rode alone, way out in front, or off the road to the regiment's side. He often stopped and studied his soldiers as they passed. The business of the march kept him occupied, but occasionally he let his mind wander. It was during one of these breaks that he became aware of the image, a piece of a repetitive dream. He would close his eyes, rest them from the sun's glare, and the image would appear: a lone rider on an empty ridge, far away, observing him from a distance. He wore dark clothing, and his horse was black. Harry never could see the rider's face, no matter how hard he focused. Once, during one of the dreams, he galloped toward the image, but no matter how fast or how long he rode, he could never get any closer. The image itself never moved, just stood there watching him like some omnipotent god. Sometimes he thought it was just a statue, but then he'd see the swish of the black horse's tail. He even tried waving once, but predictably, there was no response. Now he was searching for a meaning or message, and as of yet, nothing had come to him. It was all so vague.

They camped near Charlestown on the twenty-third, then the next morning started off again, passing a little ways west of Harper's Ferry, and settling that night along the Potomac below Shepherdstown. That evening, and some thirty-five miles to the north, General Ewell and his Second Corps occupied Chambersburg, Pennsylvania. The invasion had become a reality.

HOOVES CLICKED ON MOSSY ROCKS, AND THE sound echoed down the narrow hollow. The slave and his thirsty wards worked their way down the dry stream bed. An occasional puddle caused Cora and Hawkeye to lag. Kinchen pulled them along.

The river was low and clear and carried with its lazy flow an intoxicating, earthy smell. Bass rose in the ripples, sunfish popped and smacked near the shaded banks; the horses shook their heads and slurped. The sun was dipping below the mountains. The Potomac was a sublime green when not reflecting a pale blue sky with orange streaks. Such peace and beauty reminded Kinchen fondly of the Roanoke.

They made their way back up the hollow, and laughter burst forth from up over the rise, deep rolling chuckles that bounced off rocks, and almost caused leaves to vibrate. Kinchen couldn't help but grin, and followed the sounds of joy. Luther, Robert, and Farley were sitting around a fire, their black hair and faces contrasting the stained white wagon cover behind them. They were all servants like he, and he had met each, separately, but had never seen them together. He made straight for the gathering.

Farley, a tall, lean boy not much older than Kinchen, was sitting on a crate, bent over, mumbling. Robert sat next to him, listening intently. He was Farley's age, handsome, shy. Luther leaned back against a wagon wheel, scriggles of gray in his black nap, a tiny grin hidden behind a smoking pipe clenched in his yellow teeth. Little snickers escaped from Robert and Luther, as Farley whispered a story. Luther saw Kinchen's approach, waved an invitation.

"Wha' da talk?" Kinchen asked after securing the horses and squatting near the fire. Luther just pulled out his pipe and pointed it at Farley, a sign to Kinchen just to listen.

'Well, Caroline, she just kept takin' the breakfasses an' suppas up, rapped on da door, but dare was no call. Da Missas, now she so skinny, we was beginnin' to wonder if'n she was meltin' away."

Luther chuckled as Farley continued.

"But I was happy. I was gettin' da meals."

Robert slapped his knee.

"Wha' y'all talkin' bout?" Kinchen asked again, but was ignored.

"Well finally, some a' da food, it began ta go. A bit at a time. Den one day da plates were empty, and the next mornin', da Missas, she came out. She came down ta da kitchen, slow and 'spicious like, cuttin' her eyes."

Robert snickered.

"She sat at da table, and Caroline served her up a fine breakfass. She took a sip a' da coffee."

Farley motioned as if sipping from a cup, mimicking. Everyone laughed.
"She den smacked her lips."
Farley smacked his lips, moved his eyes.
"Den cut her eyes again."
There came a roar, Luther laughed so hard he coughed.
"Den she picked up da fork and stabbed da eggs."
Farley kept mimicking, and joyful tears began to form in Robert's eyes.
"She took a nibble, took another, den she spit it out."
Luther began to shake, cough again.
"Caroline, well, she dropped da kettle, and it made such a clatta, the Missas turned peaked and stiff."
The laughing was uncontrolled now.
"Den came such a holla ta wake da dead, and da Missas, she ran quick as a mouse up da stairs. A blur she was."
Robert and Luther were gasping for breath, and Kinchen laughed too, not quite sure at what.
"And she didn't come out again 'til da mens come home."
"Wha', wha' dat 'bout?" Kinchen asked again.
Farley just sat up on the crate and made a declaration as Luther and Robert tried to recover.
"Now I say dey all scared a' us, scared as da dickens. All dem white folks. Thinks we debils, dey do."
Kinchen insisted that he be let in. Luther, rubbing the tears from his cheeks, finally accommodated. The older slave told him that a mistress of a plantation neighboring Farley's master's had been murdered by her servants, poisoned and strangled. Of course, all the white folks were terribly upset, and the perpetrators were promptly tried and hung. There remained a mystery as to why the servants had done-in the mistress though, as she was old and kindly, and had even spoiled her slaves. During the trial all of the men folk at Farley's plantation had left to attend, and only his mistress remained, and she was scared to death that her servants were poisoning her, and of course it was funny because they intended no such thing.
Farley repeated his declaration, "I say dey's all scared a' us."
Kinchen grinned, but didn't laugh. The story had lost its initial impact, and besides, it was a little morbid. Kinchen began to think on Farley's declaration, then made his own.
"Dey's scared, but not all in da way you say." The three slaves looked at him, surrendering the floor.
Kinchen smiled. "My Missas, now she's the kindest, sweetest woman dare ev'a was. She's from da Noth, dat big city, Boston. Dey goes up dare ev'ry summer, at least 'fore da war."
His expression turned serious. "Well, she don't take too kindly ta slav'ry. But she not scared of me a t'all. She knows I likes her, and knows I won't nev'a harm

a hair on her head."

Robert interrupted. "My Missas, she da same way."

"She from da Noth?" Kinchen asked.

"No, she from Wilmin'ton."

"Well, no matta. My Missas, she not scared of me, but I sees da fear. Sees it on her face, in her eyes. Y'all know what I mean?" Luther nodded, Robert said he thought so.

"Sometime she seem so sad, so sad, and scared too. She's sad and scared at da same time. Fears for her soul, I believe. Reckons' da Lord holds bad judgment."

Everyone turned silent, and all nodded except Farley. He felt defeated.

"I still say dey all scared a' us." Farley fought back. Then a thought came in his head. You could see it on his face. He gave Kinchen a strange look, almost demonic.

"You know whar dis valley leads? You know what's ober dat rivah?"

Kinchen just looked at him, as Farley grew more excited. Farley looked over his shoulder.

"Freedom," he whispered. "Freedom," he hissed. Then he began to giggle.

"All dese sold'yas. All dese guns. Dey's fightin' ta keep us home on da plantation. But dey's marchin' us," he pointed at the other three, then jabbed his thumb in his chest.

"Dey's marchin' us right ta freedom."

He laughed loudly. "We gots an escort."

Then the jolly face suddenly frowned, looked at Kinchen.

"Robert an' me, we's runnin', first chance we get, ain't dat right." He poked Robert with his elbow. The boy shrugged, looked down.

"Dey never catch us. Dey be too busy fightin' Yankees."

Luther took the pipe from his mouth, put a finger to his lips, looked about. Kinchen knew what was coming, didn't really want any part of it.

"Dey's room fo' you," Farley said to Kinchen. "Want ta run wid us?"

Kinchen really didn't know what to say. His mind reached for something, he looked at Luther.

"You runnin'?" He asked the old man. Luther shook his head.

"Da ol' man ain't goin'," Farley barked. "Says it too late fo' him. Don't know why. Nev'a too late fo' freedom."

Luther just looked at him blankly, then got up, said good-bye. Kinchen watched him leave, wished he hadn't.

"Well, yuh wanna go?" Farley asked again. "Or are yuh gonna miss yo' Missas too much?"

Kinchen looked at Robert. "You goin'?"

Robert shrugged.

"Yep, he goin'," Farley said for him. "He got a woman at home, a little one. So do I. Don't matta. Dey's plenty a' women up noth. Ain't dey, Robert?"

Robert nodded.

"So yuh goin', ain't yuh?"

Robert nodded again. Farley looked at Kinchen.

"Yuh got a woman?" Kinchen shook his head.

"So yuh goin' too."

Kinchen thought on it. He'd heard about it all his life. Free to go where you want, do what you want. Free to buy some land, raise some horses. He had once reflected on it long and hard, but had since learned not to dwell on it. Didn't do any good to dream for something that really wasn't there. Those images in his head, they didn't really exist. He'd never be able to walk right into them. Now he wondered if that was true. Was this his chance to see? Freedom, a frightening notion.

"I dink 'bout it," he said.

"Well, don't dink long 'cause we's runnin' soon, and we's runnin' fast."

"Hey!" A soldier wheeled around the wagon, saw the three servants.

"What y'all doin' here?"

Farley's and Robert's eyes turned wide, fear all over their faces. Had the soldier heard them?

"Get on to your masters!"

The black faces turned to relief.

"Yeah suh, yeah suh."

Robert and Farley got up, peeled away. Kinchen took his time, untied the horses.

"Now who scared a' who?" he mumbled to himself.

OFF CAME THE FOUL SOCKS, THE WORN SHOES, the tattered trousers. Toes tested the cool waters, then waded in. Longstreet's and Hill's Corps crossed the thigh-deep Potomac and greeted Maryland with far less fanfare than during the excursion of the year before. That foray had been little more than a raid, but this was truly a prepared invasion. In all, there were one hundred and sixty-five regiments of infantry, well over ten thousand horsemen, and two hundred and eighty-seven cannon, not to mention the miles and miles of wagons carrying supplies and munitions. The Rebels marched swiftly and purposefully while under strict orders not to molest noncombatants. There was little straggling, and few instances of stealing or looting, despite a powerful and universal desire for revenge for the countless Yankee violations of their homeland. The men were united and steadfast in the belief of their Cause, and a more confident band of volunteers would be hard to find. Perhaps no army had greater faith in their leaders. Before them was their greatest challenge to date, and with few exceptions, they could not have been more primed.

The Twenty-sixth forded just below Shepherdstown, and put their shoes and drawers back on near the home of Henry Kyd Douglas. Since the death of Jackson, Douglas had become a Major and a staff officer in a brigade that was camped just outside Chambersburg that day—the Stonewall Brigade.

The Carolinians easily covered the three miles to Sharpsburg where they were greeted rather soberly, perhaps a handful of the locals showing any fire for their presence. The brigade marched past the scarred Dunker Church, where the fighting had been fierce during the battle of last September. The scene produced a memory for Harry; he recalled a letter from Sumner whose regiment had fought near there. The letter had described their charge through the woods, how an adjacent regiment had been decimated, and Sumner's wild leaping antics out in front of his own regiment. He had grabbed the colors, but fortunately they had been taken away from him. Such a reckless boy! How lucky he was to have escaped the day untouched. Harry tucked himself under his hat, contemplated the coming battles, and endured the heat for fourteen more miles until the regiment camped near Hagerstown that night.

He dreamed of Annie Devereux, and the next day tried many times to capture her face in his mind. But it was a very warm day and countless images whirled in his head, so he gave up the effort and concentrated on his duties. They marched through a number of small towns and saw legions of long faces. Harry ordered the band not to play; he wanted no crowing or gloating. They would portray themselves as accomplished veterans who were determined only to fight Yankee soldiers and to bring this war to a successful close. Their grim resolve would leave a favorable impression on the natives, and was apt to encourage sympathy. That was General Lee's plan, and Harry fully understood it.

They crossed the Pennsylvania border and the troops could not resist. Cheers went up, whoops, a mass shaking of hands. Harry allowed the spontaneous celebration, but advised his officers to curtail all future outbursts. The regiment tramped twelve miles that day and camped in the rolling hills near Waynesboro.

To Kinchen, the landscape, the towns, the people, the strange accents were all a wonderful curiosity. He wanted to leave the crowded road, ride up one of those marvelous hills, and look down on it all. But Harry forbade him to forage now, perhaps considering it too much of a temptation, although there was a greater likelihood that the servant would be picked up as a runaway by foraging Rebel cavalry. So Kinchen stayed with the wagons, choked on their dust, and moved into the free land, as bound to his master as any loyal slave through the ages.

On hilly, rocky roads that tore away the soles of the soldiers' shoes, Hill's Corps penetrated further into Pennsylvania. They marched in loose formations with heads up observing the bountiful countryside, the sturdy barns, the modest homes. Pointing and lively chattering were a constant, the urge to forage overpowering. Barefoot boys who walked in the grasses aside the pikes often slunk away in search of footwear. Shops in every town were visited, but not pillaged, as the proprietors' drawers overflowed with Confederate script.

Harry had never felt healthier or stronger. His appetite returned, renewed by the knowledge that they had thoroughly fooled the Yankees and were invading Pennsylvania unopposed. Scrumptious cherries and apple butter, fresh beef and lamb stimulated his taste buds. The regiment would cover fifteen miles on June twenty-seventh, their confidence growing with every step. The only bad news came from Captain Young, who reported to Harry just after an inspection of the wagon train.

"Ain't hardly a Negro left with the wagons, sir! Ran off in the night, most of 'em."

Harry didn't respond straight off, just kept his eyes on the dusty road ahead. "Just as soon as we arrived here they cut out. Even Sterling's gone."

"Sterling?"

"Yes sir, the club-footed boy who cooked for the band."

Harry nodded, supposed it was to be expected. Young assumed he would get more of a response, studied his Colonel as they rode along slowly.

"Sir? Shall I have Sergeant Crawford keep an eye on your Kinchen?"

Harry shook his head. "Won't be necessary," he said sharply, and the subject was dropped.

It began to rain as the brigade marched into a new campsite in a sheltered hollow near Greenwood. A fine spray at first, followed by a slow, steady drizzle that dripped down through the thick branches, forming tiny rivers over the leaves, sputtering as the droplets rolled and hit the warm forest floor. Makeshift shelters were constructed and Kinchen made Harry a little lean-to, but as soon as everyone was comfortably situated, the drizzle stopped and the bugs commenced their steady racket. The Colonel poured over maps. He loved maps, the crisscrossing lines that told him where he'd been and where he was likely to go. He knew the first phase of the invasion had been a great success, the Yankees left far behind, still in Virginia were the reports. Pennsylvania was fat and open to the gray columns. Where would Lee take them? This valley led straight north to the Susquehanna River. Harrisburg, the state capital, lay beside it and appeared ripe for the plucking. However, just ahead, not two miles away, was the main road veering east from Chambersburg through the mountains. There was rich country over that way, strategic railroads, and down to the southeast, a great jewel, Baltimore. Soon they would know, he figured. If they passed that road and continued north, Harrisburg would be the objective. If they turned right, Baltimore, but they were bound to run into Hooker before they got there. There would likely be a big battle soon, if they headed that way.

It was growing too dark to see the map so he folded it and put it away, then stepped out from under the lean-to and stretched. He normally wrote his letters during this time in the evening, but he didn't have a lantern, and it was too sticky and humid to sit by the fire. He looked over toward the flames, saw Kinchen sitting quietly, poking the embers. The sight made him homesick. He craved a letter from home. He always destroyed his letters from his family shortly after receiving them, so he didn't even have an old one to peruse. But he did have something. Harry ducked back under the shelter, pulled out his saddlebag, sorted through it and found the yellowed paper. He sat down, unfolded it, and could barely make out the heading, "Harry," the old poem from his mother.

Kinchen squatted, perched back on his heels, his arms resting on his knees as he played with the fire. He listened to the soft murmurings of a handful of soldiers flowing from a nearby fire, heard an occasional chuckle. Usually he'd move up and lean against a tree so he could understand what was being said, and since he had a reputation of being a cheery fellow who brought humor to the fire, the soldiers often spotted him and invited him in. But tonight it was different. The warm ring seemed foreign, forbidden. The men had not teased him today, had actually ignored him, purposefully avoiding him whenever he came near. He didn't understand at first, but then he came to know. He could no longer be trusted, he was no longer a comrade, for almost all the other Negroes had abandoned the column, and the soldiers were certain that it was just a matter of time before Kinchen would also make his break.

He felt betrayed, and angry. The mere suggestion that he might run was causing him to consider it. Farley and Robert had snuck out the night before, but he hadn't approached them. Now he was measuring his prospects, was quietly retreating within himself.

Getting caught ain't a worry, I'll get through, he thought. What will I do once I's free? Don't know nobody. Go and try to git hired, I suppose. Do dey raise horses up heah? Dey's bound ta raise horses, though I ain't seen one. What in the wurl plows up all dem fields?

"I've got news from home!"

Harry's voice startled him, he sprang lightly to his feet, but nearly stumbled on a log.

"Pardon me," said Harry, surprised that Kinchen had jumped.

The servant grinned nervously. "Say yuh got news?"

Harry always read Kinchen his letters from home, a special treat.

"Well, not really news. It's an old poem. Remember that poem Mother sent me a year back before the battles around Richmond?"

"Oh, yeah, suh."

"Care to hear it?"

"Yeah, suh, dat would be nice, real nice."

The two sat by the fire, the flames dancing on the bent figures, the soft light reflecting off white and brown cheeks. Harry read the poem slowly.

"*There I wish my boy to be.*"

The words put Kinchen in a trance, brought on images of their composer.

"*Win for thyself an honored name.*"

He saw Anna's great portrait hanging in the drawing room at Thornbury. The long, elegant dress, pure and white.

"Storm the redoubt, drive back the phalanx. Fear no sharpshooter from the wall."

He saw her with hair up, sleeves rolled, nursing the sick.

"Naught but thy compassion feel."

And he remembered the evenings she would read from the book, the Bible, and smile down at him, looking through the windows of his soul.

"As in the peaceful days of yore."

Harry read the last verse, then slowly folded the paper, glanced at Kinchen, and saw him put a finger to his eye, hiding a tear, deeply moved. Harry looked away, not wishing to embarrass him, waited a moment before he spoke.

"I wish very much to go home."

"Yeah suh," Kinchen sniffled.

"But we have a duty here, you and I, and we can't go home 'til it's completed."

"Yeah suh."

They looked at each other for a long moment, each trying to read guarded thoughts. Harry finally rose, turned slightly, clasped his hands behind his back, looked out beyond the firelight.

"Pretty country we've been traveling through."

Kinchen nodded, looked over his shoulder into the night. Harry looked up through the trees.

"Very dark tonight, very dark."

Kinchen looked questioningly at his master, who just stared out into the black, then down at the fire again.

"I think we'll rest here a day or so. Are you tired?"

"A bit," said Kinchen.

"I'd like you to run an errand for me tomorrow. How would you like to take Cora into the village to get some victuals?"

"Umm-hmm, I'll go."

"You can go alone, I have some things to do here. I'll give you a pass and some money."

"Yeah suh."

"You'll have to be careful. You understand?"

Kinchen nodded.

"Mr. Wells will have a service in the morning, so you'll have to hurry back."

Kinchen nodded again.

"Well then, good, you'll set off after breakfast. I'll sleep now."

Kinchen got to his feet, and Harry smiled at him, patted him on the shoulder, said good night. And the slave settled back down by the fire and thought about Anna's poem, about Thornbury. He let the visions wander for a long while until the camp grew very still, and the fires died away, and the darkness came and enveloped him.

⚜ 19 ⚜

WALKING BLIND

*"We looked for peace, but no good came;
and for a time of health, and behold trouble!*

*The snorting of his horse was heard
from Dan: the whole world trembled at the
sound of the neighing of his strong ones; for
they are come, and have devoured the land,
and all that is in it; the city, and those that
dwell therein.*

*For, behold, I will send serpents, cockatrices, among you, which will not be charmed,
and they shall bite you, saith the Lord.*

*When I would comfort myself against
sorrow, my heart is faint in me.*

*Behold the voice of the cry of the
daughter of my people because of them that
dwell in a far country; Is not the Lord in Zion?
Is not her king in her? Why have they
provoked me to anger with their graven
images, and with strange vanities?*

*The harvest is past, the summer is
ended, and we are not saved."*

THE CHAPLAIN, MR. WELLS, STOOD on a round boulder and read from Jeremiah: eight, verses fifteen through twenty. Tall and gaunt, he bore a solemn expression as the entire regiment, well over eight hundred men, gathered around a rocky knoll and carefully listened to his sermon. The chaplain spoke of the abomination of war, preached of its wickedness and evil, and how it distracted men from their greater duty toward God. He warned them of putting flag and country ahead of the Lord their Savior. Advised them not to take too much heart in their recent victories in Virginia and their successful journey to Pennsylvania. Through sweat and sacrifice they had come thus far, but the real struggle lay ahead.

"Do not take joy with what abounds in this land of plenty, but eat for strength and resolution, for you are about to be tested by your enemies and by your God. Look to your brothers beside you and draw strength from mutual faith. We are in the third year of war, we have marched two hundred miles, and we are not saved. Victory alone will bring no salvation, and we will not be so blessed without faith. Shoulder your arms and bind yourself to the Lord and we shall thrive. Go forward and do your duty and even though you may perish from this world, if you embrace Him, He will accept you at His Altar and Kingdom."

Kinchen stood apart from the sweat-stained uniforms. With derby in hand, standing by a jagged locust, he looked at his master on the knoll. Harry was looking down on his regiment, and the slave read his face, could tell that his master was greatly affected.

The congregation knelt and Mr. Wells said a prayer, and then they all rose and recited The Lord's Prayer. Kinchen closed his eyes and spoke the words.

A gentle, mountain shower passed over the congregation. The regiment broke up and quietly walked back toward their bivouac. Kinchen watched them pass as he waited for Harry. Then he heard a soldier speak softly to another as they paused near the locust.

"Did you notice Colonel Burgwyn during the preaching? He seemed to be deeply impressed."

The other nodded solemnly, looked at his comrade with eyes of worry. "I believe we're gonna lose him on this trip."

A SPY MADE HIS WAY TO THE Confederate camps around Chambersburg. He called himself Harrison and he'd been employed by General Longstreet before the campaign. No one had heard from Jeb Stuart's cavalry. Didn't know where they were in fact, and Harrison brought news that Jeb had failed to procure. The Federals had crossed the Potomac, were down around Frederick, in Maryland, and moving north. Yankee cavalry were much closer, and General Meade had replaced Hooker.

General Lee reacted quickly, and ordered his flung-out army to unite. Cashtown, a small town just east of the mountains, would be the concentration point.

Pettigrew's Brigade turned right on the Chambersburg Pike, cut through the mountain passes, and settled in just east of Cashtown. That evening, rumors began to filter about. There was a large store of shoes in the next town over,

Gettysburg. Seeing that his brigade was nearly barefoot after the long march from Virginia, Pettigrew asked General Hill if he might go retrieve them. Hill had no objections, except that, in the unlikely event the enemy was encountered, he was not to bring on an engagement. That was the evening of June twenty-ninth.

Harry assembled and inspected the Twenty-sixth early the next morning. All men who were not able to march swiftly were pulled out. The band was given the option to go or stay, and they elected to remain. Powder and balls were issued, and canteens filled. All the wagons were to be left behind, as were knapsacks and nonessentials. The regiment was stripped for speed. At 6:30 AM, the brigade left Cashtown for Gettysburg, Harry's regiment leading the way.

Captain McCreery came up with orders from General Pettigrew.

"Proceed with caution. You will send out flankers and advance guards. It is not unlikely you will have a brush with militia. All sightings or contacts with the enemy are to be reported immediately. You are not to advance against them without orders."

It was an overcast day with intermittent showers. Normally it was good to be first in line, no dust in the road, but today the lead held no such advantage. Instead, the regiment ranged through enemy country with poor visibility, blind to some extent. There was no gray cavalry out in front, no buffer between the brigade and the entire Yankee army.

They marched through thickly settled country, yet it was nearly void of its inhabitants. No traffic on the pike, no stock in the pastures; the houses dark and empty. The road ahead was long and straight, and it rolled up and down over low ridges that blocked their view. It was eerie, like passing through a ghost settlement, not knowing what lurked over the next rise.

The intermittent showers chilled the men. Each time they ceased, the air hung hot and humid, causing sweat to streak down grimy faces. The rain would come again, and the process repeated itself over and over.

Mounted on big Hawkeye, Harry was at his usual place at the head of the column. Every time a new ridge came into view in the distance, he would look for the image of a dark horseman, thinking perhaps, the recurring dream might have been a glimpse into the future. No such rider appeared.

Around mid-morning the sun peeked through the clouds in places. Harry passed a roadside tavern, then climbed a boulder-studded hill. The view from the top of the rise was much like those that he had left behind him; below was a shallow valley rising up to another ridge, this one lined with trees. He turned in the saddle, looked back, and saw the entire brigade filling the road. It was a splendid sight, reassuring and comforting; it sent tingles down his spine. He could almost feel the brigade's power and confidence. Harry wheeled the horse, turned back toward the east, and trotted down into the valley.

Lieutenant Jordan, Harry's adjutant, galloped into view as he rode over the tree-lined ridge. Harry had sent him out with the advanced guard, and he was returning to the column. He came up a little wild-eyed and panting.

"Begging to report, sir. There's blue riders in the town!"

"Where?"

"In the town! Beyond that ridge is another, and I was just there, and you can see the town pretty good, and I saw blue riders and many more on the hills beyond."

"In what number?"

Jordan rolled his eyes, figuring, couldn't come up with an accurate estimate.

"Hundreds!"

"Go find General Pettigrew. Tell him what you saw."

The Lieutenant peeled away. Harry motioned to Captain Wright, whose company was in first position, and together they cantered toward Gettysburg.

It wasn't much of a ridge, fairly low and surrounded by open land, but the ridge itself was wooded. Over to the right, near where the pike passed over the ridge, was a stately Seminary. A Private was standing up on a rail fence that lined the road, balanced, his hands on his forehead. He was looking down into the town. A small number of Harry's Rebels were scattered around the pike, also peering east. The Colonel and Captain Wright trotted up, and the boy on the fence pointed toward the hills beyond Gettysburg. Harry pulled out the opera glasses.

There was a camp on the hill, a lot of horses, many men, some mounted, some not. Further down the hill, where it sloped away to the south, was a column of cavalry. Off to the north, heading away from Gettysburg, was yet another column, and down in the town itself, Harry saw small bodies of horsemen moving about. He lowered the glasses.

"Well, it's not militia," he said to Captain Wright.

A Sergeant piped up from below.

"There was a big gang of 'em right heah on this ridge, but they skedaddled when they saw us. Didn't even get a shot off on 'em."

"How many?" asked Captain Wright.

The Sergeant looked at the others, several soldiers answered.

"A big gang!"

"Fifty!"

"A hundred!"

"How many on that hill?" Wright asked Harry.

"A brigade. Better if you tally those over there."

All the men looked to the north; they hadn't seen that group.

Two brigades of cavalry is a damned big scouting party, thought Harry. He sensed power behind them. Infantry were bound to be close. The whole Union army could be coming up from behind those hills as far as they knew; that's how uninformed Stuart had left them. Damn him!

Harry was directing the glasses toward the south, and watching for infantry on the road when General Pettigrew and his staff quickly came up. There was a flutter of salutes; Harry's boys stepped away.

"What do we have here, Colonel?" asked Pettigrew in a concerned tone.

"Two brigades of Union cavalry, regular," said Harry calmly.

Pettigrew took out his own looking glass, aimed it at Gettysburg; he held it for a long spell. While still examining the ground, he called for Captain McCreery.

"Go to Colonels Marshall, Collier, and Leventhorpe, and tell them to turn 'round. We're going back to Cashtown."

"Yeah sir."

"After you inform Leventhorpe, go to General Heth. With my compliments, inform him that there are two brigades of enemy cavalry in Gettysburg, Army of the Potomac, and that I am taking my brigade back to Cashtown, unless he instructs otherwise."

"Yeah sir."

"That's all."

McCreery galloped off, and Pettigrew lowered his glass. He looked at Harry.

"Your regiment will bring up the rear, Colonel."

Harry nodded. Pettigrew looked at the Union horsemen on the hills again.

"There is an abundance of good ground. Where do you suggest we establish a line?" asked the General.

Harry wasted little time in answering, pleased that the General had consulted him. "We passed a strong stream a mile or two back. Recall the stone bridge?"

"I was just there," said Pettigrew. "Yes, take your regiment beyond the bridge, and picket the stream, until we hear from General Heth."

Harry saluted, told Captain Wright to go back and turn the regiment around, then he and the General lingered for a while, surveying, and marking the ground around Gettysburg.

THE HILLS HAD EYES. Roaming bands of blue riders followed the Twenty-sixth as they retired to Marsh Creek. Again, Harry studied them as they traded back and forth over the ridges, and he groped for the slightest resemblance that they might have had to his image. But they were in parties of four and five, no lone riders, and they didn't single him out when they spied down at the column. Still, there was something vaguely disturbing about the prying Yankee scouts.

The regiment crossed the stone bridge, then marched another quarter mile before bivouacking in a large clover field on the south side of the pike. Harry immediately charged Colonel Lane with placing the pickets, recommending he spread them along the creek rather thickly on both sides of the bridge. Scouts were sent out to search for hidden fords, and the remaining troops were kept on constant alert.

Late in the afternoon, several wagons came down from Cashtown with rations for the regiment. Kinchen rode with them, on Cora. Straight off, the slave noticed the tension, as he helped hand out the food. The boys were jittery, spoke incessantly, speculating. Many openly wondered where their own cavalry were, and cussed Jeb Stuart and his merry plumed raiders. Kinchen took it all in, decided there might be a fight tomorrow, and searched for a way to avoid going back to Cashtown with the wagons. Ever since the sermon on the rocky knoll he'd been haunted by the comment he'd overheard, spooked by a premonition of disaster. His imagination ran awry, and even though he knew that war and death were one and the same, for the first time he realized that Harry might be taken away.

Down on the picket line, around twilight, four Yankee horsemen approached the stone bridge, but soon realized their mistake. They cantered off just before the Rebels could draw a bead on them. Shortly after, two women were seen toiling down the pike and were stopped by the gray pickets. The ladies were terribly upset, complaining that their house was in the dangerous area between the picket lines. The matter was brought to Colonel Lane's attention, who, with his chivalrous manner, soon had the ladies calmed and satisfied by assuring them that Carolinians did not make war on women. The pickets on the west side of the bridge were then ordered to ford the creek and extend their lines to take in the ladies' dwelling. After an escort followed the ladies home, a guard was posted in the yard to warrant that the night would pass with no further worries.

Word reached them from division Headquarters that evening. The regiment was to be prepared to march at first light. Generals Hill and Heth actually had decided that Pettigrew had seen only militia at Gettysburg, and that on the morrow, the entire Third Corps would barrel into the town and run them out. The venture would be part of a greater movement of the entire Rebel army. Lee had decided to change his concentration point from Cashtown to Gettysburg, perhaps with the hope that from the latter town, his legions would be in a better position to pounce on Meade's army while it was strung out on the march. However, strict orders would remain; no general engagement would be sought until the entire army was gathered.

Harry was disgusted that Pettigrew's report of regular Union cavalry occupying Gettysburg had been dismissed out of hand. If General Lee wanted to avoid a fight before his army was fully concentrated, then it was best not to go into the place. But the decision had been made, orders had been issued, and there was nothing a colonel could do to change them. Still, his anger simmered. It was not directed at Generals Heth, Hill, or Lee, but at Jeb Stuart, who was still missing, and who was ultimately responsible if a battle flared before all were ready.

A GRIZZLED CHIN RESTED IN A FILTHY PALM; glassy eyes transfixed on a lapping flame. A floppy hat pulled tight to the ears. Three Rebels sat, watched, and anticipated, while Kinchen cooked a stew of beef fat and potatoes. His reputation as an excellent as well as charitable cook was known by all in the ranks, and since he had not run off despite having every opportunity to do so, a fair number of the men had ceased to shy away from him. Some, perhaps, trusted him more than before, because they knew what the temptation might do to them if the shoe was on the other foot. A group of the boys had watched Kinchen build his fire at the far end of the clover field near an oak grove. Seeing that the Colonel wasn't around, and knowing that the surplus wouldn't feed all of them, they drew sticks. The three winners went begging, and the others looked out for Harry. While the three waited and watched the potatoes boil, they chattered about the Yankee cavalry. One hoped they would come galloping down the pike in the morning and charge them head on.

"We'll cut 'em to pieces."

Another Rebel didn't think they'd be so foolish.

"If they're still in that town, they'll skedaddle just as soon as they see our battle flags."

The third coveted the Yankee horses.

"My feet are wore out. Think we should surround the whole bunch and take their horses, then mount the whole regiment and go out lookin' for them foot soldiers."

Kinchen listened, mildly amused. He didn't have a comment.

"What you think, boy?"

Kinchen stirred the stew. "Dink dem horse soldiers are tellin' dare Gen'rals right where yuh at."

"So?"

"So yuh betta be gittin' ready fo' a big fight."

All three agreed.

"That's right!"

"Yep!"

"Gonna be a big fight."

Kinchen rattled the pot and three tins suddenly appeared. The slave ladled generous portions of stew on to the plates, but it all disappeared in a blink.

"Y'all still got all yuh fingers?"

One boy actually checked.

A whisper came out of the dark beyond the fire. "Colonel's comin'!"

The three Rebels disappeared as fast as the stew had.

Harry came up, leading Hawkeye. Kinchen saw that he was exhausted, yet the Colonel still looked neat and tidy, always did, a handsome boy, full of dignity.

"Evening." A tired voice.

"Evenin' suh." Kinchen got to his feet, pointed the ladle at the pot. "Gots some tada stew fo' yuh."

"Smells good," said Harry as he led the gelding to a white oak and secured him, then limped over to the fire and sat rather gingerly. He didn't complain; Kinchen poured him his meal.

"Wagons are going back to Cashtown here shortly. You better get Cora ready to go."

Kinchen didn't answer right off. He didn't want to go.

"I'll clean up ol' Hawkeye first."

"Better hurry."

"Yeah suh."

Kinchen moved the gelding to more level ground, but still within the glow of the fire. He removed the saddle and the blanket, the bridle and the bit, then retrieved a half empty bucket and a rag. He rubbed the horse and eyed the Colonel. Harry had eaten several bites, but then just poked and pushed the potatoes around the plate. Kinchen tried to break the tension by whistling an old plantation tune. Harry just glanced over his shoulder, said nothing.

Hawkeye's legs were knotty and tight, and Kinchen massaged them with both hands. On one of the hind legs Kinchen thought he felt a rough spot just above the hoof. He felt it again, looked at his hand, saw blood. He checked it closely. There was a small gash, but not serious.

"Hawkeye gots a cut!"

Harry didn't answer, perhaps was too lost in thought to hear him.

"Say Hawkeye gots a cut!" Kinchen said louder.

"Bad?" Harry asked.

"Needs doctorin'."

"Can't wait for the morning?"

"No suh, might get 'fected."

There was a long, silent moment. Kinchen stood, looking at Harry's back.

"You'll miss the wagons," said Harry, finally.

"Yeah suh."

Another long minute passed.

"Go on. Clean it up."

Kinchen went right to work, cleaned the cut thoroughly, then went to the edge of the grove. He pushed aside the moist brown leaves, the dry ones beneath, and dug a hole in the loose dirt with his hands. He poured water in the hole, saturated the dirt, then scooped the mud up with both hands, walked back to the gelding, and smeared it on the wound. He caked the mud thickly, covering the entire gash, then slowly fanned it until it was dry.

"There boy, dat'll keep da flies off 'til it heals."

Kinchen had missed the wagons. He would stay the night. He led Hawkeye back into the dark grove, away from the rich clover, and staked him beside Cora.

"My lambs, my baby lambs. Yuh safe heah. Rest good now. I'll be sleepin' right ober dare."

The Colonel's agitation had been obvious, and now he was pacing, his mind off somewhere it shouldn't be. Kinchen squatted by the fire, watching Harry from the corners of his eyes. He'd seen him like this before, but it was rare. Something was gnawing at him. Kinchen had an idea what.

"Is dey gonna be a fight tomorrow?" he asked.

Harry answered quickly, "Possibly."

"A big fight?"

"Possibly."

The answers were curt, so Kinchen said nothing more. Instead, he looked straight into the hypnotizing flames, and his eyelids grew heavy.

The Colonel jarred him with a question. "What day is it tomorrow?"

"Suh?"

"Tomorrow, the date?"

"Don't know," said Kinchen after some thought.

"The first day of July," said Harry. He'd known all along.

"Dat right?"

"Remember where we were a year ago?"

Kinchen searched, couldn't remember.

"Malvern Hill!"

The sight of piled corpses jumped into his mind; he remembered the stench. "Oh yeah, dat damned hill."

Harry, ominously: "Tomorrow's the first day of July."

"Umm-hmm."

Nothing more was said, the camp grew very quiet. Kinchen closed his eyes, suddenly felt very tired, and began to drift. Then his mind grabbed the words he'd heard after Chaplain Well's sermon.

"I believe we're gonna lose him on this trip."

⁂ 20 ⁑

WHERE IS MY SWORD?

HE WOKE TO THE SOUND OF A HORSE NEIGHING, the call of a lonely animal. His eyes squinted open and focused on the massive roots that surrounded him. He was disoriented for a moment, didn't know where he was, then the neighing came again. Kinchen rolled over, sat up and spied black Cora standing in a shaft of light. Hawkeye wasn't there. Kinchen got up, peered around the great oak, and didn't see the Colonel, but through the morning haze, he glimpsed the big pasture full of sleeping soldiers, some beginning to stir.

Massa must be out fo' a ride, he thought. Hope he don't open up dat cut on Hawkeye.

Cora neighed again. Kinchen went back to soothe. He had no forage for her, so he led her into the clover and let her graze.

The breakfast fire was already burning when Harry came back from his morning jaunt among the pickets. An officer scurried up, saluted, and Harry gave him instructions. The officer bounced away. Harry returned to Kinchen and the fire, but he stayed only long enough for the slave to reapply mud to Hawkeye's wound, which was scabbed now and healing. The regiment's adjutant came up and informed the Colonel his officers were waiting for him. Harry told Kinchen to hold off on his breakfast until later.

The apprehension didn't come suddenly, more like gray rain clouds. It started with the infectious excitement of the men, as they cooked and ate, grew stronger when General Pettigrew and his staff appeared out of the mist, and reached his consciousness when Harry rode off with them toward the stone bridge. The great mass of white men marching down the pike, the rest of the division, advanced his anxiety still further. The column was gloriously intimidating, a silent band of killers, and somehow Kinchen knew there would be a battle today. He observed the building activity while cooking the Colonel's eggs and apples, then watched Harry closely after he returned from a scout. A marvelous figure on big Hawkeye. But Kinchen couldn't dismiss his fears, strong emotions that pecked at him, urging him to strike some kind of warning.

He piled hot food on a tin and set off toward the Colonel standing by the pike, surrounded by mounted officers. Kinchen drew near, but stopped short. He didn't want to make an appearance in front of so many important folks, but still, somehow, wanted to make his warning. He tried to catch Harry's eye, but the Colonel was absorbed with General Pettigrew, who was gesturing to another general just beside the column.

The sun broke through. Kinchen waited patiently while swishing away the flies that buzzed the steaming plate. Then he heard a crack like sharp thunder. Skirmishers were firing down beyond the bridge.

A fight today, no doubt, he thought. More determined, he watched and waited. Harry was speaking to Pettigrew now, Colonel Lane in the conversation as well. They all seemed quite annoyed. Pettigrew trotted off, and Kinchen heard Harry issue an order to Lieutenant Jordan.

"Prepare the regiment to march!"

Finally, Harry spied Kinchen holding his breakfast, and steering Hawkeye towards him, he rode up to the slave and apologized for his oversight.

"Oh, yeah suh, Colonel Harry suh, I-I fixed yo' breakfast. But I's 'fraid it's got a bit cool."

Smiling, Harry reached down and gently took the tin plate from his servant.

"Eggs! They look delicious!"

Kinchen bowed his head slightly to acknowledge, and Harry noticed he wasn't smiling. There was a strange softness in the black eyes, and he seemed troubled.

"You feeling all right this morning?" the Colonel asked.

Kinchen jerked, quickly looked up at Harry and finally beamed his signature smile.

"Oooh, yeah suh, I's fine. Just a lookin' at all dem sold'yas, suh. Just can't get ober all dem sold'yas."

Harry mentioned something about there being many more, and Kinchen agreed, pointing toward the hills and saying there was a great multitude more coming.

A sputtering of shots rang out again in the distance. Both instinctively looked east, but said nothing. Kinchen bounced nervously on his toes. Harry finished eating.

"Kinchen, I believe that was the best breakfast I've had since the war. Aunt Ruthy has done just a marvelous job in teaching you the art."

Kinchen smiled. "Oh dank yuh, suh, twurnt not'n, suh. Did yuh taste da suga' on da apples?"

"Oh yes, delightful!"

Kinchen beamed, but then the troubled look returned. Harry noticed.

"Something on your mind?" he asked.

"No suh," Kinchen responded as he scratched his cropped head with a nervous finger. He scrunched his nose, trying to come up with a way to sound his warning.

"Suh, I's fixin' ta go back ta da wagon camp wid Cora."

"Yes, you do that," said Harry. "The wagons will be following here shortly. Do your best to help them."

Kinchen swayed nervously. "Well, Colonel suh, seein' dat dare might be some trouble ta'day, dought I'd take Hawkeye wid me."

Harry sat up, turned in his saddle, looked to the east, contemplating, then rubbed the perspiration from his eyes.

"No, won't be necessary. There's just enemy cavalry ahead and the Twenty-sixth will be at the end of the column. No fighting today. Hawkeye will stay with me."

Kinchen wasn't convinced, "Yuh sure, suh? Yuh a mighty invitin' target on dat big Hawkeye. Yuh sure I might not betta take him wid me?"

"No." Harry appreciated Kinchen's concern, tried to comfort him. "Don't worry. You go on back with Cora. I'll see you this evening."

Kinchen was struggling, wrestling with the barrier between them.

"Yeah suh," Kinchen said resignedly. He gave up, turned slowly away from the invisible wall and made his way back toward the grove, glancing back one more time over his shoulder.

"Don't worry," called Harry.

The regiment filed on to the road to Gettysburg, taking their place in line behind the Eleventh Carolina. Kinchen paced back and forth on Cora in front of the grove, watching the gray figures as they slipped away into the dust. Finally, he set off for the pike, back toward Cashtown, but paused just short, looked back at Harry, the Colonel, the boy he'd known all his life. He reflected for a moment, traveled back as far as his memory would take him. He saw the red curly locks, the fat rosy cheeks, remembered all the excursions, the countless hunting expeditions. The barrier had not been so strong back then, and they had kept very little from each other. That had all changed. Kinchen knew it useless to tell Harry of his fear now; it would have done no good at all. The tall young man was bound to duty and would march down that road, even if he knew he would die.

Kinchen was thinking of Anna and Henry and the children when Harry caught sight of him. The slave was back at Thornbury and hadn't noticed he had caught the Colonel's eye. He stared blankly, was finally distracted by the movement of a dirty glove, Harry's wave.

Both were studying each other from a distance, long moments, Harry a bit troubled, Kinchen thinking, perhaps, this would be the last time he'd look on his master alive. The slave read the worried face and rushed a gentle smile to his own. Harry's change of expression was immediate, so Kinchen added a tip of his derby and a flourishing bow. Harry's smile showed a flush of sentiment. It was best to part this way, thought Kinchen, and he slowly turned Cora, and cantered for the pike.

The road to Cashtown was jammed with troops from Hill's Corps heading for Gettysburg. The dust swirled around them, so Kinchen rode far off the pike through the fields and pastures, jumping creeks and pulling away small sections of rail fences that blocked him. The going was slow, and he had not traveled far before he heard the first blasts from cannon. He stopped beside a willow to listen, dismounted, and let Cora pull at grass.

Cannon weren't so bad, he thought. It was dem rifles. When yuh hears dem, den yuh knows dare's a fight.

He listened for a long while, the cannonade was not all that heavy, a good sign, so he remounted and spurred Cora into a wheat field. Then came a faint sputtering, the crackle of musketry, and Kinchen winced. But he kept his back to the fighting, trying to ignore it, and the sound followed him all the way to Cashtown.

BLINDING SMOKE FILLED THE WOODS, and he could not see the destruction at first. No return fire came. Had the Iron Brigade broken? Colonel Lane came bounding out of the smoke.

"All in line on the right, Colonel!"

"All in line on the center and left," was Harry's reply. "We've broken their first line."

"We came across their exposed flank, Colonel! Just as you said! Just as you said! They fell back, sir, and the last volley sent 'em runnin'," Lane hollered exultingly.

"We must stay on them," Harry yelled. They'll reform. We mustn't let them. We'll have to break their second line—prepare to advance!"

Lane saluted, and scampered back to the right.

About fifty yards below the wooded crest of McPherson's Ridge was another dry creek bed. It ran approximately north to south, a natural trench. Here, the remnants of the Iron Brigade were rallying.

The smoke in the grove caused eyes to burn and tear. The Twenty-sixth advanced up the wooded slope, and made their way blindly through the drifting haze. The soldiers choked, their faces caked, nostrils black with powder, mouths burning, and throats parched. A clump of Wolverines, Hoosiers, and Badgers waited for them. A line of fire lashed out. A ball whistled by Harry's head, and one found yet another color bearer. Harry was close. He snatched the flag and turned to look for another bearer. Just then, Captain McCreery from Pettigrew's staff came rushing up. Harry barely recognized the Captain covered in grime. McCreery yelled over the den, had a message from Pettigrew. Harry cocked his head, could not hear, and signaled with his hands for the Captain to repeat the order. But the adjutant was infected with zeal. He grabbed the colors from Harry's hands, stepped forward, waved the flag frantically. Another volley of balls hummed, one ball cutting through the Captain's chest. He sprawled backward, fell on the colors, and stained the banner with his blood.

Lieutenant Wilcox jumped forward, the same boy who had described Archer's and Davis's battle so vividly to Harry. He pulled the flag from under McCreery's body and advanced it three steps. The balls whistled in again. Two grazed Wilcox's head, and he went down. For the first time, the Carolinians wavered. Harry grabbed the colors.

"Rally to the colors! Dress to the colors!"

A Private from Company F bounded forward. "You ain't gonna carry them colors, Colonel."

But the Private quickly perished, the twelfth bearer to fall, and Harry caught the staff before it hit the ground. His mind was clear, uncluttered of images. No thoughts of home, of family. The instincts clicked in his mind; they had to rush the enemy. He held the colors aloft, waved the flag high.

"Charge! Charge! Charge!"

Harry ran ahead to the top of a little knoll, stopped. Rows of men in blue were but twenty yards away. The Carolinians behind him hollered like demons and charged with bayonets. The Yankees rose from the creek bed. Powder exploded. The whistling balls came twisting through the smoke. That horrible, murderous whistle.

Harry saw the flash of powder. A ball hit the scabbard hanging at his side. Two more ripped at his coat. He could feel little tugs on the staff as more hit the flag. He was still standing, none had hit flesh. He turned to his side, the colors aloft in his left hand, his sword swinging in his right.

"Charge!" his voice cracked, gave, and went unheard over the den.

A ball crashed into his side, below the arm, and ripped through both lungs. The force twirled him about, an arm catching the flag as he twisted, and the red silk enfolded him, as he sprawled backward down the knoll. The gray line faltered again, then began to trade blows with the enemy at point blank range. Bullets whirled like a thousand flying fists. Two privates went for the Colonel. They disentangled him from the colors and begged Harry to speak. There was no reply. One soldier climbed the knoll, but hesitated to wave the flag. Colonel Lane ran up, bent over Harry, grabbed a hand.

"Are you badly hurt, sir?"

The eyes were open, but didn't see. There was a soft drag from the weak hand though. Lane squeezed it tightly, then placed it at Harry's side.

"It's my time to take them now," he said. Lane wheeled about, ran for the bearer, seized the colors.

"Colonel, it's certain death for anyone," the soldier warned.

"It's my time now," he yelled. Lane stared into the smoke, thought he saw the blue line giving, breaking. He turned and faced the regiment.

"They're runnin', boys! Follow me!"

A Yankee Corporal had just rammed a charge home when his comrades began to melt away. One last shot. He rested the barrel against an oak, took careful aim at the officer holding the colors, went for the fatal head shot, and squeezed the trigger. The ball smashed into the back of Lane's neck, tore through his jaw, and careened out his mouth. The fourteenth bearer was down.

The Twenty-sixth surged up the hill, the ungodly sounds reaching their peak, the thud and crack of lead hitting tissue and bone. Balls crashed into trees, splintering them. Horrid sounds came from hundreds of mouths, yelling, howling, sobbing, laughing. They cursed their Lord, then praised Him. Captain Brewer, the last bearer, clutched the flag and advanced it. The Rebels swept the Yankees before them. The Iron Brigade rallied at the crest, trying to reform, but the Carolinians' frenzy pushed them out. The Yankees ran from the grove and into a field, heading for Seminary Ridge. The momentum of the charge carried the Rebels with them, shooting the Yankees down from the rear. A disorganized and staggering gray clump struggled across the field. Out of breath, legs burning, one by one they quit the pursuit. Then came a tremendous roar from the rear. Red battle flags, row on row, emerged from the grove, then a steady gray line. It was the head of Pender's Division.

Their hearts leaped, and they tingled with excitement. They felt joy like never before. The hoarse yells were involuntary. Arms flung high, they jumped. The fresh line swept forward, the Carolinians begging them on, pointing the way, as Pender's men passed through them. Then they fell to the ground, panting. On hands and knees, laughing, cackling and hollering, they watched their comrades roll up Seminary Ridge and beyond. More strong, gray lines pitched in from the north and chased the Federals into the town. Boys in blue threw up their hands by the thousands.

THE EYES WERE CLOSED NOW, the limbs still. He didn't see or hear, and felt nothing. Numb, unconscious, as if asleep. He lay like that for quite a few minutes. The battle passed away from him, and he lay among the stricken, deaf to their agonizing cries.

Then the eyes flung open, a frantic gasp for breath. His head jerked upward, tried to seize air. His arms wailed, his face contorted, and his whole body shook in convulsions. He coughed in uncontrollable spasms, tasting the warm blood as it filled his mouth, spitting it out. The crimson flowed from his nose. He tried to get on his side, kicked his feet, and rolled down the hill. A stump stopped him, but he was on his side now. The lungs began to hold air, he spit up more blood, but it kept coming. He kept sucking in the air, concentrated on it as if it were his only function. Suck air. The mind slowly began to grasp thought, he rolled on his back, saw the blurry green of leaves overhead, realized he was alive, and began to calm.

He felt the burning, moved his left hand to his hip, then slowly guided it upward and felt the thick fluid. He placed his hand over the warm, wet hole in his coat and pressed. It burned hot. He bit his lip, groaned, sucked more air.

The realization hit him; he was shot through the body, a mortal wound. The instincts kicked in, the most powerful of human traits, self preservation. He began to fight the wound as if strength alone could defeat it, but the pain grew worse, the breathing labored, and the coughing uncontrollable. He spit out the blood, sucked, vomited. Another voice from deep inside tried to make itself heard. He shut it out, but it was the strong voice of logic, and it gained his consciousness. This wound will take you away. Accept it, accept it.

"No!" he gasped out loud. "I will not," and the pain and suffering pulsed through him again. Then the calm voice spoke. Resignation, it is the best way. The pain subsided, breathing came easier, and the coughing passed.

"The Lord's will be done," he whispered.

He saw wet cheeks on his mother's face. He saw Annie weeping in the parlor. His own tears gathered. He closed his eyes tight and tried to hold them back, and the voice said let them come. A cry distracted him, then he heard all the cries. He listened to the helpless, and his tears dried.

He started to feel stronger, thought it queer, and for a moment he had new hope, but then quickly brushed the thought away. A wound through the body was hopeless. He struggled to get on one elbow, grimaced, then reached for the stump and pulled himself up. He managed to prop himself against the stump and the pain burned, but the breathing became even easier. His vision was blurred, but he could see the wreckage around him. He was surrounded by dead men, streaks of blood on ripped bodies. The smoke had cleared and he could see the pock-marked trees, chipped and splintered. He could hear men howling and pleading at a distance, could see some trying to crawl with filthy hands, clutching at the brown forest floor. Away off somewhere, he could hear the battle still raging. He gathered his bearings, trying to determine the direction. If the sounds were to the east, it was a victory, to the west, defeat. He listened. The rattle of musketry came from beyond the ridge, to the east. He smiled slightly, satisfied. The thought of victory made the resignation easier. He was shot at the head of his regiment, leading them to victory. It had been glorious. His men had not failed him. They were glorious.

He looked about at the cost. There were numerous clumps and piles, dozens of prostrate bodies. He tried to focus down the hill, saw men in gray and blue tangled in bloody heaps. A man was trying to get to his feet, managed it, but then grabbed his leg and fell. Men were slinking toward the run for water. The sight brought the sensation of his own thirst. His mouth was dry, his tongue thick, he could taste stale blood. He looked at a man curled up beside him, a canteen hanging near his hip. It only made his thirst that much worse. He didn't have the strength to reach for it.

He coughed, a little blood came up, not much. He spit, wiped his lips and noticed his bloody hand. Someone cried behind him. He shut his eyes against it, thought of home, saw peaceful images, and waited for death.

THE SHELL HAD FLOWN IN AND LANDED NEAR HIM, and had sent him flying. Private Cheek didn't remember it, but his head had hit a rock as big as a watermelon, and he lay there unconscious. When he came to, his head was on the cool rock. There was a pounding. He reached up and felt the big knot just above his temple. Then he realized all was black, he couldn't see.

Private Cheek managed to sit up, and sat there fearfully for a while. He heard the same sounds Harry had heard. Men wailing, the battle at a distance. Eventually he began to see light, and slowly, very slowly, his vision returned. He managed to get to his feet and staggered about as his head pounded. He fought the dizziness. He had an incredible thirst.

A terrible howling came from beyond some brush. He investigated. One of his comrades was kicking around, convulsing, foaming at the mouth, like a mad dog. He reached down and tried to calm him, but his touch went unnoticed. Cheek checked for wounds, saw only one. The right arm was shattered, but otherwise the wounded man was untouched. Strange that an arm wound would bring such a violent reaction. Cheek found the man's canteen, half full. He tried to give him water, poured some on the foaming mouth. It had no effect. He emptied the canteen on the face despite his own raging thirst. The eyes went wild, looking at him as if he were some kind of devil, and he tried frantically to crawl away. Cheek tried again to calm him, but the man just kicked and screamed in terror. Private Cheek finally walked away from him.

He made for the creek and saw many men just like the soldier with the shattered arm. That insane howling and foaming at the mouth. All the men who were conscious were so stricken. There was nothing he could do to help them.

At the run he found a small pool and buried his bursting head in the cool liquid. He drank, then filled the canteen. He crawled out of the creek bed intending to help the wounded, but immediately saw two soldiers carrying a man in a blanket. He saw fine boots hanging out the end, so he knew the wounded man was an officer. He hurried over as the panting soldiers gently set the man down to rest. He looked at the officer's face and saw it was a boy, his commander, Colonel Burgwyn. The Colonel recognized him and spoke softly.

"Private Cheek, will you assist these men?"

Cheek could see that the Colonel's wound was serious. "Yes sir, my honor, sir."

Harry grimaced, then complained of burning. He politely asked his men if they would pour water on his wound. Just then an officer appeared from the thickets near the creek. The soldiers asked him what regiment he was from, but the officer said only that he was from South Carolina. The officer assisted Cheek and one of the other soldiers in removing Harry's coat, while the second soldier went to fill canteens. They turned Harry on his side as he groaned, and right off, they all saw that his wound was mortal.

Cheek was about to empty his canteen on the bubbling gash when he spied a handsome gold watch on a silk cord hanging from Harry's neck.

Thinking the water might damage it, he reached to remove it, but a filthy hand beat him to it, the officer's hand, and it broke the cord and stuffed the watch into a pocket. The officer then turned and cantered off. Mouth sagging, Cheek was shocked. His first instinct was to kill the scoundrel straight off. He looked for a rifle, found one by a nearby corpse, and ran after the robber. He had no idea if the gun was loaded, but caught up to the officer and stopped ten yards behind. Pointing the rifle at his back he called for him to stop. The officer ignored him.

"Stop, or as sure as powder burns, I'll kill you." Cheek cocked the gun. The officer heard it and stopped, turned around.

"Give me my Colonel's watch or I'll pull on you." The officer looked at him foolishly, slowly removed the watch from his pocket, and threw it at Cheek. The Private caught it, scowled.

"You're nothing but a coward and a thief. Get out of my sight!"

The South Carolinian ran.

Cheek shouldered the gun and walked back to Harry. He kneeled, gave the watch to his Colonel. Harry's face, stained with black, dried blood, was soft and warm, full of gratitude.

"You have no idea of the sentiment attached," Harry said. "I will never, never forget you."

Harry was thankful almost to tears. It moved Cheek, and he poured some water on a handkerchief, and cleaned the dried blood from Harry's face. Cheek would never forget the look about his Colonel for the rest of his days.

They pulled Harry through the thickets around the run, then strained to get him across the trampled wheat. At the grove at the foot of Herr Ridge where the terrible attack had begun, they rested. Captain Young, J. J. Young, Harry's best friend, came upon them. The pain on the Captain's face showed his concern. Harry didn't complain, didn't groan, only soft murmurs came from his lips. Young apologized, over and over, for something that couldn't have been his fault. Harry was resigned.

"The Lord's will be done."

Young wept. Cheek decided to go in search of a litter so they could carry the Colonel with greater ease and comfort. He excused himself and ran up the ridge.

Harry could feel his life ebbing away. There was a thickness in his chest, his breathing more labored. His thoughts became disjointed. He grasped for images of home. Saw everyone, saw all the sad faces and tried to make them happy. Saw Anna sweeping away the webs, Henry fretting over a sick servant, Annie giggling while he curled her locks around his fingers. Grandpa shuffled across the room, while Minnie sang and played the piano. Sumner was shooting squirrels and flirting with the girls. Pollok rolled and smoked a cigarette behind the kitchen. Allie and Collie marched and beat the drum. Madie brushed his hair, told him how handsome he was. Ruthy skinned and stewed Sumner's squirrels. And Kinchen, Kinchen, he sat on old Alveston, the racer, tipped his hat and bowed.

Captain Young spoke to him through his tears, told Harry of the day's great victory.

"My regiment has honored me, and I am honored to have died with them. No regrets—I have fallen for the Cause of my country—and on a great day—our greatest victory. The Lord's will be done." Then Harry fell silent again, returning to his thoughts.

A stray shell landed nearby, knocking the hat from the head of Captain Brewer who had come from the front and had joined the mourners. All agreed, they had to move Harry; they were still in danger there.

It took almost an hour for Private Cheek to find their litter bearers, and he overcame the party hauling Harry over Herr Ridge. They transferred him to the litter. While they carried him across a barren field, Harry pleaded for them to stop, he couldn't breath. Over toward the pike was a big walnut tree, standing alone. They rushed him there, propping him against the tree. Harry sat quietly, said very little, his breathing growing sparse and weak. Private Cheek took one of the Colonel's hands within his own and placed it in his lap, rocked. Harry mumbled how satisfied he was, and just before the end, he drifted back to before the charge. He was standing in the wheat at the base of Herr Ridge, at the head of the Twenty-sixth, he reached for his sword.

"I know my gallant regiment will do its duty… Where is my sword?"

THE BATTLE WAS PLAINLY AUDIBLE to the thousands of gray troops rushing down the narrow road from Cashtown and Chambersburg. Most would not arrive in time to participate, nor would most of the Union troops coming up from the south. Barely a third of each army grappled on the first day at Gettysburg, just four Rebel Divisions and two Yankee Corps. They were evenly matched, yet the first day was far from a draw. The Federals put up stiff resistance at first, but when Pettigrew's Brigade broke their lines on McPherson's Ridge, the retreat was on. Jubal Early's Division swept down from the north and turned it into a rout. Over five thousand Yankees surrendered. The great Rebel mistake though was allowing the Federals to consolidate a new position on the hills immediately south of Gettysburg. For the next two days the Rebels would pay dearly in their attempts to remove them.

Pettigrew's wagons were constantly being pushed on and off the road as more and more fresh infantry poured toward Gettysburg. There was a logjam at the stone bridge over Marsh Creek, so the teams were guided into the dying orchard, until the troops were able to pass. It was there that Corporal Mordecai, Captain Young's aide, came looking for Kinchen.

"Where's the Negro, Kinchen?" asked the bedraggled Corporal.

A soldier pointed toward the wagon-park. "Ain't many darkies left 'round heah. You'll find 'im over there."

Kinchen thought he heard his name, ducked from around a wagon, saw the Corporal approaching, walking.

"You Kinchen?"

"Yeah suh."

"Cap'n Young sent me after you. Says the Colonel, your master, is wounded right bad."

Kinchen was stunned, yet he was half expecting the news. "Bad? How bad?"

"Don't know, didn't see 'im, but the Cap'n sent me to fetch you. Says the Colonel wants to see you."

"Is he dyin'?"

"Don't know. Suspect we'd betta hurry back though."

Kinchen started briskly toward Cora who was tied up in the shade back in the orchard. The Corporal followed, jabbering.

"We were in the most God-awful fight, the worse there's been, I suspect. Don't think half the reg'ment made it through untouched. Heard company F got mauled. They were in the center, in the worse of it. The Colonel was 'round there too. I was down on the left, not so bad there, but still God damn lucky to be heah talkin' to you. Look heah!"

Kinchen wasn't listening, didn't stop.

"Look heah, I say!"

Kinchen stopped, turned around. The Corporal caught up, showed him his neck stained with powder.

"See that? That's a powder burn. Damned Yankee was so close when he fired, he burned my neck. Ball passed by and caught poor ol' Homer Fitz in the head, but that Yankee paid. Got stuck in the belly for his trouble. Stuck 'im and twirled it about. Left 'im spitting blood, I did."

Kinchen shuddered, started again for Cora. The Corporal kept yammering.

"The officers got hit right bad. Ain't many left. Colonel Lane got shot through the mouth. He's dyin' for certain. Major Jones came through all right. He was down with us, commands the reg'ment now, I reckons. We bloodied them Yankees good though. Never saw so much bubblin' blood on them nice blue uniforms. Them black hats were all trampled in the leaves. Sent 'em running and we were shootin' 'em down, a regular slaughter, I'd say."

Kinchen reached Cora, untied her, mounted, asked the Corporal where his horse was.

"Ain't got one. I walked here."

Kinchen reached down, offered his hand to help Mordecai up. The Corporal hesitated, wasn't too keen on sharing a horse with a Negro, but it was better than walking. He took the hand and skittered up. Kinchen then spurred the mare through the wagon-park and aimed her toward the crowded road.

The bridge was too congested, so they waded the creek, then peeled away from the road and galloped through the fields. Troops were marching through them too, having been pushed off the road by racing artillery and caissons. All the nice planked fences that lined the pike were torn down now, and the Rebel army cut a wide swath with its hurried pace. It was late in the afternoon, the sun falling, and a huge cloud of dust swallowed all. Kinchen had no idea where he was going, but Mordecai, between all his runny news, assured him he did. Fortunately, they didn't have far to go, the walnut tree where Harry lay was just a mile or so east of Marsh Creek.

They came to a stone house just off the pike. The Corporal told Kinchen to stop, pointed up a slight hill to the lone tree. They dismounted, and the slave began to climb the long littered slope with Mordecai behind him leading the mare. Kinchen felt a slithery hesitation, as he moved toward a clump of men gathered around the tree. His feet felt heavy, almost refusing to go further. Part of him didn't want to go, but something carried him on. One of the men, an officer, looked over his shoulder and saw him coming. He tapped the man next to him and they parted, clearing a way into the dark interior of the circle. Several of the men mumbled something to Kinchen, but he didn't hear them, just continued on in. He looked down and saw the boy propped against the tree. He felt suspended for a moment, like he might be dreaming, a tingling numbness. He looked down at the handsome face, the closed eyes, as if Harry were a long way away. The face was clean, fresh, didn't look dead at all, but there was dust in the auburn hair, caught in a streak of light, shiny. He bent down on one knee, brushing the dust from the hair as he reached, then brought his black hand down and touched a soft cheek, still warm. An overwhelming wave of sadness washed over him, he couldn't speak, began to sob, tears rolling down, nose streaming. He looked up, looked at all the silent faces that surrounded him, and he covered his face and wept uncontrollably.

Two soldiers dug a grave by the walnut tree. A wooden gun case was brought up, and just before Harry's body was placed within, Kinchen cut a heavy lock of hair from his head and placed it in a fold of paper. The adapted coffin was lowered down. Chaplain Wells said the rites, a brief service, then the burial was completed, as dusk settled in over the battlefield. The slave was full of grief, could not be comforted. Captain Young made the greatest effort. Ultimately, he decided it was best to put Kinchen to work. The regiment still had hundreds of wounded helplessly spread through the wheat field, the creek bed, and the wooded slope of McPherson's Ridge. They needed to be carried off, needed water, food, and care.

A grisly night passed and Kinchen endured it in numb silence. He carried litters by torch light, until his arms ached and he couldn't lift another. He went out into the dark with a dozen canteens to find water, searched for hours, came back spent and exhausted. The field hospital was a scene of torture, not for the faint-hearted, yet Kinchen wandered in to visit Colonel Lane who, despite having a hole in the back of his head, and his jaw blown away, was somehow still alive. Fortunately, he was unconscious and did not suffer. But he would. A slow agonizing death was likely to come.

Captain Young found the Negro roaming among the stricken trying to be useful, but too weary to do any good. He sent him off to sleep, and Kinchen made his way back to Herr Ridge where the regiment was camped. A small camp now, only two hundred and fifty haggard men were left from the eight hundred proud souls who had charged the grove earlier that afternoon. The survivors were in a state of shock, too grieved by their losses to be proud of their accomplishment. Whole companies had been nearly destroyed. Company F no longer existed, not a man left standing.

Kinchen limped through the stunned camp, hardly noticed. He saw no one he knew. They were all unrecognizable. His feet carried him toward the walnut tree, which was at the far end of the camp and just outside the glow of the last campfire. He came to the new grave, smelled the freshly turned dirt, a common, familiar scent. Beneath was a silent form, a cold lifeless body that was his master's. He saw him there down in the dark, in his mind. Could not believe it. Could not fathom this boy dead and buried in this strange place so far from home. How could it be? How could the Lord take away one so young and noble and leave his body to molder in a strange land?

He tried to shut out his worst thoughts, but the images of Anna and Henry and the family hovered in his brain. His heart was breaking for them. He could not bear the thought of passing them the word, felt the weight of it, the incredible burden, didn't feel the strength to perform the task.

His emotions bubbled over, escaped. Cold despair, waves of anger, sorrow and pity. He wrapped both arms around himself, hugged his chest, paced. He mumbled curious words, shook his head violently, began to weep. Still hugging his chest, he finally leaned against the tree, slipped down resignedly, began to gather himself.

"No mo' tears," he said out loud, as he wiped his face with his coat sleeve.

The sun will rise tomorrow, he thought. It will be a new day, a day without Massa' Harry, but another day to live and breathe.

A large group of men were passing over the nearby pike. Torches disclosed to Kinchen that most were wearing blue. Yankee prisoners, several hundred he guessed, being escorted back toward the hills to the west. He watched the long line of shuffling men, until the torchlight faded over the next rise. But his attention remained with the road. He thought of where it led, to those green hills. He knew now why the mere sight of them had moved something within him. It was Scipio, and his Papa's words. So many years ago, just a boy, but it had all come back to him.

"Listen to yo' soul, boy, and da hills of freedom will always be 'round yuh'."

Mr. Lincoln had proclaimed him a free man. He was sitting right there on free soil. Massa Harry was dead. That road, it led straight to freedom.

Kinchen shook his head. He really couldn't explain it well, couldn't put it into good words, but for some reason, for him, none of the rhetoric rang true.

"Peoples go off a' searchin'—lookin'. Dey does it all da time. Searchin' for sump'n betta'. Lookin' fo' dings dat just ain't 'round. Massa Harry did it. He came up dat road, and now he's buried right here 'side me. It ain't here, Massa. What yuh were lookin' fo'. It ain't here."

Kinchen leaned back against the tree, placed a hand on his chest, sighed.

"It's here." Tapping on his chest, "Right here."

He glanced at the pike again, that dusty, faint line in the dark leading to those glorious hills. The tears began to well up again, tender pain in the brown cheeks.

His words were both angry and resolved. He spoke to Harry deep in his grave.

"No suh, I ain't gonna take dat road."

⚜ 21 ⚜

ALWAYS FAITHFUL

July 2nd, 1863
Near Gettysburg, Pa.

Mr. Henry K. Burgwyn, Esq.
Raleigh, North Carolina

Sir—

 I feel it my duty to communicate the painful & melancholy intelligence to you of the death of your son, Colonel H. K. Burgwyn, who was killed nobly fighting for his country, July 1st, 1863. He was shot through both lungs & died an easy death. I have buried him as well as possible under a walnut tree on the turnpike leading from Gettysburg to Chambersburg, 2 miles from the former place in a field about 100 yards from the road. I have all his effects, his horses & Kinchen, until I get a chance to send them off. I would like very much to send them immediately, but being in the enemy's country, it is nearly impossible.
 His loss is great, more than any of us can imagine, to his country. To me it is almost stunning & to the whole regiment. We gained a great victory the 1st of the month, the enemy losing it is said 12,000, but though ours was not a fourth so large, your son's death made it great. Poor Kinchen takes it bitterly enough.
 The Colonel, Colonel Lane, Captain McCreery & 10 others were shot down with our colors. Captain McCreery was instantly killed, & Colonel Lane seriously if not mortally wounded. The regiment went in 800 strong & came out with but 250 men. The fighting yesterday & today has been terrible & will continue tomorrow, I suppose. General Pettigrew is in command of our Division, Major Jones of our Brigade. This will give you an idea of the frightful loss of the officers.
 I have concluded to send Kinchen off towards home soon as some of my wagons will go to Winchester, though I am fearful to do so yet for somebody might possibly take both horses from him. This, however, they will have to do by force if at all, for I never saw fidelity stronger in any one. But taking everything into

consideration I fear to keep him longer, for we may advance & he fall into the hands of the enemy & there is now every prospect that this great battle will open again, so I will start him off as soon as possible. He will take both horses, the Colonel's clothes, except his arms and his best uniform suit, which is in the medical wagon & cannot be reached & a pair of shoes. Both spy glasses, pocketbook & a couple of memoranda books, both shot through by the more than cruel ball that deprived the Confederacy of one of her brighter ornaments, his watch & tooth brush will go with Kinchen.

There was in the pocketbook $135.00. I give $95.00 of it to Kinchen, leaving $40.00 in my possession. If anything should happen to me, I hereby state that Colonel Burgwyn was last paid by me to May 31st 1863. There is due him, one month & one day from the Confederacy. I will pay up his mess bill & other debts if any, I suppose there are none else, which we will arrange hereafter.

The death of one so young, so brave, so accomplished, with every prospect of being at no distant period one of our greatest men has filled all with sadness & sorrow. His fall is universally regretted, but in his regiment all are filled with the greatest sorrow.

In some way I have ever felt uneasy whenever he went into battle & always cautioned him to be cautious. My forebodings, alas, have proved too true, & I have lost one of my best friends. I can truly say, the death of General Lee himself I would have preferred. But all mortal that is lovely has to fade away, but his example ought ever to be a shining light to his relatives & friends left behind. Their loss is great but I hope & believe it is his eternal gain.

Ere this reaches you, you will doubtless have heard of the result of this great battle. May it prove a total victory for our arms and bring a speedy end to this horrid war. Please inform me when Kinchen arrives safely for I shall feel a good deal of anxiety, until I hear he is safe. With great remorse of being the bearer of these sad tidings, I am, sir, your most obedient servant,

Captain James J. Young
Quartermaster, 26th Reg. N.C.T.

WHITE TENTS SPRINKLED ACROSS a hay field, glowing faintly in the weak moonlight. No movement in the night air, the canopies hanging taut and moist in the thick humidity. Colonel Lane was there, under the canvas, awake at 2 AM, suffering, wishing he were dead. He could not call out, his jaw shattered, a bandage wrapped around his head, only his eyes and nose exposed. He lay in the darkness in excruciating silence. The only light, slivers of the moon's reflection and a dull spark in his liquid brown eyes. Sleep was hopeless. He struggled for a diversion, some kind of relief, but the pain raged like a furious child. No peace. No mercy. Trapped in agony.

There was movement beside him, a slight roll and toss from a sleeping body. Lane didn't notice. It was Private McCracken, Seth McCracken, a giant boy from one of those clans of Scots in Wilkes County. He was bleeding inside, hemorrhaging. Death was near.

McCracken suddenly woke, a violent eruption, and he screamed from the effects of a terrifying dream, then stared at Lane with a demented expression.

"No! No!" he raved. A chilling blast in a hot, quiet night. Lane cut his eyes at him.

"No! God! No!"

The Private recognized Lane, pleaded with a panicked voice.

"You've gotta stop 'em, Colonel! They's charging that hill. Oh God, the cannon, row on row. They's bein' slaughtered!"

McCracken reached, grabbed Lane's arm with a tremendous grip.

"Gotta' stop 'em. Stop 'em." Panting: "The reg'ment—murdered—chargin' with Gen'ral Pettigrew. Chargin' that hill. Stop 'em!"

The grip suddenly lost its strength, the hand slipped away, flopping to the ground. The life went out of the Private's eyes; he slumped, dead. Lane blinked, looked on with sympathetic horror, could say nothing. He closed his eyes, the pain rising back from its brief repose. They opened again and focused on the sagging canvas. The pain engulfed. Could think of nothing else. McCracken's ravings meant nothing to him, nothing at all. The wee hours ticked away slowly. It was the morning before the great charge, the morning of July third.

THE FIGHTING STARTED FRESH BEFORE SUNUP. From over on the eastern side of Culp's Hill, came the thumping of musketry and cannon. A brigade from Edward Johnson's Division of Ewell's Corps had charged the hill the evening before, overrunning some trenches, then held on to them through the night. They weren't far from the rear of the Union lines, within rifle shot of the Baltimore Pike, the Yankees' avenue of retreat. Johnson had two fresh brigades he could have thrown in to seal the road, but he held off, and planned to send them in at dawn. He would be too late. The Yankees would beat him to the attack, eliminating his advantage, and the Rebels in the captured trenches would eventually be driven out.

The roar of the fighting bounced over the hills, rolling across the shallow valleys, over Seminary and McPherson's Ridges. Faintly tapping the morning air from more than a mile away, they were the first sounds to Kinchen's ears when he woke. They were familiar now, the sharp crackles, the muffled booms. They'd been pounding the air all the previous afternoon and evening, a tremendous den. This morning, Kinchen thought little of them, the sounds having become as natural to him as chirping birds. Instead, as he cleared away the webs of sleep, his first instinct was to look for Harry. A glance over the shoulder, heavy eyes scanning the camp, but there were no lovely boys standing near. The only locks of wavy auburn hair were tucked within a fold of paper deep within Kinchen's breast pocket. Yesterday, several times, he had caught himself searching for the Colonel among the resting men. He had to tell himself repeatedly that Harry was gone. But his mind's habits were strong, and the cycle of brief, sad quests would continue yet another day.

The struggle for Culp's Hill lasted into the late morning. Kinchen passed the time toiling at his new adopted duty, the endless search for fresh water for the wounded. The nearby brooks, if they weren't dry, were putrid with blood, entrails, and excrement. Toting a string of canteens, he would range far into the hills in search of trapped puddles yet untouched by the long reach of two flailing armies.

Straps pulled tight against his shoulders, cutting into muscle, his full load made him struggle down a narrow draw, his knees burning. He stopped for a moment in a quiet place in the woods to rest, and noticed the stillness. The sky was bright now, light streaming down in hot rays. Not a sound could be heard, leaves drooping heavy. The fighting had stopped, no guns in the distance. The quiet made him anxious, and he started out again for the hospital.

He walked through a patch of wounded men spread out on the side of a yellow hill. They had limped out from the shade of the trees to listen, and were looking up into the sky. They had an eerie sense of anticipation, and Kinchen dropped his load, stood among them, infected. He looked up into the pale blue, trying with the others, to guess what would happen next. There was only hot stillness, and eventually the men began to retreat back into the darkness under the trees. Kinchen heaved up his load and started back over the rise.

He had delivered the canteens to a steward and was just setting out for another trip when there came a report from a single cannon, a signal. Kinchen didn't know its significance and carried on back toward the yellow hill speckled with boulders. With sweat beading on his brow, the early afternoon sun casting its heat, he trudged through the trampled fields. Suddenly, from over the ridge came a long discharge quickly followed by another. Then many guns, all firing in quick succession. The sound drew him up the rise, the scorched grass brittle under his feet. From the summit, he could tell the artillery were pointed away, and he looked east to see where it was directed, but a line of tall trees on Seminary Ridge obscured his view. He saw only the hot air shimmering over the trees' pointed tops. The sky was opening like thunder now, deadly cracks, enormous ripping sounds. It spread from his right to left like giant spraying shotgun blasts. He hadn't seen the Regiment since early that morning, when they had formed up and marched off out of sight. Maybe the boys were up there among the guns.

The wind shifted. Great rolling clouds of smoke rose up over the trees and drifted towards him. Beyond the white bank, the cannonade grew even stronger, echoes rebounding and bouncing off rocks and hills. Return fire came. He could see red and yellow flashes through the smoke and trees. It was the most enormous sound he had ever heard. Greater than Malvern Hill. Surpassing the deafening battles of the two previous days. Shattering, overpowering, the gun blasts went on and on, hundreds belching out their destruction.

The ground underfoot was unsteady. Smoke hung thick around him, with the bitter smell of burning powder; a taste of sulfur coated the inside of his mouth. He couldn't see any more, couldn't see the next hill over, so he squeezed down between two gray boulders and listened to the havoc. The bombardment refused to quit, surged on like a great panicked herd of braying mules. A tremendous crescendo of varying sounds and concussions. For nearly two hours the lead chunks screeched through the air, while Kinchen hunkered between the rocks, his fear escalating until he was sure the whole countryside would erupt into flames.

Then the booms grew softer, slowly died away. Suddenly it was marvelously still, like a saturated high tide under a full moon. Kinchen pulled himself up from the shelter of the rocks, peered through the clearing smoke. Over the trees, a huge black cloud was coiling high into the sky. The Yankee army. That's where they must be. He wondered if they had been obliterated. Nothing could have survived such a bombardment.

The infantry assault was forming. Three divisions. Fifteen thousand Rebels. They rose up from their shelter behind Seminary Ridge, quickly passed through the woods, and reformed in the wide clearing on the other side. Their target was a copse of trees in the center of the Union lines. A mile away, it had just been raked by one hundred and seventy guns. General Lee had previously attacked both of Meade's flanks, had come dangerously close to turning them. The enemy was massed there now, so their center was thin and weak. The Rebel guns, it was hoped, had just punctured a hole, and the three divisions were to rush in and split the Yankee army in half.

They were Lee's freshest troops. Pickett's Virginians had not yet been engaged. Pender's and Heth's Divisions, the victors of the first day, had rested since, although they were without their commanders. General Trimble now commanded for the dying Pender, and General Pettigrew had replaced the stunned General Heth. Colonel Marshall directed Pettigrew's Brigade now, and he would take it across the mile-wide valley along with the two hundred and fifty remaining boys of the Twenty-sixth North Carolina. Battle flags dancing, they stepped off as if on parade.

Kinchen sensed the grand movement, couldn't see it, but knew something big was underway. He tipped his toes, perked up, tried to squint through the summer foliage. The cannon began to play again. This time, all thundering from the Yankee hills. Then came the brutal smashes, as shells and solid shot rained down on the open ground on the other side of the trees. An enormous procession of scythe-like blasts rollicked through the unseen lines of drab uniforms. Proud boys were falling in mangled rows.

He could only hear the battle as it moved quickly away from him. Could only sense the attack. The gray troops advanced solemnly through the flying debris. There were no tell-tale screams or yells that would verify their charge.

But the rolling echoes, the great beating on the earth, the belching shots of canister, all spawned a curiosity. Kinchen rushed to the highest rock on the hill, climbed it, tried without success to see his charging comrades. He opened his ears to every sound now, and for one euphoric moment, could almost hear hoarse cheers from a thousand raw, victorious throats. Was it over? Was the war finally over?

The smoke, trees and wavy ground spared him the horror. The sight of Pettigrew's prostrate gray kicking for life. The General himself, holding a bloody hand behind thinning lines of desperate men. Colonel Marshall, unrecognizable, riddled, sprawled among the broken planks by the Emmitsburg Road. Harry's regiment mowed down, the seventy survivors recoiling from the stone wall, scurrying back, spiteful, remorseful, back to the safety of Seminary Ridge. Their stained silk flag, spun with care by Minnie and her school friends, dangling low for a hopeless cause. Kinchen had heard his world change.

THE RAINS CAME IN GREAT WHITE SHEETS, cleansing the battlefield, flooding the red streams choked with bodies. Two wounded armies stood face to face in the torrent, waiting for the other to make a move. Lee and the Rebels prayed for the Yankees to attack, but the timid Meade had no plans to follow up on the fearful slaughter his army had handed the Confederates the afternoon before. The blue troops were safely dug in atop their sodden hills and ridges and were not coming out.

Behind the Rebel lines and along the mud-soaked Cashtown Road, a huge park of ambulances, wagons, carts, and caissons was being assembled despite the confusion of the storm and a mass of numbed stragglers. John Imboden, a prim attorney-turned-cavalry leader was supervising the gathering. Progress was slow, no abatement in the downpours, but by late in the afternoon all the wounded and supplies were packed and ready for a long, miserable retreat. Guarded only by Imboden's small brigade of irregulars and various reinforcements from other units, the seventeen-mile-long train would be extremely vulnerable during its trek back to Virginia. At four o'clock the train set off for Cashtown in the howling wind and thunder. Its goal, the passes through South Mountain and the fords along the Potomac beyond Williamsport, Maryland. After dark, Lee's infantry and Stuart's cavalry would start off using a different route, so they could screen and protect the train. Meade had anticipated the move, and had already sent his marauding horsemen in pursuit.

Riding slumped forward, head leaning into the wind, derby tight over his eyes, Kinchen slogged through walls of rain. The night had thrown its shadow over the hills, utter blackness. Sparks of lightning were his only guide, as he and the wagons struggled to stay on course over the saturated roads. Drenched, quivering, he was whipped down to a state of distressed gloom. Between the splats of thunder, a chorus of hideous pleas from suffering wounded filled his ears and every thought. He tried to turn his mind away from their torture, but he saw them clearly with each lightning bolt. Soaked, dismembered, their blood running freely as they lay under ripped canvas. Spread on naked boards of springless carts, the stricken cried a litany of anguish caused by the unmerciful bouncing. Cold, shivering screams from shattered men; they pleaded with foul oaths for their Lord to take them away.

A monstrous anger mixed with his unbearable sadness. The worst hours of Kinchen's life dragged through an endless night.

He was the ward of Captain Young now, a tidy young man with limited abilities, who was being swallowed by the strain of keeping the wagons moving under impossible conditions, while men died within them. Young had lost all semblance of coolness. He was charging his horse through the deep mud, and yelling instructions to teamsters who could not hear him over the wind. He was in a fever, expelling his energy uselessly, the only way he could cover the shock of losing hundreds of men he had thought invincible. Fortunately, Kinchen had lost contact with him in the dark. He rode alone on Hawkeye, Cora's reins tight in his rain-soaked glove, surrounded by suffering he imagined not possible. He kept moving; it was his only real function. As long as the wagons moved, he moved, and their wheels churned through rivers of mud the whole long night.

There came a great flash of lightning that lit up the horrid scene, followed by a tremendous crack, right overhead, that deafened all until it rumbled away over distant ridges. As the thunder died away, Kinchen thought he heard his name spoken in a hoarse whisper. He looked about in the dark, and realized Hawkeye had drifted to the center of the road right behind a wagon. He heard his name again coming from within the cart. A strangely calm voice.

"Kinchen. Come here, boy."

He saw a pale hand wrapped tightly around the wagon's rear gate handle, and through the darkness under the canvas emerged a grotesque face he did not recognize.

"Who dat?"

"Surry," a weak response. Kinchen didn't know the name, but the soldier knew him.

Kinchen leaned forward, searched through the wet blackness for something familiar about the scarred face.

"Tell the driver to stop," said Surry with great effort.

"Wha'?"

"Stop—stop the wagon."

"Can't stop," said Kinchen over distant thunder. "Cap'n says no wagons should stop."

"Just for a while. The driver, ask 'im, just for a short spell."

Kinchen knew the driver wouldn't listen to him. "You just hold on dare. Cap'n says we be stoppin' soon. Real soon. Just hol' on a while longer."

Kinchen lied.

Surry smiled feebly, knowingly, and the slave managed to see it, knew the soldier did not believe the train would stop.

"I'm dyin'," said Surry, followed by a painfully long pause. "I'm dyin' right here. Rattlin' to death."

Kinchen fumbled for words in the pouring rain.

"Damn-it to Hell. Don't want to die like this. Ask 'im. Ask 'im to stop, so you can pull me off. Peace, just ask'n for a peaceful place to die."

Surry was serious, his last request, and Kinchen felt a cold wave of depression. A moment of indecisiveness passed. Then he guided Hawkeye toward the head of the wagon.

The driver was struggling, his hat full of water and hanging floppily over his bearded face.

"Mr. Surry axes yuh ta stop da wagon. He dyin'," shouted Kinchen over the racket of the storm.

The driver turned his head a bit, acknowledging that he had heard, but flailed at the reins for the mules to pull even harder.

"Mr. Surry's beggin' yuh ta stop!"

"Can't stop, boy," an angry growl. "I'll get stuck for certain. Hold up the whole train."

Kinchen kept his parallel course, looked at the driver with a pleading face, but the callous eyes remained buried under the wilted hat. Kinchen gave up, pulled Hawkeye to a halt, ashamed at his feeble attempt. The wagon rumbled away from him, while he stood helpless in the spattering rain. He looked down, turned his head, unwilling to give Mr. Surry a passing glimpse.

The train couldn't stop for one dying man. Kinchen knew that. About all he could do was talk to Surry, distract and comfort him. He spurred the gelding forward, caught up with the wagon, but didn't see the hand gripped to the tailboard handle, and there was an empty place at the rear of the wagon where Surry had lain. Kinchen pulled away the canvas flap for a better view, saw bouncing bodies huddled in a pile, none of which looked alive. Surry wasn't there. He must have pulled himself out. A vision of the soldier trampled in the mud jumped into his mind. A quick, jerking glance over his shoulder disclosed only darkness. He tied Cora tightly to the wagon, then set off back up the road to find him.

A dozen or more wagons passed him, and he struggled up the road about a hundred yards, before thinking he had gone too far, and turned back. No sign of Surry, the pike a black quagmire, flashing lightning the only light. Probably buried in the muck; between the white streaks he could have easily missed him. Kinchen dismounted, his search becoming frantic, flopping around in the mire. He waded a ditch beside the road, slipped up the bank, studied the ground on the other side. A flooded field, knee-deep; the soldier couldn't have gone through there. But there came a wink of lightning followed by a long, sparkling bolt. Kinchen saw something about twenty feet up, something lumpy on the bank. He scrambled up that way.

He found Surry's bootless feet, his legs falling away to a partially submerged torso, the head barely floating in the glutted field. He had drowned himself. The slave looked down at him, his face stung with pity. Aching minutes passed while he searched his memory, probing for an image of the soldier, and how he might have come to know his name. Finally he concluded that Surry must have been one of dozens of boys he had fed from the Colonel's many surpluses. Now another life was gone forever. Another piece of the regiment pulled away from its core and left to rot in a horrible land.

Kinchen gathered himself, got down on his knees and pulled the water-logged corpse out of the lagoon, then struggled to his feet. His clothes saturated and clinging heavily to his shivering frame, the derby dripping and losing its form, he stood in the deluge and looked up into the thunderous blackness. A special kind of loneliness. Feelings he had not known since the great fire at Hillside and the death of his parents. Alone and abandoned in desolation. Forsaken, he felt completely forsaken.

JOHN BUFORD'S CAVALRY DIVISION had been so badly mauled on the first day's fighting at Gettysburg that it had been sent to the distant rear to rest and refit. The blue horsemen were lounging about ten miles south at Emmitsburg, Maryland on July fourth when the dispatch arrived informing them the Confederates were retreating. Buford, a deliberate commander not known for his speed, set off to intercept them, and was able to beat Jeb Stuart's boys to the vital crossroads. The huge Rebel supply trains lay ripe for the plucking, only the storm and heavy roads would prevent Buford from seizing it.

The rain changed to a fine mist as dawn approached. Gunfire replaced the thunder. Kinchen rode like a lonely wanderer, soaking in the sounds, tabulating their distances. The fighting was both ahead and to the rear; a good three miles off in both directions, he gauged.

Completely ignorant of what was transpiring, troopers passed wild rumors up and down the line, planting a sense of doom among the teamsters. They were cut-off, surrounded, would all be captured. The train stalled in the dark. The few Rebel horsemen rode off to investigate, leaving the wagons blind and vulnerable. Kinchen directed Hawkeye and Cora off the road to the shelter of dripping trees to rest them. There, he anxiously waited and listened. He didn't know that it was just small bodies of Union cavalry that had reached the train, small groups that were doing plenty of damage. Packs of twenty or more were swooping in from the dark, imposing their terror, shooting and sabering the mules, cutting the traces, pulling out the wounded, and burning the wagons. Imboden's men were rushing up and down the train frantically trying to beat them back, but the plunderers would simply vanish only to reappear a few hundred yards down the line.

Kinchen couldn't see the sacking, but his imagination didn't fail him. He felt the helplessness of the wounded, and his contempt for the Yankees grew to hatred. What was the meaning of it all? What cause justified the savagery? He wanted to close his eyes, escape into a long cleansing sleep. Suddenly, he realized there was something even better, and it surrounded him, tempting him. The foggy wood. He could slip away into the mist and no one would see him, not a soul would notice he was gone. Out in the soggy landscape he would be free from this, free from all the suffering and torment. There was shelter in the free land.

The momentary temptation passed like a musty odor. Reality seeped into his thoughts. Nothing was certain out there. Passing into the mist offered no more than marching through the gauntlet with the wagons. Freedom was as vague and obscure as the fog. It offered no guarantees, no insurance. Instantly, he yearned for home, for Thornbury, and the warmth he had known there. He had a promise to fulfill, a task to complete, and when it was done he would return to the stables and to all the sights and sounds and scents that were familiar and safe. Beyond that churned up road and on the other side of the river was home, and that's where he wished to be.

The sky was turning gray. The train was moving again, the fighting fading away. He mounted Cora now and led Hawkeye in with the wagons.

THE CURTAIN ROSE AND UNVEILED THE BUTCHERY. The pike was lined with corpses: mules, horses, and soldiers. Between the smoldering wagons, some of the dead Rebels were laid out in neat rows, others were half buried, and still more had been thrown haphazardly along the side of the road. Crooked fingers reached out of the mud, bloated bodies immersed and floating in the sated ditches. All created a haunting vision forever stamped into memory.

The column passed through a grimy village where scores of disabled wagons littered the thoroughfare. Their wheels showed signs that they had been chopped and hacked by axes and hatchets; vengeful townsfolk had attacked them in the night. More bodies were scattered about. A small burial detail was digging graves in the yard of a dark and sorrowful home, which, a week before, had been the town's brightest and finest dwelling.

Kinchen clung to the beaten army, a witness to its wreckage. Already one hundred and fifty wagons had been claimed by the Yankee raiders, yet the train was still together, pushing for the Potomac. General Imboden was pressing them forward with no rest. His cavalrymen, aided by daylight and the dying storm, had been able to check the enemy horsemen and keep them at bay. With a little luck, they had a chance to reach safety, before Buford's heavy columns could arrive. There was a good ford at Williamsport, and at Falling Waters, about five miles down river from the town, where pontoon bridges had been placed to help accommodate their crossing. If they could get to the Virginia side by nightfall, they'd be reasonably safe.

The head of the column reached Williamsport around mid-day, but the river was high and rising, the ford impassable, and the nearby pontoons had been cut away by raiders. The Potomac, a swollen, creamy yellow, stood as a barrier. The train was trapped against the riverbank and easy prey.

Kinchen drifted with the train as it snaked into Williamsport, the wagons peeling off one by one to unload the wounded into the town's homes and neighboring farmhouses. Captain Young, cutting a brittle figure, had rejoined Kinchen, and the two followed three wagons to a plump structure just on the town's edge and helped transfer the hurt to soft, dry beds. The Captain disappeared again soon after, and Kinchen settled in, fired up a wood stove and began to prepare a rare hot meal.

Outside, there was a great surge of activity. Hundreds of the supply wagons were parked below a bluff near the river at the far end of the town. Imboden began arming all the teamsters and any wounded who could handle a gun and formed them into little regiments. Including his own brigade, he was able to gather a ragtag little force of three thousand. They were placed in a thin semicircle around the wagon-park, guarding the roads leading in from the north and west. Although they were in poor condition and low on ammunition, the Rebels had a fair number of cannon, which were carefully placed along the line to bolster the defense. If the Yankees wanted the train, they would have to make sacrifices. Imboden harbored no notion of holding indefinitely however. He hoped only to last until help could arrive.

He was not well versed in the arts of strategy or tactics, but it didn't take a keen mind to recognize the frail position he and his allies now occupied. Kinchen began to ponder the possibility of being taken by the Federals. Would they let him go his merry way, allow him to cross the river and continue his journey, or would they steal the horses and force him to cook and toil for them the whole war through? Another unbearable thought: would they haul him up to the cold, cruel north and hire him out to some mean-spirited fellow, or some sooty factory along a gray, barren river? He now abandoned the job of frying and roasting, and turned it over to the lady of the house who had been more than bothered by the commandeering of her kitchen, and who had been pacing and tapping her foot for the job anyway. Kinchen went out into the confusion to find Captain Young and offer his services in the struggle at hand.

Barely had the preparations been complete before the Federals arrived; a long mounted column veered in from the west about an hour and a half after noon. They came on rather rashly, exposing their flank to a battery hidden in the hills above the town. A barrage lashed out at them and sent them reeling. The Yankees rolled in their own artillery, a small force, but the Rebel guns pounded them to silence. Soon, all twenty-three of the Rebel guns opened and kept the scavengers at arms length for a time.

General Buford arrived on the scene and observed, as Imboden sent his entire force forward in a bluff-like show of might. Buford dismounted five regiments, sent them in, and a roaming fight drifted into the late afternoon, with the Federals only able to break into the far right of the Rebel line and destroy a half dozen wagons or so. The sun was sputtering to dusk, when the Yankees were finally beaten back with a cavalry charge. Portions of Jeb Stuart's horsemen began to creep up on the Federals' rear, and the encouraging sound of their guns sent the Rebels around Williamsport surging forward. Buford packed up and escaped to the east, as a chorus of cheers rose up from Imboden's troopers.

There was work behind the lines. While the battle swayed, the Rebel guns fell dangerously short of ammunition, so flatboats on the Virginia side of the Potomac, loaded with shot and powder, risked the flooding river. Kinchen helped to carry the ordnance to the front, and he was near the guns when the celebration commenced, a wild, jocular revelry. General Lee's supply train had been saved.

22

THE GIFT'S BURDEN

THE CONFEDERATE ARMY TRAMPED DOWN to the rising Potomac and found the river was too angry to hold a pontoon bridge. They began to trench and, after a few days, the works were so terribly impressive that all the troops and generals wished the enemy would try them. But Meade had been rather bashful in his pursuit from Gettysburg and was even more reluctant to charge once he arrived abreast of the Rebels. He had won a victory up in Pennsylvania; he would not ruin it with a defeat down here along the Potomac. Although nothing would suit Lee more than to inflict some injury on the Federals, he welcomed the respite and applauded each day that Meade sat and the river fell. Already, his engineers were busy fashioning makeshift rafts and rope-wire ferries that would carry wounded and prisoners to Virginia, and float supplies and ammunition back to him in Maryland.

He was on his sixth grave of the morning. He didn't mind the digging, it was the filling in; it gave him the tingle-neck and conjured up a vision of Harry's death face, so pale and peaceful and beautiful. As muscles pulled and sweat poured, and with each swing of the pick and heave of the shovel, the haunting image would temporarily fade until, once again, it was time to throw dirt on the anonymous soul and seal the tomb. He thought there must be some better way of ridding the dead from the living other than covering them with earth, but nothing came to mind except fire, and while that was certainly less burdensome than digging, it was not very pleasing to the nose. He knew; he had burned many a drowned heifer awash up in the fields after a freshet.

The Lieutenant had told him to dig to his belly-button for the corpses in blue and to his eyes for those in gray. He was mining for a Rebel now and was nearly through, the tip of his head bobbing up from the grave with each rise of the pick, then disappearing with every blow. He didn't see that Woodfolk, a commissary sergeant, had ambled up to the edge of the hole. The cool shadow fell over him, and he paused, then squinted up into the sun, over the faceless hulk looming just above. Kinchen covered the sun with a crusty, dirt-covered hand and the face came to view: hairy, a red cheek swollen with a plug of tobacco, fluid, green spittle trapped in the beard.

"You Kinchen?" asked the face.

"Yeah suh."

A huge hand reached down to him and, before he could blink, he was out of the grave and standing next to the giant.

"Cap'n Young says you're to come with me."

Kinchen studied Woodfolk, the great greasy beard, a dent in the nose, but eyes that were soft and blue and looked much younger than the rest of the face.

"So pack up your belongin's and gather your ponies and meet me down by the ferry."

"Wha' we goin'?"

"Over the rivah, to Martinsburg, then I'm to point you the way home."

"Home?"

"Yeah boy, with God's blessing you'll be goin' home."

With that said, Woodfolk turned and began to lumber down the hill toward wagons parked on the road. He was limping, quite a bad limp, and Kinchen thought he must have been inflicted with some grievous wound earlier in the war, but in truth, Woodfolk's shattered knee had been given to him by a yellow-toothed mule some ten years before. He'd never been a line soldier, had never fired a shot in battle. The big fella' was nothing more than a mule-driving wagoneer.

The riverbank was as sloppy as a hog pen, and all the turmoil reminded him of a killing day at Thornbury: carts and wagons snarled in mayhem, a long line jamming the road, bellowing sergeants, cursing officers, a general uproar. There was little to do but wait, and the afternoon drifted to the fringe of dusk, before he and the horses were shoved into a nook between two vehicles crowding a small flatboat of freshly-hewed pine. The river was in a fitful dander, foamy, but Kinchen wasn't too terribly impressed. He'd seen the Roanoke in a far greater tantrum. But then again, he'd never tried to ford it when it was riled. The work of the crossing was done with ropes and pulleys and bent-backed tuggers. With short jerks the raft plodded through the swift riffles. Hawkeye and Cora were irritated with the whole process, eyes cutting, manes bristling, ears flapping like flags in a windstorm. Kinchen's voice had a tranquilizing effect, and the wagons blocked the horses' view of the clapping torrent and floating debris. The entire trip took less than ten minutes, so before their fevers could rise, they were slanting up the opposite shore and dozing on a Virginia bluff. Woodfolk gathered his wagons there with their broken passengers, and soon they were off down a squishy, rutted road, until darkness forced them to bivouac well short of their goal.

The next day they made Martinsburg, where there was a hospital for the hurt, and where Woodfolk was to gather supplies to be hauled back to Maryland. The town was out of sorts for the war, a strategic spot because of the B & O which ran through the place, but now paralyzed because of the damage inflicted some weeks back by Imboden's irregulars, during their northward raids. The railroad had brought more prosperity to the town than most valley villages. Now, it had a disheveled appearance, having been fought over and occupied more than once by both sides. The clapboard dwellings and businesses were sun-bleached and chipping. The depot burned, a black shell. Shambling walkways, broken windows, pock-marked brick, streets that were quagmires of deep furrows and trapped puddles. The natives had been split in their sympathies, strong for one side or the other, but they were now sour and jaded and didn't care a dime which army prevailed. Tucked away and hidden, the townsfolk no longer ambled along the spattered boardwalks, yet the streets were full of the war's refuse: convalescents, shirkers, and those weak of leg who had fallen out during the great march North.

Woodfolk's wagons waded in. Lounging on a stoop, a one-legged observer aimed a finger toward the center of town, then crooked his wrist indicating a turn to the right, while mumbling something about the stockyards. Directions to the hospital, Woodfolk supposed. He tipped his hat at the cripple. The train turned off the main street and down another thoroughfare, until a stir in the air brought the putrid scent of infection. The Sergeant followed the stench. Rows of shops were passed, until at the outskirts of town, they came upon sprawling corrals and fences. Crated within the paddocks were cheerless prisoners, northern soldiers. The captives showed little interest in the train, it being one of many that had creaked by their compound, but some paid a passing glance at Kinchen. Haggard eyes, gray under sullen brows, rose up at the Negro, followed his progress, then blinked shut.

Kinchen chose not to gawk, but his eyes soon fell on a pig pen, wired, and woven high around a square of gums whose sparse leaves did little to shade a clump of Negroes huddled on a floor of dried manure. There, lolling side by side, shoulders leaning heavy against a splintered feed trough, were Farley and Robert. His eyes met Farley's, and Kinchen gazed upon what he thought was an expression of pure hatred. Robert reacted to a finger poke, black eyes rolling up from beneath limp lids, and there Kinchen perceived a picture, just as unsoiled as Farley's, a portrait of fear.

The two rose out of the dust, and hobbled to the side of the pen, their black fingers clutching at the wire. Kinchen felt a surge of shame, didn't slow his pace, and turned away. He could feel Farley's and Robert's stares, a shudder in his lower spine, and he reigned Hawkeye to a stop. He pivoted his chin to his shoulder, and peered back at the threatening sneers. The haunting visage had not changed: hate and fear. The emotions consumed them like the pox, spreading, a scourge on their souls. It was a common affliction these days, Kinchen thought, and if all were to catch it, the world would not be fit for living. He couldn't help but feel some pity for the lost, but this too, seemed a vain emotion; he cast it out and fell in closer with the wagons.

The hospital was situated at the end of a rail-head, and was nothing more than tarps tied together in a grove of more scraggly sweet-gums. It wasn't actually a place for treatment, but a resting place where the wounded could gain strength before more carts came and carried them further down the valley to Winchester. Woodfolk parked his wagons, and Kinchen and the drivers helped the wounded to their cots. Then the mules were freed from their traces and led to a patch of shade under scrub oaks, where they dined on the thin leaves within their reach. After all were settled, Woodfolk started the business of preparing Kinchen for his journey. They climbed on horses and made for a general store, where they would purchase some supplies.

On the way in to town they again passed the stockyards converted to prisons. Farley and Robert noted their progress, assumed their previous position, clasped to the wire. They eyeballed Kinchen closely, keen, irresistible stares. Woodfolk couldn't help but notice.

"Believe them boys are acquainted with you."

"Dey are," said Kinchen casually. Woodfolk leaned forward, rested an arm on the pummel, and looked over at the captives.

"Wouldn't trade hats with them for nothing."

"Nope," added Kinchen.

"They lookin' a bit repentive now, though. Wouldn't you say?"

Kinchen didn't look over at them. "No suh. Maybe one. The other one..." Kinchen didn't complete the sentence, chose not to elaborate. Woodfolk looked at him queerly.

"Nope, not a kind fate for them boys," said Woodfolk thinking he might gain a corresponding question. Kinchen did not respond though, so the Sergeant made his point anyway.

"Bounty-men'll be buying them up. They'll take 'em down deep for a profit, or hire 'em out to the army."

Kinchen maintained a blank expression, stared forward, an indication he had no desire to talk about them. He was not immune to their suffering, their plight, but he knew that falling in with their despair was like willfully breathing in bad, bilious air. It was all right to feel compassion, but coupled with helplessness, it often led to bitterness, which begat torment. That was the danger. Suffering began in the mind. Its cure was in the heart. It was a terrible struggle, he knew that well, so it was best to turn off the mind and close ranks with the heart.

They passed the slaves without another word.

At Lowery's Store he bought his supplies with the money from Harry's purse, about ninety-five Confederate dollars. Woodfolk recommended he buy foods that didn't need cooking: dried fruit, salt pork, bread, and the like. He knew that only the most desperate men wallowed in the wakes of armies, and that it would be best if Kinchen travel at night and nourish himself without the aid of fires. There was enough money for fodder for the horses as well and, when it was all packed on Hawkeye and Cora, together with Harry's accoutrements, it made for a bulky load. But the trip would take weeks, cover hundreds of miles, and there was no telling how scarce supplies might be on the way.

They led the horses through town on foot and paused at its outskirts, where the Winchester Pike trailed off to the south. The sun was still high and Woodfolk pointed to a lush hillside and its screen of trees, suggesting that Kinchen doze a while before setting off. He said he'd be back to wake him and help set his bearings.

Kinchen did not sleep, but lounged on the slope mulling. Not so much about the long grim ride and the perils he might encounter, but of the journey's end, Thornbury and the Burgwyns. He thought of arriving there unexpectedly, with news that would stab them. A vision of Anna's face haunted him, blistering his mind. An image, he reckoned, that would be his companion for the duration of the trek.

"IT'LL BE THE FIRST FEW DAYS," Woodfolk warned. "They'll carry the greatest risk. These valley pikes are full of trash—outlaws, deserters, bounty men, and black fugitives. They'll want the horses and the provisions. Won't be askin' no questions. Just cut your throat and leave you bleedin' in the road."

Kinchen patiently sat on Hawkeye and listened.

"Then there's the provost," Woodfolk waved a folded piece of paper in his hand, a pass written by Captain Young that was Kinchen's safe passage to Carolina. "They won't give no more respect to this than they do the Bible. You are dollars, boy. That's all they'll see, and so are the ponies and the goods."

Woodfolk squinted at Kinchen carefully, checking if his words were making an impression.

"The main road between here and Winchester will be full of wagons. There's a big store of supplies there and they'll be moving wounded. The officers runnin' the trains might not pay no heed to this pass neither. Just depends on their spirit at the time. So it's best to make like a ghost, travel at night, give a wide birth to all the towns, and make your camps far off the road and away from settled places. If by bad luck you get caught out in the open, don't run! They'll figure you a fugitive. Just show 'em your pass and pray for good fortune. In God's name—don't lose this pass. It's the only difference 'tween you and your friends back there in the pens, and I'm sure your master has more to do than traipsin' all over yonder lookin' for you. Not that he'd ever find you."

Kinchen fidgeted a bit, shifted in the saddle.

"You got all that?" asked Woodfolk.

"Yeah suh."

"Want me to say it again?"

"No suh, Mr. Woodfolk."

"Fine. Now, listen close. I'm gonna tell you the way home." Kinchen leaned forward to show his attentiveness.

"You'll be goin' south first, straight down this valley while keepin' the hills on your flanks. The first thing of any consequence you'll come across is a spur of this here railroad. I'd say, late tomorrow mornin'. There's a little depot town, Stephenson's Depot. Stay clear of it. Look for a good size creek flowing north and cross the tracks there. You had better make your first camp shortly after that."

Kinchen nodded.

"Then you follow that creek south staying close to it. That way you'll miss Winchester, which will be on your right. You know right and left?"

"Yeah suh."

"Good. Pretty soon the creek will get small and turn off to the west and you'll break off from it. Just keep on down the valley until you see a big mountain rise right up from the middle. I forget the name of it. Massa—something. Don't matter. You won't make it out at night, so when you see it in the mornin' make another camp, and mark it when you pick up again. You gonna want to keep to the left of that mountain, passin' down a narrow valley, but just before comin' to it, you'll hit another railroad runnin' by a big stream. Cross over both. They'll be two towns near—Front Royal and Strasburg. Stay out of them. This sinkin' in, boy?"

Kinchen nodded, but Woodfolk sensed he was losing him.

"The ground's not so clear to me after this, but soon the valley will widen out again. You'll pass the big mountain by and you'll be wantin' to move back towards the middle of the valley, stayin' clear of Waynesboro and Staunton. You read any?"

"Some."

"I'm gonna print a word here on your pass. The name of a town, Lexington." Woodfolk handed the pass to him and Kinchen studied the scribbled word.

"You gonna want to follow the roads to this town. Watch for signs."

"I know it," said Kinchen. "Massa Harry had his schoolin' there."

"That right? Good. Don't go into the place. Pass it by. One night's ride south of it and the valley will slope way down. There'll be a rivah at the bottom flowing east. A big rivah. The only big rivah you'll come to. The James. When you see it look off to the east, to your left, and off in the distance you'll see a big gorge through the mountains. The rivah cuts through there. You're gonna want to pass through that gorge, stayin' to the north side of it cause the roads there are less traveled."

"Ride down the valley dat away until I comes to a big rivah," said Kinchen confirming Woodfolk's directions.

"Uh huh, then follow the river east through the gorge. There are quite a few hamlets aside it, take care goin' through 'em, but keep followin' the rivah 'til you see a good size town on the other side. It'll be some twenty miles past the gorge. Called Lynchburg. Say it."

"Lynchburg."

"A bridge goes over the James there. That's how you'll know it, but keep goin' down the rivah stayin" on its north side. Oh, and there'll be a canal runnin' next to it. Once you pass Lynchburg a ways, you gonna want to cross the canal and the rivah. They should be low and an easy wade. You gotta cross 'em though, so if they're high, you'll just have to wait 'til they fall."

Kinchen nodded.

"Cut straight south now, overland if you have to, but you should find a road. Shortly you'll come to more rails trailing east. You're not half way home at this point, but the worse'll be behind you. Just follow those rails. It'll take the better part of a week, but you'll come to Petersburg. Cap'n Young says you might know Petersburg?"

A pause. "Yeah suh. Reg'ment's camped there and passed through a number of times on the cars headin' for Richmond."

"So you can find the rails trailin' straight south from there."

Finger and thumb to his chin. "Yeah suh. Believe I can."

"You sure?"

"Yeah suh. I knows the place."

"Good, cause that's the way to Carolina, boy, the way home. The rails go to Garysburg and I'm told that's your country."

Bright eyes shone beneath his derby. "Dat's home, yeah suh. Easy ride from dare."

"Won't none of it'll be easy, boy," said Woodfolk. "Lots of soldiers 'round Garysburg." He rummaged around his jacket pocket for a pouch of tobacco, pulled out a stringy glob and stuffed it in his mouth. He peered down the pike as his jaw wolfed, his eyes following it until it faded into the growing darkness.

"That's 'bout all I can do for you," his voice muffled and choked by the tobacco. "The rest is up to you and just how slinky and clever you can be."

Kinchen grinned, a stir of confidence in his eyes.

"Any of it puzzlin'?" asked Woodfolk.

"No suh. Gonna camp 'morrow mornin' along dat creek, below the railroad, some ways off from dat depot town."

"Stephenson's Depot?"

"Yeah suh."

A curved grin escaped from below Woodfolk's turgid cheek.

"Gwon, boy," a lazy gesture to the south. "Gwon home."

Kinchen made a solemn sign of gratitude, set off, and Woodfolk watched him for a spell, figuring. He thought the trip would be a trying one for a white man, and for a black—severe and bordering on desperate. He wondered if Captain Young had really deliberated about the danger of it before fixing on letting the boy go. Nothing he could have done about it anyway, Woodfolk resolved. Just did what he was told to do. That's all.

HE RODE THROUGH A FLEETING NIGHT, a brief night of summer. Kinchen kept to a slow pace, had to be alert to figures on the road and the flickering lights or dark forms of homes set near it. He encountered little: startled birds flitting from trees, the huffing and puffing of heedful deer, and at one bend an opossum waddled tipsy-like across his path. He stopped frequently to listen at the fringe of black copse, or when the road ahead climbed a hill that blocked his view. All the delays brought a frame of dim light over the eastern ridges before he was ready for it. A short time later, the rolling earth had caused a powerful sun to leap clear over the rounded peaks. He was in broad daylight and had yet to find any sign of the little depot town.

The morning was still though, and he could hear across great distances. Deadened echoes of man-made sounds: milk pails clanking, the slamming of doors. He guessed the village was a mile or so away. It was time to abandon the road and, as soon as he found a thin spot in the poke and blackberry brambles, he dismounted, led the horses through the briars, then jumped a dry ditch. He made for a swell overrun with cedar, intending it as a look out. A brief climb up the thick growth and he found a clear top, but the view disclosed no settlement, only a sweep of rolling pasture land that fell to a narrow flood plain, then a dense stand of high sycamores. He knew that particular tree found great comfort near water and judged the grove sheltered a creek. Perhaps the wide creek with a northerly flow that Mr. Woodfolk had advised him to find and track.

He did not ride out into the open, but kept to the hilltop, tracing its spine as it slanted off to a thickly wooded ravine, an ancient cut in the ridge carved by a bold current. After a sharp descent over a stony ledge, the ground planed off into lush ferns, dogwoods and other shrub-like trees. The glen was cool and moist. He could hear the bubbling creek, and when he broke through its cover, he saw it, wide, clear, and shallow with a bed of round pebbles. The creek's current was steady and rushing to the north.

Kinchen guided the horses into a pool, allowing them a drink while he studied the ground on the other side; it banked up high and could not be scaled. Noticing sandy flats and gravelly bars in the creek bottom, Kinchen worked the horses upstream, until a twisting bend caused the far bank to fall off and allow them a ford. They climbed the bank easily and found themselves in a brushy forest laced with numerous cow paths. Screened by the thick foliage, the trio made speed upstream to within eye-shot of scattered dwellings and a railroad climbing to a mountain gap. They took care now, dropped back down into the creek, plodded up it, passed under a low trestle, and did not saunter out again for another quarter mile.

By now a hot sun had climbed over the trees and he felt a pit in his stomach, his eyes were drooping, and the horses were sluggish for a meal. It was time to camp, and he looked off to the east for prospects among the hills. He spied a cove, which gullied up to a ridge waving with broom sage and crowned with shade-throwing catalpas. He had never seen trees such as these, and their exotic allurement spurred a curiosity he could not resist. A lazy brook spilled out of the cove, nearly dry, but the swale in the open fields it formed offered some cover, so he followed it until he reached the coolness of the hollow, then wiggled up its course and through a young orchard.

Tiny green apples littered the ground, tempting Hawkeye and Cora. Kinchen thought the unripened fruit victims of the many big storms and high winds of late, and to avoid the binding effect they often had on horses, he dismounted and led his wards. The high grass was so crowded with fallen apples that he nearly lost his footing several times. Then he noticed that some were rather large for the season, so he pocketed three or four thinking they may add tartness to an otherwise drab breakfast of bread and salted pork.

Kinchen angled his face to the sun and toward the ridge and realized the climb would be longer and steeper than he had supposed, but this, he admitted, would only make his camp that much more isolated, while offering a vista of all that surrounded him. They made a zig-zag advance up the rise, trudged to the catalpas, then caught their breath under the shadows of the trees' fanlike limbs. Kinchen hobbled and fed the horses there, and then went about quenching his own hunger. The apples, he soon found, were too hard for knife or tooth, so he laid them on a flat rock, got on his knees, and with a sharp palm-sized stone, pounded them to pulp. He then scooped the mush into a tin cup, added water and drank the sour mixture. It had the effect of wrinkling his face up like old Ruthy's. His lips puckered, his eyes teared, but the stimulation to his parched mouth and throat compelled him to finish the concoction. Mixing the blend had left his hands sticky, but instead of rinsing them off with canteen water, he scraped up what remained of the pulp on the flat rock and strolled over to the horses. The treat was accepted zealously, and after every nook and notch of his hands was thoroughly and completely licked; they were no longer tacky.

He wandered along the ridge top fighting his drowsiness, checking the sights, but the haze obscured all but the closest mountains, so he sat down in the yellow sage and studied the valley floor. Using the little opera glasses, he scanned beyond the sycamores and over the rolling pastures, to a tree line clouded with swirling dust that fanned in either direction. The pike he rode last night, he figured, and now it was clogged with wagons. The scene conjured up an appreciation for Woodfolk's advice, and he felt safe and snug atop his high perch.

Kinchen tossed his head back, nested down into the warmth of the weeds, and watched the delicate seeds float and mix with the sky's pale blue. He began to daydream, random thoughts that tumbled along no particular course. They were not pleasing thoughts however, and he realized that he was snared in ill humor. The effect of fatigue perhaps, or the want of sleep, but it felt more like pining lonesomeness, and he recognized that he was just plain sad. A void deep within, a swath of stirring emptiness, and his mind rested on a vision of long ago. Harry's face as a child, smooth, glowing, and framed by rolling locks. It wore a cheerful expression, pure and guiltless. The memory was old, yet familiar, and had always brought comfort, but now it was startling. The boy had always been a part of him, a fixture of his being, irreplaceable. For a moment, Kinchen feared that he would carry a faded spirit for the rest of his time.

He jerked from a shiver, then shook his head in an attempt to break the spell. He rolled, debated resting right there in the open, but thought it better in the shade, so he rose and shuffled toward the catalpas. On the way, he cut a twig from a sapling cedar, and twirled it between his thumb and finger, letting the sap drain on the padded tips. He curled down on a cool side of a trunk, placing the twig on the ground near his face, and with the gentle scent of cedar filling his nostrils, he settled into sleep.

ON HIS THIRD MORNING OF WAYFARING, the dawn greeted him with a burst of dense wind that kicked up dust in the road and hurled it against his twitching eyelids. His back was humped in the saddle. The horses' haunches were working slowly and stiffly, as if every step took great effort. Their rapid and often careless pace had caught up with them. To his knowledge, he had been seen only once, and that came one twilight when a farmer hailed him from an abode, so far off the road that Kinchen wondered what kind of eagle-eyed mortal dwelled there. Only one other close call came to mind. During the wee hours of the second night, the pulse of galloping horses had rushed upon him. With no place to hide, he had slid off the road just as three riders passed. So close, the glowing whites of their steeds' eyes were plainly visible. Yet his presence there had not even caused a break in stride; the gallopers' mission evidently was so pressing, they thought only of it and paid no heed to other traffic. Otherwise, the nights had been lonely, and as far as he could see, the rolling countryside nearly uninhabited.

They had just completed a blind jaunt down the length of the narrow vale to the left of the great mountain crowding the main valley. So swift had been the pace that the horses gave out before Kinchen realized they were even fagged. A rare oversight for him, and one he ranked as foolish on his part. Two months of campaigning had weakened them more than he had accounted.

He began searching for a place to camp, but the dank forest that enfolded the pike was uninviting. Daybreak had come on gloomy, foggy, and the air had the feel and smell of rain. He wanted cover, but none was being offered, so he pushed on through the murk.

Finally the mist commenced to burn away, some color breaking through wispy clouds. He heard the high screech of a buzzard and peered ahead. The pike climbed to a bald hill, the road sunk into it, and above was a great circle of carrion-eaters. Something dead or dying was up there, man or beast, and this stopped him in his tracks. The reek of death had been an intimate partner up to three days ago, and his breach with it had been most refreshing. He cared not for another whiff, and looked earnestly for some place near to bed down. As he scanned the lay of the land his head commenced to itch, a symptom of his having worn his hat for long stretches without washing, so he jerked the derby off to give his scalp some air.

He remembered passing an overgrown track. It couldn't have been used for years, and it hadn't offered any clues to where it led. Just a rocky path that had immediately lost itself in luxurious growth, nothing more. He turned back for it.

Due to a myriad of tangled branches, he couldn't ride the path, but led the horses with arms flung back, like a carved mermaid clinched to the bow of a tumbling ship. The track climbed steeply then rounded a knoll where Kinchen saw evidence that it once had been a substantial road, and traveled with frequency. From the crest of the rise, he threaded the faint trail down a swooping shoulder, then up to a higher ridge. Nestled there on a tiny basin at the lowest point of the shoulder were the ruins of a chapel, blue in color, having been built entirely of river rock. Only the walls stood now, the roof having burned, but it was a welcome sight to weary travelers who needed but the slightest of comforts.

He let the horses roam in the main sanctuary where he shaped a lean-to from charred timbers. Kinchen took quarters in the vestibule, which still had a semblance of a roof. Woodfolk had dared him not to light fires, but given his isolation and the gathering rain, he hesitated little before sparking a dwarfish blaze that fried some pork and boiled some potatoes. Biscuits and steaming coffee filled in the holes, then he pitched back and relaxed with his pipe. Leaning against the cool stones and mortar, he filed back and pulled out a favorite parlor tune. He whistled and hummed, but chose not to irritate the horses or any passing critters with the words. Finally he banked up the fire, let it fall scarce, and listened to a shower move in through the trees. An irrepressible sound that no power on earth could stop, forceful, commanding, yet soothing and elegant. A chime from nature that nudged his vulnerability, yet gladdened him with its beauty.

The shower matured into a slow drenching rain that would fall all day and into the night and through the next morning. Kinchen chose not to tire the horses by venturing out onto roads of guzzling mud, so the three rested in their safe haven until the trees quit dripping. It took a strong rod of sunlight to get Kinchen stirring again, and he started pacing. There were hours of unwanted daylight left, but he didn't have the patience to wait them out. He packed the horses and set off for the main road.

The forest was like a broiler, sizzling and spitting. He was slick with sweat and panting when he broke out into the light, so he soaked his kerchief in a puddle, rubbed his neck, then tied it tight around his head so it would drip and streak down his face. He eyed the road reproachfully when he mounted, marking the sky for lingering vultures. Not a soaring wing was in sight, a fair sign.

There was but a hint of rot in the air, where the road sunk into the hill, so the kill had probably been small. Perhaps the rain had partially washed the scent away, or maybe the buzzards had been thorough in their pickings. Not seeing the carcass, but measuring its slight odor, he placed it in a maze of coilberries about twenty yards to the left of the road. He had no reason to think the rot was from human remains, until he spied a broken manacle and iron chain glinting serpent-like on the pike. He did not stop to ponder, but walked the horses slowly through the place, declaring whatever happened there none of his affair. For the better part of five miles he couldn't help but mull it over though. Was the departed a prisoner, a convict, or a reclaimed slave? Which one? Or was it the escort? Why would the chain be in the road and not on the body, if it were not the escort? He arrived at nothing except, he would never know for certain who had perished there.

The pike kept to its rolling course, but the land took on a settled appearance, open and cultivated. Modest homes dotted the country at brief intervals. This started Kinchen to fretting, for he was drenched in the broad of day and raw for all to see. He felt trapped, but nothing came of his fears except the maintenance of his slow walk. Eventually, it came to mind that his nakedness might work to his advantage. Travel slow with no cast of fear or threat, for a black with horses treading south should raise no more suspicion than a flock of migrating starlings. A Negro going north was another story, but one on a southerly course was as harmless as a gentle wind.

Not a soul came into view the whole of the afternoon. The valley seemed so lifeless that he wondered if all the men folk were off to the war and their dependents refugeed in the towns or at distant relatives. No cattle grazed the fields, no fowl wandered the lawns. It was a land stripped cleaned and abandoned with little dread of pillagers. He became so confident with the state of things, that when it came time to rest for a spell, he didn't hide, but merely guided the horses to a patch of shade aside a fence-row directly by the pike. The horses cropped at the sleek grasses gathered close to the posts, while Kinchen collected his position. They would pass away from the big mountain soon, and they were supposed to tack a bit to the west, toward the center of the main valley, while avoiding several villages. Woodfolk had not been precise with his directions here, had named no road or creek to follow, no landmarks to set. Had only told him to peek for signs to Lexington. Signs had been sparse up to then, and none had had any cluster of symbols that summed up to anything close to resembling Lexington. With light beginning to wane, he determined to find some high point from where he could gain a course.

A fair-sized stream that Woodfolk had not mentioned had been rambling parallel to the pike. They had forded it at the head of the vale and had been making contact with it from time to time. Kinchen had refilled his canteens with its waters a ways back. Now it cut straight for twin hills, one barren, the other supporting a handsome mansion. Kinchen aimed for the vacant hump, but before reaching it, he passed through a scorched and dilapidated tract, which he reckoned had been witness to combat. Fences were pulled down, and there were blackened patches in the fields where rails had been fired. The ground had been churned up and plowed by solid shot, and dirt mounds were grouped in random batches where, he guessed, graves had been dug and filled with haste. No doubt, a furious struggle. The signs, however, were weathered, and the fracas, in his best judgment, had been decided some months passed.

Closer to the hills, he noticed a tiny crossroads town. The stream forked; one branch veering west and the other falling off to the southeast. The town rested directly in the slot, and he halted to explore his options of skirting the place.

The pike also split at the town, and the western wing, the direction Woodfolk had instructed him to take, looked heavily traveled, while the eastern track possessed a sleepier face. He could reach neither road without penetrating the town, which was something he was not inclined to do. Overland was his only recourse, and a southeasterly heading appeared the safest.

A setting sun aided their stealth, as they vaulted split-rail and low, stone fences. They roved without benefit of trail or path, while keeping out of sight of prying eyes. It was a secure but slow circuit, one that was prone to test one's patience, but eventually they cleared the eastern pike and slid into broken country, before making new contact with the stream. They were veiled in darkness now, and after fording the creek mirroring a starlit sky, they ranged to the west, until they struck a pike bidding a desired direction.

The night had taken on the properties of coal, no moon to speak of, merely a slit in the dark. The stars twinkled dimly. It made for anxious touring, and they prowled at the pace of thick sludge at the bottom of a molasses barrel. The black had nearly absorbed them, when the pike pierced a compact grove of hemlocks and spruces, the darkness so dense as to seem solid and impassable.

Hawkeye carried him, Cora trailing behind, and she suddenly gave in to a spell of the jitters. The gelding shied at something ahead, snorted. Kinchen paused so his eyes would adjust, but no amount of blinking could relieve the absence of pattern. Hawkeye's pawing told him something was lurking, but God Almighty could only tell him what. He cranked his head quickly to both sides, but the forest was like a wall wedging him tightly into the pike. He hesitated turning around, fearing whatever lay out there might pounce. Finally, he detected faint movement, plodding lumps, and he realized that the shadows closing in on him were but ten yards away. He prepared for strife, clutched nervously for his dagger, and pulled Cora's reins taut. He yowled a terrifying shrill as he buried spurs into Hawkeye's ribs, slashed with the blade and vaulted forward. Bare hands slapped at him, one pinching his trousers; another grappled with the reins. He broke free of them, but a sharp tug on Cora's reins caused them to slip from his clasp. She lurched away though, haunches kicking, peeling ahead. More forms and masses jumped at Kinchen. The big gelding butted something head on, slamming it to the road, a hoof breaking it like a hatchet cracking kindling. Kinchen swung the knife and sliced an arm, felt it clip flesh, setting off a squealing yelp. Now Hawkeye had momentum and made speed. There were padding feet behind them, curses. Someone yelled "Nigga," then Kinchen heard nothing but the sharp and rapid ticks of eight hooves rutting the pike.

They sped on blindly, hearts pumping. Kinchen gained his senses, could hear Cora loping ahead, but he had to keep pace with her so as not to lose her. He called, hoping a familiar voice might slow her. Finally, they cleared the pine bogs and Hawkeye's longer legs brought him abreast with the mare. It took another quarter mile before they came to a gasping halt.

Kinchen was stunned, the horses' eyes glaring and shocked. He took hold of Cora's reins again and set off walking. Slow, shuffling steps carried them for many miles, until their breathing and nerves were restored.

They lounged the next day deep in a pocket of a stone-fringed mount, where they were completely cribbed and estranged from the rest of the world. Kinchen spent part of the following evening taunting and ducking bats, as they swooped down on the pebbles he heaved. Luring the bats down from the heights with imitations of swirling bugs spawned feelings of control and superiority, like Zeus throwing thunderbolts. The bats had brought to mind one of his and Harry's favorite recreations as youths at Hillside. Baiting the flying rodents had been a cause for joy, and had guaranteed a certain quota of giggles. They would spend hours of humid twilight flinging at them, until their thin arms hung sore.

The dusky sky shaded to black. The bats were no longer visible, and the hollow began to take on the same eerie traits, as the piney bog that had nearly swallowed them the night before. He vowed right then that his night treks were through.

He delighted in this promise for a moment. For all its tribulations, the trip did offer certain gains. Like the freedom to make his own decisions. It was completely within his power to decide where to camp, when to travel, or what route to take. He had never really experienced quite that much latitude and it made him feel a bit giddy.

He took to the saddle again an hour before sunrise, tracing the path down the hollow, until he gained the pike and turned south. The stream still gurgled nearby and the pike snaked tight to the foot of the Blue Ridge. Fully aware that Woodfolk had advised him to travel through the center of the valley, he clung to this road because it suited him, and because he knew that sooner or later he would happen upon a trail that would carry him further west.

Again, the landscape became more populated, and there was traffic on the road: mule teams pulling carts, lone hikers, and women burdened with baskets filled with goods. Even slaves scampered by. Regular business was being transacted, and when it passed close, Kinchen turned on his charms and good manners. "Mornin' ma'am. 'Day, suh. Just a fine day fo' a ride."

Not a single brow of suspicion was raised at him, and he figured they all could be assigning him as a local boy running an errand. His bedraggled appearance and the sum of the load on his mounts brought him to doubt that though, so he figured them just gentle folk who clung to their own concerns.

The pike bridged the stream, veered away from it, then curled over a series of minor ridges, the last offering a view of high steeples and a good-sized clan of dwellings. Waynesboro. Kinchen debated going into the place, but concluded that his supplies were not depleted to the point of risking it. So he circled down between the ridges and back to the stream, which he tracked to a trestle of the Virginia Central Rail Road. This line offered no advantage to him though, so he kept to the stream until yet another pike aligned with it. The lane was white and dusty and a magnet for flying bugs, and they cantered it as long as they could stand the rising heat. Finally a stream's cool trickles beckoned them. Kinchen relieved the horses of their lading and tack and permitted them to stray free within the confines of sparse shade blanketing the creek bank.

The days were still much longer than the nights, and six hours of wandering time was available to them. Most of the afternoon was spent at a drowsy clip, the heat stifling their energy and resolve, the air so sultry that Kinchen was certain a violent storm would blow up and scatter the air to ground. Sure enough, the sun dipped down below a bank of ominous clouds, and great droplets of hot liquid whipped in on a southwesterly wind. His eyes had been keening for shelter, expecting a squall, and he recalled a single fodder barn a short ways back. They raced for it, as the rain bellowed up in torrents and beat down on them at a slant.

The barn was corrupt and crumbling and stood withering in a ripening hayfield. He noticed the door was in a state of advanced decay when he wrenched it open, and the interior was tainted with a strong balm of mildew. The roof leaked like a sieve and had been in that condition for so long that indentations had formed on the dirt floor where dozens of puddles were in the process of recollecting. The barn was only half full of hay, the field having been cut just once that season, so there was ample space for him and the horses. He tethered them to a stud on the east wall, removed their cargo, then wiped them dry. A fallen rafter held his own wet clothes, and he wrapped himself in an army blanket before settling down for a nap.

The rain, lightning and ripping thunder delayed his snooze, and he was never really able to fall into a deep sleep that night, for his mind was fitful and packed with dreams that kept him tossing. Once he woke quick and cranky from a maddening tickle to his left ear, and a sudden slap flushed something hovering in its vicinity. He heard whatever it was scurry away through dry hay stalks. Cutting his weary eyes, he saw the silhouette of a tiny mouse hunched in a faint moonbeam angling through a notch in the wall. Kinchen was too dazed to laugh, but realizing the mouse's silky whiskers had been the source of the tickle, he couldn't help but grin at the rodent's curiosity and boldness. Apparently, the rodent resented his discovery, for he fired an annoyed squeak just as he popped from view.

Runny, burning eyes summoned him to wake the next morning, the effects of mildew spores. He rubbed them harshly with fisted hands. When he quit and his eyes began to grasp shapes, they focused on a black snake coiled two or three yards from his feet. Its flicking, forked tongue conveyed that it was aware of Kinchen as well. The snake didn't conjure up any fear on his part, for he had had numerous encounters with them, and none had been even close to deadly. But the snake did remind him of what his people back home would say: "A bad omen for the day. Best to stay in bed."

Kinchen didn't hold with their superstitions though. The snake was simply one of God's creatures with its own function and duty. That was his mind. Superstition was a symptom of mistrust in the Lord, and a sign of a frail soul.

Kinchen embraced what had been his father's beliefs. That the world was like the sky, always changing, chaotic. That only the Lord's power and His teachings kept men from flying into the pattern of the stars. Mistress Anna was similar in outlook, had always been a great source of wise sayings, her most famous being: "One touched with the grace of God can withstand and thrive in all manner of famine." Colonel Harry had echoed them both in certain respects. Kinchen remembered a particular dinner fire after the fight at Malvern Hill, the night after they visited the Yankee corpses. Harry had said that good and evil dwelled everywhere and within everyone, but not in equal increments. That the two forces had struggled against each other since creation, and that man, being the only creature obliged with higher intelligence, was burdened by God with the responsibility of directing the fight to the best of his ability, so that nature and mankind could benefit from his efforts. He went on to say that the current war was an extension of that policy, but Kinchen didn't remember much about the specifics. He did recall what Harry had said about the burden of man and the various ways men parried with it. Some refused to carry the burden and had cast it away. Others were afraid of it, shied away. They were tumbling souls, folks like Farley. Still others didn't carry the burden, as much as help those who did. Harry thought they were the majority. Lastly, and he had implied his father and mother as being among their ranks, were the few that carried the strain hard and fast on their shoulders, were weighed down and struggling with the stress of it.

At the time, Kinchen wasn't sure where he fell within Harry's four categories, but it had come to him most assuredly some months later, during his spring furlough to Thornbury. Three plow mules had come down with a common malady: wheezing chests, frothing mouths, and eyes running with creamy mucus. The affliction could spread easily and was often fatal, but with the right care and treatment a full recovery was possible. He and Driver Jim were charged with the curing, which was an arduous process that usually involved staying with the animals night and day for some weeks. The prescription was simply to keep them on their feet, for if they lay down, which was a sick mule's main preoccupation, they would not have the strength to rise again and would suffocate. The Driver also had a treatment that he thought worthy and effective: a mixture of dried oats and hickory ash that he claimed would clear the breathing passages. Kinchen had no faith in it and held firmly to the belief that there was nothing better in the world for infirmities than a kind touch and soft words. A singing chorus accompanied by gentle strokes on a fiddle was good too, but instruments and chanters were hard to scare up, so the mules mostly settled on and benefited by his own solo humming. The two men went about the work of keeping the mules standing in shifts, and the mules were in the midst of turning the corner when Jim was called out on an errand. Some nights later, a mule tossed, and all of Kinchen's straining and pleading couldn't get him up again. By morning, he was dead. After receiving the facts, Master Henry ordered the remaining two mules destroyed. Kinchen protested. But Henry feared a widening of the scourge and cited a message from Harry calling for Kinchen's quick return to the army. The risks were too great, and there simply wasn't time to save them, was the master's view. So ten days of affection went to waste, and not without a weighty dose of bitterness on Kinchen's part.

The memory of the killing haunted him, while he eyed the coiled black snake. It had felt like a deep betrayal, to dispatch those he had vowed to revive. A broken promise to beasts-of-burden whose existence was little more than toil and trouble with little reward. But he had always been faithful to his masters' biddings, and the killing of the mules was no exception. And when he struck the match that would flame the carcasses, he came to realize his place in Colonel Harry's hierarchy. He was among the bulk who served those who carried the burden. Whether by circumstance or talent, that was his lot, his station in God's plan, and there was solace in that. He was in no position to judge. His purpose was simply to do, to endure loyally the disrespectful sneers and petty jealousies from those above and below his situation. To be taken for granted, overlooked. He was part of a process as old as time. Like a stone cutter for a Pharaoh, like a sheep shearer for a Scottish Duke, like the blades in a reaper machine.

He had grown tired of the snake's company, so he simply tapped the earthen floor of the barn with his bare heal. The vibrations had an immediate effect on the snake, which turned and slithered for a heap of rotting hay against the far wall. Kinchen could see that the snake had recently fed, as there was a bulky expanse to its sleek form about eight inches from its head, the distorted outline of a small, bewhiskered rodent.

THE ROAD RAN AMBER THROUGH MISTY HILLS, the landscape round and bulged, like so many rumps of grazing beef crowded together in a great herd.

They had woven through puddles that morning, until the pike split, the more traveled fork cutting east through the Blue Ridge, the seldom used path veering westward into a wavy country. Lexington, and the broad James some fifteen miles below it, was still the goal, and Kinchen harbored a notion that this westerly route might bring him to the meandering river.

It was the warmest morning of the summer, the low, gray sky a barrier to the thick air, plugging it, and he could feel the heat soaking down through him. When shafts of sunlight shifted through the canopy and scorched the pike, it felt like passing through fire. Slumped and brooding, he trudged through the vapors until they dissipated. Finally, the power of white-hot stillness forced him to cover.

He found a shade tree near a shallow gully, a swollen creek rushing through it, so he bathed himself and the horses there. After fashioning a tent resembling something shaped by an Arab in haste, he slept long and hard, dreamlessly.

Steamy haze of late afternoon received him when he woke. He spilled out of his cover, tottered to his feet, stretched and arched until he could stand straight, then splashed his face with waters from the silty brook. Bent and stiff, he made for the horses, and judged them just this side of spent, a troubling prospect. He itched to move though. Kinchen spoke to them with a coaxing voice, and Hawkeye responded, a sturdy horse, willing, while Cora's great soft eyes told him she had lost all but the desire. They had rested most of the day though, so he loaded them up and cast off down the shimmering road.

A quiet darkness spread over them. Great mountains, looming purple, looked misshapen and strange in the waning light. But it was a lovely evening, cooler, and the outlined ridges carried a hint of peace. The three paused in the gathering dusk, while Kinchen mulled whether to camp or break his vow and sally forth into the black. The likelihood of more sweltering days in comparison to the soft, blowing nights the Lord now provided, caused him to spur old Hawkeye and walk purposely into the blessed dark.

There were patchy forests, but mostly they traversed open grazing land. The night wasn't nearly as ominous, for a yellow crescent moon had risen and the roof overhead glowed with stars. His eyes quickly became accustomed to surveying the dark, and he was surprised at the things he picked out. When passing through groves, instead of filling his mind with bleak thoughts of courting danger, he played games. His favorite was the practice of spotting the hunched silhouettes of owls perched low in the branches of tall pines, peering down at the pike as they used its contrasting color to pick out crossing vermin. His questing eyes and ears could pick out a great range of critters, from bleating deer to chattering coons. At a rock fence, vined and scented with honeysuckle, he heard two fox cubs playing. So lively and intent were their snarls and nips that Kinchen walked Hawkeye within feet of them and gazed with amusement at their antics for some minutes, before their fearful scent finally sent them scurrying. Shortly after, Kinchen glanced at Harry's watch and noticed the night had just rolled into a new day. He declared the time his favorite. Not just for its calm, or that it was rare and seldom seen, but because it was at the brink of a fresh offering, a promise of time, of miles soon to be passed, and of one more day closer to home. Getting home—he was single-minded in that purpose.

The dawn broke while he was resting in a wood, listening to speckled birds flitting in the trees. The roamers had just finished their breakfast, the horses filling whatever space left in their bellies by chomping at tender leaves. The rose glow over the ridges and the buzzing mosquitoes hailed a warning, though. In a few short hours, the air would set to simmering again, and all roving would cease. The little scrap of oaks they now occupied was a good place to wait out the heat, but Kinchen was feeling a bit lost. They had been offered just one small token of their whereabouts. The streams they now came across all trickled south. An indication that they eventually fed the James. How close the river was, he did not know, but those first bearable hours of the day just might shed the river's mask.

Soon they were making their way through the soft morning haze, and they had not traveled much more than a mile when a sleepy crossroads settlement came to view. A quick and silent jaunt through the place, and Kinchen found himself angling south on the main valley pike. He kept the horses at a canter, raising dust, the weedheads and wildflowers waving at the pike's fringe. His confidence blossomed. The thoroughfare, the proper course; he began to sense real progress.

A sign came to view, one meant for the benefit of travelers heading north. Kinchen passed it, turned to cipher its face. He saw: "Lex. 12 mi."

A great surprise. He was much further along than he had supposed. Lexington was behind him! The river was close, and the morning still young.

He rode with new vigor and in just a few minutes came to where the valley sloped way down into a bowl. There was fog deep in the bottom, white and sheet-like. He crouched forward, but didn't detect any flashes within the mist, no water casting a reflection. Then he recalled what Woodfolk had said. Search for the gorge. It would be within sight. He looked off to the east, to the Blue Ridge, and there it was, in plain view in the bright morning light, magnificent, a great cleft in the green hills. The river's passage.

A gentle breeze rolled up from the bowl, he felt it, and it carried a moist scent, the smell of water, yet not the clean fragrance of a clear stream flowing over rocks, but of a deep, thick current like a lowland river's, like the Roanoke's. Mixed with the aroma of the horses' sweat and tack, to Kinchen, the breeze carried a scent of Carolina.

Kinchen rubbed the back of his neck, cast his head back, squinted upward. Jittery fingers reached for a vest pocket, extracted the fold of paper containing the lock of hair. It had the same look and feel as when he first cut it from Harry's head.

The moment was very quiet, and feelings of guilt swayed within him. The awful beginnings, the first lapping waves of sadness; he wrestled with the rumblings and held them back. But the vision boiled, a firm image of Anna's grief-stricken face quivered, until it lapsed away into the sight of the hazy gorge.

Hawkeye pawed with his hoof. The gelding was restless, complaining of the heat, so Kinchen walked him back and forth across the rise. Then it came to him. He reigned Hawkeye and paused in the dust. Here, in the middle of summer, Thornbury would be vacant. The Burgwyns would be sheltered from the bad air in Raleigh, in the rented house. They wouldn't hear of Harry's death from him. He wouldn't see Anna for months. Not until Autumn.

He felt a vast release. He perked up, smiled inwardly, felt a small ripple of joy. The long flowing sigh he exhaled left him slack and placid.

Kinchen pivoted the horse, looked off again at the brilliant gorge. He knew when he passed through he would leave the hills behind, the sense of splendid space they gave, and the independence he had shared with them. And even though he had never tired of their ripples and folds and their smoky terraces, he knew his time to breathe was drawing to a close. He would miss the mountains, but wouldn't hold their memory too dearly. To wander among them aimlessly lent nothing to the soul. For what was freedom without a purpose?

ON A BACK ROAD IN MARYLAND, a lone Yankee cavalryman hid in a patch of strategic brush and waited for Rebel stragglers to happen by. When little packs of the gray beggars passed his way, he leveled his revolver and demanded their surrender. So wild was his success that in a matter of an hour he had over fifty prisoners to his credit. Then a boy from the Twenty-sixth North Carolina stumbled within his web. The Yankee repeated his tried and true tactic and called for the tattered soldier to give up, but the Rebel quickly leveled his rifle at the horseman and said:

"Won't neither, damn you! You surrender!"

The Yankee promptly dropped his gun, and was led back to the Confederate lines with a large escort.

In the early morning of July fourteenth, the same morning Kinchen hit the rails below Lynchburg, the last of General Lee's army was crossing the Potomac to Virginia. Stuart's cavalry forded at Williamsport around eight o'clock, leaving just one infantry division to defend a series of works around Falling Waters. The remnants of the Twenty-sixth North Carolina were a part of the Rebel rear guard. Federal cavalry were pressing from front and flanks, attempting to cut the division off from their pontoon bridges.

Barely visible in the thick humidity, a party of forty horsemen appeared several hundred yards from the entrenchments. The Rebels, lounging with rifles stacked, watched the riders curiously, and thought them scouts from their own army. Only after the blue covey broke into a wild screaming charge did the southerners realize they were a squad of drunken Yankees.

The Union troopers were a part of the Sixth Michigan, some of George Custer's bunch, and they easily broke into the Rebel works with sabers slashing. But for all their flailing about, they didn't scratch a single Confederate. The Rebels went after them with fence rails, in a savage skirmish, then they fired into the mass of mounted men.

During the scuffle, a Confederate General with a sling on one arm had his horse rear, and both fell. The General managed to gain his feet, then aimed his pistol at a nearby cavalryman, but it misfired. He calmly checked the piece, moved closer to get a better shot, but the Federal fired first and the ball punctured the General's left side. Private Staton from B Company of the Twenty-sixth assailed the Yankee, knocked him off his mount, then cracked his chest with a whack from a boulder.

Thirty-three of the Union cavalrymen were killed, six captured. They had hurt only the Rebel General, Johnston Pettigrew. His wound was so serious that a surgeon recommended he be left behind to the Federals, but having been captured once before, Pettigrew refused. Four bearers carried him twenty-two miles to Bunker Hill, Virginia.

The last man from Pettigrew's Division to cross the river was Captain Cureton from the Twenty-sixth. He cut the pontoons on the Maryland side, then rode them as they swung over in the current to Virginia. His effort was a bit premature, for there were well over one thousand Rebel stragglers still trying to make their escape from northern soil. Most would be snared.

⁙ 23 ⁘

AT PARADISE'S GATE

Camp, 35th NC Regiment
at Drewry's Bluff
July 20th, 1863

My dear Father,

 I have a good opportunity to write a letter & I take advantage of it to write you. I received a letter from Mother yesterday dated July 17th. I am truly glad dear Mother appears so resigned, & I can only acknowledge, dear Father, how much you feel Harry's loss, for it was easy to perceive how completely you were wrapped up in him. But now, since God has taken him from us, I hope you will not let it break you down, and I thank God you bear it outwardly so well, though Mother says it is easy to see the agony you endure. We all will try to make up for him we have lost, and by unvarying deference to your wishes, will try to imitate him & therefore, dear Father, may the pain of losing forever poor Harry be lessened by the increased affection of your other children.

 Immediately upon receiving Mother's letter of the 14th advising me to write General Pettigrew applying to get on his staff, I wrote him & sent it off, but I soon heard afterward that he had been killed at Williamsport, while defending the rear of Gen'l Lee's army. Though he was not really killed, he was desperately wounded & has since died.

 I wrote day before yesterday to Mother proposing, as I saw no other chance of changing my present position, to get a position as Lt. Colonel or Major in the NC Troops. But saying to Mother, I would not take any more steps until I had heard from you and your opinion of it. If you approve, I wish you would help & try to get me such a position. I would always be near you & would have an opportunity of doing something for myself.

 Bob Peebles has some time since, written to his brother to get him such a position, & General Matt Ransom told him he might get him one, & would try, & that he would as soon have a position of equal rank in those troops as his present one, for he said he thought they would be kept in service as regular troops. If you think it advisable, I will get recommendations.

Our regiment was sent here Friday in anticipation of an attack on the Bluff, but as the Yankees have gone back below City Point. I imagine we will go back to Petersburg, though you had better direct here.

I am truly glad to see how we are getting on at Charleston, & I am in hopes that if we defeat them there, the present unrest in New York will so much increase that we may have peace. But it seems too good to happen.

Mother has not mentioned whether Kinchen has returned & whether Harry's baggage has been sent to Raleigh. I should think Kinchen might have brought the horses through the country. Has he been able to do so & has he arrived?

If you are able to write, I would like very much to hear from you Father, and I should think it would do you good to write a little.

Give my best love to all & tell Mother I am truly thankful her health is so good.

>Your Most Affectionate Son,
>W. H. S. Burgwyn

THE RAIL LINE SOUTH OF PETERSBURG passed over a flat country, tedious and dull, a straight iron ribbon besieged by stark yellow pines. There were few depots, a virtual wasteland. He couldn't pick out any landmarks, even vaguely familiar, until he reached Belfield. At that moment he knew he would make it. Garysburg was but fifteen miles further down the line, and he thought he might reach the town that very evening.

The afternoon wore on them, stifling heat. The horses were dragging, he had pushed them too hard. There was plenty of light left in the day, but it wasn't prudent to drive them further. Kinchen saw a tiny dent in the earth that trailed into a thick stand of young pines, guessed it the beginnings of a creek. He steered Hawkeye away from the rails and, with Cora bringing up the rear, drifted down the draw and followed the dry bed. After a few hundred yards without so much as a trickle, the ditch ran into a wider bed, and he followed it to a shallow pool trapped between a pile of gravel, where the stream had cut into the bank. The horses went right to the liquid, sucked it down to a puddle.

He walked the mounts further, found another pool, bigger and deeper, but didn't let them drink. Instead, he stopped by a fallen pine and slowly slipped off the big gelding. He felt a sharp pain shoot up his legs when his feet hit the ground. His legs were actually trembling, so he rubbed them, and walked stiffly in a circle. After wrapping the reins around the fallen tree, he squatted and unbuckled Cora's saddle straps. He could hardly get upright again, and had to push off with his hands.

Fishing out a soiled handkerchief, he wiped the perspiration from his face. Finally he pulled the saddles and bags off the animals and draped them over the tree, then drank warm water from his canteen. After the horses cooled off, he watered them again, cleaned them up, and rubbed them down. He fed them from a dwindling grain sack bought in Petersburg. Lastly, he started a fire and cooked his own meal.

That windless night he listened to a symphony, the cicadas, the crickets, the frogs. He heard the sad whistle of a train passing in the dark, rested silently, and fell asleep to visions of war and home.

The morning was still and noiseless, the air so thick and moist it seemed to drip from the pines. He woke from the sound of snorting horses, jerked, peered around the piney thicket, realized where he was, and immediately thought of Thornbury. He'd get there today, couldn't be more than ten miles away. The image of the wide frame house got him to his feet, but his stiff lower back and sore legs sent him off at a limp. He hobbled among the pines trying to get the blood to flow, the inside of his thighs so tight that rubbing them brought only a tingling numbness. He had ridden nearly three hundred miles and could feel every one of them. He knew the horses had to be worse.

He had a little coffee and some bacon. The horses ate the last of the grain, and he watered them again. He packed, saddled up, and was off before the sun was high; he linked with the steaming iron rails again and followed them south. The horses had no fire though, couldn't be pushed. They didn't know home was near. He chattered to them constantly, and coaxed them up to a trot every once in a while. Cora had a little hitch in her stride, so Kinchen dismounted and checked her legs. They were just stiff, but he decided to ride the stronger Hawkeye instead for the last stretch. The big chestnut responded to his gentle, loving voice, and he broke into a nice gait, while forcing Cora to keep up. Several trains passed them puffing north. They had a full head of steam, so Kinchen knew there was still a ways to go.

The sun was directly overhead when he heard a train's whistle off to the left, toward the east. The train was on the line that trailed off from Garysburg to Seaboard and Norfolk beyond. That meant the depot was very close, and not long after hearing the whistle, Kinchen was able to make out the water tower over the tops of the trees ahead. He grinned, told Hawkeye they were almost home, and gave him an encouraging nudge. They'd be at Thornbury in a matter of hours.

Garysburg was an armed camp, and even though war had changed it drastically, the town still bore a welcome familiarity. He'd been sent to the depot on numerous missions through the course of his life, whether riding on errands with York as a boy, or as an escort on the first leg of the northern escapes the Burgwyns had taken every summer. He had picked up Minnie, Harry, Will, and Pollok countless times, when they had returned from months away at distant schools. Someone could blindfold him now, spin him around, and Kinchen could still find his way home.

Two Rebel pickets noticed his approach, eyed him suspiciously. As Kinchen drew near, one grabbed Hawkeye's reins and the other thrust his hand at the slave's chest, demanding a pass. Kinchen reached into his vest pocket and produced Captain Young's note. The soldier didn't read well, perused it for what seemed like minutes, then circled the horses, studying them.

"Says here your name is Kinchen," he finally said.

"Yeah suh."

"Says you've come from Pennsylvania?"

"Yeah suh."

"These are your dead master's horses and effects?" Kinchen nodded.

The Private looked at his comrade. "Bring him," and they led him with Hawkeye and Cora to the sergeant of the guard. The Sergeant meditated over the pass then led them to the center of the little town, until they stopped in front of a two-story frame house. The Sergeant went in, leaving Kinchen and the two privates to broil in the mid-day sun. A quarter-hour later an officer came out, a captain. He eyed Kinchen from the porch, then walked down the flight of stairs and strutted around the horses.

"You're Kinchen?"

"Yeah suh."

"On the way to Thornbury, are you?"

"Yeah suh." The Captain paused in front of Hawkeye and rubbed his nose, and the gelding shook his head to avoid the affection.

"You were at Gettysburg?"

"Yeah suh, sure was," Kinchen said with pride. The Captain looked straight into the liquid black eyes, hesitant to ask about the battle. He didn't want to show too much respect for the Negro. Kinchen sensed it and very simply, described the battle for him anyway.

"The debil's harvest," he said ominously. Kinchen's expression told the Captain he spoke the truth, his black diamonds staring into the officer's eyes, until they finally blinked and dropped.

The Captain stepped back, glanced at Kinchen from head to toe. "So you've brought Colonel Burgwyn's horses all the way from Gettysburg?"

Kinchen shifted restlessly in the saddle. "Yeah suh."

"By yourself?"

Kinchen nodded calmly.

"Well, I suspect your master will be very pleased to see you."

The slave blinked, felt a little flushed by the officers show of favor.

"I just spoke with Mr. Burgwyn this week. He and your mistress came up in the cars from Raleigh on Thursday. I spoke to him briefly, takes the Colonel's death poorly, I believe."

"Massa Henry, Missas Anna?" Kinchen asked with a squeak of surprise in his voice.

"Yes, they passed through here on the way to Thornbury. They're there now. Wanted to be out of town and alone, I believe."

Kinchen sank back in his saddle, looked in the direction of the plantation and pictured them there. He was stunned. Since the war, Henry rarely went to Thornbury during the summer months, and Anna almost never. He'd been certain he wouldn't see them until the fall. Shortly, he'd be face to face with them, wasn't prepared, wished it wasn't so.

The Captain handed back the pass. "Suspect you should be on your way, boy. You can water your horses at the stream just out of town."

Kinchen was well aware of the creek, he stared with glazed eyes at the Captain's hand, took the note and pocketed it. The Captain turned back toward the frame house, the Private released Hawkeye's reins, and the slave spurred the gelding lightly. Moments later they were drinking at the creek, and Kinchen took an inventory of Harry's effects.

HE KNEW EVERY BEND IN THE ROAD, every dip and hill, every tree and stone, he could tell you the number of windows on the front of every farmhouse he passed. The sights bathed his eyes, washed away the pain in his limbs. He sat tall in the saddle, his back straight as a ramrod, would have been smiling if the grief of Harry's death hadn't weighed on him. The horses seemed to know where they were, too. They trotted at a confident pace, a second wind and renewed strength in their rippling long legs. Kinchen kept up a nervous chatter, stayed alert, as visions of the unseen road ahead darted through his mind.

"Listen heah, Hawkeye. We's goin' round dis bend up heah, den straight down da hill ta da Occoneechee bridge, over da creek, den up the windy hill. Yuh 'member da windy hill, don't yuh? Den at da top, we's gonna turn a little ta da left, downhill a short spell, den a wide right turn, and we'll be at da gate. 'Magine dat, da gate. You knows it's just a straight flat ride ta da house from dare."

It had always been known as the Hoburn Gate, had been called that long before Henry Burgwyn ever arrived, and perhaps even before his Uncle George Pollok had acquired the land. Since all the locals had called it that for over a century, the name had stuck. From force of habit, most of the locals still called Henry's plantation its original name: "Bull Hill." Only family, friends, and new arrivals called it Thornbury.

Kinchen came to the end of the wide bend and pulled Hawkeye to a halt. Leaning against the pummel, he focused on the huge square columns that rose up from both sides of the plantation lane. The columns were white, and board fencing of the same color curved down to meet smaller posts just off the main road, where the fence then turned and ran parallel with the road for fifty yards in both directions. The gate and fence weren't functional. They were purely decorative.

The gate had been in disrepair when the Burgwyns had arrived and had remained that way for years, until Henry found the excess capital to recreate a threshold worthy of the glorious estate he had built. It had always been Kinchen's task to keep the entrance in order and well painted, and the white sign with black lettering displayed the first word he had ever traced or written. He had never learned the significance of the name Thornbury, never knew that it was the name of the village near John Fanning's birthplace in England. Thornbury, to him, had always conjured up an image of a holly tree with bright red berries and prickly leaves. The tree had been the favorite of one of the main women in his life, Anna. The Mistress had once said during a Christmas season that the holly was a good representation of the natural beauty and danger of God's world. Marvelous with its shiny leaves and tempting berries, but any effort at harvesting the juicy red spheres would invite a painful prick. Venturing to eat them would leave a sour taste on the tongue, and some said they were poisonous.

Straight off, he could see the gate had suffered from his absence. It needed a fresh coat of white wash, some of the boards were tacky and rotting. Thornbury was barely legible on the sign. Getting it back in order would be one of his first chores, he thought.

Mostly, the gate brought on a flood of memories. Beyond those massive posts was the home of his large family, white and black. It was a warm, safe place, a haven from the horrors he'd seen far away. It was the setting of all his pleasant dreams, the scene of all his joys, the stage where his life had unfolded. Every sight was familiar and intimate, every face close and personal. It was regular, routine, common, relaxed. He was accepted there, and all were aware of him. Where was there a better place in the world, a spot he held more dearly?

Hawkeye began to pound at the hard-packed road. He knew exactly where he was, wanted his paddock and the clover field. Kinchen patted the glistening, dripping neck, lightly squeezed the belly with his legs, and they trotted up between the pillars and into the enchantment beyond.

The sun was bright and cheerful. He hardly noticed the heat, except for the shimmering waves that danced above the immense fields of cotton spread before him. The bolls, bursting, looked like a great multitude of tiny white flames licking at the blue skies. The southern planters, in patriotic defiance of the Yankee blockade, continued to grow their cotton. Henry had gone with his peers, and had shifted from wheat back to the white gold, even though the nutritious grains would have served the Confederate Cause far better. Profit was also a motive for the change, the blockade had brought on a shortage overseas, and prices had soared. Most planters would never see the return though; the bales would sit in barns, warehouses and wharves, eventually being captured and burned.

There was a long, slight rise to the plantation lane until it reached a majestic maple. Then it sloped backed down and leveled off. He paused under the shade of the tree and from that vantage point could see the wide, white manor in the distance with its high observatory. Between, he saw wagons and carts and a long line of pickers in the field, the colorful bandannas wrapped around the women's heads, the green cotton plants behind them, and the white laced unpicked ones out ahead. On the road, he could make out the foreman, the unmistakable silhouette of old Driver Jim. Images of past experiences with the Driver shot through his mind. He was the glue of the place, loyal, hard working, taciturn, more motivated than all the other hands. He took reward from a job well done, wasn't favored much among the people, and hardly showed much respect for other Negroes. But Kinchen liked him. Jim was a lover of horses like himself, and as a boy he had spent time with him, had seen his softer side.

Kinchen let the images go and soaked up the familiar sights. Listened to that haunting click of insects within the still crops. They seemed to be applauding his return, and to him the sound was as comforting as a music box to a baby.

Big Hoseanna was the first to see the lone rider under the maple. It figured, she being the top picker, the top dog in the pecking order. Her scarred and ravaged fingers and hands were evidence of that, but she knew the tricks now, could pick all day without receiving so much as a nick. She moved easily through the field, like the veteran she was, and didn't have to watch what she was doing. It was natural that she should be the first to see him. She didn't recognize him though, the rider was blanketed in shadows. Distance and glare obstructed her view. Driver Jim noticed Hoseanna putting her hand over her eyes, then turned and looked up the road. He had a better angle, better eyes, and the big chestnut was one of his own children; he had raised and broken Hawkeye himself. Kinchen's derby was also a giveaway. Jim didn't react to the new arrival though, only stared.

When the rider broke into a trot and into the sun, and when she saw the second horse trailing behind, Big Hoseanna realized who it was.

"Lawdy, lawdy, Kinchen." Lucy heard her, looked up.

"My, oh my, it's Kinchen. Look yond'a, it's Kinchen," and all the pickers looked up at the rider.

"Kinchen..."

"He's back..."

"Look dare, Kinchen..."

"Kinchen's home!"

Big Hoseanna reached down and checked the canvas sack hanging from her hips, thought it full enough and made for the lane and the carts. The other women followed, all looking at the rider, all talking among themselves. Kinchen pulled up next to Jim, who didn't say a word, but reached right up and shook his hand, which was quite a gesture from him. Then the Driver immediately went about checking the horses. Kinchen watched the women filing out of the field towards him, beheld the sweating, shining, black faces, and the spontaneous smiles. He took off his derby, bowed in the saddle.

"Aft'anoon, ladies." Big Hoseanna grinned and frowned at the same time.

"Get on off a' dat hoase boy, come down heah," Hoseanna admonished. Kinchen jumped down and his little frame was immediately swallowed up in a bear-like embrace.

"Oh, we worried, worried sick," she said, then looked over her shoulder.

"Weren't we?" There came an immediate and loud response, as the girls and women gathered around.

"Thought you'd nev'a come home." Kinchen smiled politely, embarrassed with the warm welcome.

"Whar yuh been, up in B'aginia fightin' Yankees?"

Kinchen nodded. "B'aginia, and up noth," he answered.

"Noth!" was Hoseanna's surprised response. The word shot through the women like blowing fire.

"Yuh been up in da free land?"

"Yes'sum."

Hoseanna yelled back to the troop of women. "He's been ta da free land!"

"Why yuh come back?" Lucy piped up. Hoseanna gave her an elbow, a nasty glare.

"I axes da questions heah." Then she turned to Kinchen.

"Why on's God's earth did yuh come back?"

Kinchen glanced over his shoulder. "Had to bring back da horses and Colonel Harry's dings," he said sadly.

A hush came over the women. They looked down, whispered a little among themselves.

"We heard 'bout lil' Harry. Massa Henry and Missas Anna are heah," said Hoseanna. "Dey called us all up to da house and told us 'bout him bein' kilt in a great battle. Were yuh dare, Kinchen?"

"Yes'sum."

"Did yuh see 'im kilt?"

"No ma'am, but he died brave, as brave as could be." Hoseanna nodded in approval, as did all the women.

"Whar's he lay?" Hoseanna asked.

"A pretty place," he said. "Und'a a big walnut in a pretty field, all's by himself. He lies in da free land, in Penn—Pennsylvania."

All went silent, the women tried to picture a lonely walnut in Pennsylvania, but it was a world they didn't know, so the images were hazy and uncertain. Lucy tapped Hoseanna on the arm, whispered in her ear. Hoseanna nodded, passed the question on.

"Lucy wants yuh to tell us 'bout da Noth. Wha' it like? Did yuh see any folks likes us?"

Kinchen was about to rattle off all he had seen, all the wonderful and strange sights, but he stopped short. Really, he had witnessed the worst scenes of his life, more suffering, more death, more destruction than anyone would dream of in a lifetime. He had lost a friend, a brother, and had sobbed like never before. Whenever anyone talked of the North, these would be his first images. His mind would have to cross a terrible bridge first, before the more pleasing memories could flow into view. Whenever there was any little reminder of Harry, of which there would be many, he would instantly see the beautiful, peaceful face, his death face, and he would recall that he had felt and seen his passing long before it actually came.

But why burden them with that? Why ruin the fancies in their heads? He didn't say a word about the fighting, but spoke in a low, solemn voice. He didn't look into their eyes.

"Didn't see no folks like us, 'cept fo' other servants like me. But I seen da prettiest c'untry in da wurl, I dinks. Big mountains and hills, green valleys, wide, shallow rivahs, nice lil' towns, big sturdy barns, fields fulla corn an' wheat. Just ever'ding a body would want fo', just da richest an' prettiest c'untry in da wurl."

The women cooed and ahhed and chattered among themselves and were universally pleased with what Kinchen had described. It had supported everything they had ever heard. But this all came to an abrupt halt when Driver Jim stepped forward with hands on hips and a fierce glare. The women immediately moved towards the wagons and carts to empty their sacks, but Hoseanna and Lucy, who were closest to Kinchen and could see the pain on his face as he made his description, were stuck in place with gaping mouths. They sensed an absence of sincerity in his voice, knew something was not quite right.

Jim cleared his throat, caught their attention, pointed to the wagons, and they both moved off slowly, while stealing little glances back at Kinchen. He then put his hand on Kinchen's shoulder and commented on how well the horses looked, considering the distance they had traveled. Kinchen nodded in acknowledgement, said he was sorry for holding up the picking, then slowly remounted Hawkeye. He guided the horses around the carts, waved and said his good-byes, then sluggishly moved off toward the big house. Big Hoseanna and Lucy paused at the wagons, watched him draw away.

"Da Noth sounds like heaven," Lucy said. "I's nev'a would'a come back. You?" Hoseanna shook her head, agreed.

"Why he so sad?" Lucy asked.

"He was close to lil' Harry."

"No, why he so sad when he talked 'bout da Noth?"

"Don't rightly know."

Lucy was full of questions. "Why he come back?"

"Silly woman, don't yuh know," Hoseanna said wryly, as she gazed at the rider drifting away. "He home now."

GRIEF WAS NOTHING NEW TO HENRY, and he coped with Harry's death the same way he had with the many other deaths in his family— by pitching into his work. While Kinchen paused and reminisced at the Hoburn Gate, the master was down in the English basement, in his office, pouring over his ledgers. The books weren't consoling. Harry's death, the defeat at Gettysburg, and the fall of Vicksburg had all gone a long way in convincing him the war was lost. Other than his land and slaves, all his assets were in Confederate bonds. If the Yankees prevailed, they would be worthless, as would the slaves. His real estate was mortgaged and, without labor to plant and harvest the crops, there would be little income to pay the debt. Defeat would bring ruin, and he knew it. He was hopelessly entangled in the Confederacy's fate; could see disaster's approach and could do nothing to prevent it.

The war had already hit him hard, had eaten deeply into his plantation's profits. Now he had lost his oldest son, an incredibly promising boy. Young Sumner was still in the ranks, and fifteen-year-old Pollok was biting at the bit to join him. The Lord simply had to preserve them.

The stress of his helplessness was a struggle. He had frequent headaches, strange pains in his neck and shoulders, dizziness after he climbed stairs or rode on horseback for long distances. His health was failing, and its decay only added to the war's curse.

ANNA WORE THE LONG BLACK DRESS of mourning, now a frequent attire for women of the South. She sat at her sewing table in the drawing room off her bedroom and suffered from both the heat the dress absorbed and the loss it signified. Harry's demise had sent her into a deep depression. While in Raleigh, where she and Henry received Captain Young's first letter, she outwardly showed strength and resignation. For a week she endured the respectful callers she was obliged to receive. Solitude was what she really craved, and she would retreat to her lonely room at every opportunity. While there she sank into despair. Finally, she could no longer bear the callers, and begged Henry to take her to the isolation of Thornbury.

She retreated to her rooms and refused to come out. The first day was spent in silent grief. She gathered up every letter that Harry had written her, even the ones that dated back to his first years away at school. She poured over them and she let the tears flow, hoped she would cry until the ducts were empty. The ploy didn't work, and with red eyes and aching cheeks she retired to her bed. Perhaps she could sleep the gloom away. But Anna had too much energy for this, so she decided to employ Henry's tactics. Entrenched at her work-table, she started to sew, to repair the people's clothing, and to make new garments after the old were restored.

While Kinchen was making his way down the plantation lane, Anna's sewing came to a halt. Her stiff and swollen fingers could take no more. She leaned back in the chair, closed her eyes, and tried to empty her mind. The vision of a bullet wound to her darling Harry's side would not disappear, and when she opened her eyes to escape it, they focused on a spider's web and the dark prince within. She stared at the silvery strands and the snared victims, and felt a compulsion to attack. She called out for Polly, got up, rushed to the hallway and called again. She hurried to the head of the stairs and hailed the chambermaid once more, but there were no replies. Since the house had been unoccupied and closed up all summer, and since Anna had not been her usual self, there were many little imperfections about. Numerous webs littered the long hallway and high-ceilinged foyer. She saw them all, and grimaced, overwhelmed. These had been frequent feelings throughout her life, and now she lacked the strength to face them. She was wounded by the death of her oldest son sacrificed for a cause she had never believed in. She scowled at the webs, let go of her burden, and surrendered to the insane, unfair, yet natural order of things. She leaned against the stair-rail, then slid down and sat on the top step. After pulling her knees to her chest, she folded her arms tightly around them, and rested her chin in the cleft between. She would put total trust in God now. It was His fight, His world.

YOUNG SHAD WAS THE ONLY HOUSE SERVANT to see the strange congregation up on the plantation lane. He, who had once filled in for Kinchen as Harry's body servant and was now the temporary coachman and stable hand, was hauling manure to the garden when he saw the rider and two horses break lose from the group, and walk slowly toward the house. He saw the derby, knew who the rider was, clapped his hands and ran for the kitchen. Old Ruthy was napping within. Shad startled the old cook out of her slumber, made the excited announcement, and was gone before it was fully absorbed. With difficulty, Ruthy got to her feet and shuffled for the house. Shad ran and found Polly hanging clothes to dry, told her to find the Mistress—Kinchen was back! Then he ran to the basement door under the rear piazza and knocked vigorously.

Henry was writing at his desk, didn't like the interruption. He got up slowly, stretched, took deliberate steps towards the door, and found Shad's excited black face on the other side.

Shad saw his cross expression. " 'Cuse me Massa, 'cuse, thought I'd betta tell yuh, though. Kinchen's comin' down da lane!"

"Kinchen?"

"Yeah suh!"

Henry closed the door, went to lock up his ledgers, then made for the stairs. Shad ran for the lane to meet the returning hero, while pretty Polly dropped what she was doing, sprinted for the rear piazza and entrance, then rushed to the front door. She flung it open, and saw the dark rider a hundred yards down the road. She then closed the door, turned to go up the stairway, and was surprised to see her mistress huddled at the top. She climbed the stairs with slow concern.

"Missas Anna, you awlright?" Anna looked at her sheepishly. Polly moved up and sat beside her.

"You awlright, ma'am?"

Anna lifted her chin from her knees, blinked resignedly.

"Yes Polly, I'm fine."

The servant sighed a relieved breath.

"I have some fine good news," she said. "Kinchen's right out front."

"Kinchen, really?" Anna asked.

"Yeah ma'am, he's right out front."

Anna started to get up and Polly helped her, and they slowly made their way down, just as Henry entered the foyer from below and made for the front door.

KINCHEN EYED THE BIG HOUSE SHYLY as he drew nearer. He dreaded the coming encounter. He didn't want to see their grief, was afraid it would set him to sobbing again. He also felt a strange responsibility for Harry's death, knew it wasn't his fault in the least, but still the feelings were there within him. They came, no doubt, from that old promise to Anna to keep her son safe, a promise he could hardly have been expected to keep. Still, to him, a promise was a promise.

A strong sense of duty pushed him on. He had to complete this task, nothing else seemed more important. He needed to show them that he also mourned, that he, too, had suffered a loss.

Shad came bounding up, clapping, grabbed Hawkeye's reins.

"If yuh ain't a sight," Shad said with an excited smile.

Kinchen tipped his hat.

"Get on off dare, I'll take 'em in."

Kinchen dropped the stirrup from his boot, and swung his right leg around. He looked at Shad gratefully as he found his legs.

"How's all?" he asked.

"Mighty sad, been mighty sad 'round heah, but dey'll be glad to see yuh."

"Me?"

"Oh yeah, dey been worried. Said it was an awful brave ding yuh were doin'. How long yuh been ridin' anyways?"

"Don't know. Wha' day is it?"

Shad shrugged.

"Well, I set off on da holiday, Independence Day. Three weeks maybe.

Betta dan a fortnight, I suppose."

"Uhh," Shad grunted. He noticed Kinchen seemed very tired, wasn't his usual cheery self, and decided not to ask about the Colonel.

The little greeting party filed out on the front piazza, Anna, Henry, Polly, and old Ruthy. Kinchen saw them, but looked quickly away. Shad saw the apprehension on his face.

"Gwon Kinchen, dey wanna see yuh," he said encouragingly.

Kinchen swallowed, his mouth and throat were scratchy dry, and his hands trembled a bit.

"You gonna take da hoases up?" he asked.

"Said I would."

"Dey need water and feed," Kinchen said, as he reached into one of Hawkeye's saddlebags. "Turn 'em in da orchard pasture. And da bags, dey have some a' Colonel Harry's dings in 'em. Would yuh bring 'em in when yuh's done?"

"Sure will."

Kinchen found what he was reaching for, pulled it out of the saddlebag, and stuck it in his vest pocket.

"Dank yuh, Shad."

"Gwon now."

Kinchen took a deep breath, looked at his master and mistress waiting for him, and started up the oyster-shell walk. Already he felt a swelling in his cheeks, that tiny, dull pain right before tears. He squinted, tried to smile. He noticed they all seemed pleased, but detected quite a bit of effort on their part. He kept his own face expressionless; he was trying not to appear sad, but couldn't possibly show any cheerfulness.

As he drew closer to the steps, he reached for the silk cord around his neck and pulled Harry's gold watch from under his vest. It flashed in the bright sunlight. He paused, removed his derby, pulled the cord from around his neck, and held the watch flat in the pink of his palm. Kinchen then climbed deliberately, made straight for Henry, while avoiding to look at his face, then wordlessly placed the piece in his master's outstretched hand. Henry looked down at the watch, and Kinchen could see his jaw tighten. His color wasn't good, he seemed exhausted and worn, and the air went right out of Henry when he closed his fingers firmly around the gold. Anna was moved, reached out and touched Kinchen's shoulder.

"We're so proud of you, Kinchen, so glad you were with him," she said in a weak voice.

Kinchen's mouth trembled as if to cry, but he managed to reach into his vest pocket and remove the fold of paper. He offered it to his mistress. Anna opened the paper slowly, until the auburn locks were revealed. Instantly, the tears rolled down both cheeks, she wavered, leaned toward Kinchen, embraced him, and began to sob on his shoulder. The slave held her loosely, awkwardly, and still managed to hold back his own tears. He looked at both Polly and Ruthy in the doorway, saw that both held their color-coded handkerchiefs to streaming faces. A glance at Henry revealed a solitary tear just under his left eye. His own grief burned, felt like a match ready to burst.

Kinchen had carried his gift, his honor, like a torch. He had shouldered it bravely and unselfishly for many years. It was there plainly for all to see, but few had ever noticed. Strangely, even he had been unaware of it. Now, as they all shared their grief, and all openly wept, he felt a surge of self-awareness. A curious feeling of power mixed with the sadness. Suddenly, he realized his value. It wouldn't change him, but from that moment on he would know, and the gift, along with the knowledge, would insure a long, rich life. That was his reward.

AFTERWORD

IN COMPOSING THIS STORY, I discovered that a wealth of letters, journals, papers, and first-hand accounts were available to me. Many of the events, even some of the minor ones, really happened. Portions of the dialogue are actually quotes from these various sources. Their contributions were immeasurable, and they enabled me to create a much richer story than any I might have dreamed. Truth will always be more interesting than fiction.

Anna Burgwyn, in the years immediately following her marriage to Henry, wrote volumes of letters to her friends and family in Boston. They helped form the core of the events starting with her descent to the south until she settled at "Hillside." The letters Anna sent her mother, which were by far the bulk of the collection, were in journal form. They were quite candid and gave me tremendous insight into her personality. I sadly admit that I couldn't possibly use all of their interesting tidbits, but one good example was Anna's unsuccessful attempt to help nature reclaim the little red bird in New Bern.

Her admiration of Julia Burgwyn and her frustration with the town's social life were obvious. The natives' manners, their religion, and their political beliefs both disturbed and stimulated her. The prevailing theme of Anna's letters though was her desire to return to and live in Boston. Of particular interest were her observations and views of slavery. Unfortunately, we would have learned more of her transformation from a Unitarian abolitionist to an Episcopal slave mistress, if her mother had not died in 1843. The collection of her letters addressed to Jamaica Plains come to an abrupt halt in that year.

Anna also kept journals from time to time. They disclosed such things as Minnie's near death from fever at White Sulphur Springs, and Harry's presence at John Brown's hanging. After her son's death and as her years advanced, Anna's journals became more detailed. Some of the thicker volumes were lost however, and with them the answers to riddles left unsolved.

The poem "Harry," which I attributed to Anna, was found in her son's, John Alveston's, childhood scrapbook. Allie was just twelve years old at the time, so it's a safe assumption that Anna at least had a hand in its writing.

Anna's wartime letters to her sons, of which there must have been dozens, will be lost forever. For fear that their mother's sentiments might fall into a stranger's hands, Harry, Sumner, and Pollok destroyed the letters soon after reading them, a common practice in those days.

Henry Burgwyn's letters, in sheer numbers, did not compare to his wife's, but I found his plantation journals to be just as resourceful. They roughly covered the period of 1840 to 1848, the years he developed Hillside. They were hardly as personal as Anna's letters, but they did offer many little morsels to chew on. He struggled with his slaves, both in managing them and in keeping them alive and content. It was a very active time for Henry, and contrary to many people's perceptions of southerners, he had little time to lounge on verandas sipping mint juleps.

The journals formed the basis for five chapters in *Kinchen*, and they gave me the raw materials for painting a very different picture of the times Henry lived. The Burgwyns may have been an exception to the rule, but it was obvious that their labor force entrapped them as tightly as the slaves were themselves. Anna was quite right with her analysis of the institution, yet she and Henry fell right into the muck. Nothing conveyed that as clearly as the failed experiment with Irish labor.

Like Anna's letters, there was more material in Henry's journals than I could use. I gave the bitter legal battles with Thomas Devereux only a light brushing. The same goes for the day-to-day tedium of plantation life, and I feared Henry's many heartaches, as well as his various advancements in agriculture might bore the reader. I spent more time with his relationships with slaves, but even here, I merely scratched the surface. The journals gave me the impression that they consumed much of his time and energy, and that he felt tremendous responsibility for their welfare. Henry lost two of his children within the period of the journals, and it was interesting to note that he once entered slave deaths on the plantation within the same paragraph he marked his child's passing. There seemed to be some justification in Henry dubbing his slaves as his "black family."

Of Henry's letters, none were more personal or touching than the host he sent Anna while he was abroad in 1851. They conveyed a deep love for her and an unmistakable loneliness for his children. It was my observation that their youngest child was born nearly nine months to the day Henry left for Europe.

When sectional strife began to bubble over in America, Henry took up his pen and expressed his concern. He wrote friends, newspapers, journals, and government officials. Several of these documents contributed to a fictional scene within the chapter, "A Peculiar Situation." Henry's speech in the courthouse in Jackson depicted the dilemma facing North Carolinians after South Carolina's split with the Union. Fear, of course, was the motivation for secession, the perceived threat to the southern lifestyle by northern radicals. Seeing no compromise solution that would hold for the long run, and being tied to an economic system based on slave labor, secession was Henry's painful, yet logical choice. A majority of southerners agreed.

By far, the largest collection of letters and journals came from Harry Burgwyn. The first letter, written to his mother at West Point when Harry was just fifteen, shows his remarkable maturity. His six letters that made up the chapter, "Letters Home," were actually a conglomeration of over two dozen letters I edited together. Few of my own words, however, can be found in the new editions. I took great pains to keep Harry's style intact.

Fragments of Harry's first war journal contributed to Chapter 14, "The Boy Colonel." It covered six and one half months, the period after he was first elected Lieutenant Colonel of the Twenty-sixth to the Battle of New Bern. This diary was also lightly edited. As told in the following chapter, the journal was lost during the battle, and its recovery by the Burgwyns was due to the special efforts of a Union officer. Captain James M. Drennan of the Twenty-fifth Massachusetts found the journal on the battlefield, carefully preserved it for three years, then made a special trip to Boston after the war, so he could hand it personally to Anna. As for Harry's trunk and other effects also lost at New Bern, they never turned up and were probably looted.

The Sevens Days Battles around Richmond in the summer of 1862 were described in Harry's second war journal. This source helped me in my depiction of the events leading to and including the Twenty-sixth's disastrous charge up Malvern Hill. In that journal, Harry also mentions his pilgrimage to the Yankee dead after the battle.

Harry wrote at least one more journal that was found on his body at Gettysburg and was described in the letter to Henry Burgwyn from Captain J. J. Young as "...a couple of memoranda books, both shot through by the more than cruel ball that deprived the Confederacy of one of her brighter ornaments..." To my knowledge, this journal either never made it back to Carolina or was subsequently lost.

Harry's wartime letters to his family were both plentiful and well preserved. They covered a much wider period than I chose to cover with this story, and mostly dealt with minor campaigns in eastern Carolina. However, several that described the events leading up to the Gettysburg Campaign were quite beneficial. From them we learn such things as Kinchen's value as a cook, General Ransom's attempts to exclude Harry from commanding the Twenty-sixth, and the hot, dusty marches of his regiment on the way to Pennsylvania. Harry's last known letter to his mother really did contain the line "And now, I must bid you farewell."

Supporting the story of Kinchen were the letters and journals of William Hyslop Sumner Burgwyn, Harry's younger brother. He, too, was a prolific writer, and his preserved documents went a long way in confirming my perceptions of the story's main characters. Several of his accounts of certain events also corroborated and authenticated claims made by others. For example, within Sumner's letter to his father, which opened the last chapter, we find confirmation of Kinchen's trek from Gettysburg.

Also enhancing my grasp on persons, places, and events was a journal kept by John Fanning Burgwyn during the middle to late 1850's. My great-

great-great-grandfather's personal notes made considerable contributions to Chapter 9, "Thornbury."

Finally, letters and documents composed by several members of the Twenty-sixth North Carolina were critical in forming this tale, specifically, the recollections of John R. Lane, Joseph J. Young, George C. Underwood, Julius A. Lineback, and William M. Cheek. These participants fertilized the battle scenes with vivid details. From them I learned such things as the loss and recovery of a company's pay among the dead on Malvern Hill, Colonel Lane and Harry sipping brandy before the assault on McPherson's Grove, the overhearing of a soldier predicting Harry's death after a sermon near Chambersburg, the attempted theft of the Boy Colonel's watch by a South Carolinian while he lay wounded in the grove, the swimming of the horses across Bryce's Creek near New Bern in a hail of bullets, a dying soldier relating his dream of Pickett's Charge to Lane on the morning before it actually happened, and finally, Kinchen's bitter remorse upon hearing of his master's death.

For those readers who may be interested in the fate of the characters who survived Harry Burgwyn and lived beyond Kinchen's return from Gettysburg, I have submitted some brief biographical sketches which follow.

THE 26TH NORTH CAROLINA REGIMENT suffered unparalleled losses at Gettysburg. Colonel William F. Fox, a New Yorker, who drew from official U.S. War Department records to compile his book "Regimental Losses in the Civil War," cited the Twenty-sixth North Carolina for having sustained the greatest casualties in both numbers and percentage of any regiment on either side, during a single battle of the war. Of the 800 soldiers who went into action on July 1st, 714 were killed, wounded, captured, or missing by the end of the third day. A grisly aggregate of 89%.

The Regiment's antagonist on the first day, the Iron Brigade, was also decimated, its ranks losing 1,154 souls. The Twenty-fourth Michigan was most damaged. Going into the fight with 496 officers and enlisted men, only 97 escaped unscathed, a loss of 82%. Three other Union brigades that were engaged, at least in part, with Pettigrew's Confederates, suffered an additional 1,861 casualties. The Iron Brigade, perhaps the best unit in the Federal Army, would never recover, and soon after the battle, would cease to exist. Undoubtedly, the struggle for McPherson's Grove was one of the bloodiest single combats in American history.

The Twenty-sixth would remain with the Army of Northern Virginia for the rest of the war. Just three short months after Gettysburg, it would sustain 100 more casualties at the Battle of Bristoe Station. Again, it lost more men in this contest than any other regiment on either side. The Regiment was so broken down and demoralized after Bristoe that it nearly fell to the same fate as the Iron Brigade, but due to the efforts of its officers, the consolidation with another regiment was avoided. By the spring of 1864, new recruits and conscripts had swelled its ranks to better than 750 men.

Harry's old regiment would also participate in the terrible battles in The Wilderness, around Spotsylvania Court House, and in numerous engagements during the Siege of Petersburg. Attrition took its toll. Just 120 soldiers stacked arms at Appomattox.

In 1990, the National Park Service broke decades of precedence and allowed a monument to the Twenty-sixth to be laid in McPherson's Grove.

HARRY BURGWYN'S body remained in the gun case under a walnut tree two miles west of Gettysburg until the spring of 1867, when it was removed and reinterred at the Soldiers' Cemetery in Raleigh (now Oakwood Cemetery).

Henry and Anna marked the spot with a grand monument.

Few detailed accounts of Gettysburg fail to examine his regiment's contributions to the Confederate successes on the first day of the battle. Glenn Tucker devoted an entire chapter to the struggle between the Twenty-sixth and the Iron Brigade, in his noted appraisal of the battle *High Tide at Gettysburg*, (The Bobbs-Merrill Company, Inc., 1958). Harry possessed unusual maturity and skills for his age, and it is believed he was the youngest full Colonel to serve in the war. Historians have christened him "The Boy Colonel of the Confederacy," and a biography with the same title was published in 1985, (Archie K. Davis, University of North Carolina Press.)

Harry's name is cherished in the Burgwyn family. It can be found in four succeeding generations. Henry King Burgwyn VI was born in 1987.

As for Harry's effects which Kinchen brought back from Gettysburg, few remain. The watch is in the possession of my cousin who still farms a tract that was once a section of Thornbury. At least a part of Harry's lock of hair is in my possession. It lay within a container at my desk while I composed this novel, the curls as fresh as the day the Colonel was killed.

COLONEL JOHN R. LANE survived the terrible wounds he suffered at Gettysburg and returned to duty in the fall of 1863 as commander of the Twenty-sixth, an amazing recovery. He was wounded on three other occasions, and sustained an injury thought to be mortal at Ream's Station during the summer of 1864. Shrapnel tore his flesh to the bone above his heart and fractured three ribs, but he returned to command the following November. Finally, he broke down from his wounds and exposure and was sent to a hospital at Danville, Virginia, where he remained until his regiment surrendered. He was paroled at Greensboro in May, 1865, then returned to his birthplace in Chatham County. After the war, he prospered as a merchant and large landowner. Born July 4th, 1835, he died an old man.

Colonel Lane remained devoted to the veterans of the Twenty-sixth and returned to Gettysburg for the 40th anniversary of the battle. He left many detailed accounts of the fight, which I found indispensable in telling this story.

CAPTAIN JOSEPH J. YOUNG served as Quartermaster of the Twenty-sixth North Carolina from beginning to end. He surrendered with the regiment at Appomattox. His touching letters from Gettysburg to Henry Burgwyn reveal the sadness of Harry's death along with Kinchen's grief and loyalty. He was thirty-three years of age at war's end, and my limited research did not reveal his fate. He probably returned to Wake County.

JAMES JOHNSTON PETTIGREW'S accomplishments as a soldier, as it would turn out, would overshadow his many other achievements. His Brigade broke the Federals at McPherson's Ridge on Gettysburg's first day. His Division would make the deepest penetration of the Union lines on Cemetery Ridge on the afternoon of the third. Until lately, Harry's Brigade commander hasn't received much recognition for his participation in Pickett's Charge, but more and more modern accounts of the battle are calling the famous assault, "The Charge of Pickett, Pettigrew, and Trimble."

Pettigrew lost his mount and received a wound to his hand during the charge, which may have contributed to his awkward fall and his subsequent wounding at Falling Waters eleven days later. He was carried to the home of a Mr. Boyd at Bunker Hill, Virginia, where he lingered until July 17th. His body was brought to Carolina shortly after, and it lay in state at the Rotunda in Raleigh. He was buried at Bonarva, his plantation in eastern North Carolina.

COLONEL ZEBULON B. VANCE contributed much more to the Confederate war effort as Governor of North Carolina, than as Colonel of the Twenty-sixth. During his tenure, he was often at odds with authorities in Richmond, but was a tremendous motivator, his leadership probably having much to do with Carolina's disproportionate assistance to the "Rebel Cause" in both manpower and materials. Vance was reelected governor in 1864, but the war ended before his term. Imprisoned at Old Capital Prison in Washington, he was later paroled and sent home. His state voted him into the U.S. Senate in 1870, but since he was still under parole he was not allowed to take his seat. He was elected to a third term as Governor in 1876, then won a U.S. Senate seat again in 1878. With reconstruction waning, he was permitted to serve, and died while holding that office sixteen years later.

EDMUND RUFFIN would never see the "Grand Southern Epoch" he had envisioned, but instead witnessed "A Superior Culture," laid to waste. Disputably, Ruffin fired the first shot at Fort Sumter, then joined the Confederate army for the ruckus at First Bull Run. The cannon fire nearly rendered the old man deaf, so he retired to fight a war of pen and words at his plantations east of Richmond.

The war would take two of his children, and his plantations would be vengefully plundered. After the South's collapse, he took refuge at his small farm in Amelia County. Just before his death in June, 1865, he wrote "And now with my latest writing and utterance, and with what will be near my last breath. I here repeat and would willingly proclaim my unmitigated hatred to Yankee rule—to all political, social, and business connections with Yankees, and the perfidious malignant and vile Yankee race." Moments later he discharged a pistol in his mouth.

An innovative agronomist and a pioneer in soil chemistry, Ruffin is better remembered for his Southern Nationalism and advocacy of secession.

HENRY KYD DOUGLAS, the youngest officer to serve on Stonewall Jackson's staff, is famous for his often quoted post-war memoirs which are, at times, questionable in their validity. His encounter with John Brown (alias Isaac Smith) before the raid on Harper's Ferry was reported in his memoirs published in 1940 (*I Rode With Stonewall*, University of North Carolina Press).

After the war he practiced law in Winchester, Virginia, and Hagerstown, Maryland. He died in December, 1903.

JOHN FANNING BURGWYN'S journal came to an abrupt halt in 1856, and I have found no further correspondences by his hand. He is mentioned frequently in the letters and journals of his children and grandchildren. Affection seemed always to be associated with his name.

Like nearly all the Burgwyns, he took refuge in Raleigh during the war, and he was quite an elderly man by then, his health feeble. Henry's children constantly requested letters from their "grandpa," but the act of writing may have been difficult for him.

His grandson, Sumner, was wounded during the war in June, 1864, and while he was recovering in Raleigh all of John Fanning's living descendants were close at hand. The patriarch died at Will's Forest, the home of Major John Devereux, within a few days of Sumner's return. He was in his eighty-first year. His grave is in Oakwood Cemetery in Raleigh.

One final note of interest. Since John Fanning was born, reared, and educated in England, and since he traveled frequently and resided in the Island Kingdom on several occasions, he probably did not speak with the slow southern drawl commonly associated with planters, but with the accent of a cultured Englishman.

THOMAS POLLOK BURGWYN, John Fanning's favorite son, sold most of his land and slave interests before the war due to ill health. Thomas remained close to his father in Raleigh throughout the conflict. He is seldom mentioned in Harry's or Sumner's wartime letters, but at least on one occasion, his donation of blankets to Sumner and his comrades was warmly noted.

He never remarried after Matilda Barclay left Occoneechee. As recounted in this book, their only son died an infant. Thomas's health steadily failed him, until he passed at Cypress Plantation in 1868.

SARAH EMILY BURGWYN [Vixen] abandoned Philadelphia and took refuge in the south with her family during the war. Affectionately referred to as Aunt Emmy by Henry and Anna's children, she seems to have been quite favored by them. Sumner declared a letter he sent her in 1863, "the longest letter I ever wrote or expect to write in camp."

She returned to Philadelphia after the war. Having lived in Florence, Italy for an extended period, she continued to travel around Europe with her niece Kate McRae (Julia Burgwyn McRae's daughter). Her obituary in a Philadelphia newspaper read "a lady not only widely known and greatly esteemed in this country but also throughout Europe, and one of the most noted belles of the fifties."

Emmy never married and passed the last twenty years of her life living quietly in Philadelphia with Kate, who likewise never married. Emmy died in 1905, at age eighty-two.

HENRY KING BURGWYN, SR. lost more than simply his life's work and estate to the Civil War. Within four months of Harry's death, he suffered a stroke, which limited his mind and movement. Shortly after Raleigh was occupied by the Federals in May, 1865, he was weakened further by a second stroke.

Henry was a Colonel of Militia before he was stricken, and in a request for amnesty to Governor Holden in June, 1865, he wrote that he had not been an advocate of secession until after John Brown's raid.

Holden, who had replaced Governor Vance and had been a political enemy of Henry's, suspended his request. The Burgwyns were trapped in the turmoil that surrounded Raleigh, until Major General John Schofield took pity on them and granted them a pass. They fled to Thornbury, but only long enough for Henry to make arrangements with an ex-Confederate officer (Mr. John Randolph) to look after his plantation and personal business affairs. By the end of June, Henry, Anna, Minnie, Allie, and Collie were safe in Boston.

In September, Henry commenced another mysterious trip to Europe without his wife or children. He probably left for the dual purpose of escaping his miserable affairs and regaining his health. While he was away, Mr. Randolph died at Thornbury, and Henry's financial affairs were assumed by a friend and neighbor. Henry returned to Boston a full year after his departure with a small treasure of valuable art and antiques.

Why he risked his dwindling assets and invested in the items is unclear. He may have wanted to refurnish Thornbury, or perhaps he wished to turn the items over in America for a quick dollar. Eventually the imports were sold at auction with little or nothing gained.

Over the next several years, Henry scrambled to save his estate. The burning of his cotton, gin house, and gristmill at Thornbury in the later part of 1866 hurt his chances immeasurably. With the financial noose tightening, the only way to relieve his debt was to sell off portions of his plantations. He was unsuccessful at this until February, 1868, when he managed to sell Cypress Plantation after his brother Thomas' death. It was too little too late. A few weeks after the sale, Henry filed bankruptcy.

The Burgwyns moved to Richmond about this time, checked into the Exchange Hotel, but were soon forced to move to a boarding house. Fortunately, Anna was the beneficiary of a small real estate trust left to her by her stepfather, General W. H. Sumner. With these funds, she was able to purchase a modest home at 301 East Main Street in Richmond.

Henry would be very dependent on Anna during his remaining years. He had been an intelligent, hard-driving man who had hoped to overcome human bondage with science and innovation, but instead, and like most southerners, became ensnared by slavery's legacy. He died at his home on February 2nd, 1877, and is buried at Hollywood Cemetery in Richmond, just a few yards from the tomb of Jeb Stuart.

MARIA GREENOUGH BURGWYN [Minnie] attended St. Mary's School in Raleigh and took shelter in that city during the war with her family. Harry noted in his journal that Minnie and her school friends spun the silk battle flag of the Twenty-sixth North Carolina.

Minnie stayed near her mother's side after the war and probably assisted her in taking care of her father and younger brothers. She traveled back and forth with her parents from Carolina to Boston and remained with them when they moved to Richmond. She must have met T. Roberts Baker, a Confederate veteran, about this time, and the two eventually married in Boston in 1868. They settled in Richmond. They named their only child and son Henry King Burgwyn Baker, for Minnie's father and dead brother.

Minnie, in all likelihood, was responsible for preserving most of the Burgwyn family papers and heirlooms. She lived near Anna and Henry as they grew older and was probably closest to them. Many of the letters and papers that were donated to the University of North Carolina came from her descendants.

Minnie lived in Richmond until she died in 1908. She is buried in Hollywood Cemetery.

WILLIAM HYSLOP SUMNER BURGWYN [Will or Sumner], at the time of Harry's death, was just seventeen and a captain commanding Company H of the Thirty-fifth North Carolina in Brigadier General Robert Ransom's Brigade. In January, 1864, Sumner joined the staff of Brigadier General Thomas L. Clingman, who had been a U.S. Congressman before the war and a friend of Henry Burgwyn.

Six months later, Sumner was seriously wounded at Cold Harbor, but returned to duty later that summer. On September 30th, he was slightly wounded and captured during an assault on Fort Harrison below Richmond. He languished as a prisoner at Fort Delaware until paroled and released in March, 1865. He returned to his family in Raleigh too broken down and discouraged to rejoin the army.

After the war he attended the University of North Carolina at Chapel Hill, and like Harry, graduated with first honors. Later, he graduated Harvard Law School, moved to Baltimore and was admitted to the Maryland Bar. A short time after, he received his diploma as a Doctor of Medicine from the Washington Medical University of Baltimore, but never practiced medicine.

The rest of his life was full of diverse activities. Among them, was more soldiering. He commanded two Maryland regiments in the late 1870's. Much later, he was appointed Colonel of the Second North Carolina Volunteers during the Spanish-American War.

In 1882, Sumner relocated to Henderson, North Carolina from where he founded seven banks in eastern Carolina and one in Florida. He served as President for most of the institutions. He also established an electrical system, waterworks, and tobacco company in Henderson. Later, he served a five-year term as President of the Henderson Female College, and was named to the Board of Trustees of the University of North Carolina at Chapel Hill. He also received the post of National Bank Examiner for the southern states, and served in that capacity for nine years.

In addition to his varying careers, Sumner was an excellent public speaker and an author of several books that contributed to Civil War history and literature. His Civil War letters and journals were edited and published in 1994 by Herbert M. Schiller and White Mane Publishing Company. Titled *A Captain's War, The Letters and Diaries of William H. S. Burgwyn, 1861-65*, the work details his family and war experiences. Perusing it will reintroduce some familiar characters. Kinchen is mentioned several times.

Sumner died while visiting relatives in Richmond in 1913 at the age of sixty-seven. He is buried next to Harry in Oakwood Cemetery.

GEORGE POLLOK BURGWYN [George or Pollok] inherited Harry's horse Hawkeye upon his brother's death. He was attending U.N.C. at the time, but the war interrupted his studies.

In August, 1864, and at the tender age of seventeen, Pollok was on the staff of General Ransom in Petersburg. Stories differ: either Ransom sent the boy home about that time for being under age, or Henry had him removed from the army. I am personally grateful whichever the case, for Pollok is my great-grandfather.

Before the end of the war, Pollok joined the Corps of Cadets at the Virginia Military Institute, and in the spring of 1865, helped man the defenses of Richmond with the Corps until the city was evacuated.

He married Emma Wright Ridley at her home Bonnie Doon in Southampton County, Virginia, in 1869. They had six children.

After Henry's bankruptcy, he assumed many of his father's debts and was given the opportunity to keep a large portion of Thornbury in the family. He succeeded, but not without considerable difficulty, and eventually became a prosperous farmer. He built a new home on the plantation, renamed it "Hillside," and operated a gristmill, commissary, and barroom on the premises. He also owned a home in Jackson, "The Elms," and spent most of his domestic life there. Later, Pollok acquired White's Hotel in Jackson and changed its name to the Burgwyn Hotel, which would remain at the center of the little town's activities until 1921. Pollok was active in civic affairs and was a Layman at the Church of the Savior. He died in 1907, and is buried in the Burgwyn plot in Jackson.

JOHN ALVESTON BURGWYN [Allie] was too young to have served in the Civil War, and consistently suffered from poor health. I never came upon a full diagnosis of his illness during my research, but it seems Allie was either born with a weak heart or suffered a childhood disease that damaged it. An entry in Anna's journal for March 10th, 1867 quotes a doctor: "Alveston must be kept out of doors with constant exercise to ensure the recovery of his health, and that he could never be a professional man, for a sedentary life would surely cut him off, and that he ought not study more than an hour a day."

After the war, and when the family was in Boston, he attended the Chauncey and the Commercial Schools, but because of his health, he never had the opportunity to expand his education at any higher institutions.

Allie eventually returned to Carolina. The Reverend Cameron McRae, Henry's brother-in-law, held several mortgages on Thornbury, and after Henry's bankruptcy, acquired a large portion of the plantation, including the house site. After the Reverend's death in 1872, this land was split between his son and daughter, John and Kate McRae. Kate lived in Philadelphia with her Aunt Emmy, so Alveston took the job of managing her farm. He lived as a bachelor in the old Calvert house in Jackson.

Later, he served as treasurer of Northampton County for seven years, and was the Senior Warden at the Church of the Savior. He was considered a great friend to local African-Americans, and since he was an extremely popular man, a huge throng attended his funeral. He died unmarried in 1898, just shy of his forty-eighth birthday. He is also buried in the Burgwyn family plot in Jackson.

COLLINSON PIERREPONTE EDWARDS BURGWYN [Collie or Coll] was just eleven years old when Kinchen came home from Gettysburg, yet the slave's singular act of sacrifice and devotion made a lasting impression on the boy. In 1889, Coll wrote and published a little novel, *The Huguenot Lovers*, in which Kinchen played a minor character, a loyal coachman. But in the brief preface to the story, Coll asked for indulgence from the reader for "his effort at portraiture of the character of devotedness in the Negro. If an excuse is needed for this, he trusts that it will be found in his desire to put upon record, so as to be remembered whenever this book is read, the act of one of that race who protected the dead body of his brother on the battle-field of Gettysburg."

Henry's and Anna's youngest son graduated from Harvard University after the war, then completed courses in civil engineering at Harvard's Lawrence Scientific School in 1876. Shortly after returning to Richmond, he accepted the job of designing an extension of Hollywood Cemetery, and would later be the consulting engineer for the entire cemetery for fourteen years. Perhaps the most historic burial grounds in the south, Hollywood contains the remains of two U.S. Presidents, six Virginia Governors, and the only Confederate President. Among the Rebel notables who were mentioned in this story and who are also buried at Hollywood are Jeb Stuart, John Imboden, Edward Johnson, George Pickett, James Archer and Henry Heth. Nearly three thousand Confederates who died at Gettysburg are also interred at Hollywood, among them at least nine known members of the Twenty-sixth North Carolina.

Coll was just twenty-five when he became an engineer, and his work at Hollywood would kick off a distinguished career. He assisted in the improvements of the deep water terminal on the James River below Richmond, and he laid out the design for Monument Avenue, a Confederate shrine, and one of the most beautiful boulevards in America. He was also a consulting engineer for the Robert E. Lee Monument and was commissioned to sail to France to procure the stone for the giant sculpture. He also supervised the construction of Richmond's old City Hall, a unique and interesting structure that stands near the state capital building designed by Thomas Jefferson.

Coll settled in Richmond for the remainder of his life. He married Rosa B. Higginbotham, but the couple had no children. Coll died in 1915. He is buried in the section of Hollywood Cemetery he designed.

ANNIE LANE DEVEREUX [A.L.D.]. The Civil War was a period of modesty in America. It was not uncommon for soldiers, when composing letters and journals, to refer to young ladies they were sporting by the admired's initials instead of by their names. Harry practiced the same discretion within his own correspondences.

There was never a formal marriage engagement between Harry and Annie, but several of Anna Burgwyn's grandchildren claimed there was an "understanding" between the two. Also according to family lore, Annie was so devastated by Harry's death that she never married and wore the black of mourning for the rest of her life. She was barely twenty when Harry was killed.

Miss Devereux and Anna maintained a close friendship over the years, and Annie was a frequent guest at the Burgwyn household in Richmond. Anna's diary entry of July 10th, 1886 states: "When I went to breakfast I found a box in my parlor left by Express which contained a worsted shawl as a gift from Annie Devereux. It was very kind of her to remember me in this way, & I shall doubtless find it a most useful addition to my wardrobe & always wear it with pleasure as she made it for me."

ANNA GREENOUGH BURGWYN. When reading the numerous letters directed to Anna from her family, I could not help but notice the universal feelings of love and respect. I detected a kind heart and strong personality, which I believe trickled down to her children. She seems to have been capable of rising to any occasion and weathering any storm.

When Sherman's troops occupied Raleigh in the spring of 1865, Anna found herself in a potentially dangerous situation, while bearing the responsibility for a broken husband and dependent children. She was constantly forced to move her family to safer dwellings. Evidence of the danger she was exposed to can be seen in a childhood painting of little Harry that had hung in the parlor of their rented home. It bears sword slashes from a Yankee looter. Eventually, Anna was able to persuade Major General Schofield to give her family safe passage from the city, so that they might find refuge in Boston. The family took rooms at Mrs. Putnam's in Pemberton Square, and probably feeling at least a bit estranged from her friends and relatives there, Anna went right to work getting her family circle back to normal. Allie and Collie were entered into the Latin School, and shortly after Henry sailed for Europe, she established a Spanish Class in her parlor taught by a Señor Luares. In January, 1866, she attended a lecture on Reconstruction given by H. W. Beecher.

Anna would stay in Boston for sixteen months. Pollok and Will, who had stayed in the south, would pay visits from time to time. Mostly, her diary noted the comings and goings of friends and relatives, both northern and southern. When Anna finally traveled back to Carolina, she only visited Thornbury briefly, then moved her family to Richmond and checked into the Exchange Hotel.

Over the next decade Anna renewed the old habit of wintering in the south and summering in Boston and Cohasset. Since all her children eventually settled in the south, Richmond gradually became Anna's permanent home. In 1868, she bought the previously mentioned home on Main Street, and in 1869, was appointed one of the mangers of the St. Paul's Orphan Asylum. Her first grandchild, Minnie's son Harry, was born at her home in Richmond during the same year.

There is a large gap in Anna's journals between 1874 and 1886. Several more grandchildren were born during these years, and Henry died in 1877. We know she kept diaries for most of the period, but they were donated to a library and promptly lost. Her last journal survived, and it takes up with her living cheerfully in Richmond. She seemed in good health and constantly made notes on the activities of her offspring. The memory of her oldest son never left her. On February 25th, 1887, she wrote "The anniversary of my last parting with dear Harry."

In her later years, Anna made sizable donations for the improvement of the Church of the Savior in Jackson. Even though she was no longer a member of the parish, she had played a key role in the church's founding, and two of her sons were still active members of the congregation. In April, 1887, the local Bishop planned to visit the Church and view its improvements. Anna made plans to be present at the visitation and stopped in Henderson to visit Sumner on the way. She contracted a severe cold there and did not recover. Anna died on the twenty-sixth anniversary of the firing on Fort Sumter. She is buried next to Henry in Hollywood Cemetery in Richmond.

KINCHEN. Even though it carries an abstract meaning, freedom has always been a word adored in America. The underground railroad will always be a great symbol in American history. Slaves who broke their bonds and escaped the oppression of the plantation system will always be praised and esteemed. But what about the African-Americans who stayed behind? What about those who remained loyal to their masters, or even fought for the Confederacy? Were they subhuman? Were they too ignorant to know better? Should we just label them "Uncle Toms?"

Many of us lack a well-rounded perception of American history. It is much easier to understand the past if we choose to see it only in black and white. Actually, our past is always more complex than that. It is gray, always gray, and the story of Kinchen stands as a reminder.

Those of us who live in the twenty-first century share very little common ground with Americans who walked within the same borders in the 1860's. Values have changed. Our personal missions and our perceptions of ourselves have changed. In the nineteenth century, once an American was born into a certain class, it was very difficult to move beyond it. A citizen may not have had money, but being an honorable person was the next best thing. Honor was a cherished word then, and that is a perception that many of us have lost today. We might fail to recognize that to Kinchen, being honorable may have been more important than being free.

Kinchen could have been ignorant, he may have been comfortable as a slave, or he may have known a free black had no better opportunities than he had. We can never know, and, we are in no position to judge him. However, we do know he was human, and as a human he carried the same strengths and frailties we all carry. He had emotions, he had loyalties, and he had motives. Who are we to say he made the wrong decision?

I chose to portray Kinchen as a man with a certain resiliency. One who not only had the instincts to survive, but also the confidence to be content with himself, a man who did not fear to show affection, and who also possessed the grace to accept it. I believe many African-American slaves carried these qualities. How else could they have thrived despite the harsh times they endured?

What we know of Kinchen after his return to Carolina is sketchy at best. His name does appear on a post-war list of freedmen living and working at Thornbury. A ledger shows him being paid for fodder he'd collected. According to family lore, he worked for my great-grandfather, Pollok Burgwyn, and lived at Hillside for the rest of his life. It is said that the Burgwyns never forgot his brave trek from Gettysburg, and that Pollok accepted him as one of the family, taking care of him in his old age.

There are two known photographs of Kinchen. One shows him standing next to the massive gelding, Hawkeye, holding his reins. It graces the cover of this book. Some have claimed that this photo was taken at Thornbury shortly after his return, but a closer examination discloses a canvas tent in the background. Probably it was taken at one of Harry's various war-time encampments. A second photo shows Kinchen with pure white hair and beard and grinning broadly, while sitting in a rocker on a porch. Written below the photo, by an unknown hand, is "Uncle Kinchen, eighty years old." I have heard that children would often gather around him and listen to his war stories. He loved to tell war stories, and this assertion is supported to some extent by Coll Burgwyn, who portrays him telling a tale of the battle of Drewry's Bluff in his novel, *The Huguenot Lovers*.

In 1893, a severe pneumonia epidemic swept through Northampton County. It claimed the life of Pollok's wife, my great-grandmother, Emma Burgwyn, who was just forty-seven at the time. According to her youngest son, my great-uncle Sumner, Kinchen passed in the same year. Perhaps he died from the same cause.

I have heard from some of my kinfolk who still live around Jackson that there are several cemeteries on the ground that was once Hillside Plantation. On my latest visit, I was in hopes of finding a local who could show me the sites, but most of them were not sure if they could locate them. They say the cemeteries are overgrown with thickets and brush, and the grave markers are gone or worn away. I was disappointed in hearing this. I am certain Kinchen is buried there.

ACKNOWLEDGMENTS

I WOULD LIKE TO THANK the descendants of Henry and Anna Burgwyn for preserving the family documents that inspired this story. Many of these were loaned to the archives at the University of North Carolina at Chapel Hill, and I thank the professionals there for their assistance. They treated me with kindness and respect, and it will be a great pleasure to visit there again. Not all the letters, journals, and scrapbooks are deposited in archives. Some remain with individual family members, and I am grateful to the late Jack Baker and Emily Burgwyn Sneed. Special thanks must go to my father, Nat Burgwyn, who not only tracked these documents down from his vast repository, but also spent many an hour and quarter copying, then passed them to me in nice, neat binders. My cousin, Stephen White Burgwyn, also loaned me several documents that I found invaluable. Steve and his wife Jo-Jo endured several inquiring visits from me, and they were most gracious. Steve gave me a driving tour of the old plantations, and filled me in on local history. An amateur historian like myself, Steve also read one of the first drafts of the novel and lent me his input. My visits to Jackson and Occoneechee gave spirit to the novel and I am happily in Steve's and Jo-Jo's debt.

I must acknowledge my editor, Sofia Starnes, an award-winning poet. I went to her with plans to make great cuts in the manuscript, but after reading it, she talked me out of it. She did not bathe the manuscript in red ink, but polished it with great care. Her support and encouragement gave me confidence, and I can't wait for our next project. I am grateful to Dr. Robert Christin for pointing me in Sofia's direction.

Thank you also goes to Tammy Deane and Marshall McClure, for their valuable time and talent. I am fortunate to have them as friends. Affectionate thanks goes to those who read the manuscript in its various forms, and for their support. My sister Emily Burgwyn, Carla Garber, Tammy Deane, Patty McBride, and the late Bill McBride, whom I miss very much. My mother Margot will never know how valuable her opinions are to me. Same goes to my "Pop," who read the manuscript more than once. It was essential to be true to the story, to the characters, and to history, and I feared I would offend some of my large, extended family. I felt confident that if it got by old Nat, I was reasonably safe.

Lastly, there is my wife, Ellen. It would not be too kind to say that this book would not exist without her. She shared with me all the pains and pleasures of its making. She is a treasure, and I am a rich man.